FLESH AND BONE
RISE OF THE NECROMANCERS

Compiled by Alva J. Roberts
Edited by Jessy Marie Roberts

Copyright © 2010 by Pill Hill Press

First Edition

All stories contained in this volume have been published with permission from the authors.

All Rights Reserved

No portion of this publication may be reproduced, stored in any electronic system, or transmitted in form or by any means, electronic, mechanical, photocopy, recording, or otherwise, without written permission from the authors. This is a work of fiction. Any resemblance to any actual person, living or dead, events, or locales is entirely coincidental.

ISBN: 978-1-61706-001-4

Printed in the USA by
Pill Hill Press
First Printing August 2010
Cover art by Chandra Kusuma
Cover design by Alva J. Roberts

1 2 3 4 5 6 7 8 9 10

Flesh and Bone
Rise of the Necromancers

Compiled by Alva J. Roberts
Edited by Jessy Marie Roberts

Pill Hill Press
Chadron, Nebraska

Table of Contents

The Blade of Tears by Lydia Sharp......................................1
No Man's Land by K.G. McAbee..12
Wrists by Shennandoah Diaz..24
All the World a Grave by Michael McClung....................33
Blood on the Beach by Anne Michaud............................49
The Scarlet Cat by Rebecca Lloyd..................................56
The Mortician's Secret by Kelley Frank.........................81
The King's Accord by Alan Baxter....................................107
Necrodance by Darin Kennedy..121
The Ghost Walk by Marianne Halbert.............................130
Blood Brothers by J. Matthew Saunders......................141
Bequest by Greg Mellor..149
9 Mystery Rose by Eden Royce......................................157
In the Dark Kingdom by Brandon Berntson....................165
Jenna's Awakening by TW Brown....................................194
Queen of Bones by Aubrie Dionne...................................207
Small Matters of Immortality by Michael R. Colangelo..219
The Stoner Bride by Matthew Fryer...............................231
Sedenberry's Pest by Jon C. Forisha............................244
A History of the Wraith King by Chris Poling................261
And the Greatest of these is Love by David McDonald..275

The Blade of Tears
Lydia Sharp

"Alinor!" The bellows of Lord Ghislain intensified. "Stop!"

She spurred her heels into Shadow's ribs, forcing him into a gallop. The landscape transformed into a blur of muddy green. Blazes from the fiery sunset sunk into the distant horizon.

Alinor embraced the wind. Ahead of her lay the dreaded Forêt Noire. Behind her, a life of misery.

"We'll take our chances with the legends and myths," she confided in her ebony steed. A smack of her crop against his shoulder urged him onward. "Hyah!"

Don't look back.

"Alinor de LaRoux!"

Don't look back!

The hoof beats of Ghislain's stallion thundered behind her. Her freedom was within reach. Ghislain would not dare follow her into the forest. He was a man of outward bravery and inward cowardice.

The wall of trees welcomed her entry with arms of sticks and foliage. Alinor eased Shadow's gait and circled him around to face her enemy. He pranced in place, agitated.

"Easy," she soothed, slacking the reins.

He hesitantly obeyed her command. Unexplained fear rippled through his tightened muscles. He tossed his head and let out a sharp snort.

Through the dark branches, Alinor saw Ghislain on the crest of the hill. He raised his longsword in a threat.

"Don't be a fool, Alinor! Retreat from the Black Forest and accept your judgment."

She cursed his impudence. Judgment was only required when a crime had been committed. She had merely taken what was rightfully hers.

"I am not a criminal!"

Shadow sidestepped and threw her off balance.

"Whoa," she scolded. It wasn't like Shadow to scare so easily. He must have sensed an unseen danger. Alinor scanned the trees, considering any option for escape.

Ghislain charged toward the forest with a valiant roar, sword held high.

Stunned, Alinor spun Shadow around and kicked into his sides. "Hyah!" The beast refused. He back-stepped, sliding his hooves through the forest floor as he vacillated between fear and obedience.

She spurred him on. "*Remue-toi!*"

He reared and teetered backward. Alinor pressed her feet into the stirrups, gripped the saddle between her knees, and clutched the reins against his neck. Shadow toppled over her with crushing force.

Alinor screamed. Searing pain consumed her.

She dropped the reins and slipped her feet from the stirrups. Shadow flopped about the ground like a fallen fledgling. Digging her fingers into the dirt, she crawled away from the chaos. Although sorely bruised, no part of her felt broken.

Ghislain drew closer. As Shadow regained his footing, Alinor conceded she must let him go. She stood and smacked his hindquarters, urging him toward the open landscape. She turned and sprinted into the sea of black. Deeper into the woods.

Lightning flashed. Thunder clapped overhead. Alinor ran as fast as she could. Rigorous winds ripped at her braided hair. The loosened red locks raged about her head like angry flames.

The hoofbeats grew louder. Ghislain would reach her soon. With a swift glance over her shoulder, Alinor made a decision. His stallion would not purposely harm her; she had trained it herself.

She unsheathed her rapier and dropped to the ground. As the mottled gray horse leapt over her, Alinor rolled to her back. She swept the edge of her blade under its belly and sliced the girth of the saddle as it passed.

Hooves pounded into the dirt. Ghislain yelled. An awkward thump preceded a painful groan.

Alinor sprung to her feet, ready to fight. Ghislain's horse released a high-pitched whinny and galloped away from the depths of the ominous forest.

Ghislain lay on the ground, clutching his shoulder. Alinor grinned. Although minor, his injury would give her an advantage.

Determination surged through her. She would not run from him anymore—it was time to end this. As she closed the gap between them, she was confident she would not die today.

The storm rumbled in and the clouds burst open. Even with the thick canopy above, a ponderous deluge beat upon Alinor and her opponent. A web of tiny rivers spread across the forest floor, forming a mosaic of puddles and floating debris.

Ghislain caught sight of her splashing toward him and pushed himself to his feet. He held his longsword ready with both hands, legs spread in proper stance, but his expression betrayed his inner thoughts. He did not believe she would fight him.

Alinor stopped a few feet short of his position. Rapier in hand, she shifted her arm forward and angled the slender blade toward his smug smile. With her left hand, she unsheathed her dagger.

"You dare to challenge me, woman?"

"It is you who has challenged me, Ghislain. I'll offer you one more chance to walk away before I strike."

He laughed. "Striking with the very weapon that brought this shame upon you?"

Alinor glanced at her rapier. It would never bring her shame; Ghislain had accomplished that on his own. "The Blade of Tears belonged to my father, you swine, and now it belongs to me. You'll not put a finger to it while there's still breath in me."

She focused on his piercing stare. There was a time when those brown eyes had given her a feeling of warmth and security. All she could see in them now was sorrow and hatred.

"If you wish to mimic your father's temerity, Mademoiselle LaRoux, then so be it."

Alinor tightened her grip. Anticipation coursed through her. Ghislain had insulted her for the last time. "I will not die today," she whispered.

She thrust toward him. Ghislain raised his sword and engaged her attack.

Right. Clash! Left. Clash!

Alinor caught his bulky blade with both her rapier and dagger, creating a metallic star between them. Flashes of lightning reflected off the pear-cut sapphires in the hilt of the Blade of Tears, her father's most prized possession. She swept her hands to opposite sides and shifted back. The ring of iron sliding against steel hung in the air.

They locked glares. Wind howled through the branches and rain mauled the ground.

"Stop your foolishness," Ghislain said. "We've played this game too many times."

Alinor seethed. "This isn't a game. This is about my family's honor. Something you could never understand."

"You can't defeat me." Ghislain gave her an arrogant sneer. "Perhaps we can come to an agreement. I'll allow you to keep the Blade of Tears...for a price." He looked her up and down with lustful eyes.

"I've already paid you more than enough in that regard. I would rather die." She spat at his feet.

Ghislain softened his expression. "You know I won't kill you, Alinor. I love you."

"Liar!" Alinor charged him, slashing. "You lying sack of donkey entrails, all you've ever done is cause me pain!" Her words had a force that matched every thrust of her blades.

Ghislain merely blocked her attacks.

The Blade of Tears

"Fight me, damn you! You've already murdered me with slander. Finish it!" She kicked his legs out from under him and sent him to the mud.

Ghislain released his sword and pushed himself to his knees. Before he had a chance to stand, Alinor stationed herself behind him. She placed her rapier alongside his neck and pressed the point of her dagger against his back.

"One move and you're dead," she growled.

He remained on the ground. His shoulders rose and fell with every heaving breath.

Memories of his abuse resurfaced. "Why couldn't you just let me go?" she shouted over the thunderclaps. She'd spent years being subordinate and mocked, being used only for his selfish pleasure. Hadn't they agreed to be equal partners for life? Why had he turned against her? Pain clawed at her chest. Tears threatened to flow. She forced them back with a hard swallow.

"If you must kill me, do it now," he said. "I won't fight you."

Alinor's hands trembled as Ghislain's words battled with her thoughts. No matter how deserving he was of death now, he wasn't always so. He must have known she wouldn't kill him in this manner. Under the cover of a seeming defeat he still challenged her. She clenched her jaw, wishing she could forget the man he used to be, and dispose of the man he had become.

A brash rustle among the foliage stole her focus. She kept her blade at his neck and shifted her gaze upward.

Three pairs of blanched eyes emerged from the trees. Alinor withdrew her rapier.

"*Mon Dieu*," she whispered. "They do exist."

Ghislain stood quickly and readied his stance. Her conflict with him suddenly took second place. They were *both* victims now.

Every flash of lightning revealed more and more bodies trudging toward them from all sides. They shuffled, as if their limbs were a burden, and moaned a somber melody. A distant look of death emanated from their eyes, among the sallow skin that hung from their bones. Overgrown ropes of twisted hair draped across their shoulders. Ragged clothing covered them.

No armor. No weapons.

Alinor stood back-to-back with Ghislain and contemplated her defense. Within seconds, they were surrounded by the unnatural creatures that had incited the horrifying legends of long ago.

But this was no legend. This was a living nightmare.

"Send your prayers now," Ghislain said. The bodies slowly closed in around them. "No man has ever journeyed through the Black Forest and lived to tell of it."

"Then we shall be the first. I will not die today."

Cracks of lightning created split-second visions of terror. Alinor's heart thumped against her chest. She rushed her breath hard through her nose, uncertain of what to expect. The eerie moans grew louder, drowning out the sounds of the passing storm.

Alinor tightened her grip. Ghislain tensed behind her. "I won't let them hurt you," he said.

For a moment, she thought she heard the voice of the man she'd once loved.

Alinor stabbed and slashed at the nearest bodies, but with no effect. The group in front of her opened their mouths wide and roared. Their arms stretched forward with clawing fingers. They looked like men but behaved like beasts. Her blade sliced through the limbs with ease, dropping them to the ground.

Alinor gasped. No blood poured from the open wounds and the creatures did not cry out in pain. Only a corpse would have such a reaction. These beings weren't dead, and neither were they alive.

"We can't defeat them," she cried, hacking into whatever came near. "They won't die!"

She turned to Ghislain who had severed the legs of one. It kept moving toward them, using its hands to drag itself across the ground.

Ghislain looked around at the growing swarm. There were too many to number. "Our only chance is to outrun them."

Alinor spun and kicked a creature square in the chest, sending it sprawling into a group of others. A narrow path cleared as

The Blade of Tears

they scrambled to regain their footing.

"Now!" Ghislain yelled.

She bolted across the slick mud and brush. Ghislain was right on her heels. The trudging gait of the creatures had deceived her, for she had believed they weren't capable of moving any faster. One quick glance over her shoulder confirmed the stampede behind them. Ear-piercing shrieks erupted from within the throng and echoed through the trees.

Alinor's legs felt like sacks of wet sand. The black of the forest ahead seemed eternal. "We can't run forever."

"We don't have to." Ghislain quickened his pace and grabbed her arm, dragging her toward the edge of a cliff.

She didn't have a chance to question. Ghislain forced them both into a free fall.

Alinor's scream was cut short by an abrupt plunge into rushing water. Blind and disoriented, she fumbled for the surface. A familiar hand grasped hers and guided her through the current. As they swam, bodies dropped in around them, thrashing.

Alinor brushed against what she guessed was the bank of the cliff. Relieved, she pulled herself up for air. With a desperate gasp, she surfaced under the overhang of a massive tree root. Ghislain popped up beside her.

Bodies continued to drop in front of them and swarm through the river. They were trapped. The only way out was through the ghostly horde.

Alinor's chest heaved. Every breath stung her throat. She silently pleaded Ghislain and hoped their deaths would be quick.

"Don't give me those eyes, Alinor. Don't you dare give up. We are not—"

He spun away from her and she heard a cracking sound. She hadn't noticed the creature's presence until she saw the end of Ghislain's blade jutting from the top of its skull. He retracted his sword and the limp body floated downstream.

She caught a spark in his demeanor.

"Their heads," he said, betraying a smile. "If they can die, I can save you from them." His smile disappeared. "Stay under here until I've drawn them away, then get out of this forest as fast as you can."

"What are you saying?"

Ghislain pulled her to him and gave her a firm kiss. For a fleeting moment, Alinor forgot about the peril around her.

When he withdrew his lips, reality slapped her across the face.

"I'm saying that I'm willing to die for you."

Before Alinor could protest, Ghislain forged his way through the waist-deep water, directly into the swarm of beasts.

"No!" she shouted.

Waves of water enveloped him as he swept his sword against the attacks. An innumerable amount of bodies streamed toward him from all sides. More and more dropped over the cliff above Alinor, unaware of her position, and headed straight for Ghislain. For every one that he disposed of, two more stepped into its place.

Alinor's head swam with dizzying speed, attempting to comprehend the turn of events. How could someone who had caused her so much pain be willing to sacrifice himself in her behalf? Had he remembered their youth? Had he mentally traveled back to the time when the only thing that mattered was protecting each other from harm, at any cost?

She wouldn't leave him to die. Not now. Not ever.

The pile over Ghislain grew. She could no longer see him, but only heard his exerted groans accompanied by the cracking of skulls.

"Run!" he shouted through the mass of clawing hands.

No. She wouldn't run like a coward. Pride-driven rage boiled within her until it steamed its way out and forced her to action.

She treaded through the floating bodies. A creature dropped behind her and grabbed her shoulder. She spun and thrust her dagger, stabbing it in the eye and then twisting the blade with an upward motion. Two more met the same fate within her next few steps closer to the chaos.

The Blade of Tears

Alinor's feet were swept out from under her. She sunk into the water and then pushed herself up with a roar.

Her father once told her that the Blade of Tears was so sharp it could separate a tear from a widow's cheek and remove only the pain. Whether or not that was true, it certainly had no trouble removing the heads of the monsters around her.

As if in a dream, Alinor slashed through the swarm without regard for danger. She didn't know how many fell at her hands, only that there were many more to follow.

Upon reaching the pile of thrashing limbs, Alinor made quick work of thinning the horde. Her arms moved about her like a well-rehearsed dance. No forethought was needed; instinct guided her.

Alinor finally caught a glimpse of the victim within the mass. Blood covered his face, flowing as freely as the rain that fell upon it. His movement had slowed, weakened by the fight. Alinor continued to slice her way toward him.

Ghislain managed to step backwards far enough to find the opposite bank of the river. Once out of the water, he slumped to the ground and let out a strained shout.

"Run, Alinor!"

The swarm crumpled over him with moans of pleasure.

Alinor quickened her attacks and sloshed through the mud of the riverbank. The rushing water was no longer visible beneath the thick blanket of decapitated bodies and floating heads. The creatures became a blur around her until, one by one and two by two, they were motionless.

The sudden silence overwhelmed her.

Alinor shifted her stance every few seconds, searching through the trees for more of the monsters. She turned a complete circle. None remained.

The storm passed, moving toward another victim of the night. She grabbed Ghislain's wrists and dragged him away from the pile of death, toward the base of a nearby boulder. With a sigh, she dropped her weapons.

Alinor released a flood tears. A torrent of emotions overtook her. Sorrow and anger. Triumph and defeat. Ghislain's screams echoed through her mind, reverberating off the terrifying visions of his final moments.

Her knees buckled and she collapsed beside him. Gaping bite wounds covered his face and neck. His skin was pale, drained of its life-giving blood.

Alinor pounded her fist on his chest. "Damn you, Ghislain!"

The cost of her freedom was greater than she'd anticipated. She stroked a single finger down the length of his nose and then across his parted lips.

His body jolted upright. She scuttled backwards, fixing her stare on the blank look in his widened eyes. He reached for her. Bared his teeth like an animal. Grabbed a clump of her hair and yanked it backward.

Alinor fumbled her fingers through the mud and found her dagger. She thrust the blade upward under his chin, disabling the attempt to bite, and then pushed herself away. She grasped her rapier and jumped to her feet. Before Ghislain's corpse could do the same, she sliced through his neck. His head thumped to the ground followed by his mangled body, returning him to rest.

Hoof beats steadily approached. Alinor wiped her cheeks and saw Shadow a short distance away. Her loyal steed had returned. A deep sigh of relief escaped her chest and she looked at Lord Ghislain one last time.

"*Au revoir, mon amour*," she whispered.

With the Blade of Tears in the hands of its rightful owner, Alinor de LaRoux mounted her horse and then spurred him on. "Hyah!"

Alinor embraced the wind. Ahead of her lay a life of freedom, alone. Behind her, a victory over the dreaded Forêt Noire.

ABOUT THE AUTHOR:

Lydia Sharp is an author of science fiction, fantasy, women's fiction, and young adult fiction, both novels and short stories. She

The Blade of Tears

is a lover of life, people, nature, animals, science, the cosmos, and has an incurable addiction to coffee and chocolate and all things Star Wars. This is her second Pill Hill Press anthology. She lives in Ohio with her husband and son. You can follow her blog at www.lydiasharp.blogpspot.com and her tweets at @lydia_sharp.

No Man's Land
K.G. McAbee

The worst, the absolute worst, was the smell.

The cold was bad, cutting into his very bones like long sharp knives. The constant rain created the slimy mud that clung to his boots and weighed him down even more than his kit—that was bad. The rats, fat and clever, their beady eyes filled with a knowing look, their heads cocked to one side as if wondering how tasty, how tender he was going to be—they were bad. The incessant barrage from the Huns, shells bursting day and night, so loud his teeth rattled inside his head and his bones shook—that was bad.

But the smell was the worst of all. The sweet, bitter scent, so strong he could taste it, of rotting flesh. Rotting human flesh. Masses of it, surrounding him in all directions, from the thousands of dead bodies trapped and sinking in the mud. He was always afraid he'd drown in the reeking, disintegrating flesh of his brothers-at-arm and his enemies.

But that was then, when he was in the front-line trenches, before he'd been wounded and sent back. He promised himself then he'd never return.

But that was before he found out about Esme.

Now he was near again; the front was a mile away, the guns were blasting, and he was in the very last place on earth he wanted to be. He stood at the top of an abandoned trench. Below him, he could see bits of bodies, hands and feet and other, less identifiable parts, sticking up through the thick mud. Some of the hands looked like they had just at the instant of death, as if they had just stopped scrabbling at the muddy soil. It was almost like they were still trying to escape their fate, even with all life drained from them. Feet, some bare, some encased in ragged boots, seemed to still be trying to run away from danger, from despair, from death itself.

But there was no escape from death. That is what he'd been taught, and that is what he had believed...until he'd met the tall man with the white face and the anthracite eyes three nights ago. The man who introduced himself as Doctor Hezekiah Smith...and had offered Hopkins a miracle.

Smith said it might just be possible to bring her back. His darling, his Esme DuPre. Hopkins could hold her in his arms again. He could hear her laugh, see the love in her eyes.

There was a price. Naturally. Is not there always?

But Captain Hopkins was willing to pay anything, everything, to have his Esme back.

He dropped the things he'd brought with him down into the trench, nearly a mile from the front lines and empty of living men. But to put off that moment he'd been dreading, when he must follow down, down into the place he dreaded of all things, he began to remember...

I met her on 31 October, 1914, my first day in France after I'd joined up, after the rush of training. I was a captain; that made me laugh a bit, to think of myself, Josiah Matthew Hopkins, a captain in His Majesty's army. We were all convinced the war would be over soon. We'd have the Hun on the run, wipe things up and be home by Christmas.

We weren't. Not that Christmas nor the next...nor the next.

And now we've been fighting and dying for years, and look to go on doing the same—for years.

That had started it, of course. Dying; dead. Esme thought I was dead. She read, in the newspaper every day, the list of wounded, missing and dead. And she saw my name. Hopkins, Josiah M, Captain, Fifth Northumberland Fusiliers, missing, presumed dead.

Are there any sadder words in the language than presumed

dead? Well, yes. When they told me Esme had taken arsenic so that she could join me in the next world—three days before I was found, wounded, wandering, confused, but remembering at last who I was and where I must go—three days before I could tell her I was not dead, presumed or otherwise.

But she was.

Dead. And gone.

Then the man in the little café, the man with the black, black eyes, told me he could bring her back to me.

Captain Hopkins shook the images away and looked around him, forced himself to take a deep breath of the fresh spring air. The land, once green with life, was sere and battered and pitted, and in the distance, he could just hear the *boom boom* of the German barrage.

Then he looked down. Down into that pit of Hell, that noisome grave of unburied men, that trench for which he and his brothers would fight and give their very lives, only to abandon it and go forward—or backward—to another, so alike as to be indistinguishable. The Great War had created this way of death; let the Great War take all responsibility.

It was time. He had to do this thing; he had no other choice. He had to bring Esme back.

Hopkins started down the rickety wooden ladder that led into the depths of his nightmares. He had vowed never to return to a trench. That was before he'd found out she died. Now, he had no choice.

At the bottom, the smell was stronger. He pulled his scarf up over his face and gathered up the things he'd brought with him.

Two large buckets, with tight-fitting lids.

A shovel.

He found a good spot almost at once. It was impossible to take all the dead men from the trenches, whether friend or enemy; often, the bodies were simply piled in out-of-the-way side trenches and left to decay…and to the rats.

His boots squelching in mud that was more rotted flesh than

dirt, he began to methodically fill his bucket with the thick, viscous matter Smith had said he needed.

Needed as raw material.

Needed to bring Esme back.

Needed to make her live again.

***

The air in the small café was thick with smoke and the scents of unwashed men and cheap wine. Hopkins peered through the murk until he saw Smith in the most distant, darkest corner, a bottle and two glasses on the table before him.

Hopkins made his way through the milling mass and pulled out the opposite chair, sat down, and poured thin sour wine into both glasses.

"Good evening, Captain." Smith's voice was smooth and low, with a hint of an accent. "I take it you have obtained...the necessary?"

Hopkins upturned the glass and drained it in a single gulp, then reached for the bottle. "I have," he said after another glass followed the first. "And may God forgive me."

"God, my dear sir, has nothing to do with it. He—if indeed He exists—did not start this war; Man did. And what Man provides us, we shall use." Smith sipped his wine and made a face. "Do you have my payment?"

"I do." Hopkins took an envelope out of his pocket and passed it across the table. "It's all I could get my hands on for the moment but, by God, if you can do what you say, it's worth it."

Smith just took the envelope and smiled as he tucked it into his jacket.

He waited, but Smith continued merely to smile.

When he could stand the silence no longer, Hopkins rapped out, "When?"

Smith cocked his head to one side, giving his smile an odd cantilever. "Eager, aren't we, Captain?"

K.G. McAbee

"When, damn you?"

"What about…in three days time?"

"What about tonight?" Hopkins demanded as he filled his own glass yet again.

Smith raised one long-fingered hand, the skin as white as paper against his dark sleeve. "Tonight is not…propitious, captain. Three days—or rather, three nights from now. Meet me in the abandoned chapel at the edge of the village."

"The one with half its roof missing?"

Smith nodded. "That is indeed the one. Bring the…material. And I shall need something of hers. A lock of hair, perhaps? I suspect you have such a thing, do you not?"

"I do." Hopkins poured the last of the wine in his glass and drained it. "I'll be there. What time?"

"Just before midnight, my dear sir," said Smith.

The pale man's eyes, black as coal, seemed for a moment to shine from within, as if they reflected some internal hellfire. He rose and disappeared into the crowd.

Hopkins shook his head and eyed his glass. This wine must be stronger than he'd thought. No man has internal fires. Must have been some chance reflection of an open fireplace. He turned around, surveyed the room.

There was no fire.

***

The first two nights passed at last, though the time dragged like an overloaded cart pulled by mules with broken legs. Finally, the sun sank on the third night.

Hopkins sat in the small room he'd rented from a local farmer. He sipped wine as he fondled the golden lock of Esme's hair—all he had left of her. He remembered that hair, so long that when she unbound it from her usual braids, she could sit on it. He remembered how it would fall over his face in bed when she straddled him, the smell like a thousand orchards, sweet and rich.

No Man's Land

In the other room, the farmer's old clock bonged eleven times. Hopkins looked out the uncurtained window onto darkness. It was a five-minute walk to the old chapel, but he would be heavily burdened.

And he could wait no longer. If...*if*, what a small and yet supremely powerful word!—if indeed this Smith could do as he promised, then before the clock ticked off two more hours, Hopkins would hold Esme in his arms again.

He tucked the lock of hair carefully into an inside pocket, then grabbed the handle of one heavy bucket in each hand and began his short journey.

It took longer than five minutes, far longer. The thin metal handles kept cutting into his palms; his hands would tingle and go numb, and he'd have to put the buckets down to shake some life back into them. His breathing was not what it had been; the mustard gas had seen to that.

The tumbled mass of the old stone chapel rose before him at last. He walked up to the broken steps and put his buckets down yet again, then dragged out his pocket watch. He could see by the light of a fat full moon that it was just a quarter of midnight.

But all around was silence. Even the insects were silent, as if frightened of what was coming.

The door to the chapel, hanging by one hinge, creaked open before him and a brilliant yellow light dazzled his eyes.

"In time, Captain, well in time," said the shadow that held the lantern, in a voice he recognized only too well. He blinked, and the shadow became Smith, wrapped in a black cloak. "Come inside, Captain. It is time to begin."

Hopkins followed the shadow named Smith though the little chapel to a small room opposite the main door. It smelled musty and forlorn, as if it had been used to store mildewed cushions or ancient hymn books and was haunted by their smells.

Smith set the lantern on a tiny wooden table just inside the room and motioned to Hopkins. With a sigh that was very near a groan, Hopkins set the two buckets side-by-side next to the table with the lantern. He shook some feeling back into his hands as he examined the room, made bright as day to his night-attuned eyes by the sizzling lantern. It was small, not more than a dozen feet square, with a stone floor. On the opposite wall, he could make out a drawing done in black, bold, crude strokes; he could not make out exactly what it portrayed and started forward to see it better.

"No, if you please," said Smith as he flung out a hand and grabbed Hopkins' sleeve. "The drawings on the floor must not be disturbed."

Hopkins looked down, to see more bold black marks on the pale stone floor. This image, however, he could make out: a five-pointed star, with a circle and a triangle in the very center, and odd signs at each point. In the very middle of the star sat a low rectangular stone coffer, the sides no more than a foot high, the entire thing perhaps two feet by three.

"If you will be so good," murmured Smith, motioning with one pale hand to the stone coffer, "as to pour the contents of your two receptacles into that?"

Hopkins pried the cover off the first bucket and, in an instant, the musty smells in the small room were replaced with the rank, bitter odor of rotten flesh.

"Do not, as you value your life, spill any of that in any place other than the stone box," Smith hissed suddenly.

Hopkins, who had just started to pick up the first bucket, started and set it back down. He examined it carefully, but nothing seemed to have spilled. He carried it the three steps necessary and tipped the contents into the stone box, then repeated the performance with the second bucket.

"Now, just set those outside in the nave, will you please? And close the door?"

Hopkins set the buckets outside, the stepped back in and shut the door behind him.

Smith was correcting a few smudges in the artwork on the floor. He rose and turned to Hopkins.

"Now, Captain," he said, holding out one milk-white hand,

No Man's Land

"the lock of hair?"

Hopkins thrust his hand into his pocket and, for an instant, his heart stopped within him. Was it gone? Had he lost it? His treasure, the only bit of Esme he had left?

But no; it was there. He pulled it out, relishing as always the smooth texture. He held it to his nose and could just detect, over the reek in the room, its faint and flowery scent. He kissed the hair, kissed the green ribbon that bound it—the ribbon he'd bought Esme because it matched her emerald eyes—and handed it, though not without a sudden reluctance, to Smith.

"What...what are you going to do with it?" he asked, his voice husky with fear and a horrible sort of desire. "Will...will I get it back? It's all, you see, I have left of her."

"Now, perhaps, Captain, it is all you have," said Smith, a little smile flickering across his shadowed face, "but soon, you will have no need of such a remembrance. You will have her back again, flesh and bone, fire and stone."

"What do you mean?" Hopkins asked, or tried to but his voice seemed stuck in his throat.

Smith ignored him; instead, the pale man pulled the green ribbon from the hair and tucked it away, then moved towards the stone coffer, the bit of golden hair caught between two pale fingers.

Smith hovered over the coffer with its putrid, unspeakable contents and Hopkins listened as the man began to murmur soft words, blasphemous and obscene, that chilled the air and made Hopkins' very heart go cold within him. He wanted to cover his ears with his hands to block out the words and the images they called up, but he did not dare.

The voice went on for what seemed like days, though could only have been minutes. The room grew brighter, and Hopkins looked up, to see a hole in the roof and the moon peering in, as if interested in the events transpiring.

And events were transpiring. The thick substance in the stone coffer began to bubble, as if a fire below was heating it. Hopkins did not want to know where that fire originated; he did not dare think of it.

Then the lazy bubbles began to burst, one by one with tiny pops, filling the air with noxious fumes that grabbed Hopkins by the throat and set him to gagging.

Smith continued to speak, but now his words were in some strange arcane language that Hopkins did not recognize—for which he was extremely, exceedingly grateful. Smith raised the hand holding the lock of hair as his voice rose to a crescendo of indecipherable noise.

Then he dropped the hair into the bubbling muck.

Hopkins started forward with a cry of dismay, but Smith raised his other hand and the captain felt an invisible force shoving him back against the wall. Smith followed him, laying one arm across Hopkins' chest as he stood beside him, both of them with their backs against the wall.

"Stay here, away, well away. We must watch now. Watch… and wait."

Hopkins was afraid, more afraid than he'd ever been, even when the guns were blazing above him and men were dying around him. Death was in this room, with him, closer than it had ever been before. Death and…something worse, far worse, shared this small space with him and Smith. What was he doing? What was he risking?

"See!" hissed Smith, though he did not remove his arm from across Hopkins' chest. "See there!"

Hopkins watched in fascinated horror as the thick mud in the coffer started to raise itself, as if it wished to escape its stony bounds. Up, up, higher than the topmost edge, it rose, somehow clinging together in a single mass. A bone stuck out here, another there, fragments that had been in there when Hopkins shoveled the mud into the buckets; he remembered the cracking sounds they'd made as he drove his shovel into the muck.

The mud column rose ever higher.

And horribly, began to take on a shape—a recognizable shape.

Arms formed, mud-colored and shapeless at first, though

growing firmer and paler as he watched. A blob on top began to shape itself to resemble a head, and he almost screamed when golden curls began to sprout like weeds and tumble down to cluster around the coalescing figure.

"From dust we come, to dust return," intoned Smith. "But sometimes, to those of us who know the old ways, who can utilize the ancient powers, the dust can be brought back…for a time." On the last two words, Smith's voice rose into a sort of ecstatic wail, and Hopkins could feel the arm still rigid across his chest, tremble.

The figure was now almost completely covered with rivulets of flowing golden hair. It stood perhaps five feet high—just the height, Hopkins thought, of Esme, her lips at the level of his heart.

A tremor ran though the figure, and then a low, soft voice, a voice he almost, nearly recognized, whispered, "Jo…si…ah?"

"Well, Captain," said Smith, his voice smug and satisfied. "Do you scoff? Do you doubt, now, with proof before you? Man can raise the dead—at least, one man can. *I* can."

"You…you…" Hopkins stuttered, trying to control his tongue, which seemed to tremble as did the rest of him, whether in fear or desire he could not say. "Is she…is she…"

"Dare you, now, with this before you, doubt my power?" Smith shouted, his anger blazing white hot. "Dare you, with all you have seen? Frail mortal, do not mock me!"

"I…do not doubt," Hopkins managed to say, though his tongue felt dead and dusty in his mouth. "I cannot doubt you. But is she…can she….will she…?"

He could not go on, could not frame his questions in his mind or on his lips. He could not take his eyes off that gently swaying figure, so close to him, the golden hair flowing down all around it in gentle waves.

Then two arms, white as the face of the moon above, snaked out from the mass of curling hair. They extended upwards in the bright moonlight, as if reaching for the beams that fell from above. Fingers grasped but could not capture the silvery dancing beams.

Then the figure began to turn, and Hopkins held his breath.

His Esme, returned to him from death itself. Could he—*dare* he—believe it?

Limned by moonlight as bright as noon, the figure finished its turn and he could see, within the masses of hair, two brilliant green eyes.

With a horrible squelching sound, one foot raised up to the edge of the coffer and balanced there for an instant, then stepped over to the stone floor. The other followed, and two small white feet stood, their little toes just touching the black line of a single ray of the five-pointed star.

Hopkins flung Smith's arm away and stepped forward—only to be stopped by a hand on his sleeve.

"I fear, Captain, that I did not mention one tiny little detail." Smith's voice had lost that anger and once again was smooth and low. "One small, insignificant, quite minor detail."

"Let me go, you bounder," Hopkins shouted. "Let me go... to her."

"Oh, of course, of course," said Smith, though he did not turn loose of Hopkins' sleeve. "But let me tell you just one thing before you fling yourself into her arms, shall I?"

"What thing, damn you? What thing did you *forget* to tell me?"

"Only this, my dear sir."

The golden-haired form stepped forward, and one little toe touched one black line of the pentagram. She—*it*—hissed and drew back, lips wide in a snarl of rage and pain.

Hopkins saw rows upon rows upon rows of tiny, sharp white teeth inside that mouth that, an instant before, he had longed to kiss.

"Only one thing, my dear Captain," Smith said, and though he could not see the man's face, Hopkins knew he was smiling. "I can only work with the raw material I am given. You brought me death in those metal buckets of yours, sir, decayed bodies of men... and rats. And other things too, no doubt. I fear, sometimes, such substance is less than...desirable."

Hopkins gazed at the thing in front of him, and saw long

claws where its nails should be. Worms erupted from the pale cheeks and waggled obscenely. The green eyes were round and bright, and there was the glint of hellfire within them.

Hopkins screamed. And screamed. And went on screaming as the abomination that was not, and had never been, his Esme reached out pale arms to him and gnashed its bitterly sharp teeth in dark and eager anticipation…

About the author:

K.G. McAbee writes fantasy, pulp, horror, mystery, YA and steampunk; she has had more than a dozen books and nearly seventy short stories published. Her work has won a variety of awards, including the Independent E-Book Award for Best Reference Book and the Dream Realm Award for Best YA Fantasy; she is also a Derringer Award finalist in mystery. She and her co-writer, Cynthia D. Witherspoon—writing as Cynthia Gael—just signed a contract for their first collaboration, an urban fantasy called BALEFIRE AND MOONSTONE, Book One of THE BALEFIRE CHRONICLES. For more information, visit http://kgmcabee.books.officelive.com.

WRISTS
Shennandoah Diaz

Morgan huddled in the crook of the concrete structure. Once a two bedroom home, only a few walls remained of the old stone cottage. Its frame fell away, broken and dissected so that it looked as though decades of erosion and neglect etched it down to its somber bones. Morgan knew the truth. She knew the damage occurred in less than a few hours and by her own hand.

She caught the sobbing gasps in her chest. Listening for footsteps, she clutched the stone. The cold surface soaked into her skin and permeated her bones with a chill so deep and fierce that she believed she never again would feel warmth.

The laughter of children grew closer.

"There you are."

The air rushed from her chest as the pain of fear dug into her. She pushed herself deeper into the stone. Her swollen eyes searched and begged for the demon children to fade into the darkness like any normal nightmare.

"No, you can't make me. I won't do it again."

The black creature smiled, revealing silver fangs. "You don't have a choice."

Morgan tried to stand, but her bare feet slid on the slick stone. The demon child jumped on top of her and bit down. The instant it's venomous teeth pierced her flesh she felt the overwhelming sensation of sleep take her. She saw three more demon children join the first; their laughter followed her into the darkness.

Wrists

***

Hands brushed the hair across her face.

"Wake now. You've slept long enough."

Morgan blinked. Damp grass formed a bed beneath her. She looked up at the iridescent black orbs, at first not understanding.

She scurried back. "No."

"My dear. You needn't be afraid of me."

He reached out a kind hand. She saw beneath the glamour to the black sick feeding within him.

"You can kill me if you like. I won't do it again."

"Why would I want to kill *you*? You're more valuable alive. In fact—" He considered for a moment, "—I think you're the only human worthy of life."

The pile of bodies in the center of the grove stared at her with cold eyes. Morgan searched for a way out. Shadows moved on the edge of the moonlight. Their teeth reflected in the silver rays.

"There's nowhere for you to go."

Morgan swallowed the lump in her throat and forced herself to her feet. Tremors rumbled through her muscles, threatening to send her tumbling to the ground once more.

"Then I guess you don't have any choice but to kill me."

"I always have choices. It is you who does not."

He stepped closer, the serrated blade held firmly in his right hand. She stepped back on bruised feet. Demon children nipped at her heels.

"Why are you trying to stop this? You were made for this. This is what you are supposed to do."

She wrapped her arms behind her back, hiding the scars. "I'm a freak. At least I realize that."

He smiled. "A freak, no. You're a demigod, a queen—and a queen always serves her king."

He yanked her right arm out from behind her back. The blade tore through her wrist before she could pull it away. He dragged her toward the bodies. Blood stained the grass and dripped along the ashen flesh mangled and clumped together on the forest floor.

A demon child brought forth a goat. Wind coiled around Morgan's legs and whipped the fabric of her skirt. Electric currents reached up from the ground and bolted her in place. The wretched creature released his grip on her and grabbed the goat by the ears. He pulled back its head.

A sickening yelp erupted from the goat's strained throat, followed by the sound of blood gurgling and choking in the open wound. The animal's life-force mingled with her own atop the lifeless mound. Morgan fought to stop the currents growing around her, but her blood craved the sensation and she could no longer withstand the pull of power beckoning her forward.

The pile quivered.

Morgan clenched her teeth, fighting against the intense yearning. The need to plunge into death and bring forth life called to her blood. Every molecule in every vein hummed in anticipation, begging to be a part of the primal dance.

Limbs shifted.

A deep hunger twisted in her stomach. Her body wanted to continue, wanted to feed the frenzy building around her.

Fingers stretched. Moans echoed in the night air. A cold hand wrapped around her ankle. Morgan screamed.

"That's enough." The demon master placed a bandage over the open wound. "This is my army to command, not yours."

The flow of blood ceased, and so did her hold over the animated flesh. He tied a knot and squeezed her arm below the cut. The bodies continued to stand and situate themselves into a subdued and willing army.

"Why," Morgan fought against the swirling sensation, "why do you keep doing this?"

"Because they have to know." His fingers wrapped into her hair and forced her within an inch of his face. "These people forgot what fear is. They create a false fear, laugh at it, sell it, then beg for more."

"They don't deserve to die."

WRISTS

The heat of his breath brushed against her cheek. "They don't deserve to live."

Prompted by a silent command, the makeshift squadron marched forward. A muffled mew escaped her lips. Among the ranks, a twelve year old girl walked forward, her eyes blank and hollow.

"Now, my dear. If you don't mind, I have work to do." He released her. Morgan swooned and fell to her knees. Demon children surrounded her. Their small hands sent electric currents through her body. "Wait here for me, won't you."

He walked ahead of the somber parade. Morgan turned away, not wanting to watch the disjointed bodies drag their feet across the field.

"Damn you," she mumbled through clenched teeth. She wrapped her good hand in the grass and yanked out a clump of sod. "Damn me, too."

A tiny hand slid across her shoulder.

"Don't touch me." Another hand poked her side. "I said, *don't touch me*."

She looked up at the bastard child. He smiled. Behind him, dead bodies marched forward. Slack jawed and dumb, their heads lobbed about as they slid forward in an uneven cadence.

"You beast."

The child darted away from the airborne clump of earth. He clapped his hands and danced, proud of what he had done.

Morgan's head fell forward. She beat her good fist into the earth. The mad dancing of the demon children swirled around her as she sank deeper into the soil. She pushed her arms against her ears, protecting herself from what she knew was coming.

***

The screams stopped.

She heard his footsteps above the giggles of the demon children. She did not raise her eyes to meet him. The weight of the past few hours held her down.

"Come." An icy hand pulled her up. "See the marvelous work we have done."

Blood throbbed beneath the scab on her wrist. The pulse intensified and worked its way through her body, until it pushed the boundaries of her skull. She felt the blood flowing in her veins. It called out. It wanted to taste the power again. It wanted death.

Too weak to fight, she let him drag her forward.

Silence filled the woods surrounding the tiny hamlet. Even the birds remained quiet. All life abandoned.

"You really should have been there. It truly was quiet marvelous."

Worms wriggled in her stomach.

"You have a gift, my dear. You are a," he smiled in search of the word, "treasure."

"You're a bastard."

"Don't be angry with me. Soon you'll see."

Worms burrowed through the lining of her intestines, filling her insides with twisting, turning knots of sick.

Tendrils of smoke peaked in the sky above the trees. The bitter cold settled in her bones, accumulated, until it deepened into a harsh chill. A small gust blew through the forest, carrying with it the stench of burning flesh. Her steps faltered.

"Hold on, my dear, we're almost there."

He wrapped his arm around her waist to keep her steady. She tried to hold on to the numb creeping over the edge of her heart. At least the numb would kill the pain.

The trees thinned. The first outbuilding emerged. A man hung over the stone fence. His head lay at an awkward angle, the result of a severe break. They walked past the gate. Through the opening, Morgan saw another body. The woman's arm lay a few feet away from the rest of her. The muscles of her face, contorted in pain, froze into an everlasting expression of agony.

"The best is over here."

Acidic goo burned the back of her throat. She doubled over.

Wrists

He yanked her upwards, forcing her to swallow the rising bile.

"Hold on, we're almost there."

The familiar sound of laughter echoed around the next building. Morgan braced herself as they turned the corner.

Bodies littered the city square. The demon children worked quickly, dragging each body to a makeshift pile in the center.

"Isn't it beautiful?"

Morgan wailed. Her knees buckled. The master let her fall. Her shins smashed hard against the cobblestones.

"Now we'll have an even bigger army."

Spit foamed through her clenched teeth. "Never."

He grabbed a handful of hair and dragged her toward the pile. "Oh, yes we will."

He threw her down in front of the bodies. The many faces—too many faces--stared back at her, questioning her, asking her why. Why did they have to die this way? No answer to give, she moved back onto her knees, but couldn't seem to tear her eyes away.

The bodies from the previous town began to show advanced signs of decay. Knives, bullet holes, and other countless wounds also mottled the zombies' flesh. Morgan dug her fingers into the cracks between the cobblestones. She looked closer at the twice dead bodies.

They fought back. Despite their obvious terror, despite the unstoppable foe marching right at them, the people of this town fought back.

The demon children added more bodies and severed limbs to the fray. Something bright reflected in the growing sunlight. Morgan glanced over at the master. He paid no attention to her, and continued delegating the placement of more bodies.

"Excellent work, my children. Just toss them over there. If we have too many, we can always start another pile."

Morgan crawled forward. The hilt of the blade stuck out above the shoulder of a young man's body. She wrapped her strong hand around it. She pulled. Reluctant to release the steel from its insides, the flesh held tight. Morgan maneuvered to get a better grip on the blade and eased the knife from the wound.

She glanced over at the demons and their master. Two children tossed a severed foot back and forth. Another pulled the body of a young woman by her pigtails. Her face scrapped against the stone until it flung her onto the pile with the others.

Ignored, she carefully undid the knot and unwound the bandage, discolored pale pink from her blood. She pulled the blade across the wound, breaking open the fresh scab. A thick stream of crimson flowed down her arm. She reached out, letting the droplets saturate the still flesh.

Electric currents pricked at the hairs on the back of her neck. The power danced on the edges of the imaginary circle surrounding her. With each drop of blood, the circle shrank until the electric tendrils wrapped themselves tightly around her.

The mound before her trembled.

The master called out.

She squeezed her arm, forcing more blood from the wound.

Fingers stretched. Heads rolled to the side. Something groaned.

"What do you think you are doing?"

Morgan placed the blade between her knees. She held the naked flesh of her left wrist against the blade and pulled up. Blood gushed onto her skirt. She swung her arm over the rumbling hill of flesh.

The master grabbed her shoulder and twisted her around.

"Stop it. Stop it now!"

He reached for her arm. She hid both hands behind her back. More blood saturated the soil. The red liquid tied her to the electric currents. The chain grew stronger with each pulse.

A hand reached out and pulled on his ankle. The master jumped back.

He feigned a smile. "Morgan, dear, stop this now."

The first bodies left the pile and made their way toward the master and his children. His eyes darted round, as bright and fearful as the slaughtered goat.

WRISTS

"Now, I mean it."

Morgan held out her hands, letting the blood flow across her palms and into the frozen earth. A slight warmth filled her hands. The heat rose, filling her arms then flooding her chest with its comfort.

Fingers crawled passed her, dragging along a detached arm. Bodies on the outskirts of town began to stir, beckoned forth by the blood permeating the soil. The demon children snarled and clawed.

The master shrieked. "Stop this at once. I order you."

The loss of blood left white spots in her vision. Morgan fought through the dizziness. "You can't order me."

"Yes I can. You were made for this. You were given a gift. You must use it. It's who you are." His head shifted back and forth between the approaching zombies. "Morgan, you don't have a choice."

A slight smile curled her lips. "We always have a choice."

A cold hand fell on his shoulder. The master pushed the first zombie away. The zombie righted itself, and pursued again. More bodies clustered together, forcing the demon children into a tighter circle around their master.

A demon child bit into the leg of one the zombies. The demon pulled back and spit out the tainted flesh. The zombie reached down. The demon fought against its grip. The dead man leaned over. With a gaping mouth, it chomped down on the child's shoulder. The demon screamed. Frothing at the mouth, the zombie noshed and chewed. He pulled back, ripping the ligaments from its neck. The demon screamed. The zombie pushed the child's neck against its mouth. The demon fell silent.

More spots filled Morgan's vision. She held onto the electric currents, channeling them to a single target.

The master screamed. She recognized the sound. It was the sound made a dozen times over by innocent people sleeping in their beds awoken to find their nightmares are real.

Another scream, an awkward pitch of pain and fear, filled the town square.

The currents permeated the entire basin. Morgan felt the

fading pulse of life beating beneath the sea of death. The pulse slowed. She listened. The screams stopped. The master's life force ceased its ragged beat.

She fell on her side. Her own pulse slowed to a trickle. With each beat the currents receded. One by one, the bodies fell where they stood. The wave ebbed inward, pulling the power back toward her.

Morning rose in full glory. Sunlight filled the square. The orange rays warmed her skin and thawed her aching bones.

The electric waves fizzled. A single breath escaped her lips, followed by the last drop of crimson from her wrists.

ABOUT THE AUTHOR:
Shennandoah Diaz' work has appeared in *Sex and Murder* and the *2010 Elemental Horror* anthology. Diaz was also recently named a finalist in the 2009 Writer's League of Texas Manuscript Contest.

All the World a Grave
Michael McClung

They called this place the Abode of Wraiths.

It is a very old place in a very old city, this pile of stone set high on a hill overlooking the Vanach bay. It is—was—the black heart of a twisted body, steeped in history and foul deeds. It's home, now.

They used to bring the Witches here to execute them, and later, when the Witches took power, they in turn brought their various enemies of the state here to be executed. Untold gallons of blood have soaked the flagstones of this windowless edifice of despair. The stone walls have echoed back centuries of doomed, terrified wails, and absorbed fierce amounts of psychic terror—so much that the spirits move about freely through the empty rooms and black hallways. It is never quiet here. There are always shrieks and moans, and less identifiable sounds.

Once the Witches were ousted, the place was abandoned. It has lain empty, as far as I know, for nearly a century. But time means little to the wraiths. Or me, for that matter.

And who am I? Nobody. As I was never given a name by the whore who abandoned me at the doorstep of the Yshevine monks, and the monks never saw fit to call me anything other than 'boy', Nobody is who I am, and who I have become comfortable in being. Malthus called me Ulik, but that's just the Hardreshi word for 'bitter'.

Ahenobarbus, the only wraith with any wit in this place, finds it amusing to haunt nobody. He was an augurer in ancient times. He had power enough to retain some sense of self beyond death. Most of the other wraiths are barking mad, full of rage and terror and pain. Ahenobarbus suffers mostly from a deep if antiquated sense of irony. He foretold the rise of the Witches, and then was executed by them for having supernatural powers once they'd administered their bloody coup. Seemed they thought that the true Power was strictly a woman's prerogative.

This is possibly the least pleasant place in the world, the Abode. But it is never quiet here. And I've grown sick of silence.

***

I awoke this morning from a dream about my mother. I've never dreamt about her before, nor my father that I can recall. I seldom remember my dreams at all. This one was little different; only fragments, images; flashes of white and red, and eternal, monotonous coughing. It was not a pleasant dream, but then, who would expect pleasant dreams in the Abode? But it brought forth old memories.

I found my mother when I was ten. She was consumptive by then. I tracked her down in the Order of Mercy infirmary. She was curled up on a narrow cot, wearing a clean white shift. Her dirty blond hair was sweat-streaked, and lay wild about her face and on the thin pillow. Her eyes shone fever bright. When I told her who I was, she laughed. Laughed until she hacked, and spit up a pink froth into one of the small supply of kerchiefs on the stand by her narrow bed. She didn't argue. The resemblance between us was very strong.

"What do you want from me, then?" she finally managed.

I had planned to slip a knife in her heart, but there seemed little point.

"I want a name," I finally replied.

"I haven't got one for you. I haven't got anything. Go ask your father, that fecking blood-specked turd."

"I will, if you tell me who he is." And she did.

"Is there anything you want me to say to him for you?" I asked.

All the World a Grave

"Tell him I'll be waiting in Hell to tear his miserable Gloinish eyes out." She cackled, then coughed, and a gobbet of blood flew out of her mouth to spatter down the front of her clean white shift. The look of surprise on her face was almost comical.

The Sisters had sharp eyes; one darted past me to clean the old hag up. Another took my arm in a painful grip just above the elbow and dragged me away, whispering fiercely all the while about torturing a damned soul. I would have snapped the old bird's neck, but there were too many people about. Besides, I'd got what I wanted.

***

It took me two more years to find my father. He was a sailor. I tracked him down in a cold, filthy inn in Gloine. He was a used up wreck. He was of the Gloinish clan of Cluanghe, which means 'Son of the Ship' or sometimes 'Son of the Sea'. A poetic name for an unpoetic breed.

I left him in a darkened corner, face-down and eyes open on a scarred, filthy table, hand still curled around the drink I'd bought him. When you slip the blade in right, a heart will stop instantly, and the dead man won't even let out a sound. The Monks taught me well, though I doubt they'd approve of some of the uses to which I put my knowledge.

It was only after I'd left the inn that I realized I'd forgotten to deliver my mother's message. I didn't bother to ask him for a name; by then I'd gotten used to being nobody.

So much for my parentage.

***

Ahenobarbus says I must be the most evil person who's ever lived. He says it with a smile, but I really think he believes it. He can't understand how I could care for no one and nothing. He says even the old Emperors, as sadistic a lot as they were, had appetites and enthusiasms. Metitus, butcher of Cispades, built toy boats. Aphranus, the man who plucked out his mother's eyes and, supposedly, ate them, loved horses. Whereas I, he says, have no enthusiasms. He says he could not imagine me caring for another living thing. He is wrong in this, though I do not correct him.

There was a cat. A one-eyed tom that fed from the monastery's garbage. The thing was more scars than fur. We had much in common, that cat and me. I'd throw him scraps from my meager portions. He would take them, hissing and growling the entire time, fur raised and needle-teeth bared. The one time I tried to touch him he nearly took my fingers off. We suited each other.

Then one day he disappeared.

A few days later, Brother Movel gave a class on poison delivery systems. We walked into a room full of cages. The cages held rats, pigeons, dogs, and cats.

I got to feed the cat poisoned meat. That particular poison was called red death. It is distilled from lathanberries and is odorless and nearly tasteless. It causes massive internal bleeding and is among the most painful poisons known to the Monks. The victim bleeds from every orifice and every pore.

I can still see the tom staring at me as the blood poured from his one eye, his snout, his mouth, his anus. The look of hate in his eye. The rumbling yowl. Then the final swaying collapse.

I was eight. A week later, I pilfered a vial of red death from the poisonarium, dosed the Brothers' ale keg and went over the wall.

It took them three days to find me. They dragged me back to the monastery and broke my legs. Then they set them, very expertly, and locked me in a lightless cell. Once a day they would come and feed me, and check on the progress of my healing. Two months later, they brought me back up into the light and held a feast in my honor. I was their prized pupil.

They never asked me why I did it. They knew. I learned my lesson well. I spent two more years at the monastery, perfecting the art of death by stealth. Then the brothers sold my contract to the Duke of Malthus.

All the World a Grave

He was a tall man, and handsome in his way. They called him the Pale Duke. He had watery blue eyes and ghostlike skin. His hair was white and straight, falling down around his shoulders. The only color to him was in his lips, which were crimson.

He installed me in his palace, in a room just off his own. There I became his catamite and his assassin.

***

We are all born with a death sentence hanging over our heads. It's inescapable, despite alchemists' chatter about the philosopher's stone and with due regard to the dark arts. Longevity is not immortality.

If we were immortal, perhaps we would be just and reasonable creatures. We are not, and so those who can grab all they can while they live. It is human nature. Those few who are ruthless enough to dominate, do, and the rest suffer and toil. Malthus taught me that. He also taught me that it doesn't matter who is in power, the result will be the same. Let the slaves rise up in bloody revolt, unable to endure their miserable lot in life. Let them take power. What will change? Titles. Only titles. But I didn't need Malthus to teach me that. Time and again, history has proven it so.

We are, at best, selfish creatures. Such is our nature, inherent in our own mortality. Malthus believed the only thing to be done about the human condition was to make sure all the other humans were in a worse condition than himself.

Ahenobarbus is the opposite. He says that man, given the choice, will choose good over evil. He says that love is stronger than hate. He thinks that suffering is not a natural consequence of mortality, but rather love is. Just goes to show you that being dead doesn't make you any wiser.

I don't subscribe to Ahenobarbus's point of view, that much should be obvious. But I didn't agree with Malthus, either.

In any case, it's all theoretical, now, isn't it? That's all right. Idle speculation passes the time. And time is the one thing I have lots of.

Michael McClung

***

I almost went for a walk today, outside the Abode. I just stood there at the great key-shaped entrance. I couldn't seem to make my foot cross the threshold. I tried to remember how long it had been since I went outside, and I couldn't. For a crazed moment, I thought I might have died and become a wraith myself. Nonsense, of course. Wishful thinking, perhaps.

Finally, I turned to go back. Ahenobarbus blocked my path.

"Going out?" he asked.

"I was. I changed my mind."

"Why?"

"Nothing to see I haven't seen before."

"Oh, now that is an untruth. In all the time I've known you, I've never known you to lie. It is perhaps the most refreshing thing about you."

"If you say so. Now please move. I don't like walking through you lot. Gives me the mimis."

"Go take a walk, Nobody. Get some fresh air, some sun. Take in the sights."

"I don't want to. Please move."

"I don't think so."

I stared at his wispy face. There was something…something feral, almost, in his expression. Normally he was very civilized for a wraith, even friendly after a fashion. But wraiths feed on negative emotion.

"Move," I said, "or I will abjure you."

He moved.

***

Malthus. Nobleman, lover of boys, consummate politician, practitioner of the Dark Arts. If Morgani had a human face, it would be his. He personified this wicked city. I hated him, and I admired him. During the day he treated me as a near equal. He respected my abilities. At night, in his chambers, I was his property to do with as he saw fit. What he saw fit to do was always degrading, and often painful. It was the perfect classroom. I learned to hate him, and I learned to hate myself. And I learned to hate and pity life.

I killed twenty-three men and seven women in the six years I served Malthus, not including my father. I killed him in my free time. It amused Malthus to grant me the time and resources to track down my parents. "Anything to keep my young protégé amused," he'd say as he handed over fistfuls of gold. "Do be a good lad and make yourself available on the twenty-eighth, though; there's a merchant who's positively truculent about grain prices." Or a count who'd said this, or a courtesan who'd done that. Or occasionally someone who'd done nothing at all save be born into the wrong family. It was all the same to me.

The last year I served the Pale Duke, he had less and less use for my body or my blade. I was getting older, and his tastes ran young. But the reason wasn't that, or at least the bulk of it wasn't.

Malthus had always dabbled in the Dark Arts. He enjoyed nothing so much as doing what was illegal and immoral. That last year, though, it blossomed from a dalliance into a torrid affair. And it all started when he got hold of the Black Book.

There's no telling where he found it. Those who dealt in the bizarre, the horrific, the sacrosanct and the contraband always had a patron in Malthus. Room after room in his palace were devoted to subjects twisted and vile. One room housed jars of aborted fetuses; another, two-headed beasts of every description, stuffed and mounted, some of them human. A third was composed solely of precious artwork of every size and description—the only common theme among them being murder, torture and rape. And these were the rooms that were open to any visitor. Deeper into the labyrinth lay darker places locked away from prying eyes.

The first time I ever saw the Book was on a chill autumn afternoon three days into the new year. I was passing through one of the courtyards in the interior of the palace on my way to the kitchens when I saw Malthus sitting at his portable writing table. Sheets of fine paper were scattered all across the surface. There was an ink pot as well, and quills. To his left was a bookstand; a heavy tome was chained to it. To his right was a flickering brazier.

There was a look on Malthus' face akin to ecstasy, or rapture. Slowly, he tore his gaze away from the Book and bent to write. The tip of his quill snapped, he bore down so hard on the paper. He cursed and flung the quill away. Then he took up another and quickly pared the tip with a small knife from one of the pockets in his robe. He held the newly pared tip just above the coals of the brazier to harden it, and turned back to the Book.

After a time the quill caught fire. Malthus didn't notice. When the flame reached his fingers he still didn't notice. When the air began stink of charred flesh, I turned and went back to my room. I wasn't hungry any more.

After that he stopped going to court, stopped taking me to his bed, stopped giving me assignments. He locked himself away in his private quarters for weeks at a time. At first I was glad. Then things became worse than they ever had been before.

***

I never drew any pleasure from killing. Malthus and others I've known seemed to delight in it. Killing, inflicting pain. Pain especially, be it mental or physical or—best of all sordid worlds—killing after torturing some poor wretch to the point of madness. I never took any pleasure in it. Ironic, wouldn't you say?

Malthus thought so. I think Ahenobarbus would, did he believe that what I did was done out of necessity, not some dark urge, not out of evil. I've never tried to convince him otherwise. What would be the point?

***

Darby was the first Malthus fed to the book. He was a kitchen boy, and he was all of eight years old. He had a sweet face under the soot and grime—big gray eyes and a quick smile.

The Book had demanded of Malthus the blood of an innocent. Darby had been nearest to hand. I only learned this later, you understand. I had nothing to do with the boy's actual death—though if Malthus had instructed me to kill him, I most likely would have. Such is my innocence. When Malthus summoned me to his study one early morning I went, rather gladly as I remember. He hadn't been seen out of his chambers for over a week at that point. I knocked quietly and opened the door. The first thing I noticed was that Malthus had taken every stick of furniture out of the room. I first got only the sense of a large clear space in gloom. The maroon velvet drapes were drawn across all the windows, and the candles in the crystal and gold chandelier had almost all guttered out.

As my eyes adjusted to the semi-darkness, they were drawn to something at the center of the floor. I could not at first tell what it was. All that could be made out plainly was that it was lumpy, and had a certain wet sheen to it that spoke of freshly slaughtered meat.

Darby, of course. What there was of him.

"It has begun," said Malthus from a darkened corner of the room. I had not noticed him where he huddled, facing the wall.

"What has begun, your grace?"

"My ascension, Ulik. Come and see. Come. Help me up. I fear this first task has weakened me."

I went to him.

He was naked and shivering, his forehead pressed against the marble wall. He clasped the book to his chest with both arms. Always slender, he had lost an incredible amount of weight. I could count every rib through the pale skin of his back. The vertebrae of his spine stuck out like the teeth of some strange serrated sword.

"Am I not more godlike, even now, Ulik? Can you not see in me the rising mark of the divine?"

"No, your grace." I had no fear of him, not in the condition he was in. The slow, steady pulse of his carotid drew my eye, and my hand itched to plunge a knife in it. Not for the first time. But then what?

"Stupid boy. Stupid, lovely boy. You will see. Serve me well, and you will know."

I helped him to his feet, careful not to touch the Book. Nothing could have persuaded me to touch it. I helped him hobble to his bedroom, deposited him in the depths of his monstrous bed, pulled the coverlet over his shaking frame. Turned to go.

"Ulik. I will need a whore tonight. The most withered hag you can find."

I closed my eyes. Put a hand on the doorknob. "Yes, your grace."

"Clean up my study, Ulik. Dispose of the refuse. But leave as much blood as possible."

I left, saying nothing, and did my master's bidding.

***

The wraiths cannot force themselves on a person, should he know how to prevent it. When I first came here, they gathered around me so thick that I walked in a cacophonous fog. They had been starving and I was a feast. The feast to end all feasts. It was Ahenobarbus who told me how to beat them back, whispering the words in my ear as all the others shrieked and gibbered and plunged themselves through me to taste my soul. I repeated his words. I abjured them, one after another, until only he was left.

"Welcome," he'd said. "I knew you would come eventually, World Ender."

He had been an augurer, after all.

***

Before the whore, I had killed for Malthus to protect or advance his interests, be they political, social or commercial. I had fulfilled my contract as the Yshevines intended.

I didn't kill the whore myself, but what's the point quibbling?

All the World a Grave

I picked her out of the line on Gash Street, where she stood shivering, nearly toothless and in tatters. I put the gold haemon into her grimy, tremor-struck hand. I escorted her back to Malthus' palace in the two-and-two and watched her try to compose herself on the velvet seat across from me, looked on passively as she cinched up her sagging breasts and tried to tame her matted mop of badly dyed hair, to make herself more presentable for 'the laird'. I opened each and every door that led to her end, from the lacquered carriage door with its gold scrollwork to the featureless mahogany door of Malthus' study.

No, I didn't kill her. If I had, she wouldn't have suffered as she did. If I had killed her, the filthy scrap of aether that was her soul would at least have gone on to whatever afterlife she had earned.

Instead, it was devoured by the thing Malthus called out of the book with her pain and her terror and her blood. And in exchange, Malthus received a little more of the power he craved, and became a little more monstrous, a little less human in appearance.

No, I didn't kill her. Nor did I kill all the other sacrifices Malthus had me collect.

I just served them up and cleaned up the mess.

***

One day the servants just disappeared. I thought at first the lot of them had finally decided to seek employment elsewhere. I thought they'd packed up in the middle of the night and slipped out the back way.

They hadn't.

In the kitchen, a kettle of tea had boiled away to nothing on the stove. Not so much as a muffler was missing from the cavernous cloakroom, despite a light dusting of snow on the ground outside.

Slowly, I trod the back stairs up to Malthus' private quarters. A sluggish rivulet of blood passed me as I neared the top, pooling on each step as if to gather strength before descending to the next.

The headwaters of that stream of blood were behind Malthus'

study door.

I almost turned away. I had all but decided to leave the palace, leave the city, take ship to Karharna or Gloin or anywhere, take the first berth outward bound I came across. Instead, I found myself with one hand on the doorknob and the other stroking the hilt of my knife.

I don't know why I decided to kill him then and not in the weeks or years before. It wasn't that I hated him, though I did and always had. Nor was it that I pitied him. I feared him, and always had to a greater or lesser extent, but looking back I realize that wasn't it, either. I think it was because killing was the only thing I knew how to do well, and something had to be done. Some action had to be taken.

I just didn't know if he *could* be killed any longer.

***

"How long will you hide here, scribbling among spirits?" Ahenobarbus asked me today.

I put down my pen. "What do I have to hide from, wraith?"

"An interesting question," he replied. "What do people usually hide from? Let's see. The law. Very popular to hide from the law. But there is no law anymore. Then there are debt collectors—but no, there are none of them left either, nor debts for that matter. I personally was fond of hiding from relatives, and the occasional angry husband. But—well, you take my point, I'm sure."

"And you make mine."

"So what is left to hide from, Nobody, World Ender?"

"Nothing, wraith. I do not hide."

"Do you not? Then why don't you take a walk outside?"

I threw the journal that I had been writing in at him. It tore a ragged hole in his chest that reformed immediately. He smiled, shook his head, disappeared.

"I had no choice! I did not know what would happen!"

Only silence answered.

All the World a Grave

***

When I opened the door to Malthus' study, I was assaulted by the spirits of the dead.

They swirled around the room, shrieking, clawing for purchase they could not catch. At the center of the room, naked amidst the carrion that had been his household staff, Malthus stood—or rather crouched, as he could no longer stand straight. His spine had curved nearly double, and his legs had grown an extra joint. Before him, on a pedestal of flesh, rested the book. Above it a hovered crimson ball of light, into which the spirits were being sucked one by one.

"It is nearly time, Ulik," said Malthus. His jaw had distended and his tongue grown hard and hornlike; I could hardly make out what he said. "Soon I will be immortal, all-powerful. Soon I shall be a god. I have come to the last page. Can you see it now?" He looked at me, and his bulging eyes had no irises, no whites. It was as if they consisted entirely of pupil.

"Yes, your Grace." I made my way carefully toward him across the bloodwashed parquet. I held the knife hidden in my sleeve. "How can I assist you?"

"Ever faithful Ulik. Nothing need be done now. Once these shades are consumed by the Orb, catalysm will be achieved. I need only place my hand in its divine fire." He stared up at it with a longing that was as naked as it was disturbing.

I stopped a pace or two away from him, from *it*. "What would happen if you touched the Orb before it was ready, your Grace? Before all the spirits had been consumed?"

He tore his gaze from the glowing orb. Even as inhuman as his face had become, I could read the suspicion that flared to life there. I plunged my knife into his coal-dark eye and he screamed. I turned to the Orb and, as his claws raked my back to bloody ribbons, I plunged my fist into the heart of it.

And all the world was made a grave.

Michael McClung

***

When I woke, Malthus, the spirits and the orb had disappeared. Blood and gore surrounded me, and atop a pile of severed limbs lay the Book. I reached out for it and my back shrieked its protest of pain, of the agony of torn flesh.

I stumbled out of that charnel room, down the bloody stairs, outside and into the snow. Laid on my back in it, waiting for the cold to numb the pain. I clutched the hated Book to my chest. Stared up at the steel-gray sky. Listened to the whisper of the wind through the bare branches of Malthus' plum trees. There wasn't another sound, besides my own ragged breath.

There is always noise in the city, day or night.

I clawed my way to my feet and stumbled, shivering, down to the postern gate past the perfect carcass of a newly fallen sparrow. Opened the gate with numb, clumsy hands. Looked out on death.

Bodies were scattered all along the Ponce Nobless. Men, women, children, horses, dogs. All fallen in the same instant, it seemed.

I wandered the city for hours, and found only death.

***

I went out today. It was not as difficult as I thought it would be.

The sun was shining. I had almost forgotten what it felt like to have the sun on my face, the tangible weight of light.

The city was as silent as ever. It is summer, now. I had expected there to be at least the chirruping of the boyne beetles in the trees, but it seems even insects were not beneath death's notice, and the trees are all skeletons raking the blue summer sky.

The bodies have not decayed.

They could almost be sleeping. Almost.

I made my way to the rocky cliffs above the bay. I don't know what I thought—perhaps that the sea would not, in all its vastness,

All the World a Grave

hold a hint of the dead that surround me. In that I was disappointed. The corpse of a leviathan rose and fell on the waves, pale belly to the sky, its flukes splayed out to either side.

I rubbed my eyes, coal dark as Malthus' had been, and turned back to the Abode.

Ahenobarbus was waiting for me, just inside the shadows.
"You've taken that walk we discussed."
"So?"
"So what do you intend to do, now?"
I laughed. "What is there to do, wraith?"
He smiled, a little sadly, and said "That is entirely up to you. Whatever there is to be done, you are the only one left to do it."

***

Poisons are what I know best, though there are any number of ways I could do it. Blood brought the Orb to life, though, so I think it best that there be blood involved at the end. All the Arts, dark or otherwise, demand a certain balance be reached, and once reached, maintained.

I've no idea if it will work. Frankly, I don't much care. In the end, it isn't guilt or remorse that drives me to it. It isn't hope that leads me on. I've no interest in sacrifice. Only a little pity. For myself, maybe, or for a cat that I fed poisoned meat to, or for a palsied hag of a whore, or for a kitchen boy who had an easy grin.

I finally abjured Ahenobarbus when he wouldn't stop following me around with those sad, spectral, cowlike eyes of his. In a little while, I will recant the abjurations I laid on all the others. Blood and spirits. I will open the Book to the last page.

At first, I couldn't decide which vial to take from the poisonarium, so I slipped one of each into the velvet-lined case and brought them all back to the Abode with me. But as I said, blood will probably be best.

The red death is odorless, and nearly tasteless.

Michael McClung

About the Author:
Michael McClung was born and raised in Texas, but now lives in Singapore. His first novel, THAGOTH, won the 2002 Del Rey Digital first novel competition and is available as an ebook. He enjoys kickball, brooding and picking scabs. He can be contacted at mcclungmike@yahoo.com.

Blood on the Beach
Anne Michaud

It started with a light, the end of a tunnel. A flash, intense and blinding, then everything changed for me. Forever.

I open my eyes; all I see is blurred and deformed. What could have been images of reality seem to have melted, always out of focus. And that smell. Decayed flesh, dried blood and bones. I leave, the room so cold. *Rise...*

I'm alone. The street is deserted, cars have been left where they've crashed, pieces of clothing and shoes wait to be picked up in the middle of the sidewalk. A breeze blows newspapers and garbage into the wind. Where do I go? *Rise...*

I remember bits, images, my life? Hands grabbing hair, clothes, faces. Tongues searching for blood all over a stranger's skin. Teeth tearing muscles, flesh pierced then ripped off hard bones. I smell urine, from fear and the excited expectation of death, eyes closed from pain and terror.

And that feeling of letting everything go, letting go of all strengths and hopes, letting dreams slip into oblivion. Nothing can be done, it's too late. No turning back, ever again. *Rise...*

So I walk, no destination in mind. My left leg drags behind me, flesh and bones. But it doesn't hurt, I don't feel it. My thick sole drags on the asphalt, the only proof it's still there. I can't move my right hand, my wrist bitten, open, pain-free. I feel nothing.

I can breathe but don't hear my heart beat, don't feel it in my chest. I can't move any faster than this; I can't make any complicated movements. There's something controlling me other than my conscience. I've lost it, like everything else. *Rise*, it says, *rise and rise again…*

The sun is too hot. My skin itches and I scratch, my nails falling off one by one. I'm slow; I'm not myself. But there's nothing I can do, none of my limbs move as they used to. Something controls me, but what? Who?

When one of Them sees me, and they let me walk past them. I look into their eyes, but find nothing. They're empty. They've been transformed like me, only their shells remain. Or maybe their voices are trapped inside. I can only pronounce words with one or two syllables, nothing more. Not like I have use for them. I'm alone and when I'm not, no one talks, they only stare and growl.

I come out only at night, the sun too intense, making my skin fall off where its rays touch. I hide in a building, the elevators too complicated for the others to understand, but not for me. Although it takes a while before I can press a number, any number, the closest to my good hand. I enter into what used to be an apartment, photos of strangers hang on the walls, there are clothes everywhere. There's food in the fridge, but I don't want any, finding the smell unbearable.

From the window, army trucks, men dressed in black fatigues walking down the streets. They hold glistening weapons, looking for others, others like me. I know I should be scared, I know I should try to hide. Maybe they're protecting me? Maybe others have pieces of souls left and the army is defending us instead of hunting us down?

I hear someone walking down the hall. The fast pace proves that it's not one of my kind. I hide in the kitchen pantry, my head slowly falling to its side as I'm too tall to get in otherwise. As I close the door on my face after having taken a deep breath—useless, old habits die hard—a soldier walks in, aiming his weapon at everything in sight.

The soldier searches for something in the bedroom, furniture pushed aside and tipped over, restless. My brain registers everything seconds after it actually happens. And the worst part is I know it. Every time I hear something, I know it's already in the past.

The guy speaks into a radio device he wears on his shoulder, and then takes off his hat. He thinks he's alone in the apartment. He thinks one of Them wouldn't be intelligent enough to hide in such a high-scale building.

It's not the smell of his skin. Or the sweat beading down his neck. His blood pumping from his heart to his veins. His tight muscles rippling under his uniform. His tender flesh hiding, for only me to find. It's the entire package. The way he looks around, still a bit nervous, as if only now realizing what's been going on for the past endless three days. How he sighs at the sight of personal pictures of strangers. How his eyes dance over every unknown object. I need to feel his heat. I want to taste him. He looks finger-licking good.

No, this can't be. I can think. I can formulate thoughts. My mind is at work. I'm not like the rest of Them, I'm not. I refuse to be. I refuse to give in to that instinct. It's just not me. Me from then and me from now.

But it's too late. Before I can stop myself, my body moves towards the soldier, my hunger too great to suppress. He doesn't know what's going on, waiting for further instructions as to where to look for survivors. Hey boy, I'm right here, I'm behind you. And I could eat a horse.

As he turns to face me, I plunge my bleeding teeth into his soft neck; my movement slowed only a short instance by his strong perfume. He tastes divine. I can't stop myself; I have to eat every part of him. I drink his blood, eat the big vein in his neck, swallow his left eye in the process. I don't care, I'm hungry and he's already dead by the time I've lost my left ear, the earring having caught on his uniform. Oh well.

When I leave the apartment, the dead soldier will wake up soon. I can't bear the thought of having to see him as anything less than what he was minutes ago. My first, he was delicious. And he will rise, too.

I wait for night to fall before I leave the building, hoping to find someone else like me. It's hard to avoid the army trucks, with their huge spotlights searching left and right. And the soldiers, all eager to stay alive and kill anything moving in the shadows.

Anne Michaud

Electricity seems to still be working in most of the neighborhoods, although no one has the courage to try it, people on my side, anyway. Hiding from building to building gets boring after a while, especially when I can't walk any faster. But most of the trucks are leaving the area, finally.

I jump as I feel a hand on my shoulder, although my body doesn't show any sign of panic, too slow to react. Another one of Them, looking a lot worse than me, with his face half-eaten off and the skin drooping from his chin. He signals me over to a group by an old Gap store, its windows and contents destroyed. Another conscience, another one like me. I follow what's left of the guy and stare at the others. The girl is almost naked, but no one is looking anyway. Her sagging skin seems to ripple off her frame. The old guy is missing an arm and his lower jaw, his face almost intact from the nose up. We exchange knowing glances, unable to talk, forever silent.

Then, a kid comes out of the store munching on a woman's arm. Its tendons have been sucked out and only a few mouthfuls remain on the bone. The girl fights for it until the kid grabs her shoulder and pulls down. If she'd been alive, the girl would've screamed, the skin from her upper body falls off like a banana being peeled. There's nothing she can do, although she tries to retain most of it with her arms, modestly. The kid stares at her with a blank expression and eats the remaining few bites off her radius. When he's finished, he drops it to the ground and two men go for it, as slowly as their deranged bodies allow them to.

I remember pieces of it, a former life, estranged from now, so far away in my mind, it sticks to my brains. There was pain in the chest, tests, machines and beeps, one last breath, half of me frozen, attacked by my own heart. Then a voice, distinct, when there shouldn't have been any: *Rise, rise and walk, rise and obey. Rise* for a second chance. *Rise* for something better, things I never had the chance to finish. *Rise for us*, rise for them. So when I opened my eyes on this world, I rose like they asked. What was I supposed to do? I'll never know, but arise I did, like a good soldier.

Blood on the Beach

From what I can see, maybe many rose, but not many survived. An army of undead, followed by an army very much alive. They're killing us, destroying us for destroying them, the people, the ones who have a right to live. But not me, not us, we are to be taken down, to be forgotten like a bad dream. I never asked for this, so why should I have to pay? All I did was follow orders, too.

The guy leading us starts to scream, or what should sound like a scream. Deformed mouth, distorted noise. I can see them, a platoon of soldiers rushing our way. I stop, so sudden that I lose my balance for a second. When I turn around, I notice that my fellow flesh-eating friends are following me, all desperate to get away from the huge spotlight coming from the tank down the street. We hide in a subway entrance, protected by a thin layer of metallic shingling, but there are already many hiding in the dark, the reflection of the street light in their eyes, some with only one opened, others without any.

It takes forever, but as soon as the troops leave the streets, my people become vicious, a commotion breaks at the back, I can't see why. One of them pushes a little kid to the ground; it takes him half an hour to get back up again. The ones who were there first want us to leave; they push us towards the subway entrance, their hands grabbing my body. I can't control it, can't think of what to do. But I do, I fight back.

Claws. As if the meat at the tip of each finger has fallen off, revealing only pointy bones. And that putrid smell of unwashed skin mixed with rotten meat. No wonder even the dogs run away when they sniff around us.

I fight them off, but there are too many. I try to speak, but can't, so we leave it at growling at each other. By the time I see the soldiers waiting by the subway entrance, their weapons aimed at us, it's too late to escape. They move so fast, I can't even follow them with my eyes. I back off, hoping it will be enough for them to aim at someone else.

I back off, deeper into the darkness where fewer bullets reach me. I've never felt such an urge to live before, the little adrenaline left in my dead body pushing me to walk towards the subway's lower tunnel. It's full of decomposing bodies, a few rats pick at the remains here and there. I think the kid is following me, I can hear something very slow trying to reach me, but turning to check would be too hard. Then I hear heavy footsteps, fast paced. Not ours, theirs.

I fall to the ground, ripping off my knee in the process. I pretend to be dead, hiding my head under the railway, seemingly decapitated days ago, such was my fate. I wait. And I wait some more. It's hard to hold my breath; my lungs slowly fill with air seconds after I feel light on my back, my skin so sensitive that it hurts. Soldiers shoot close to my body; for once I'm glad my body reacts ten thousand years later. I feel a bullet go through my thigh, blood dripping under me. If nobody was around, I would drink it. I'm dying of thirst.

A soldier's boot touches my hand, slowly pressing down on it, pushing it deeper into the dirt. I don't feel it, I just know something's on top of it, and dirt is filling its grasp. The soldier kicks my body a couple of times and after they all conclude that I'm really dead—and are they ever right—they leave me alone. When I stand up an hour later, I see the kid's body, decapitated, dead for real, unlike me. The tunnel is cool, wind rushes over my decaying skin, the darkness heaven for my tired eyes.

I walk. For days. Sometimes, I can hear what's going on above ground, in the streets above me. Bombs, gunshots, screams. Nothing good, for me or for anyone. I see a couple of others like me but none notice my passage—without blood or flesh, we slowly die, feeling our hearts stop beating, the air leaving our lungs, our souls lifting from what's left of us. I've seen it happen, more than once, but each time I can't help but think that there's a part of us that never goes away, even when we're transformed. Maybe I'm the last survivor still walking the earth, maybe I should try to mate with another of my kind. Maybe not.

I finally see the light at the end of the tunnel, blinding, painful and alluring all at once. There's a beach, waves come crashing down where there used to be land. I find no one, night or day; no one

Blood on the Beach

survived, dead or alive, no one but me. I walk to the sea, a leg falling off slowly as my flesh rots in the salty water. I'm drained, hoping my death won't be too painful. And my mind wanders for a short while, as I bleed.

About the author:
Anne Michaud lives south of Montreal with two devious cats in a house full of books, some of which are hers, as yet unpublished.

THE SCARLET CAT
Rebecca Lloyd

"You're such an odd child, Danica," Grandma said in Russian as she fussed her wrinkled fingers through the ash-blonde hair of the girl sitting on the porch at her feet. Danica was thirteen and tolerated it, barely showing her annoyance as her shoulder-length locks became stubby pigtails—again. What she learned at times like these was more than worth being treated like a doll for a little while.

All she had to do was wait until Grandma got into one of her mumbly periods. Then she'd start absently spitting out the things she denied even knowing about when she was feeling less senile and more Catholic. Bits of incantation; scraps of lore. Danica had learned early that her family had only one inheritance to offer her, and it was locked away in the brain of the aged woman in the chair behind her.

Magic. Necromancy, one of her horror comics had called it: the magic of the dead. Scary stuff, but Danica needed scariness right now. They were the only "Russkies" in a west Nevada craphole: population 840, insular as hell. It might be 1980, well past the era of Red Scares, but the locals apparently hadn't heard the news—and they could get very loud about it. But from poverty or inertia, her parents never mentioned pulling up stakes and moving. Maybe it was because the house was the only piece of real property that pair of sad drunks had ever managed to hang onto. Whatever the case, Danica was stuck looking for a way to fend off the locals, and protect her own. Ordinary methods weren't working. She needed… an edge.

The Scarlet Cat

She was distracted from her brooding by her twin, Marina, singing off-key to the leggy bundle of white fluff tumbling through the grass at her feet. She couldn't help but smile as she watched her sister with the cat. Both of them got depressed, but Marina never let herself fight back against anything that troubled her. Maybe she thought it was the Christian thing to do—turning the other cheek, only to invite another bruise.

Danica was the one who stepped in when the local wannabe-gang teased Marina in the schoolyard. Her sister would just stand there and cry. Marina could keep that martyrdom crap; it just made a hard life worse. Some nights, holding her awkwardly while Mom and Dad screamed and crashed plates downstairs, Danica wished she could shake her twin out of her passiveness. Cody the cat could at least comfort Marina without getting irritated by her need to play victim, so in spite of fleas and hairballs, Danica liked the fuzzy little thing.

But she had work to focus on now. "The bird, Grandma," she urged again. The tiny brown-feathered corpse sat still warm on the porch railing next to her. "Can you fix it?"

"Oh, dear," Grandma replied, taking it in her soft, seamed hand. "Another little one. You're always finding them." She lapsed into mutterings in Old Slavonic, which her granddaughter strained to hear correctly. Then, back to Russian, her tone still cheery. "Did you break its neck yourself?"

Danica blinked, then snorted. "Yes, Grandma, I snatched it out of the air like Cody does butterflies. Of course not. Why do you think such things?" Actually, she had scared a stray cat off of it—after calmly standing by and letting it make the kill.

"You're too cold, Danica," Grandma insisted, cradling the bird. "You're too much like my father. So strange to see it in a young girl, but yes, you get your temperament from him."

"How, Grandma?" *It's because I'm strong like him.* Great-Grandpa was the whispered-about one of the family, a legend whose grave was never visited. The stories had a quality of black fairytale to them: an aged necromancer, forced to leave his lands lest his family starve, raising the contents of a whole cemetery to lead them safe across the Iron Curtain. *A hero.*

There was fear now behind the soft reproach in the old woman's voice. "You are too angry, and you have a taste for blood."

"...Oh." *Pah. Not around here I don't*, Danica thought with a faint smirk.

They had become vegetarians because of Grandma, though of course Mom and Dad insisted it was for health. Nobody but Danica was willing to discuss the real reason meat was banned from the table. Grabbing a burger on the sly after school every day, she savored the taste of beef that didn't squirm under her teeth.

That was life with Grandma. A drive to church was once disrupted by an amazingly coherent treatise on corpse preparation. When they were nine, Marina, going weeping to Grandma about her dead hamster, was comforted by strange rhymes—and found the little corpse running on its wheel when she went back to her room. (Mom wouldn't let Danica keep it).

And then, the fatal dinner scene, two years ago: a headless Thanksgiving turkey, fully cooked, starting to thrash on the platter and wiggle its half-severed limbs as Danica's drunken father kept trying to carve—in front of a full house of twelve people. Aunts and cousins screaming, Mom screaming, Marina wailing in the corner—and Danica, clamping a hand over her mouth to hold back laughter as the pathetic thing stubbed around on the gravy-spattered table, jumped off the edge, and waddled off into the kitchen.

In the aftermath, there had been talk of sending Grandma to a home. But the idea of this "awful" family secret getting out in a public facility was even worse than cornering the market in tofu and greens. They had adapted instead, going into convenient denial. Danica hadn't. She was hooked. And so she started visiting with Grandma at every opportunity—and taking lots of notes.

She went back to listening as the old woman started whispering over the bird again. She had her battered black-covered notebook with her as usual; she always told Grandma, who could not write in English, that it was for homework. She wrote down

The Scarlet Cat

each syllable phonetically, to compare against her other notes, and watched for something to happen.

There was a tiny pop, like the noise Danica's back made when she stretched. The bird's head righted itself suddenly on its wobbly neck. It blinked, and then fluttered its wings.

"There. Oop!" the old woman laughed as the bird pecked her and a small red dot appeared on the heel of her hand. "Heh-heh-heh. They like blood, they do. Like blood, hate salt. Blood for life, salt for death." The bird pecked her again, then tipped its head back, letting a ruby droplet slide down into its gullet. Its glazed, still eyes became bright. The restless movements of its wings strengthened.

"Off you go!" Grandma called softly, and tossed the bird into the air. It flew off awkwardly on slightly-mangled wings. "Good as new."

Danica knew it wasn't; it would rot away within a week. She had caught several creatures after reanimation and studied them. They were very lively, and seemed almost immune to pain. Decomposition stopped them eventually. Dismemberment only resulted in a handful of wiggly pieces. Fire did the trick, but it took a long time, even with all those flammable feathers.

(Dad never used his basement workbench anyway, so he never noticed the few stains Danica wasn't able to clean up. She burned the evidence in the ashcan with the yard sweepings).

A stone smacked into the grass just between Cody and Marina's reaching hand. Danica stood and looked over as the cat skittered up the stairs to hide behind Grandma's feet. "Dammit, not again," she growled under her breath. There were three of the usual five gathered on the sidewalk: eighth-graders led by big redheaded Jim, the local beat cop's boy, now bluff-faced and grinning at them as he hefted a small chunk of asphalt.

"Marina, take Cody and get in the house." Danica's voice was hard. Behind her, the window-blinds rattled; Mom or Dad, up early at noon—watching but staying hidden, as usual. Her sister hurried up the stairs, groping for the cat between Grandma's feet.

The boys jeered. "Hey, what's that big white rat on the porch?

You keepin' it as a pet?"

"It's a god-damn alley cat. Oughter be killed." That was Steve, the lanky blond. Short Sammy with the braces grinned at his elbow.

"Don't you hurt my kitty!" Marina shrieked at them through her tears, clutching the captured Cody to her chest as she stormed inside. The screen door banged.

That just left Danica...and Grandma, the creak of her rocker slow in the sudden quiet. Everyone knew the rumors. It was part of why they hated Danica's family. As the creaking stopped, and the old woman's housecoat rustled as she rose, the boys all backed up a step.

Danica felt a surge of malicious joy. Now Grandma was angry. What spell would she choose? Would she summon ghosts to haunt them? Would their dead relatives claw their way from their graves to pay the bastards a visit?

The old woman pointed a narrow finger at them, and rasped in her broken English, "God see you pay for this."

The three looked at each other as Danica's heart sank. Sammy snickered. Then Jim dropped his rock and turned away grinning and shaking his head. "Senile old Russkie bitch." Laughter rippled through the knot of boys, and they drifted off down the street.

Danica stood there with her face hot and her fists clenched at her sides as she glared after them. She kept her back turned to keep the old woman from seeing her expression. Instead, after several deep breaths, she asked in pained tones, "Grandma, why didn't you do anything to them?"

She heard a grunt and a creak as Grandma settled back in her chair. "Do what, Danica? What did you expect me to do?" Her tone was baffled—and a touch reproachful. She was too lucid now; she was denying the magic. Again.

Danica felt her temper slip its leash and turned, the look in her eyes making Grandma blanch slightly. "I don't know," she snapped. "Make them pay. Scare them off." *Certainly stop playing stupid.*

The Scarlet Cat

Grandma squinted in the direction the boys had walked. "They're gone now."

"They're laughing at us. They made Marina cry again." Danica's voice softened into exasperated pleading. "I know you can do something about this."

"I'll do rosary." She was always doing rosary. When Dad lost another job, she did rosary. When Marina cut herself, she did fucking rosary.

"I know you have power, Grandma. You have to do more. You're the only one that can!"

Grandma's eyes clouded for a moment, and then she glared at Danica sullenly. "I'll...do...rosary."

Danica stared at her, all her anger dying down into disgust. *Am I the only one in this whole family with any strength?*

She stalked inside, and found her parents shut back up in their bedroom and Marina sobbing on the couch. She brought tissues and a cup of water, and sat beside her twin quietly until the sniffing stopped and Marina looked up. "Keep Cody indoors from now on, okay?"

Her sister nodded. Danica went upstairs to go over her notebook of Grandma's stolen phrases again, and daydream about revenge.

What Grandma knew was her key to getting the boys to leave her family alone for good. Danica could fight until she was black and blue, but it only made them let up for a little while. They needed to be taught respect—forcibly. *I just don't get why Grandma sits on her butt and lets the family suffer like this. Magic is power. Why not use it?*

Four months later, Grandma stood up in the middle of tofu-and-greens, pointed in horror at an empty corner of the room, and collapsed.

The hospital said stroke. Danica was quietly frantic. She knew she had not gotten all the words to the incantation the old woman used, and she needed it. The boys were starting to come around the house at night, throwing rocks at the windows and scaring

Marina. One well-aimed casting could stop them; Grandma had never had the guts, but Danica sure did. She imagined reanimated bones from chicken dinners and buried pets, road kill and cat kills, all scrambling from their rude graves and chasing Jim and his cronies through town. She had to find a way to make it happen before those ignorant thugs graduated from scaring Marina to hurting her.

It was past one in the morning by the time they left the ER with news that Grandma was stable. Mom and Marina dozed in the back of their battered sedan, wrapped in the bliss of hospital-issue sedatives. Dad drove white-knuckled, licking his lips so constantly from twitchy booze-cravings that Danica wanted to slap him. She rode shotgun with her hands knotted in her lap, face white. Grandma being stable was good, it was great, but she was trying as hard as she could not to think about brain damage. Of irreplaceable knowledge lost.

She helped Marina into the house and got her tucked into bed. Her parents vanished into their room as usual. She sat up for a while, reading her notebook again by the dim light trickling in through the window by her bed. These days, she found herself doing it whenever she was upset. The thought of power was what she had for comfort now that she was too old for teddy bears; study had become ritual, like Grandma and her rosary. She read until she nodded off.

Nobody noticed that Cody was missing until around four.

Danica only got a glimpse of the alarm clock's glowing dial as the screaming in the back yard jolted her from bed. It was interspersed with male jeering that sounded hideously familiar. She was on her feet and racing down the stairs in her pajamas before she realized the screaming didn't sound like a human. Then she heard her sister upstairs:

"Cody! Oh my God, *where's my kitty?*"

"No," she said through gritted teeth as she raced through the kitchen, snatching a butcher knife out of the block on the counter as she ran past it. "*No. No.*" She flipped on the backyard light and came crashing out of the door.

All five of them stood in a ring. Something on the grass

The Scarlet Cat

between their feet. Dark stains on their hands and pocketknives.

The screaming had already stopped.

"...that was cool," Jim's voice was breathless. He stepped back...and she glimpsed the thing they were looking at: slick and red and still twitching. Cody. His fur hanging like a stained white rag in Jim's grip.

Adrenaline roared through her; she was off the back porch before she realized it. She crashed into them, swinging the butcher knife like she was felling a tree.

They fought back, yelling in surprise: fists slammed into her, hands grabbed at her, but she twisted and kicked and slashed wildly, fending them off while trying to do as much damage as she could. Three times the blade-tip caught in flesh: Jim stumbled back, clutching his thigh with red drizzling between his fingers; another boy's cheek gashed open, showing the side of his teeth. Sammy grabbed for the knife and got just a shallow slice across his palm, but it was enough to make him gasp and pull away.

She kept fighting. Because of Marina, wailing and struggling against Dad's grip in the back doorway. Because Cody was just a poor stupid innocent cat that never hurt anyone, and he had made Marina happy, and they needed to be punished *now*. Because she knew Dad wouldn't help, so she couldn't let up, or they'd pull her down and stomp her into the dirt. So she slashed, and stabbed, and elbowed until they broke and ran, screaming about the crazy bitch— three bleeding and at least one with the crotch of his jeans darkened.

She stood there panting and trembling with the red-painted blade gleaming in the porch lights. Triumphant. Hating. Bitter, as she looked down and saw the little corpse lying there in the dust like a butcher-shop castoff. Her knife arm dropped to her side, the rage curdling inside her with her powerlessness.

She glanced back at her family cramming the doorway. Marina was sobbing, reaching out to the mess at Danica's feet and then drawing back in horror, crying out over and over about her poor, poor kitty. Mom kept to the background, puffy eyes squinted in incomprehension. Danica's gaze trailed up to Dad's thin hand around her sister's wrist, the awkward half-hug that was his only gesture of comfort.

She locked eyes with him, dark determination welling up in her heart. "Get her inside. Lock the doors. Take care of her. *I will take care of this.*"

Dad nodded wide-eyed and pulled Marina back into the darkened kitchen.

Danica realized she was hugging herself and folded her arms. She glared down at the skinned cat in disgust. These chuckleheads couldn't even come up with anything original in their acts of cruelty.

But I sure can. Blood of my great-grandfather willing.

She took a few minutes to compose herself, then set the knife down and went inside. No time to wash, bruised and dusty and blood-spattered as she was. She walked into her room and saw Marina huddled on her bed with Dad hovering ineffectually nearby. She slipped past them, stepped into her sneakers and grabbed her notebook off her bed.

"Danica, wha-what are you going to do?" Dad, his chin trembling like Marina's.

Child. "Just keep the place locked up until I come back." She stalked out.

She had only a fragmented spell to go by, but she remembered something Grandma had said about the dead, and blood. She looked at the knife. She had blood from three of the boys on it. If a drop could animate a whole bird, couldn't this much work for a small cat?

She had imagined that her first spellcasting would be at least somewhat grand: candles and robes, incense fogging up the basement and something cool on her tape player. Not bending in her pajamas over Cody's corpse, straining to read phonetically-spelled Old Slavonic by the chancy porch lights. She knew it probably wouldn't work at all, but she was too desperate and pissed-off to care.

The syllables felt strange on her tongue. She tried to remember Grandma's inflection. She had no idea what the words meant or what part of the incantation she was actually missing. She tried to focus her whole mind on getting it right; doubt nibbled at her and she pushed it away stubbornly. Incomplete or not, the spell had to work. She was going to give those boys the scare of a lifetime, no matter how many tries it took.

And then none of them would make Marina cry ever again.

She didn't know how long she stood there, repeating the same phrases while the corpse cooled and stiffened. She knew it was long enough that her neck hurt and the chill sank straight through to her bones. Long enough that her mouth felt thick, and her fingernails bit crescents into her palm that kept hurting even after she noticed and pulled them free. Long enough that tears of frustration dripped on the dirty meat of the cat's face. And she still kept going.

Finally she finished the incantation a last time, trembling with rage; dropped the notebook, and took up the knife, still dark with the boys' drying blood. "Get up," she ordered the dead cat.

It didn't move.

She clenched the corners of her jaws. "I said, get up!"

Not a twitch.

Danica felt another storm of adrenaline break through her veins; she lifted the weapon and brought it down with all her strength. "Get...the hell...*up!*" The knife bit home in the cat's chest—and something like a silent thunderclap slammed up Danica's arm.

Its filmed eyes flew open.

For a moment, she thought her blow had shaken them open. But then Cody started to thrash, struggling against the blade that pinned it to the ground. Claws gouged the dirt. It hissed at her, sounding as annoyed by the knife as if she were simply holding it down.

"Cody." The word was breathless. The cat stopped squirming and stared at her with eyes like lusterless pearls. Its raw, ratlike tail curled and uncurled.

Real. This is real. I did it. Absolutely thrilled, Danica crouched down; the cat rumbled warningly at her and lashed out a claw.

"No!" It stopped. "Not me. You know who hurt you. Their

blood's on the knife."

It could have been her imagination, but the cat seemed to be listening to her, its talons flexing impatiently. With the pads stripped off, they looked larger than they had in life.

Danica fought the crazy, bitter grin that pulled at her lips, and took hold of the knife again. The boy whose cheek she had mutilated would have had to go to the hospital for stitches, and would be out of the cat's reach. But the others would have tended their wounds as best they could in secret, to keep their bloody "prank" from their parents. "Jim Carnahan and Sammy Mathers. Want to go visit them?"

She didn't know how well it could move; she might have to carry it to the boys' houses. Coatless in the cold—but she didn't care. The looks on their faces would repay her for her goose bumps.

She yanked the knife free—and the cat took off, scrambling over the fence and vanishing. Danica blinked after it. "Crap!"

At least she wouldn't have to carry it. That would have implied, well, putting her bare hands on it. Anyway, she knew the direction it was going: straight for Jim's house.

She hurried down the street, and into Jim Senior's weed-strewn side yard. The whole time she was whispering: "I did it. I *did* it." Feeling a trembly-sweet thrill of power all through her. So long in coming: years of dead birds and pigtails and waiting for senility to put enough cracks in Grandma's denial. The spell was cast—successfully. Now, all she had to do was watch the fun.

The yard was a mess of hidden lawn furniture and tumbled car-junk rising from the overgrown grass to bite her shins. She stumbled her way along, mouthing her full thirteen-year-old's compliment of juicy swear-words.

Jim's room was on the first floor. Danica knew because she'd smashed the big jerk's window in last year with a board. Now, the replaced sash was up perhaps four inches in spite of the cold, and she could see dark smears on the windowsill. She sniffed, and smelled blood. The cat was here, all right. *Fast work. Good kitty!*

Inside, she could hear slow breathing. The bastard snored; his

The Scarlet Cat

breath rattled like his throat was half full of fluid. Boy was he going to scream when the cat jumped on him in the dark, all wet meat and claws and attitude. Danica waited for it, listening to wheeze after bubbling wheeze.

When Jim's snores slowed after a little, a line of confusion appeared between Danica's brows. And why...why was the smell of blood getting so strong? The cat must be right under the window. She bent down, listening, and heard a faint sound beneath the strangely erratic breathing. The rhythmic rasp of a cat's tongue lapping at something.

What the Hell? Suddenly she wished that she had brought a flashlight. Had the thing she'd raised from the dead stopped to wash its butt before making with the scary?

She slipped her hand inside the gap and tried to pull the curtains aside to let in some moonlight. They budged perhaps an inch; she tugged harder—and was horrified when the runner came loose from its hooks and crashed loudly to the floor. She ducked out of sight as moonlight flooded the room—but glimpsed something that had her peeking back up over the sill immediately.

Something dark on the floor around the bed, like an irregular black rug that gleamed. The cat was crouched in the middle of it, head down. She looked closer, even as another drawn-out, bubbling wheeze trickled out from under the sash.

"Jimmy boy, you drop something?" called a male voice from somewhere in the house. "Y'all right in there?"

Jim drew in a whistling breath...and then let it out in a thin hiss. Nothing followed.

Footsteps neared the bedroom door. She tensed, but couldn't tear her eyes away from the window. *What's going on in there?*

The door flew open and the light went on, and the darkness blazed into five-alarm red: arterial gouts on the walls and bed sheets, the floor around the bed covered with pooled gore. Squinting in the wash of light, she gaped at Jim's claw-ravaged neck and choked on a scream.

And then her gaze fell on the cat, its face pressed greedily into the sticky red puddle, purrs vibrating the gristle of its throat as it lapped. Its blood hadn't settled into its extremities; its exposed muscle and arteries were still vibrantly red. And it looked...no, it couldn't be right, but somehow it looked...bigger.

Its muscles bulged. Its talons glittered like knives. When it raised its head to stare at the man in the doorway, she saw that its ears had grown back.

Jim Senior stood there with his donut-gut lopped over his belly as he stared at his son like he couldn't see the cat or Danica or anything else. His voice broke on his scream. "JIMMEEE!"

He lunged for the bed and the cat's re-grown ears flattened; it exploded toward the window. Danica threw herself to the ground and covered her head with her arms as the glass smashed outward and showered her. She heard something heavier than it should have been land a few feet away and tear off through the high grass. Jim Senior's screaming kept on and on as lights blazed on in the windows of the surrounding houses.

Danica scrambled away from the window before the light could catch her, crawling on all fours in the glass-strewn dirt. Her repeated whisper had changed its tune: "What-did-it-do-what-did-it-do...what-did-*I*-do?"

It killed him, she thought as she hitched her way to her feet and ran after the cat as fast as she could, the butcher knife still clenched in one fist. *How did a little dead cat manage to rip out someone's throat? It...it killed him. (I killed him). Then it drank his blood and now it's growing—I swear to crap I saw it growing....*

Sammy. Sammy was the other close target. His house was two streets over, and the cat's spattered trail through the grass pointed straight in that direction. As if it could scent the boy from here.

This wasn't how it was supposed to be. It was only Cody, Marina's half-grown kitten. It was supposed to scare them. Maybe claw their faces. There wasn't supposed to be a gashed-open corpse in Jim's bed. The big burly cop that Danica had grown up fearing wasn't supposed to be wailing like her sister behind her.

She forced herself to focus, breathing deep and steady as she

The Scarlet Cat

ran. She had to figure out a way to put the cat safely in the ground before things spiraled even more out of control. She had no idea what it would do once it ran out of targets. Pick new ones, maybe. *Like Marina. What if it comes home to her? What if it's still hungry?*

The cat was definitely growing stronger by the minute. She realized this for certain when she heard splintering sounds up ahead in the darkness, and found a hole clawed in Sammy's back fence. Cody had gone through the pickets in seconds, and the sight of the gouged wood sent a cold surge of nausea through her stomach.

How can I stop this thing?

On the far side of the yard, she heard something slamming repeatedly against a door. Lights started coming on inside the house as she groped her way around to the side yard in search of the gate. "Good, good, they're up," she mumbled. "Please, be predictable rednecks. Somebody in there have a shotgun or a hunting rifle handy—and don't point it at me."

From behind the door, a sleepy female voice: "Charlie, honey, what is that?"

"Sounds like someone's trying to break the door down. Hey! You out there! I got my Colt right here in my hand. Get the Hell away from my door!"

The slamming stopped. Silence, for a moment. And then…a drawn-out, ululating yowl, raspy from a death-swollen throat, far louder than it should have been. Not of pain; nothing plaintive about it. It was a cry of blood-madness and rage.

The woman in the house gasped. But then someone started fiddling with the locks, and a fresh chill went through Danica as she remembered all those experiments. How even the severed pieces would move….

"Don't open the door," she heard herself mumble. "The gun won't stop it long."

The latch clicked. "No."

A line of light from the opening door washed across the lawn.

"Don't open the door!" she screamed just as something slammed into the wood and claws started tearing at its edge eagerly.

"Jesus Christ! What—"

"Oh God, Charlie, close the door, close the doooor...."

"Mom?" Sammy's voice. A light went on in one of the upstairs windows. The cat snarled.

"It stopped! Where did it go?" The door opened a little more and Danica tensed, but nothing attacked. She stopped the last few feet from the gate and dared a peek over the fence again as the backyard floodlights went on.

A bloody streak ran up the side of the house like a slug trail, each strip of white siding puckered outward slightly where it passed. A third of the way up the wall already, something the size of a large raccoon was muscling its way upward, drizzling scarlet fluid as it went. Its talons dimpled and tore the aluminum as it climbed. It was heading straight for Sammy's window.

"Crap!" She yanked the gate open and hurried in. "It's climbing up the house! *It's after Sammy!*"

To his credit, Charlie only raised the hand-cannon in his fist halfway before he stepped outside and peered at her. "Ain't you that drunk Russkie's girl? What you doin' out here?"

She spread her arms, showing her bloody pajamas. "It attacked our place first! It goes after kids!" Congratulating herself for the quickly-thought-up lie, she gestured frantically at the side of the house, where the cat was more than halfway up. *Look! Monster! Get shooting, idiot!*

"What—sweet Jesus God—" He raised the pistol, his screaming punctuated with sharp cracks as he pulled the trigger. Danica didn't wait to see if he succeeded in slowing the thing down. She shoved her way past Sammy's mom and raced into the house, hoping she'd get to the stupid boy before the cat did.

Sammy doesn't deserve the rescue, she thought as she found the stairs and took them two at a time. *He and his friends are the reason this is happening.* If they'd kept their pocketknives and sick cat-torture fantasies to themselves...if they'd just left her and her family alone, none of this would be happening.

But she hadn't meant to kill anyone, she really, really hadn't, and now she had to find a way to put the cat back down among the properly dead before things got even worse.

She had the knife, but she needed the notebook. She had left it back in the yard, stupid fool that she was, and now she had nothing that could have helped her figure out how to cancel the spell. So she did the only thing she could think of: put herself between the cat and its target, and try to get Sammy far enough away that it couldn't follow.

"Sammy! Where are you?" she yelled as she reached the top of the stairs. "Get out of your bedroom! Hurry!"

A door opened down the hall and Sammy peered out. The fingers curled around the edge of the door were bandaged. "Oh shit!" he said when he saw her. He yanked his head back in and slammed the door fast. "Crazy bitch and her knife again—how did you get in my house?"

"I should let you get killed, you ungrateful crap-sack!" She raced up to the door and kicked it, then started pounding. "Sammy, it's the cat! That's not the TV, those are gunshots! Your dad's shooting at the cat! It's climbing up the wa—"

Inside the room, glass shattered and Sammy let out a terrified screech. "No!" Danica yelled, and started twisting and yanking the door handle. It wouldn't budge, and Sammy was screaming and the cat was yowling and things in the bedroom were crashing and thudding while she wasted seconds fighting with the door. Outside in the yard, she could hear his parents calling out his name in desperation, and wondered why in the hell they weren't running up to help.

Then suddenly, he was struggling with the handle from the other side, and she let it go, and he spilled out of the room with a red malignancy on his back that spat and snarled and must have weighed thirty pounds. One of its eyes was shot out, and as it lifted its head to glare at her she saw the bullet slip out of the drizzling wound and bounce off the back of Sammy's neck. A fresh orb, pale as milk, rolled into place from the depths of the socket a moment later.

Danica couldn't scream; she stared, thinking *I had no idea I had this much power*...and she was thrilled again, in spite of herself. But sickened as well, because Sammy's pajamas were shredded and spattered with blood, and the thing's fore-talons were dug into the meat of his shoulders like hooks. He collapsed at her feet and wailed, trying to cover the back of his neck and getting fresh gouges in his arms for his trouble.

"No!" Danica shouted, shaken from her reverie. The cat hissed its derision and lashed out at her. "No! Damn you, let him go!" She stabbed at it ineffectually, forced to avoid hitting Sammy, then finally and started sawing the knife against one of its forelegs to try and cut it off the boy.

It snarled and lunged at her, talons disengaging from Sammy's back in little pops of blood, and she knew in that moment that she couldn't control it, any more than she knew how to make it stop. She swung the knife two-handed and missed with the blade, but her forearms smacked into the cat awkwardly and it missed as well, slamming into the wall beside her.

She whirled and drove the knife into the side of its neck before it could slide down. It squirmed and screeched, and clawed trails of fire down her belly and one of her arms, but she pushed until the blade crunched through cartilage and meat and then stuck fast in the drywall beyond. The cat became a storm of talons and spattering gore; she stumbled back with another rake across her hand and caught hold of Sammy's less-injured shoulder.

"Come on," she panted, heart pounding. "That won't hold it. We have to get you out of here. Is the car out front?"

Sammy stared at the writhing thing on the wall through a half-mask of blood that squinted his left eye closed. He was breathing hard and had probably pissed himself, but at least he wasn't gouting everywhere. "Jesus...is that the cat we skinned?"

Her arm was dripping on the floor: a deep scratch, but she could still use it. "Yes, it's the cat you skinned. It came back to life just like the damn turkey you guys like teasing Marina about. It's trying to gut all you idiots for what you did to it, and I'm caught up in the whole damn mess trying to stop it. Okay? You should never

The Scarlet Cat

have messed with us."

He gawped. "But—but Jimmy said your Grandma was in the hospital, and she was the only one what did that kind of witchy stuff—"

"Leave my Grandma out of this, buttwad. She's a good Christian." The bullshit was just rolling off her tongue tonight. She started tugging him down the hall as fast as she could. "Our family's cursed. This kind of crap happens anytime anybody screws with us too much. Now answer me, idiot. Where's your dad's car?"

Sammy, in a panic of confusion over the crazy Russkie bitch taking a beating to save his ass, seemed to buy the whole mess; at least it made sense of things. "I-in the garage."

"Take me. Hurry."

The screams and scrabbling of the cat trying to free itself grew fainter as they raced down the stairs. Danica's foot touched the bottom step—and she heard an ominous clatter as the knife fell to the hallway floor above them. Sammy's parents were still freaking out uselessly in the backyard, his mom gibbering and Charlie still yelling his name. *Have they locked themselves out or something?*

She was really getting sick of useless people.

Talons scrambled on hardwood upstairs. They raced for the kitchen and the door to the attached garage—just as footsteps finally came thundering in through the back door.

"Where's the monster?" Charlie yelled. "I gotta git the shotgun, I'm out of rounds!"

"I hear it upstairs!"

"Is he still in his room? Sammy! You hear me, boy?"

"Dad! I'm here, Dad—" Sammy stumbled as his attention was caught in mid-step, and Danica was pulled nearly off balance.

"No, don't stop!" she yelled, dragging at his arm. "It's faster than us!"

Behind them, the cat and Sammy's mother screamed in unison—then someone slammed hard into the wall.

"Marge! No, get off her, fucker—wait—oh no—wait! Sammy! Run, boy, it's after you!"

She glanced back and saw the cat racing around the corner toward them. Its claws were easily as long as her fingers now, and it gouged up the floor in its eagerness to reach them.

She threw the garage door open and pushed Sammy through it as the cat tried a sharp turn on linoleum and slid splay-pawed into the cabinets. Somewhere back in the dark, Marge was screaming: injured doubtless, but lively enough to be noisy about it. Charlie would be helping her and then going for his shotgun; meanwhile, Danica had to hold Cody off on her own. She lunged through the door and slammed it just as the cat skittered up to the other side.

Sammy was tugging at her arm like a small kid. "My Mom—we can't leave them!"

"Your Dad can get her out the back door and come around. The cat's not after them. It's after you. Now come on." She groped for the light switch and hit it, revealing a powder-blue station wagon with Bondo-and-dent detailing, flanked by shelves of gardening supplies, tools...Danica looked around quickly, and finally hefted a shovel. "Know how to drive?"

"Dad was giving me l-lessons." His eyes were glazed with tears. At least Sammy would walk away from this with the proper scare she'd been meaning to give him—if he survived. Something slammed hard into the door, and he jumped and whimpered.

She shook her head. "Good. Where does he keep his spare keys?"

He gave her a deer-in-the-headlights look until she scowled at him; then hurried over to a stack of driveway-clearing supplies tucked in the corner. He reached behind one of the bags of rock salt and pulled the key off a low hook on the wall.

Slam. Slam. The cat was damned persistent. Worse was when it stopped and changed tactics. She heard the solid hardwood start to splinter under its claws.

"Shit! It's digging its way through. Get in the car and start the engine. I'll get the garage door."

The garage door was a piece-of-crap automatic, and pulling the cord only made it grind open a hand-span and then rattle to a

The Scarlet Cat

stop, belching out the stench of an overheated engine. "Dammit!" She ran for the door, grabbed the bottom edge and started trying to yank it up. As the kid fumbled with the keys and Danica shouldered at the door ineffectually, the sound of splintering wood grew louder. A line of light appeared in the bottom of the kitchen-access door; a talon poked through and started tearing it wider, gouging out curls of wood as if its claws were made of steel. "Crap! Sammy, we've got to crash through the door to get out of here!"

"We can't! I can't! The c-c-car won't start!"

Danica let go of the door and grabbed her shovel. "Fine! Lock the car! Hide under the dash and don't say a goddamned word!" Hopefully the stench from the garage-door opener would mask his scent from the cat.

The talons tore another chunk away from beneath the door. The cat's face appeared, blank eyes gleaming; it snuffled, then hissed and redoubled its efforts to widen the hole. As she raced over, it started pushing through the gap, ignoring how the thicker splinters ripped gouges in its sides as it heaved itself forward.

Danica hefted the shovel, slamming it against the thing's head the moment it poked through; the cat snarled and flattened against the floor, then started hunching forward again, claws digging into the concrete. It just kept pulling more of itself into the garage as she swung the shovel down with all her strength against its steel-hard skull. It lashed out and its claws shrieked against the shovel blade, striking sparks. She flinched, but struck it over and over; then it was through and darting under the car.

The shovel had barely stunned it; she needed a better weapon. *Gas can. Goddamn gas can.* She started looking. Fire was slow, but it always did the job in her experiments. It would spread in here, make a real mess, but there was no way anyone would blame her as long as the kid lived and the monster died. *Gas can. Kerosene. Lighter fluid. Stupid bulk bottle of corn oil.* She didn't care. But there was nothing. How could a garage full of so much junk not have anything flammable?

A whimper behind her made her turn. The cat was on the

hood of the car, face pressed to the windshield, white eyes wide and unblinking. Sammy hadn't listened. He was still sitting up frozen behind the wheel.

The cat started clawing rapidly at the windshield, talons skreeking on the glass and splintering the wipers. Sammy recoiled but still sat there, eyes huge and stupid with terror.

"I told you to stay hidden, crap-for-brains!" Danica yelled as she lunged up to the side of the car and swung the shovel just as the cat was backing up for a charge. She hit it solidly; it was too big now for her to knock around, but its paws went out from under it briefly. Running on adrenaline and desperation, she took another swing, feeling something pop in her shoulder. The cat slipped off the hood and staggered into the pile of snow supplies, knocking it over. As it bounced to its feet atop one of the fallen sacks, she reached it and drove the edge of the shovel into the meat of its neck.

It was slippery, the bare muscles gristle-hard against the rusty edge; she bore down with all her weight, and it squirmed and shredded the burlap beneath it. The head wouldn't sever. She wasn't strong enough. It was pushing the shovel back up, magic-fed strength straining as it braced against the bag.

Then the sack ripped under it—and she heard a sizzle like water hitting a hot grill. The cat shrieked in unmistakable agony and twisted away, bolting off into the far corner. Danica staggered and fell to her knees with the split-open bag in front of her.

It was full of road salt, for melting driveway snow. Only at the sight of it did she finally remember:

Blood for life, salt for death

"Thank you, Grandma." Danica plunged her hands into the bag, muffling a grunt at the sting in her wounds, and grabbed two fistfuls.

The cat leapt back up onto the hood and stared at her balefully. Its paws looked thinner now, greyer and more withered. That was where the salt had touched it. It was even limping.

Danica squared her shoulders and rose. "Get back in your grave."

The Scarlet Cat

It hissed at her and she flung salt at it. It recoiled, one pale moon-eye squinting closed as its skin sizzled. Then it spun and slammed its head into the windshield. The glass spiderwebbed, and Sammy flinched back against the seat, covering his face with his hands.

She flung another fistful, and the creature squalled and toppled off the far edge. She turned quickly to the bag to rearm herself—and felt its cold greasy weight slam against her back.

No!

It hissed in her ear and started raking, shredding her pajama top and starting on the skin beneath while it dug its fore-claws into her shoulders. Twenty curved knives tore into her, and she writhed and shouldered under it like a two-legged bull, tired muscles fueled by frustration and betrayal. *Not me—get off! You were supposed to be my creature! You were just supposed to make them hurt and afraid of us! You weren't supposed to make them dead!*

But the cat had decided otherwise. Maybe it didn't figure pissed pants and bloody skin were payment enough for being tortured to death. *Maybe it's right. But this is too much. And if I don't stop it...it will never stop!*

Screaming defiance, she spun and threw herself backward onto the ripped-open bag.

Talons braced in her flesh painfully as she felt the cat go taut, its screech drilling into her ear; then it let go of her and thrashed, trying to right itself and squirm out from under her. She rolled over, grabbed it around its sides, lost her grip, tried again, dug her fingers grotesquely into the fibers of its muscle—and heaved the cat into the pile of salt, pushing it down with all her strength. "I said...get back in your grave!"

The cat wailed, and she heard again Cody's agonized screaming as the boys cut his pelt from his body, and she closed her eyes against sudden tears as she bore down. Acrid smoke rose from the struggling form, and its flesh started to bubble and run like a slug's; she heard Marina screaming *my poor kitty* in her head and choked back a sob. *I didn't mean it...not like this. I just wanted something to go our way for once. I just wanted justice!* Her arms were two bars of lead; she felt her grip starting to give...and then the cat's struggles faltered and it collapsed under her.

Bleeding from half a dozen places, she braced herself on a shelf and rose, staring down at the dog-sized corpse now corrupting rapidly into foul-smelling red sludge. She swallowed, and suddenly the rage she'd been running on all night long drained away, leaving her with only wet cheeks, wounds and a deep, bitter ache in her chest.

I'm so sorry, Cody. I'm so sorry, Marina. I'm no kind of protector or avenger at all.

The car door opened behind her. "Is it dead?"

Go play in an industrial blender. She pushed the scowl off her face and glanced at him over her shoulder. "Yeah."

He hesitated up and looked down at the puddle. "Eugh. It's dissolving. Is that really the cat we killed?"

"Yes, it is, for the eighth time. You sick little assholes bought us all a lot of trouble."

She wanted to punch out his teeth, but at least her glare made him blanch gratifyingly. "Wuh-well, we didn't know about the curse then!"

She fought a smirk in spite of her foul mood. He really had bought it. And now, at least, she could capitalize on that.

She poked a finger into his chest and lifted her chin imperiously. "Well. Now you do. Just consider yourself lucky I was here to save your butt. You screw with my family again, and I won't get between you and the curse." She turned on her heel and stalked away, leaving him nodding like a bobble-head doll behind her.

His parents were standing in the kitchen when she opened the half-wrecked door. They nearly knocked her over lunging for Sammy. "Ow! Oh *now* you're in a hurry. Where the heck were you idiots when we needed help?"

Not a glance her way. "Oh God, my baby, we were so worried about you...." Marge wailed melodramatically as she tried to scoop the equally short and blocky teen into her embrace. He squirmed and

The Scarlet Cat

winced, hugging her back with his one good arm.

"I was the one who actually risked my butt to save him," Danica snarled loudly as she stalked out the back door. But the storm of happy tears behind her didn't toss any scraps of gratitude her way. She didn't exist to them now.

At least they'd have to clean up the mess in the garage by themselves.

"Oh, praise Jesus that you're all right...Sammy, honey, we love you so much!"

She winced as if slapped. *Love! That cat-torturing trash—I should have let it kill you!*

But all she did was walk away.

She dripped quarter-sized blood drops behind her for half a block, dime-sized for another two, and by the time she reached home she thought she might not even need stitches. Good thing; the hospital was two towns off, and she couldn't go there herself. Mom and Dad would have had another drunken fight over the expense of an ER visit even as she kept bleeding. She could deal with a few scars to avoid that kind of drama. *I'm just lucky I'm in good enough shape to have the option. It felt like the damn cat hit bone. But maybe necromancers heal faster than...lesser people do.* Comforting thought, but she figured she'd check the mirror anyway as soon as she got inside.

The house was dark. They hadn't waited up for her, not even Marina. The tomb-like quiet made it easy to hear all that screaming: Jim's family and the wailing siren, Sammy's parents howling with joy to still have him.

Danica stared down at the blood on the scraggly grass and swallowed the lump in her throat. "Screw all of you," she hissed.

She found the notebook and picked it up, folding it closed carefully before turning to limp inside. She clutched it to her chest as she went through the black, silent house on her way to the bathroom. Now that she knew how to destroy the dead things she raised, she could conduct her experiments much more discreetly. Even safely whip up some more nasty revenge if she needed to. She had a grasp of the magic now. She didn't need anything or anybody else.

Maybe, once her shower was done, she could get a little more studying in....

ABOUT THE AUTHOR:

Rebecca Lloyd published her first short story in *Marion Zimmer Bradley's Fantasy Magazine* in 1994, and her stories and articles have appeared in several magazines and anthologies since then. She lives in Oakland, California with her fiancé, and recently completed her first novel.

The Mortician's Secret
Kelley Frank

Although his name sometimes put off the average passerby, Kyle Zernt was still the best mortician in town. He was always discreet and, without fail, managed to care for his clients in a sympathetic and financially-viable way. He was quiet, polite, and most importantly, a local. This made a big difference in a small town where everyone knew your daddy and granddaddy, and sometimes still talked about them as though they still worked—granddad had been dead for years, and his father had retired from the business—but the name Zernt made people think of the funeral home and mortuary. It was as ingrained as the Saving Grace Baptist Church or the Christmas Parade each winter. When the Chambers' son had been eviscerated by a malfunctioning chainsaw, for example, Kyle had made an open casket funeral possible. Those in attendance had remarked that the boy looked as though he could have stood up and started laughing at any moment, which was exactly the point. Makeup and a bit of skill were magical in the right hands, and Kyle was a product of generation-spanning expertise.

His father had been an interesting man in his own right. A collector of exotic and sometimes rare trinkets in his spare time, the sort that didn't get moved to display shelves in reputable museums. He had a vast collection of shrunken heads, various animals and organs suspended in alcohol and sealed in jars, but also, most importantly, tomes he'd picked up while drinking his way across the world. There was no telling where the original notes had come from, and Kyle had nearly donated it to the local museum, a tawdry

Ripley's Believe it or Not-style curiosity near the town square. They should have gone along with the rest of the stuff, but they were in his father's third grade-level penmanship. The level of vocabulary made it clear that it hadn't been just made up by the guy—he wasn't nearly as creative as he'd liked to believe before the Alzheimer's began eating his brain. Copied, most likely, and from some text his father hadn't been allowed to purchase. There was no indication of where it came from or even of the original title. The collection of hastily stapled, wide-ruled pages might have been mistaken for any other bit of trash had Kyle not happened to glance over the material before tossing it out.

At first Kyle had thought it was yet another of his father's faux occult experiments, but he'd taken the notes home anyway purely on impulse. There really hadn't been much to keep from his father's place aside from a few family photos in poor condition and his father's legal documents. Kyle had read the whole manuscript in one evening, time he'd normally have spent preparing dinner, playing with his cat, and watching an old movie before bed. He grabbed a frozen meal, ignored the cat, and didn't sleep until hours later than he should have.

What he'd read in those pages had at first disgusted him. The crude drawings of supposed magic circles, the instructions to do mad things like create an article of clothing from the body of the dead one wishes to reanimate, the means of communicating with the dead, even cannibalism. When he finished it, amazed at the time he'd spent, he put the pages on his nightstand and quickly went to bed. His dreams were strange, but he woke feeling better than he had in days and, in his opinion, far more clear-sighted. He was able to work through most of the legal proceedings for his father's transfer to a home before his first customer could arrive.

***

He didn't have any caskets in stock that appealed to the grieving man, so Kyle walked Sonny Green through the process with the

The Mortician's Secret

more reputable dealers online—the man was apparently not internet savvy. The less trouble a grieving father went to for his eighteen year old son, killed in a car crash by a drunk driver, the better it was for all involved.

  The boy, Al Green, had been in the running for the Braves draft pick. He'd worked hard for the glory, and was rumored to be one of the best and most gregarious players for the team since John Smoltz. And then, while leaving a downtown play with a group of his GSU friends, a drunk driver had forgotten to stop for the pedestrians. It had happened within moments, and in front of the rest of the theater crowd. The police got a slew of 911 calls all at once, but none of it mattered: promising young Al Green had been struck head-on. His upper torso was through the windshield, his legs twitching for an agonizingly long time to those on the scene. The driver had instantly sobered up, adding to the group calling 911. Despite the prompt ambulance response and the fact that Crawford Long Hospital was just across the street, Al Green had been dead by the time help had arrived. Some things couldn't be fixed, no matter how long the doctors worked or how much time family and friends spent praying for their loved one's survival.

  The boy's father was doing well navigating the website until an ad popped up for lawn care. It featured a smiling boy of about thirteen with a baseball bat slung over his shoulder and a glove on one hand, his ball cap at a jaunty angle. Kyle suggested some coffee and Mr. Green had agreed quickly, fingering a pack of cigarettes. There was no smoking indoors, so Kyle poured two mugs of the brew he kept ready for his long nights and stood on the front porch as Mr. Green smoked. They didn't say anything, but there really wasn't much to say about it. When they went back inside, it was as though nothing had happened. Later, before he left, Mr. Green shook Kyle's hand. He didn't have to say anything, so neither of them did.

  Kyle knew what Sonny Green would do with the notes his father had taken.

***

His next customer was quite different, arriving near two that afternoon with her children in tow. "She has to look perfect. It will make her mother so happy." The aunt, Carol Styles, had a long list of standards and expectations of the family for the big funeral day. At the moment, she was attempting to choose a suitable coffin from the midrange selection. She examined the handles, the woodwork, and hinges, and the lining as though she were choosing a house instead of a box in which to bury a body in preparation for decay. Her two small sons scurried around the room like a small cloud, playing and laughing amongst the displays while she browsed.

As Mrs. Styles began rubbing the light blue satin of a mahogany model, Kyle cleared his throat. "You could, perhaps, rent a casket for the funeral. I have several very nice models…"

She laughed, a sound that might have been lovely once but grieving had left it a biting cackle. "Rent? You mean lay our darling Julianna in a coffin others have used before? Then what will she be buried in? Will you just toss her into the ground like she was nothing?"

"No, what I would do is help you choose a cheaper casket, and then use that one for the actual burial. The rented casket will be used for presentation during the funeral allowing you to—"

"No. I'll choose her resting place before God and that will be that. It will be beautiful for her funeral and it will be just as beautiful for her burial."

The absurdity of his job flooded back to him, not for the first time. So much fuss for a husk, a dead thing that was no longer human, no longer felt pain or joy, and would never take pleasure in anything again. Unfortunately, Carol Styles represented a fairly typical approach to death—make it beautiful, for the dead are watching us and want beauty too. She was not attached as Sonny Green had been—the girls' mother was of course too deeply in mourning to be made to think of the dreaded funeral proceedings— but she was still grieving in her own materialistic way. Kyle had long ago resigned himself to such an approach as therapeutic. "If that's what you want, then I'll happily help you, Mrs. Styles." She

The Mortician's Secret

nodded, already turning to the caskets again. The lining of course would have to be rose pink...

The pages are upstairs. It was a completely random thought, but it smacked of a craving: he suddenly wanted nothing more than to read those pages again. It was as sudden and unexpected a thought as a cat scratch. As he spoke to Mrs. Styles, assuring that the lining could be made of whatever fabric she brought to him, he thought of his father. The man who could fix anything, the man who had seemed like the tallest person in the world when Kyle was a child, had been paper thin. His hands, callused from years of side projects on cars and gardening around the mortuary, had grasped at Kyle desperately, "It's a dying place. I'm not dying. Don't let them take me!"

"It's for the best, dad. You can't take care of yourself anymore and Alzheimer's is dangerous."

"A man has a right to die with dignity! You've got no right, Kyle, no right at all!"

***

It really started with the frog in his driveway. Shortly after obtaining his father's papers, Kyle had pulled into his driveway late one night after finishing up with the rote paperwork necessary for the success of any small business. He lived in a townhouse off the square, beneath the watchful gaze of sodium light and behind a sidewalk barrier. Each night the lamppost was lit, it had safely guided his few visitors to their cars and Kyle to his short but adequate driveway. It was a landmark—the house by the second lamppost on the right was as good a marker as any in a place where all the homes were side-by-side and looked alike. It was dependable. This time, though, the lamppost betrayed him as it cast a shadow in just the wrong place. As he pulled into the driveway, probably a bit too fast, he noticed a pale shape only because his headlights outmatched the deep shadow. The thing was little bigger than a rock, and even as he applied the brake it was under the hood of the car. There was a faint thud, but then the car was in the garage. Knowing what he would find, but still hoping that he'd somehow straddled it, he got out of the car and approached the place where the frog had been.

He knew it was a frog, the frog, precisely because he'd saved it from being hit so many times. Since moving in, Kyle had pulled into his driveway often to see the little creature sitting smack dab in the middle of the driveway. And each time Kyle had stopped, gotten out of his car despite the warning dings, and caught the little thing in his hands. If old Mrs. Pearson had looked out her window, she might have wondered why the quiet young man next-door was hunched over trying to catch some small thing in the dark as his car idled in the driveway. When Kyle finally caught it, he always returned it to the back yard. He'd had to cup his hands around the little thing, feeling its frantic breathing as tiny feet pressed against his palms. It wasn't a pet, but he felt that he and the frog understood each other. The frog was cool to the touch, but not cold and hard like something dead. Its skin was supple, pulsing, and alive.

As he approached the familiar shape, he thought that it must surely still be alive. Perhaps it was in shock from a disproportionally large vehicle passing over its head. The orange street light was bright, but this only made the shadows deeper so that anything shaded by even the scantest of leaves was swathed in inky black. But the vague outline was there, head upturned as though watching the sky, a dark shape among dark shapes, framed by the unnatural glow on his concrete driveway. As he drew closer, however, it became clear that the frog would move no more.

At first, it seemed unnaturally lengthened, but slowly Kyle realized those were the amphibian's innards stretched behind it. Kyle had occasionally and with the careless cruelty of childhood stepped on caterpillars, morbidly fascinated when he lifted his sneaker to see the tiny thing had basically shat its gooey yellow innards. The frog was like that, its innards blasted out its backside, leaving froggy entrails and dark blood gleaming faintly in the deep shadow. It stared back glassily, head upturned as though in prayer.

The next day, he used the garden hose to spray the dead frog

The Mortician's Secret

into the grass. As the week passed it resembled a dried out husk, but it was still there if he chose to look.

***

It was a week later on a Wednesday, the hottest day so far that summer at a swelteringly humid 102, when he decided to take the plunge. He'd never moved the papers from his nightstand, but he leafed through them each night before bed. The drawings no longer disgusted him, though he often wondered what the originals had looked like before his father's sloppy hand had attempted to duplicate them. Obviously they were still legible, but were they usable? These were thoughts he mostly banished during the day as work kept him occupied. In his office between phone calls he could hear birds chattering as they nested in the old sugar maple outside his window. But when he descended to the basement where the embalming and crematory equipment lay carefully cleaned and ready, he thought of Al Green moldering in the dirt and Carol Styles glowing throughout her niece's funeral as she pointed out to her fellow mourners the evidence of her good taste. Even the dead frog on the side of his driveway, half covered by grass and slowly decomposing, resonated with him. It wasn't something he could pinpoint, but a deep feeling that he had the power to do something and was wasting it.

Was there really much difference between the things detailed in his father's notes and his own profession? Yes, he finally concluded as he prepared a pair of bodies for cremation. On the one hand, he helped the living by making their loved ones more palatable in death, thereby making the death itself easier to stomach. This was all he did, though. To his customers, he was the embodiment of the gateway between life and death. They saw him as a sort of warden, a person who saw death so often that it no longer affected him. He wasn't someone people went out of their way to spend time with, though he did get a fair number of friendly greetings as he walked down the street. Hardly anyone stayed to chat though, and it had taken him some time to realize why: they were scared of him. They avoided him as though death was contagious. They didn't want to speak to him because his presence heralded disaster. No matter how calm or orderly he appeared, they equated him with the very thing he sought to protect them from: the reality of death.

For a time, before he'd begun his own mortuary, he'd worked in the morgue at one of the Atlanta area hospitals. Working with so many victims of violence—from stabbings to shootings, to car accidents—wasn't a job for the squeamish. He'd seen just about everything, but there was always that subtle dread that sometimes haunted the moments before he fell asleep. When he'd found his first gray hairs—first one then four which he regularly plucked like mutant fruit—he'd begun to have the feeling more often. In it, he imagined his own funeral: Who would pronounce him dead? Probably Vick, he was the one the locals called more often than not. He was a good doctor, and Kyle knew that if Vick pronounced him dead there would be no mistake.

But who would clean his body and perform the cremation ceremony? Here was the thought that bothered him: He was relatively sure that task would fall to Stephanie Roster, owner of the only other local mortuary, Roster and Sons Funeral Home. She had a bad temper and could be somewhat pushy, which was another reason Kyle tended to get more customers and, eventually, their families. What she lacked in interpersonal skills, though, she made up for in good work. On invitation, he'd attended Jack Lampton's funeral, the former sheriff and a man no one would have dared disrespect in life. A simple heart attack one lazy Sunday evening had left him slack-jawed and dead as could be on the floor of his newly constructed man cave during the Super Bowl. Her work on Sherriff Lampton was some of the best he'd ever seen. Unfortunately, she hadn't been ashamed to tell him so, either. She'd buzzed after him like a horsefly for a good part of that service, "That's just a sample of what I can do, Mr. Zernt. Unlike you, I am an artist. Look for a flaw; you won't find one." Her breath was minty in his ear, hissing like static.

"As long as the family is happy." His hands were steady as he sipped his Coke. "That's really the only thing that matters."

The Mortician's Secret

She'd smiled, all red lips and blonde hair, long and ironed like a model's. "I'm nearly ten years younger than you. I have more personality, talent, and appeal than you'll ever have. Stay on if you want, but my sons and I will be taking over this town soon enough."

"Your sons are children, Mrs. Roster." And they were. At twelve and nine years old, although they greeted the mourners dutifully at the door in their matching suits, they surely weren't helping with the actual preparation of the bodies. At least he hoped not.

Yes, he would think to himself lying in bed staring at the ceiling, Stephanie Roster or one of her young sons would be responsible for cremating him. Sometimes this action would be the subject of his nightmares.

The pair he was about to cremate that day had been in a car accident; both had been in the backseat when their friend, texting furiously to his suddenly ex-girlfriend, had swerved off the road and into a ditch. The car had flipped three times before it hit a tree. The driver had come away with only a broken arm. His two best friends hadn't been so lucky. The one on the passenger side had been cut in half by his seatbelt and flung from the car, which had later burst into flames. That body hadn't been a priority for the medics and firefighters who arrived on the scene. The other friend had his skull crushed by the impact, the whole left side of his face destroyed, but no one had been able to tell for sure until after he'd been cut from the mangled car. Supposedly, he'd been dead on impact, but rumor stated that he'd died from his injuries as the rescue team fought to remove the car door. Regardless, Kyle was left with two bodies and two grieving families. One body was mostly whole, the other was missing most of its lower half. The police had told him the legs of the halved boy were glued to the leather seats and, since both families had requested cremation, Kyle hadn't needed them.

He looked at the bodies, one mangled but intact and the other greatly diminished. An image of his father's notes flashed before his eyes like the flash of a camera.

No, it was too ridiculous. He began laying out his tools.

The body closest to him, the one with the missing lower half, stared sightlessly at the ceiling. His head was slightly upturned as though in prayer.

No one will know. I can try and no one will know, and when it doesn't work, I can cremate what's left.

Half a body. He knew from experience that he would be processing the remains once they came out of the crematory, sifting them for large fragments to be discarded, and then processing them until they were a fine yet slightly greasy powder. The urns provided by the families were upstairs waiting for him on his desk. Had they been down in his basement workroom, particularly the one bearing a small photograph of the deceased, he might have discounted his idea. It was mad, certainly, but reading and rereading the notes had made it more familiar.

When it doesn't work, I can cremate what's left and finally sleep without thinking of those damn pages. I'll send them to Ripley's and that'll be the end.

He barely noticed that he had begun the work. It didn't take long, with the tools at hand, to clean the halved body, close the eyes, and wheel the gurney toward the furnace. It would take two to three hours for the body to burn to ashes. He slid the body into the furnace, turned on the heat, then looked back at his work space, breathing heavily. He still had a complete body with a half-crushed skull. He should prepare that body for cremation as well, but he hesitated. Ideas were swirling in his head so quickly that he barely registered them, each more insane than the next.

His heart was hammering in his chest. He leaned his head against the wall, a freezer door, and sighed. Inside the furnace, flames were already licking the body up and down. Coffee was what he needed, with a splash of rum from his stash in the bottom of his desk drawer. He set his watch timer and climbed the stairs, leaving the corpse to burn.

Between the mysterious manuscripts and the stolen body parts, he may as well be starring alongside Vincent Price or Peter Lorre. Except those actors were dead and had only been participating

The Mortician's Secret

in fiction. This was something so different it seemed beyond the human experience; yet, someone must have done this before. Someone must have for the writings to exist at all.

Unless, of course, it was all fiction. Nice practical joke on little Kyle you played there, Dad.

Okay, no problem. The best thing to do then was to test his theory. He'd find a small incantation from the pages, use it, and see what happened. *If I'm going to do this, I'm not going to be sloppy about it. Besides, this is the best chance to test it I've had yet.*

But for that he'd need the notes, and they were still at home on his nightstand.

Kyle stopped halfway up the stairs. He only lived five minutes away from his funeral home. It wouldn't be a big deal to go get the notes and come back, but regulations insisted that he stay to monitor as the body since he'd already begun the burning process. That left a few hours for him to kill, and by that time he was pretty sure he'd lose his nerve. *It won't take long. I've run this business for ten years and nothing's gone wrong yet.* Still, there was always a chance that the building would catch on fire. And what a headline that would be: Cremation Kills Mortuary. And it would be just that, because while he was rebuilding, Stephanie Roster would be the only mortuary in town. Sure, she didn't have an onsite crematory, but neither would Kyle if he managed to let his burn down. And if it were proven that his negligence had caused the fire to get out of control, he'd have more than state lawmakers on his case—the families of the two dead teenage boys would sue. Things could get ugly. Was it worth the risk just to get a stack of yellowed notebook paper that may or may not hold some arcane secret?

Of course it is. I've run this business for ten years, but hasn't it felt like longer? Isn't each day just the same as the next, melting into dead and living faces that never meant anything to me? And if the place goes up in smoke, so what? At least it'll be a good excuse to change careers, maybe even do something around the living for a change.

His keys were in his pocket. They were in his pocket and

it was a sweltering weekday, meaning almost no one in their right mind would be outside. Sure, someone might recognize him, but no one knew the crematory was running. He could be out and back in the blink of an eye. He nodded to himself as he strolled out the back door. The old wooden steps made their familiar creaks as he thumped down to the gravel parking lot. The whole area was shaded by a giant oak tree. Sunlight spattered the ground through the leaves. A June bug buzzed past his head. Kyle's car, a battered Dodge Neon, dozed in the deepest patch of shade at the far end near the hydrangeas, their blue flowers clustered into soft sprays. To his left and around the back of the house-turned-funeral home lounged the hearse. He kept it out of the way, covered with a blue tarp that kept the pollen and bird shit at bay. It made the customers feel more at ease. On the road to his right, where the shade retreated and the gravel surfaced onto asphalt and blinding sun, an SUV rolled past, a bird tittered, then all was still again.

Coast is clear. He crunched across the gravel and unlocked the car. The air was thin inside but not yet stifling, the steering wheel warm but not scalding. It was ten in the morning on a Wednesday and, if he played his cards right, he could avoid the lunch rush. The engine turned over without a hitch and quite painlessly, he backed the car up a bit, turned it in a little half circle, then drove for the sunlight. When it hit, the temperature changed immediately and Kyle fumbled with the A/C for only a moment before it was blasting at the second highest level.

He didn't drive too fast, mostly because he didn't want to be detained, and still he made it to his little townhouse in less than five minutes. He pulled into the driveway, his eyes sliding reflexively toward the small frog's body in the sod, and put the car in park leaving it to idle as he rushed inside. He unhooked his house key and bolted for the door. Was that smoke he smelled? No, no it wasn't. The neighbors were grilling. No matter. He flung the door shut behind him and bounded up the stairs, his cat, Nicodemus, scrambling away to the safety of the kitchen.

Kyle found the notes exactly where he'd left them and,

sliding them into his inside jacket pocket, he raced back down again. It didn't take long to lock up, he had only one house key after all, before he was back in the car. The A/C had been busy while he was away, and he relished the icebox cold as he put the car in reverse again, this time backing out of his driveway and heading back toward the road.

It's on fire. It's burning because these things always happen when you turn your back for a moment. I'll still have my precious notes, but I'll never be allowed near a dead body again. He was practically standing on the accelerator so he let up. *If it's already burning then rushing there won't solve a thing.* He kept his speed steady for the rest of the drive, even stopping for a yellow light instead of hurrying on through. *Yes, just an average driver passing through town on a hot, humid Wednesday afternoon. Nothing out of the ordinary here, folks!*

He pulled into the driveway, and immediately was submerged in cool shade. He parked in his usual spot, turned off the car, and got out. No smell of smoke greeted him. A weak breeze ruffled the trees, making the sunlight dance fairy patterns on the grey gravel. Kyle took a deep breath and mounted the stairs. It took him a moment to make his hands stop shaking enough to fit the key in the lock, but when he did it turned smoothly and he let himself into the cool dark.

His basement area was secure, a simple glance at the crematory told him as much. He needn't have worried. Everything was running smoothly as ever. The other body with its crushed face was still staring at the ceiling with a semi-shocked expression that reminded Kyle of the I Can't Believe It's Not Butter commercials. For the first time, he was a bit bothered by the chill in the room, the too bright fluorescent lights that revealed every pore and laceration on the dead boy's face, and the way the stainless steel cabinets and instruments gleamed. The room was still except for the dull sound of the crematory working away at the other boy and the buzz of fluorescents, so he turned his attention to the papers crammed indelicately in his inside jacket pocket. They were rumpled, but no more so than they'd been in the trash heap of his father's belongings.

Kyle spread them out on his counter as he had so many times at home—he'd long ago removed the staples to better see some of the diagrams his father had copied so hastily. He was looking for one incantation in particular, one that was supposed to allow some sort of communication. He'd skipped it for the more juicy stuff, but now he searched for it again eagerly.

There it was on the bottom of the seventh page: Fore the Speaking Withe and Demanding Advice from The Departed. He didn't know if the minor spelling mistakes were in the original or the result of his father's ineptitude—most likely the latter. He read over the directions carefully. Not much needed, really, just the dead man's clothing and the dead man himself. It might have been difficult for a layman to procure such things, but Kyle dealt with dead people all the time. The clothing he'd removed and placed in a bag to return to the family or destroy on their consent. Being that it was torn, bloodied, and mostly destroyed anyway, he doubted they'd want any of it but he always held onto the items just in case.

He pulled the dead boy's shirt, once a white tank top but now a gruesome two-tone in red and white, from the carefully labeled bag and, using one of the many pairs of scissors he left nearby, cut a small patch from the material. He didn't bother with any that had been tainted by the blood, keeping to the mostly clean side. That done, Kyle took the roughly three inch strip of fabric back to the corpse. It was still staring up at the ceiling as corpses do.

Following the instructions with the studious care of a man accustomed to tedious work, he folded the cloth at right angles until it was roughly the shape of a paper football. This he then pushed into the dead boy's mouth just past a set of straight white teeth. Kyle looked at the book carefully then, looking around a moment, he finally spied his trusty scalpel cleaned and sanitized amongst his other tools. Snatching it up, he considered his own left hand, held out in front of him over the dead boy with the crushed face. It was a soft and unmarred hand—the hand of a man who as a boy never broke a limb or shattered a tooth in the typical childhood accidents. He stared for an instant before cutting a straight line across the meaty bit where the base of his thumb became his palm. The blood fell, as it should have, straight into the corpse's mouth and onto the cloth where it blossomed cherry red.

Kyle sat that way for a full minute, watching the red slowly overtake the white between the dead boy's teeth and thinking about what he wanted to ask. It had to be specific. Part of him hadn't thought anything would really happen at first, but the ceremonial aspect of the whole thing had focused him in a way he only felt when he was deeply involved in his work. Had the phone on his wall a mere fifteen feet away rung just then, Kyle might have been disgusted with himself. He would have bound his injury, called himself a fool, and answered the phone. Following that, he would have cleaned up his mess, chastised himself roughly, and burned the yellowed pages alongside the boy with the half-crushed skull.

As it was, though, no call came. Kyle remained focused, so that when he asked the question he had supreme faith that he would get an answer. "What is your name?"

There was no sound for a moment, and in that instant the phone call still might have saved him. But suddenly the corpse shuddered as though a current had passed through it. Then, like a death rattle forming words, he heard an answer: "Caleb ... Robert ... Smithson." Each word was like an exhaled breath, though the chest didn't rise or fall.

Had Kyle been thinking normally, he would have stumbled back from the body and rushed upstairs. He would have been badly shaken, perhaps so much so that he might have given up the business forever. But he was focused, calm, and he had expected those words to come. Had someone been present to ask why, he would have looked at them as though they'd asked why he expected rain on a cloudy day. "Where are you right now?"

"With...you."

"No, I mean, where were you before you spoke to me?"

There was a long pause, then, "Dark." Kyle was about to ask more when it spoke again, "Cold...Nothing."

"Okay." His hands were shaking again as the spell lost its

grip on him. "That's okay. Do you know you are dead?"

The face made no change, yet the husking voice when it came was fused with more despair than Kyle had ever encountered, even at all the funerals and among all the grieving families he'd ever met. It was the way fathers like Sonny Green tried desperately not to sound as they handled the events following the death of a child. "Yes."

The words were out of his mouth before he could catch them. "If you could, would you want to move again and see even if you weren't really alive like you were before?"

There was no hesitation. In fact, the voice nearly cut him off. "Yes."

"I'm not sure if this will work or what will happen, but should I attempt it on you?" He waited, his heart pounding in his wrists and neck. There was no sound, and as he waited he realized that it wasn't going to answer. The little sounds around him had all come back: the crematory working, the clock above the stairs ticking through the hours, the faintly buzzing lights, and the peculiar humming sound of silence itself which he knew was really just the blood rushing through his own body. He thought back: How many questions had he asked? Four, hadn't it been? No, there was that one about where the boy was that hadn't been specific enough. He'd wasted a question. He'd used up all five.

Well, Caleb himself had seemed utterly depressed about his situation. And he'd said as much that he would like to move about and see the world, although Kyle wasn't entirely sure if that part would even work. But Caleb hadn't seemed to mind.

Caleb. The corpse had said its name was Caleb.

The corpse had said this. The dead body.

Kyle knew he should have been disgusted but somehow he wasn't. He should have fled screaming from the room but he had no intention of doing such a thing. No, what he planned to do instead was make a nice big pot of coffee. The other dead boy would be done in a few hours, but Kyle had no intention of adding Caleb Robert Smithson to the crematory. He'd burn something else and

The Mortician's Secret

pass it off as Caleb, but Caleb himself was going to be the beginning of an experiment. Talking to the dead! That was spectacular enough, and had he been a more ambitious man, Kyle might have thought of ways to capitalize on his discovery. But he was not ambitious, working alone and friendless in his small town. The old Kyle had wanted nothing but to be left alone. But experiences could change a man, and Kyle was indeed changed. Now he wanted nothing but to be left alone to discover more about this tenuous link between life and death and the truths about death itself that his species so longed to possess. Clearly his father had been foolish not to use the notes he'd taken. Kyle didn't know how he could have been so stupid as to never try them for himself...

Coffee. Yes, that's what he needed.

He slid the body—*Caleb Robert Smithson*—into one of the cold storage freezers. Then he gathered the notes and put them back in his inside pocket and moved up the stairs. He was barely aware of the feel of the wood creaking under his feet when he reached the top floor, or the musty smell that had pervaded the locale for as long as he'd used it. He poured his coffee, adding a shot of rum from his bottom desk drawer. The birds were faintly singing outside. The trees made their unique Pollock splatters of light and dark on his face and hands. The clock on his desk ticked softly.

The two funerals were to be held together in three days, but the wake would be tomorrow and the family wanted the cremation over as soon as possible. They would use the urns for the wake instead of the actual bodies—yet one more way people avoided looking at death.

Outside, a pair of children biked quickly past the funeral home, slowing and laughing once they passed the property line. Whistling past the graveyard. It was so strange to think that people feared him, even feared the remodeled house with its neatly painted white porch and inviting shade trees. His grandfather had bought the place and slowly the family had worked together to make it whole. It was beautiful and inviting, but no one rested beneath the shade trees despite the heat. It was human nature to fear a place known for housing the dead, he supposed, and to deal with death by avoiding it altogether. Parents put off discussions of death yet allowed their children to watch films in which heroes mowed down armies of villains. And what good did it do? It sure didn't keep kids from dying. It didn't even keep their parents from dying.

It was such a foreign concept for Kyle. His father had been a mortician just as his grandfather before him. It was something Kyle had lived with all his life, and though it had taught him that the dead weren't a cause for fear, it had also alienated him from his peers. People avoided those that associated too closely with death. But was it for cultural or instinctive reasons? He'd often asked himself but was no closer to finding an answer. He'd actually gone to medical school, the first of the Zernts to change professions. Forensic psychology, that had been his specialty, and he'd looked forward to using his insights to reveal nuances that put an end to criminal behavior. But his father had laughed when Kyle had finally invited him to the graduation, the first response Kyle had gotten from the old man in years. "You're wasting your time. The work's in your blood, Kyle, and it'll come back to you."

And it had. Oh boy, it had. Kyle had student loans to pay and no place to work. Then mom and gotten sick, and he'd been faced with a decision: prove that he could make it alone or go back home and help. He'd caved, of course, like a dutiful son. And once he'd come home, dad had been the first to offer him a job. It was meant to be temporary, but somehow once his father had retired Kyle had never gotten around to selling it. Ten years had passed since he moved back home to his small southern hometown: the high school was still the same, as was the square and the general disposition of the populace toward outsiders. He could navigate the area with his eyes closed. And he was one of them. Unlike Mrs. Stephanie Roster, Kyle wasn't from out of town.

Mom had died and he and dad had made her look her best for the funeral. Some people had found that morbid, but Kyle hadn't thought anything of it. This was his life, it was in his blood as his father had said so long ago, and there was no escaping such things.

The Mortician's Secret

They'd washed and prepared her for her funeral and burial as an act of love. It was the first and last time he'd felt anything while working with a corpse.

Kyle took a long draw from his coffee and watched the dying afternoon sunlight. He had a body in mostly good condition, but what to do with it? He had a strong feeling about Caleb—that ritual had made things pretty damn obvious. Something would have to be done. He couldn't just waste the opportunity, just as he couldn't bear to leave a restaurant without a to-go box. He'd paid for the full meal and he'd eat it in his own time, thanks very much. He leaned forward, his palms flat on the desk. He was sweating, his clothes felt tight. He loosened his tie.

Outside, a bird landed on the windowsill. Its beak was open as it panted in the heat. A frog was croaking endlessly, the only thing besides the cicadas unbothered by the relentless summer sun, and Kyle wondered if it was in the old koi pond his father had let return to the wilderness out back. There'd been heavy rains lately, and the thought of that koi pond overgrown with blackberries and kudzu still holding enough water to please the local wildlife hung there in his mind like a photograph. The frog croaked on and on like the happiest thing on the planet, the cicadas hummed a mad chorus, and slowly Kyle steadied himself.

***

Kyle didn't go home at his usual time that evening. It wasn't unusual for him to stay late, so he did keep a modest amount of food on hand. He was munching a Slim Jim when he called the boys' pastor to confirm that the bodies were prepared and ready for pick up. He shook hands with Rev. Jared Stevens, a prematurely balding man with an unfortunate moustache. They chatted on the front porch for a little while, enjoying the cooling air as the sun retired for the evening. It was always depressing when young hotrods got themselves killed, yet it always felt inevitable. Rev. Stephens was troubled but unsurprised by the tragic fate of the two young members of his flock and Kyle was a good listener.

In the end, the good reverend took the two carefully filled urns with thanks. Kyle would be welcome at the service, naturally. Then, turning around with a crunch of gravel, the ashes were long gone. It was unlikely that anyone would notice the lightness of the one boy's ashes, the one whose body had been torn apart. That was to be expected. And no one would suspect that the other urn—Caleb Robert Smithson—was nothing more than a combination of his friend's ashes and some excess ash from the crematory and processing unit. If it didn't upset the dead man in question, then who were the others to be offended? He locked the door behind himself then fetched a Coke from his office before descending once more to the task at hand.

Before fetching the body from cold storage, Kyle wanted to make sure he knew what he was doing. The notes hadn't been terribly specific about how exactly he was to create the summoning circle, only that it must be drawn deliberately. Not sure what this meant, and not really one to have heaps of occult information lying around, Kyle kneeled on the linoleum unsure how to proceed. He held a black wet-erase marker in one hand, but like an artist facing an empty canvas, he couldn't for the life of him decide what to do. Should he draw upside-down crosses or something like that? It didn't feel right, for one thing, and for another it just didn't seem to reflect the purpose of necromancy. The notes had been adamant that the thing he was about to do was something in the gray area between good and evil. Besides, upside-down crosses felt too Hollywood, too high school rebellion, for something so somber. The leaf-rustle voice of Caleb Robert Smithson came back to him and he shuddered. He measured the ten by ten area the circle would encompass, moving some equipment as he went, then drew the outer and inner circles. Then, not sure what else to do, he simply wrote the man's name over and over in block letters: Caleb Robert Smithson Caleb Robert Smithson Caleb Robert Smithson.

That was step one. Retrieving the bag of ruined clothing once again before pulling the body from the cold storage unit, he cut

The Mortician's Secret

a small amount of flesh from the upper right shoulder blade along with a few squares of cloth from the clothing: a bit from the faded denim jeans, a bit from a singed and bloodied cotton Marlins t-shirt, more from the bloodied wife beater, and a tiny circle from the heel of each sock. He arranged the bits of cloth on his favorite worktable and produced a needle and thread. It took some time to stitch the fabric, as he was more accustomed to the toughness of dead flesh, but in the end, he had a rough square of patchwork cloth.

This he carefully folded around the piece of flesh and put in his pocket. Then, grabbing the corpse under its arms, he moved the upper body to a gurney he'd placed nearby. The head lolled back against his chest a bit, but rigor mortis had taken hold for the most part. Kyle suddenly had a horrible thought: he would get Caleb Robert Smithson up and running, jumpstarting him like a jalopy, but the rigor mortis would never go out of the limbs. It was a stupid notion—he knew from his studies and plain experience that rigor mortis only lasted about seventy-two hours—but the thought wouldn't go away. Focusing instead on his work, a tried and true method that hadn't failed him yet, Kyle lifted the corpse's legs then simply rolled the metal gurney into the center of the circle.

Kyle spent a few minutes perfecting the position of the gurney. He had a notion that the head should point north, but it might be more symbolic to face the head east with the rising sun. In the end, he compromised by placing the body so the head faced northeast. Then he was left staring dumbly as though he'd never seen a dead body before and wondering what in hell he really thought he was doing. It was crazy enough to think about bringing a dead man back to life, but it was even crazier if it was really going to happen. This wasn't some sick fantasy, the kind he'd heard some serial killers had where they collected bodies, dressed them up, and pretended they were having a two-way conversation. This was the real deal. Just thinking about it made his hands shakier.

Kyle himself was no magician: all he had was the fastidiousness that had always made him good with both the details that mattered to his customers and the ones that kept the bills paid on time. A little fastidiousness went a long way. But more than that, Kyle wasn't really a spontaneous man. His one big leap from the family business had landed him back in the same place his father and grandfather had both so humbly filled. Looking at the dead man in the center of that circle, surrounded by his one name in big letters carefully inscribed in wet-erase marker on the dark green linoleum, made him wonder. Was he crazy? Had the conversation with this shell of a man been a hallucination? Had he, in fact, murdered this man and simply blocked it out, all for the sake of a psychotic fantasy that might have made Ted Bundy blush? These thoughts, and much worse, scratched at the corners of his mind scrabbling for purchase like a rock climber who has suddenly lost his footing. If he did this thing, would he be able to live with it? That seemed to be the crux of the matter. And if he didn't do it, if he just cremated the body anyway then called up Rev. Stevens to say there'd been a mix-up, would he be able to live with that instead?

If something goes wrong, I can find a way out of it in dad's notes. They were right about making the dead speak, and they will be right about this. If something goes wrong, I'll just find a way to fix it. He imagined Caleb Robert Smithson shambling outdoors to lumber down the center of the road towards town like something from a Cesar Romero movie. It might have been a premonition, but it just as well could have been the very real fear of a man about to do the impossible. He closed his eyes briefly, and when he opened them, the words came clearly though he hadn't planned them. It wasn't anything complicated, just the man's name repeated in a chanting monotone. At first it felt silly, but then the words themselves seemed to feel heavy coming out of his mouth.

He had no desire to step into the circle where the body lay. He said the words heavily, plodding like footfalls.

After the fifteenth or so repetition, mostly when it just felt right, he reached into his pocket for the bundle wrapped in patchwork cloth. He hadn't seen anything in the book about what he was supposed to do with it, but in the middle of the chant, it seemed as natural as breathing to unwrap the bit of flesh like candy from a

The Mortician's Secret

wrapper and reverently pop it into his mouth. Later, he would briefly wonder where the tiny bit of meat had gone, but for the moment, he stared at the body blinking so little that his eyes glazed over, his jaw mechanically chewing the cold flesh. He didn't annunciate well as he chewed, but the rhythm stayed the same and, more importantly, the words were still repeating in that same monotone in his head—

Caleb Robert Smithson Caleb Robert Smithson Caleb Robert Smithson

—and had the fingers twitched? They might have, but suddenly it was as though all the strength went from his legs. His eyes were heavy, like he hadn't slept in days, and his vision was going dark. He wanted nothing more than to sleep. The last thing he heard as he slipped into a dreamless sleep was a rasping as of the winter wind through branches full of dry leaves.

***

When he woke, the lights were still buzzing their faint fluorescence. The linoleum was cool under his head, and a naked man was looking at his own hands as though he'd never seen them before. Kyle sat up gingerly—he felt like he'd been hit with a baseball meant for the outfield—and looked around. It was his basement, just as he'd left it. The circle was still on the floor, smeared in places but still bearing identifiable letters which, strung together, made a name. He swallowed, "Caleb Robert Smithson."

The man who'd been examining his hands turned. He was missing an eye, the upper left half of his face still crushed in, but his good eye fixed Kyle with an unwavering stare. "Yes?" The voice was like the one that had haunted him all the way into unconsciousness, dry leaves on concrete skittering in the wind. The eye fixed on Kyle so studiously was a clouded blue.

"You're...you're alive." His voice was high and stringy.

"Not alive. Something, but not alive." He was speaking in barely a whisper. He seemed to remember Kyle was there and looked at him more clearly again. "They were trying to cut me out of the car. I died. I remember that."

"Are you upset?"

Caleb managed a slightly awkward shrug. "It was empty being dead. There was nothing. Now there is something. I'm not alive, but I at least can feel." He looked at his hands again, turning them so the shadows caught the light. The fingers had a jerky range of motion, but they moved well enough. One might have merely thought the man suffered from arthritis if not for his face. The raccoon-like darkness around his right eye indicated brain damage, and the left eye was a ruined mess of partially-scorched flesh. His mouth was unmarred, as was his nose, but the rest of that face was too horrific to be real. Most of his hair was gone on that side. The skull, a nice round shape on the right, was dented on the left as though it had struck something. The top of the sports car, maybe. Regardless, the man should not have been capable of motor function at all. He should not be able to turn, fixing his cold pupil on Kyle once again, or to move his lips to speak. "Don't be scared of me. You made this possible."

"I guess I did." The notes were still there on the table. It looked just like an innocent stack of notebook paper, wrinkled horribly and bound with a binder clip. It could have been leftover from college maybe, or even a journal of some kind. It wasn't tidy enough to be anything important. Kyle tried to regulate his breathing. "What will you do?"

"I don't know. I wanted to go to law school but that's probably shot. Has my funeral started yet?"

"I...no, it's going to be tomorrow morning. Or...I guess today. They want to get it over with."

"Will Jason be there? You know, the guy that was driving."

"I guess so."

"Sweet. Hey, you got any clothes around here? And maybe something to help me look more alive?"

Kyle felt laughter bubbling up from his chest, but he forced it down as much as possible so only a snort came out. That was good. If the laugh came out, he wasn't sure it would ever stop. "I think we can, um, find you something." Caleb smiled, a winning boyish smile if not for his lumped and mangled head, and followed Kyle up the stairs. It was still dark. They had plenty of time.

***

"We really appreciate all you've done for us, Mr. Zernt. You're more reliable than your father: he couldn't shake the devil drink once it got its hooks into him."

Kyle nodded and smiled pleasantly. "I do try, Reverend."

"Well, I appreciate you getting this done so quickly. Those poor boys' parents are broken up enough without dragging this tragedy out for weeks."

"I'm glad I was able to help. Have you met Chris? He's a friend of mine from college who'll be staying for a while. He was in a car accident recently that nearly killed him."

"That's...that's horrible. Welcome Chris. I'm very pleased to meet you. I hope this isn't too much for you, attending a funeral like this."

So-called Chris smiled winningly. "My pleasure, sir." His voice was still a bit slow, but his mouth moved well enough to form the words clearly. "I'm not bothered by it as much as I thought I'd be. It's good to face your fears, you know?"

"Yes. Yes, I do." The Reverend seemed a bit concerned for the newcomer but not terribly suspicious. Which was good.

Kyle had felt nauseous all morning. What if Caleb began to smell? What if he began to rot? What if bugs infested him? But Caleb didn't smell, and a bit of makeup specifically made for the dead worked wonders on him. His pallid flesh was now pale but relatively healthy. The contact lenses made his eyes seem normal, though he had to keep applying Visine to make sure they stayed moist. And now that they were actually there, Kyle was practically humming. No one had screamed or become startled when Caleb walked in, wearing a black and white skull cap and an eye patch but otherwise dressed quite normally in jeans, blazer, and tie. Kyle mostly sampled some of the food and kept Caleb close as he made the rounds, introducing him as they went. They didn't question him when he explained that Chris had been in a horrible car accident that left him a bit disabled and somewhat disfigured.

The Reverend patted Caleb's gloved hand before releasing it, nodding at him and at Kyle. "If you have need of anything at all, don't hesitate to contact me. Troubled times find all of us, I'm afraid, but we can only keep our faith and continue as best we can."

Kyle tensed. *I hope he's sensible—a religious guy doesn't want to hear about an empty afterlife. I'll have to come up with something about Caleb's loss of faith or something, and then I really don't know what I'll say.* But Caleb only nodded sagely. "Yes. We should take every opportunity available to us."

"That's right, Chris. You'll lead a happy, fulfilled life if you do that."

Maybe we both will. Caleb had already become welcome company. Kyle thought of the notebook pages back at the mortuary. It was an opportunity to save these people from a void after death, wasn't it? He looked around at the other people going about their lives.

Stephanie Roster had brought her sons and, as usual, was hobnobbing among the guests. Most of them paid her as much attention as they would any other stranger, but a few allowed her sweet smile and charm to amend their interest. She may have been genuinely better at making the dead look alive, but there was something she'd never been any good at: returning them to life. *And who knows—maybe when I finally die, Caleb will read the ritual for me in return.* Yes, they might indeed live very fulfilled lives.

About the Author:

Kelley is an adjunct professor of English at Clayton State University. She has never forgotten the ghosts she met as a child.

The King's Accord
Alan Baxter

The King's blood soaked his white sheet, scarlet slowly spreading. Royal eyes stared wide and horrified at velvet hangings above the bed, seeing nothing. Queen Sylveen, face drawn in torment, pushed the King's guard aside and threw back the heavy, wet sheet. A gaping wound across the King's stomach, clutched in one desperate hand, yawned up at her. With a cry she turned away.

The King's Guard trembled. "Your Highness, I am so sorry. The assassin, he was like a shadow, on the King before I even knew he was there." He gestured to the ground, a black-garbed figure lying in another pool of blood. "I struck him down with all the speed I had, but I was too late."

Sylveen turned her back on her dead husband, lifting her chin. "My husband..." Her voice hitched. Clearing her throat she tried again. "My husband is not dead."

"Your Majesty..?"

"Rythell, you will tell no one of this. Send for Andur Mylan."

"My Queen, the King is well beyond healing..."

The Queen's face hardened. "Rythell, do as I say! Tell no one, send for the Court Mage and wait outside this room until he arrives."

"Yes, Your Highness." Fear and confusion on his face, the King's Guard slipped from the room.

The Queen turned, fell across the body of her husband and gave free rein to her grief.

Alan Baxter

***

Andur Mylan hurried through the castle, taking stone stairs two at a time. It was a long way from his basement rooms to the King's tower and it didn't pay to keep Their Majesties waiting. Out of breath, he reached the iron-banded wooden door and met the stony gaze of the King's Guard.

"Rythell, I've been summoned."

"I know. Brace yourself for a shock." The guard turned and rapped on the door. "Your Majesty, the Court Mage is here."

"Enter."

Squaring his shoulders, Rythell opened the door and strode in. Andur paused. A shock? With a wash of trepidation, he followed. The Queen stood in the center of the room. In a pool of blood at her feet was a man dressed all in black, apparently an Ethentian assassin. Andur's gaze swept across to the King's bed. His breath caught at the sight of blood and the King's face, a rictus of agony in death. His jaw dropped. "My Queen...?"

"Shut the door."

"My Queen, are *you* hurt?"

"No. An assassin gained entry and murdered my husband in his sleep. If I had not been outside, unable to sleep, I'm sure I would be dead, too. Rythell killed the assassin, but his end was already achieved."

Andur narrowed his eyes, trying to take it all in. Rythell stood beside him, head hung in shame. The King dead? It was inconceivable. "Your Majesty..."

The Queen silenced him with an upheld palm. "As you are aware, in three day's time the delegates from Ethentia arrive to sign the Accord Of Diam."

Andur nodded. "The entire Kingdom is aware, Your Majesty."

"Obviously someone disagrees with it."

Andur crouched to inspect the body of the assassin. "Definitely Ethentian, not just in appearance. He carries an Ethentian blade and..." He paused, sniffing at the blood covered steel. "Yes, I

The King's Accord

can smell Slybane."

The Queen raised an eyebrow.

"An Ethentian poison. This assassin wasn't going to rely on steel alone to achieve his ends."

Sylveen nodded. "There is clearly a part of Ethentian society that doesn't want to see an end to this war."

"There are many, Your Majesty. Here too, I'm sure. A healthy trade exists for the unscrupulous during wartime, not to mention the political aims of some."

"Indeed. So this accord must be signed. Therefore, the King is not dead."

"I don't understand."

The Queen crossed her arms tightly over her chest. "My husband spent many, many years negotiating a treaty with Ethentia. It's been his life's work. Our son will take over the throne and he will rule well, but he is not King Monvald of Trear. If the King is dead, the treaty will fall apart and it will become my son's life's work to rebuild it."

"Maybe not, Your Majesty. Could not Tellon simply declare his support of his father's work and sign the accord as King?"

"No more than I could as Queen. The Ethentian's are a proud and stubborn people and this accord is with King Monvald and Emperor Qoh. The drafts have all been written in these names, the last year has been spent agonising over every single letter of this thing to the contentment of all. Any change now would scupper everything."

"Then the accord is lost."

The Queen approached Andur, taking both his hands in hers, a gesture unimaginable. Andur trembled. Rythell turned away. "The King cannot be dead, Andur."

"Your Majesty, I'm sorry, but..."

"Andur! The King is *not* dead. The King is very sick, but insists that the signing of the accord will proceed. Only you, Rythell and I know the truth. Why have I called for you?"

Andur's trembling increased. He wondered if the Queen's

grief had driven her mad. "Your Majesty, I don't know."

"What can you do that Rythell or I never could?"

Andur stared into the Queen's deep green eyes as his hands trembled in hers. Their proximity overwhelmed him. The shock of the killing, the stench of death, disoriented him. He squeezed his eyes shut, trying to think, even as realisation rose in his mind. "No, my Queen. Surely not."

"There is no other way."

"But I don't know how."

"You're the only one that can learn. And learn you must, in just a few days."

Andur shook his head, eyes still tightly closed. "It is against nature, Your Majesty. And I don't even know if it can work."

The Queen put one finger beneath Andur's chin, tipped his head up. His knees threatened to fold beneath him. "Look at me, Andur Mylan."

With a supreme act of will, Andur opened his eyes.

"Think how many lives are lost in this futile war every year. Can we, in all conscience, *not* do everything in our power to see this accord signed?"

Andur's heart pounded in his chest, stunned at the Queen's touch, the slaughter that surrounded them. "But Your Majesty, I don't know how."

"Teskelleth does."

***

He packed in a haze of confusion, unsure what he might actually need. The Queen insisted that she and Rythell would take care of the body of the assassin. He was to focus entirely on his task. Already word was spreading as the castle awoke; the King was unwell and cancelling all engagements to be recovered in time for the delegates' arrival. Deciding that little beyond food and water would be of any use, and would only slow him down, Andur threw his pack across one shoulder. With a handful of medications, he returned to the

The King's Accord

King's tower.

"Your Majesty, I have brought medicines and ensured I was seen bringing them. As Court Mage and Royal Physician, it seems strange that I will be leaving. At least I will have been seen attending now."

The Queen smiled, though it couldn't push through the grief to reach her eyes. "You are a good man, Andur. I will make it known that the King is stable and you have traveled to collect medicines to hasten his recovery."

Andur nodded. "It will take me most of a day to reach Teskelleth. Another to return. I must learn while I'm there and have enough time to perform whatever is required when I get back. This may be an impossible task, my Queen."

"I know. We have three days before the delegates arrive. Tellon, as leader of our forces, will not return from the war until the accord is signed. No one else needs to know or has any business enquiring until then. If you can learn what you need, and get back in time to make it happen, we stand a chance of keeping this accord alive."

"What if Teskelleth won't teach me?"

"Do *anything* to convince her. And the Blessing Of The Six go with you."

Terrified at the thought of what "anything" might entail, Andur reached the stables as the sun cleared the city walls. Weighed down by trepidation, he walked his horse through cobbled streets, leaving the city gates as the morning mists lifted from the plains. Turning his horse to the north, he rode towards a place he had promised himself he would never go.

Teskelleth, the dark witch, once a respected citizen of Trear. He had looked up to her as a young child, when he was apprenticed to the Court Mage of the day. Her potions and her skills were legendary. Her ability to heal unrivaled. But darkness had crept into the heart of Teskelleth. Her magic had taken ever more blasphemous turns. Eventually, she had been denounced as evil and tried as a dark witch. Found guilty, they had burned her at the stake. And she had laughed. Laughed as her magic protected her from the voracious flames. When the ropes binding her had burned away along with her clothes she strolled, casually naked, from the pyre. It was well known that she had exiled herself to the north. The King kept a close eye on her with spies and scouts, but she ignored everyone and everything. Concentrating, presumably, on her black arts.

Andur had no idea how he was supposed to ask this creature for help, especially without raising her suspicions to his reasons. Though, as the Queen had suggested, what choice did they have?

***

He rode all day, careful to avoid exhausting his horse. Eventually, he reached the foothills of the Skaren Peaks, malevolent, jagged gray rising endlessly beyond. The light was fading from the sky as he walked his horse warily among the broken shale, watching for landmarks and signs. He guessed he wouldn't have to look hard. A large black crow landed on a lightning struck tree limb, its blackness stark against the pale grey of the dead branch. Signs of magic swirled about it, obvious to Andur's mage eyes. He nodded softly to himself. "You going to lead me then?"

The crow tipped its head, looking with one eye then the other.

"Ready when you are," Andur said.

The crow tipped its head again.

Andur narrowed his eyes, feeling his way into the crow's mind. "Ah, you're watching through the crow? Teskelleth, I seek your counsel."

The crow sat motionless.

"Teskelleth, I am Andur Mylan of Diam. I am a mage and a seeker. I have great need of knowledge I believe you can impart. I'm willing to pay whatever price you see fit to charge." For emphasis, he hefted a large bag of ducorts that chinked softly, though he doubted the witch would set her price in gold.

The crow took off and flew to another blasted tree, further up the hill. Andur followed until he was led down into a valley, swallowed by darkness. He cast a bobbing ball of light and walked in magical silver brightness. Eventually a cave mouth appeared, firelight flickering against the silhouette of the mountainside. Frightened by something that should have been a welcome sight he dispelled his orb of light. Teskelleth stood at the cave mouth, hands on hips, a featureless shadow with the fire at her back. "You have balls of iron, I'll give you that."

"I'm not afraid of you." He tied his horse to a stunted tree.

"The stench of fear I smell in waves makes a liar of you, boy."

"Boy? I have close to forty years."

"And you call yourself a mage? You're a child in the arts."

Andur refused to be drawn into an argument about who may or may not be a mage. "I need knowledge of a magic that I believe you have."

"So?"

"And I'm prepared to pay handsomely for it."

"So you said. What use have I for money?"

"Then name your price."

Teskelleth turned and walked into the cave, slim, attractive, moving with a courtesan's grace. Andur knew it to be artificial youth through magic. She had been old before he was born, tales of her healing predating him by generations. Before she had turned. He followed her into the cave, partly grateful to be in from the wilds, partly cautious that he was willingly jumping into a spider's web.

Her cave was a network of small caverns, packed with all manner of equipment, the bottles and cauldrons of the potioneer, the books and scrolls of the scholar, the tools and tinctures of the physician. There were caged animals and birds. At the back in deep shadow a large, dark sheet covered what appeared to be a huge cage. Andur thought he could hear a low keening floating through the smoky air from its depths.

"Best not to look on that, mage, let alone consider its contents."

He turned his attention back to the witch. She sat before a

fire, spooning a lumpy soup from a pan into two wooden bowls. She offered one. He paused, suspicious.

"Eat, you bloody fool. If my aim was to kill you, I wouldn't be so boring as to poison you with soup."

Suppressing his urgency, he took the bowl, sitting opposite her, the fire between them offering a small sense of security. Surreptitiously sniffing the rising steam, using a simple magic to feel for threats, he heard her soft chuckling. She began swallowing large spoonfuls, eating as though starving. Smiling at his paranoia, he followed suit. The soup was good, meaty and thick.

"I'm really not as evil as everyone thinks, you know."

Andur watched, chewing, choosing not to reply.

"You're the young Court Mage apprentice, eh? At least you were when I left."

"I used to idolize you."

She smiled, but it was sad. "You still could."

"I can't condone what you do."

"And what do I do exactly?"

Andur paused, spoon halfway to his lips. That was a good question. He took the spoon to his mouth, buying time to think.

"You're all told how evil I am," Teskelleth said quietly. "I'm really not evil. I just followed my studies down darker paths."

"Darker but not evil?"

The witch made a noise of disgust. "Magic is not all about love potions and healing royals! There are wonders to be unlocked, Andur Mylan. Secrets of the void. Going where others fear to tread is not courting evil."

Perhaps the things she said held merit. What did he really know of her after all? As an orphan child he had been apprenticed, taught the ways of the mage. Her reputation had been a light to guide him, her achievements a benchmark to live up to. She had ever been a free agent, never beholden to the royal family or anyone else, though always happy to help. She had often advised the Court Mage. Then tales of her slipping into black magic and dark experiments had preceded her trial, burning, escape and exile. But what had she

The King's Accord

actually done?

"It's all politics, Andur."

"Politics?"

"Of course. You cross the wrong people and, if they're powerful enough, they leak poison about you. Everything is political. Even you, here now. This is political, is it not?"

Andur shook himself. None of it mattered. He had a very specific task and a very tight schedule. "No. Not political. I need to know how to return someone from the dead."

Teskelleth rocked back with laughter. "Is that right? And for what, pray tell, if not politics."

It suddenly seemed pointless to make up a story the witch would swallow. He had had plans to talk of a murdered lover, a visceral desire to have her back, but it all seemed so juvenile. Teskelleth was old and wise, despite appearances, and not easily fooled. "Please, my need is desperate. Can I not offer you a payment that would buy the knowledge without explanation?"

Teskelleth barked a short laugh. "Politics. But you need to know something. You can't bring someone back. Or if you can, I haven't learned how yet. You can reanimate a corpse, create a profane marionette that used to be a person. That unnatural thing can even do your bidding, though by the Six, it's a horrible thing to observe. Is that what you'd like, mage?"

Andur sat stunned. He had not planned on Teskelleth being quite so open about her abilities or successes. Or lack of them. He was not really sure what he had expected, though perhaps this was enough. A war between nations was the source of their desperation, thousands of lives the wager. His eyes were hard. "Can you show me?"

Teskelleth was mildly surprised. "Must be dire straits indeed in Court."

"Can you show me?"

"Yes."

Andur's heart was racing. "How long would it take to learn?"

"A few hours. The doing is rarely complicated. It's the desire to know and the finding out that take time."

"And what is your price?" He wondered if he would be able to pay. He was willing, with a nation at stake. He would give his life for his Queen and his country, if that's what it took.

"You really shouldn't play politics with magic, Court Mage."

"Please, name your price."

Teskelleth smirked. "I need nothing. But you will pay a price one way or another, I assure you of that. Politics and magic do not mix well. Look to me for proof of that."

Andur was stunned. They would certainly pay a price if their audacious plan didn't work, but could he really get this knowledge for nothing? "You would give me this knowledge freely?"

The witch shook her head. "I will give you this knowledge, but nothing comes freely."

That was good enough. The magic was all he needed now. Without it there was little hope in the future anyway. "So, what do I need to know?"

"You will need potions to pour into the body, which I can supply. And even you know, I presume, how to draw a storm and tame the lightning?"

"I do."

***

Andur stood looking at the body of his King. "I hope I got back in time."

Queen Sylveen's face was grim. "The odour and pallor we can conceal with perfumes and make-up. The looseness of the skin is easily explained by His Majesty's illness. It's whether your magic works or not that matters."

"Teskelleth assures me it will. I just hope we can be convincing."

"It's the only chance we have. You say he..." Sylveen stopped, her face creasing as she strove to control her emotions. Andur couldn't begin to imagine how hard this must be for her. She

THE KING'S ACCORD

truly loved Monvald, had since her teens. Theirs was a marriage envied throughout the land. She tried again. "You say he will be able to remember simple instructions? Enact them?"

"Yes, my Queen." Andur's voice was tight. "We can instruct him to touch his throat should anyone speak to him, while you explain that the illness has taken his voice. We can instruct him to enter the chamber, bow as expected, take his seat, sign where indicated. You will have to guide him, you can whisper instructions in his ear, if necessary. If we prepare carefully he should act properly. And he will clearly be unwell in the eyes of those gathered."

Tears coursed over Sylveen's cheeks. She ignored them. "This desecration of my husband *has* to work, Andur!"

"We'll do everything we can to ensure it does, my Queen."

***

The Ethentian delegation arrived through the wet cobbled streets of Diam. People lined the roads, waved hands and flags, craned for a look at Emperor Qoh. Much discussion centered on whether the freak, unexpected storm of the night before was auspicious or not. Queen Sylveen met the Emperor at the Palace gate.

"Emperor Qoh, Your Royal Highness, welcome to Diam. I trust your journey was good?"

The Emperor stepped from his carriage, resplendent in blue satins and jewels. He smiled warmly. "It was, my thanks. Word reached us on the journey, and your messengers reported that King Monvald is sick?"

"He is. I'm sorry to say that he is very sick, but has insisted that the signing of this accord go ahead. He is saving his strength to attend and sign, ensuring that this moment in history is not lost."

"Unfortunate this accord could not be sealed under better circumstances."

"It is. But after so much work, as my King himself suggested, this formality is but the end of a marathon. Perhaps, on his recovery, we might travel to Ethentia and celebrate the accord there, as it should be celebrated?"

The Emperor inclined his head. "A fine idea. I'm honored by the suggestion."

Standing behind his Queen, Andur breathed a sigh of relief. The delegation was led into the palace.

Andur took his place by the throne room doors. The room was adorned suitably for such an important event, rows of seating surrounding a central table. Guards patrolled every corridor, their armor polished to mirrors. The Emperor and his party were sat and offered fine fruits and wines. Tumblers and jugglers filled the space between the table and those members of the court lucky enough to receive an invitation to attend. Heralds raised their trumpets, the royal flag of Diam hanging beneath each one. Andur's heart began to race as they fanfared the arrival of the King.

From behind the thrones, Queen Sylveen led King Monvald through the gathering. Her face was soft but even from the other side of the room Andur could see the hardness in her eyes. The King leaned on his wife's arm, shuffling unnaturally across the smooth flagstone floor. His head hung forward, his eyes rheumy and sagging, his mouth loose. The court drew breath as one, horrified to see the poor health of their King.

Sylveen whispered in his ear and he raised one hand, offering a wave left and right as he approached the table. Emperor Qoh stood as the King arrived. "Your Majesty, it gives me a heavy heart to see you so unwell." His face barely concealed his horror at the sight of the King's infirmity.

Monvald bowed, touched one hand to his throat. "Emperor Qoh," the Queen said in a strong voice. "The illness has taken King Monvald's voice, his throat swollen and raw. Our Court Mage is treating his condition, but fears his voice won't return for some days. My husband wrote a few words for me to say on his behalf."

The King nodded, his head wobbling, seeming too heavy for his neck. Sylveen cleared her throat. "Your Royal Highness, Emperor Qoh of Ethentia and honorable gathered guests. I apologize most profusely for my condition, but thank you all so much for joining

The King's Accord

us here for this momentous occasion. Every citizen of Trear and Ethentia, I'm sure, desires to live in peace. After so many years, let us not wait another moment before that peace is sealed. May the Accord of Diam be signed here and now and celebrated in Ethentia on the new moon."

Cheers and applause rose throughout the throne room. Emperor Qoh bowed again to the King. Monvald raised both hands, looking vacantly around the room, eyes unfocussed. Sylveen whispered in his ear and he returned Qoh's bow. Andur wiped at the sweat that ran from his brow. They might pull this off yet.

Qoh and Monvald sat at the table and the parchment of the accord was set before them. Qoh took up a quill, raising it above his head. "Let this moment be noted by all here and spread to the four winds!" he cried, his voice carrying over the throng. "Let there be peace!"

The roar of approval was deafening as Qoh put his quill to the parchment. Monvald sat limp, no emotion on his face. Qoh slid the parchment across the table.

The King reached for the quill in front of him. Andur held his breath. He felt sick. Just sign, make the necessary excuses of illness, and lead the King away and it was done. They would have ended the war. That the King would die of his illness in a few days time would only add to the legend of his legacy.

King Monvald raised his quill as Qoh had before him. The crowd roared ever louder. As Monvald lowered his hand to the parchment he rocked back violently in his chair, dropping the quill as his arms spasmed. Cheering died into gasps and shouts as people saw a thick black crossbow bolt protruding from Monvald's forehead. The Queen clapped her hands over her mouth, Qoh leapt from his chair.

Andur distantly heard sounds of scuffling through the rushing in his ears. Guards had fallen upon someone to his right. His knees turned to jelly as Monvald sat forward, his expression unchanged, and picked up the quill he had dropped. Paying no attention to the room around him or the bolt between his eyes, he signed the Accord

Of Diam and raised the quill once more, as screams rang through the throne room.

Color drained from the Queen's face, her skin instantly ashen. Qoh staggered backwards. "What foul sorcery is this?"

Monvald placed his quill back on the parchment and sat motionless, expressionless. Queen Sylveen turned to Qoh, her eyes pleading as he backed away in horror. "My Lord, the accord is the thing that matters. Peace in our lands is what matters!" Tears ran from her eyes.

Qoh continued to back away, his mouth working like a beached fish. "What barbaric sorcery?" he finally managed.

"Please, Emperor, let peace reign!"

Qoh shook his head. "There will be no peace." He shot forward, snatched the parchment from the table, shredding it with disgust as he called out to his retainers. "Clear the way and prepare my carriage. We leave this instant. I will not spend another minute in this evil nation!"

Amid the screams and wails bouncing off the walls Queen Sylveen dropped to her knees, face in her hands, sobbing openly.

Andur felt as if he would pass out at any moment. His knees knocked, his hands shook. "What have I done? Oh, by the Six, what have I done?"

A large, dark bird landed on his shoulder, chuckling in his ear. "You played politics with magic, Court Mage. I tried to warn you."

ABOUT THE AUTHOR:

Alan is an author living on the south coast of NSW, Australia. He writes dark fantasy, sci fi and horror, rides a motorcycle and loves his dog. He also teaches Kung Fu. Read extracts from his novels, a novella and short stories at his website—www.alanbaxteronline.com—and feel free to tell him what you think. About anything.

NECRODANCE

Darin Kennedy

I clean up nice. A little gel in the hair, polo shirt, nice jeans. I look like the kid brother they never had. Makes doing what I do pretty easy.

Plus, I can spot a damsel in distress from about six miles out.

Take this one. Seven-thirty on a Wednesday night, frozen food aisle, weighing options from the fine people at Lean Cuisine. The few stray cat hairs on her black jeans tell me all I need to know. If I wanted her, I could have her back at the dollhouse tonight, but her auburn hair and freckles remind me of my first girlfriend.

And I do so hate to repeat myself.

I head down to Warehouse Hardware, or as I like to call it, "The Fish Tank." I wander around for a few minutes until I see another potential.

No ring. Shopping alone in Flooring. *Kitchen Renovation for Morons* lying askew in her basket. A bit of wear on her UVA t-shirt. I'm guessing twenty-six, fresh out of grad school, moving into her first house. I sniff the air. Yep. Dumped about a month ago.

"Redoing your kitchen?"

"The backsplash." She avoids my gaze. "Getting ready to sell."

"For a project that big, you might want to wait till this weekend." I point to the sign above her head. "The Labor Day Weekend sale is usually pretty good."

"I'll be all right." She glances up at me, the corners of her mouth turned up in a tight grin. "Got a coupon."

"You ever put down tile before? It can be kind of—"

"Look. It's been a long day. All I want is to walk out of here with some reasonably priced tile and not get hit on by everything with a Y-chromosome and a pulse, okay?"

Damn. I was kind of in the mood for Italian.

"No problem."

I head down the center aisle, meandering from side to side as I take in the scenery. I stop for a moment in Lighting where a couple is deciding which chandelier to put in the front foyer. A few seconds watching them together confirms my suspicion.

The withering looks. His fretful smile. Her eyeing the salesman's crotch. Dude hasn't given his wife an orgasm in over a year. Maybe two. I make a mental note of her hazel eyes in case I run into her somewhere down the road. I have a sneaking suspicion she'll be alone.

I pass the paint aisle and catch movement from the corner of my eye.

Ah. There she is.

The main attraction.

Straight from the gym, her baby doll t-shirt sleeves just kiss her supple deltoids. Her calves strain as she balances atop a plastic stepstool reaching for a gallon of paint from the top shelf. I see it coming a good ten seconds before she starts to fall. The can just beyond her reach, she goes up on her toes, her fingers grazing the handle as the stool starts to wobble. I rush over, diving forward and catching her before that firm ass of hers can hit the concrete. Her voice cuts out mid-scream as she falls into my arms.

"I've got you."

She scurries out of my grasp and gets her feet back on the floor. Five-foot two at best, she looks up at me with a mixture of bewilderment, fear, and gratitude. She brushes a caramel-colored curl from her face. The deep blue of her eyes reminds me of an autumn sky.

"You the Warehouse guardian angel or something?"

"Something like that."

Necrodance

"One less trip to the ER, I suppose." She cracks a crooked grin. "Thanks."

I put on my no-fail smile. "I take it you've been down this aisle before."

Her gaze flashes downward for a second, then back up to mine. "When I was twelve, my mother took away my roller skates and told me I could have them back after I graduated from college. True story."

She's funny. I like funny.

"You know, they've got the same primer right down here." I gesture to the stack of matte white on the bottom shelf. "Something special about those on the top shelf or are you feeling suicidal tonight?"

She bites her lip, cranes her neck around the stepladder at her feet and smiles. "Hm. Not paying attention, I guess."

I retrieve the paint can and hand it to her. The lid's intact but the bottom corner's crushed in. If not for me, might've been her skull.

But the night's still young.

"So, what are you working on?"

"My dining room," she says. "I was thinking red."

"My favorite color."

We talk for a couple of minutes before she glances down at her watch.

"I'd better head on. Going to put down the primer tonight so I can work on the actual painting this weekend. A lot of mid-eighties pastel to cover up." She lets her foot brush the overturned stepstool. "Thanks for the save."

"Y'know, I've got some experience with paint."

She raises an eyebrow. "I'll bet you do."

"No, seriously. Back in college, I worked with a couple guys flipping houses during the summers so we could eat the rest of the year. I did all the dry wall and painting."

"All right, Bob Vila. Which brush should I get to do a twelve by twelve room?" She gestured to Warehouse's arsenal of painting implements.

"I'd use a roller for the big stuff. Looks a lot more professional, and it's faster. As far as brushes, a small one for the trim should be all you need."

"What about painter's tape?"

"Painting's all about prep. You can skip a step if you're brave, but I wouldn't recommend it. A little pre-work makes clean up a lot easier."

"Hm." Her wheels turn. "You got a minute?"

"Sure."

I help her gather everything she needs to lay a decent base coat and carry the basket up to the front of the store. She pays with plastic, then shoots me a sidelong glance as she steps away from the register.

"Here's the thing," she says. "I'm not much of a painter and you at least sound like you know what you're talking about. Want to give me a few more tips over a beer? My treat."

"Sure."

I do a quick mental check.

"How about Ed's, down on the corner."

Four months since I last set foot in that shithole. I never become a regular at any particular bar. Hard to stay nondescript if they know your name.

"All right." She flashes me a winning grin and extends her hand. "I'm April."

Her skin is soft, but her grip is firm.

"I'm Dan."

She smiles. "You look like a Dan."

I help her carry her purchases out to an old school Volkswagen bug done up in gold and blue, then follow her to the bar. We take a couple of seats by the front window, and talk for half an hour about whatever she wants. I learn more than I ever wanted about her new one-story house and its previous owners: the pastel blue they left on all the walls, the mildewed carpet, the leaky water heater. It's all I can do to stay focused in such a target rich environment. She nearly

NECRODANCE

catches me making eyes at a pair of brunettes playing pool. I'm ready to write the evening off when the conversation takes a turn.

"So, Dan, you hang around hardware stores waiting for women to fall off ladders?"

"Only on Wednesdays." I let out a chuckle. "You're lucky I was there browsing."

"Lucky? Maybe." She holds up two fingers to the bartender and shoots me a wink.

I wait until she's had a couple more beers before offering to help get the primer coat on the walls.

"I don't know," she says.

"Come on." I cock my head to the side and give her my best smolder. "It's past eight already. You'll be up half the night if you try to do it yourself."

"But—"

"Don't worry. I'm the best." I hold up my half empty glass. "And I work cheap."

She puts up a brave front, but I can see in her eyes that I'm in. Another push and she's giving me her address. I follow her to a little bungalow on a cul-de-sac a few miles from the bar.

"Pardon the mess," she says as we come in the front door.

"Mess?" The place is immaculate. "Looks pretty good to me. You have any plastic we can use to keep the paint off the hardwoods?"

She raises an eyebrow. "Don't tell me you actually came here to paint."

I feel my mouth turn up in a surprised grin. "What do you mean?"

"Do you really want me to spell it out for you?"

I can tell from her flushed cheeks that she and the alcohol mean business. She's petite, but I hadn't pegged her for a lightweight. "I guess not."

"Give me a minute."

She steps through a door into what I guess is her bedroom. She flips on a lamp, the dim light golden as it falls through the door.

"Okay," she calls after a couple of minutes. "You can come in now."

I enter her inner sanctum, and for the first time in a couple of years, I'm the one surprised. Decked out in a red leather bustier and a black miniskirt, emphasis on the mini, she flashes me a wicked grin.

"Do you like to play games?" A riding crop rests on the bed.

"You have no idea."

I slip out of my shirt as she pulls down the covers. I move in to take her and she shakes her head, waving her finger in my face.

"No, no, no. Got to play by the rules tonight, Danny boy."

All right. I'll play her game for now.

She slips off my pants, letting them drop to the floor, then directs me onto the bed. At her direction, I get down on all fours and wait.

She gives me a light tap with the crop. Then another, a little harder than the first.

"Have you been a bad boy, Danny?" Her sultry voice no more than a whisper, she delivers another stinging pop.

"Yes."

Another pop. "I mean, really bad?"

I grit my teeth. "Yes."

"In that case…" She scoots across the bed. She slides open the top drawer of her nightstand and gets out a pair of silk scarves. "Perhaps we need to step up your punishment."

"Wow." Even I'm surprised by the nervous laugh that escapes my lips. "Do I need a safe word here?"

She raises her eyebrows. "Do you really want one?"

I lie back on the bed and give her my hands. She straddles me and ties one wrist to the headboard. I resist as she reaches for the other hand.

"What's the matter, Dan? I thought you liked games." She leans forward, her breasts straining against their red leather prison. "You're not afraid of me, are you?"

What the hell. She'll have to untie me at some point, and

Necrodance

then it'll be my turn.

As she secures my left arm with a knot that only a boy scout should know, I notice a change. The smile is gone, but the storm in her eyes has come to life.

She rolls off me and somersaults to the foot of the bed, sticking her landing like an Olympic gymnast. "So. Whatever shall we do first?" Her words send chills through me, but not the kind I had expected. "Come on, Dan. Tell me what you want." That devilish grin of hers comes out for an encore performance. I wish it hadn't.

"I think the real question here is what *you* want."

"That's better." She sits at the foot of the bed, just out of reach. "For now, I suppose, I want you to think."

I feel my heart accelerate. "Think about what?"

"I'm guessing you're already thinking about it." She rises from the bed and goes into the next room. The bowie knife in my pocket might as well be in the next state. I struggle at the tight silk binding me to the bed until she returns.

"Don't bother. You'd have to break a couple of bones in each hand to get out of those knots." She stares absently out the window and sips at a glass of red wine.

"I think there's been a mistake." I try to catch her eye. "You see, I—"

"Oh, there's no mistake." She takes another sip of wine. At least I think it's wine. "I had a very interesting conversation a couple of weeks ago with a gentleman named Robert Davis. You may remember him. He was all over the news back in July. CNN, Headline News, MSNBC. He was even on Larry King if I remember right."

"Yeah, I heard about that whole thing. What does it have to do with me?"

"Mr. Davis is in a lot of pain, Dan. A lot of pain. To lose a daughter like that…"

"I don't know what you're talking about, you crazy bitch. I—" My voice catches in my throat as she jabs me in the gut with the riding crop.

"Be nice, Dan. You're in a precarious position to be calling people names."

"Sorry. I'm a little freaked out here. Whatever it is you think I've done, you're wrong." The fear in my voice actually gives me some credibility. "You've got the wrong man."

Her laugh chills my blood. "Perhaps." She walks to the closet and opens the door. The smell of freshly turned earth fills the room.

"Is he the one?" April asks. After a long pause, a voice that sounds like a comb being dragged across wool whispers a quiet response.

"Yes." The hairs on my neck stand on end. "That's him."

"Sorry if she's hard to hear," April says. "I did the best I could, but her vocal chords were damaged pretty badly."

"What the hell is going on here?" I stare into the darkness of the closet and see a hint of movement. I inhale to ask who waits beyond the shadowy threshold, though a part of me already knows. As she steps into the room, sweat trickles down my chest like cold fingers.

"Abby."

"Hello, Dan." My breathing grows raspy as her lips turn up into what used to be a smile.

"But…you're dead."

"And you would know." Abby takes a step closer. Her head doesn't sit on her shoulders quite right, sort of how you'd imagine a discarded puppet resting at the bottom of a drawer. Then again, I did take her head off with a shovel.

"One night?" Abby raises a shriveled eyebrow in April's direction.

"One night." A morbid glee colors her words. "Make the most of it." She takes a step backward out of the bedroom, then turns and meets my gaze as she closes the door behind her.

"Sorry I can't stay. I'd love to stick around and play third wheel, but I'm guessing you two have a lot to talk about."

Necrodance

About the Author:

Darin Kennedy is a graduate of Wake Forest University and Bowman Gray School of Medicine. When not writing contemporary fantasy, he practices family medicine in Charlotte, North Carolina. You can visit his website at www.darinkennedy.com.

THE GHOST WALK
Marianne Halbert

Mattie Wilson couldn't keep her eyes off the kids. After a long cold snap, today was the first day that really felt like spring since she'd come to town. She got to the park around sunrise. It'd been awhile since she'd rollerbladed. Sitting on the park bench, slipping on knee and wrist pads, she hoped to not make a fool of herself this morning, and hoped no one was watching her.

Fiddling with the helmet strap pulled too tight under her neck, she watched the boys, both of them probably around ten years old. She wouldn't have noticed them at all, except that one of them went up to the bronze statue. This one was a crossing guard, near the park entrance. A lanky uniformed man standing erect, one hand held up in a "halt" gesture, the other raising a whistle to within an inch of his metal lips. One of the boys, the one missing a tooth on the top left side of his grin, had run behind the guard, and on tip toes, reached up and used his hands to cover the guard's eyes.

It was a simple gesture. Kids playing peek-a-boo or hide and seek with a stationary authority figure. But it stirred a sense of déjà-vu in Mattie. The kids ran off behind a clump of red chokeberry bushes. Mattie ignored the crossing guard's warning to stop, and pushing off with one foot, then the other, she began to make her way along the paved trail through the park.

Warblers twittered and chirped at each other from the skeletal branches of treetops. Gradually, cyclists, joggers, and women pushing strollers began to emerge throughout the morning. The farther Mattie went without falling, the more confident she began

The Ghost Walk

to feel. Her strides became longer and more controlled. She came to a fork on the paved path, and saw a water fountain off to the left. A girl with a skateboard propped up alongside her was taking a long drink. When Mattie got closer, she saw the girl's coppery ponytails shimmering in the rays of the sunrise.

Another statue.

Mattie went around her to the fountain across from the girl. She bent down to drink, bringing her eyes within inches of the child-like statue. For a moment, she saw movement there in those eyes. Mattie pulled back, her feet spinning out from under her. She gripped the edges of the fountain to keep from crashing down. *Sunlight.* It was just the sunlight glinting on the girl's face that had made her eyes flash. Mattie wiped her mouth with the back of her hand, tasting the black leather of her wrist guard.

She tossed her rollerblades in the back of a taxi cab about ten minutes later. The cab smelled of sweat and cigars. The town seemed too small to really need a taxi, and she'd heard some women at the park complaining that the driver used it more as an excuse to people-watch and lurk, than for income. And for such a small town, the driver seemed rude, talking more to himself or the traffic around him than to Mattie. When they came to a stoplight a block from her loft, Mattie spotted another one of those statues. This one was a chubby old woman, clutching a shopping bag under one arm, her other hand raised as though hailing a taxi. Crazy as it seemed, Mattie had to catch herself before suggesting to the driver that they stop for the lady. The driver drummed his thumb on the steering wheel, waiting for the light to turn green. Suddenly, a teenage girl in a midriff top and jeans, *barely* teenage by the looks of her, walked up to the old lady. She put her fingers over the woman's eyes and waited a moment. She lowered her hands, and then ran across the street, through the intersection, bumping into the hood of Mattie's cab. Her auburn hair was pulled back in a sloppy loop, long bangs blowing in the breeze.

The driver rolled down his window and shook his fist at the girl.

Marianne Halbert

"You dent it, you pay for it!" he yelled. The girl looked at him, and then locked her eyes on Mattie. In spite of the horn blaring, she took time to shake her head at Mattie before darting down an alleyway.

"I know you, little miss. Little Miss *volunteer at the church and the old folks home*. Little Miss *no one sees me and Billy Britchett making out behind Old Man Hester's five and dime*. But I know you. I drive every road in town, I know every street corner, every street walker, and every alley." He took a long inhale from his cigar before placing it back in the ashtray. "I see you unbuttoning your top for Billy. I see you and your friends smoking weed and giggling behind the auto shop. *I see you.*"

"She's just a kid," Mattie said. He sounded so judgmental. So personally offended by the girl's antics. And even though the girl was gone from sight, he was fixated on the alley where she'd disappeared. Mattie couldn't stop staring at the man.

A blaring horn from behind them snapped Mattie back to attention. She looked up and saw that the light had turned green at last.

"All right, all right," the driver growled, and accelerated.

After she got home, Mattie took a quick shower. She turned the knob all the way up, but the water still ran cold. Shivering, she lingered over a cup of coffee on the balcony of her apartment. She could see the park from here. Sunlight danced across small ripples across the lake, while swans and paddle boats moved in lazy arcs across the water. The clock tower at the center of the park chimed the noon hour, the gonging of the bells carrying to her on the breeze. With each tolling of the bells, Mattie saw coppery sunlight glinting off the town statues. Lighting up like that, she noticed a pattern. Around the lake, down Main Street, past the library, ending at the dance studio.

She left her half empty coffee mug sitting on a planter next to her balcony chair. Mattie walked several blocks to the library. As she ascended the steps, she passed a statue of a young man wearing wire-rimmed glasses thumbing through an open book. Once inside,

The Ghost Walk

an older lady behind the counter almost looked at her, but then a dad holding his son's hand walked up, stepping in front of Mattie.

"Just returning these," he said, handing the librarian a few books. "I was wondering, the statue outside the entrance, the ones all over town, what can you tell me about them?"

The librarian leaned her head forward, looking over her glasses, revealing her eyes.

"What is it you want to know?"

"I don't know, I've just never seen anything quite like them. It's like they're their own little community, within our little community. And something about their eyes."

"Their eyes?"

"Well, the town kids, even my own son, seem to have a habit of covering their eyes."

"Wait here a minute," she said.

She lugged a coffee table book over and onto the counter. Flipped it open. Mattie stepped closer, peering over the boy's shoulder as he stood next to his father.

"The artist's name is Pitch Founder," the librarian said. "He subscribed to the old artisan style, the lost wax method."

"Must be pretty pricy for the town to purchase all those statues." The boy slowly turned his head to the side, glaring at Mattie out of the corner of his eye.

"Never showed up on a town purchase order. Rumor is they're donated, or a benefactor arranged for the payment. They just show up. One at a time. First one was the ballet dancer, in a perfect Arabesque en Point. Her entire frame supported by one dainty foot on her tip toes, her other leg stretched out behind her in a ninety degree angle, one hand gingerly resting on a bike-rack railing, the other tenderly reaching forward, her gaze fixated on that delicate reaching hand. The following week, it was the fisherman, sitting on the dock at the park. A couple months later, the crossing guard. That was about two years ago, and there must be dozens of them around here now."

"He can make them that quickly?" the dad asked.

"I wouldn't think so," she said. The boy darted out from behind his father's legs. He sprang at Mattie. Everything went dark, and she felt the warmth of his small hands covering her eyes. She heard the man's voice.

"Caleb, show some respect." He held the boy in his arms. "I'm sorry, you were saying?"

"You know, he's somewhat of a legend around town. He's supposed to use a clay mold, then make a plaster mold from that. When he pours the wax into the hollow plaster mold, and pours the melted bronze into the inside of the wax, the wax disappears. Some say he's a vigilante. According to the newspaper, his little sister was studying ballet. Was murdered walking home from the studio one night. He lit a candle down at St. Agnes' in remembrance of her. Then another, and another. They say he placed a lock of her raven hair and a tattered pair of her ballet slippers in his kiln. Along with the remnants of those red candles that had burned so brightly. Those candles had captured the essence of her spirit. And that's the wax he used for the mold. That's what he poured the molten bronze into, until it took shape and hardened."

The man shifted uncomfortably. "Do you really believe that?" he asked.

"All I can tell you is that when there's a murder within a ten mile radius of Twin Oaks' borders, St. Agnes knows to have her prayer candles stocked and the town knows Pitch Founder's about to fire up his kiln.

"The adults in this town just pass by those things like they were no more than a parking meter or a yield sign. But the children, the children are wary of them. Some will cross the street, take the circuitous route just to avoid them. To avoid those eyes. They say the eyes follow them. Sometimes they cover them up, just to get them to quit watching."

The man thanked her and guided his son back toward the children's book section. Mattie thought of asking the librarian more about the artist, but the woman was already closing the book. Mattie heard a voice behind her.

The Ghost Walk

"You know, if you're really interested, there's a ghost walk at midnight. It meets in front of the dance studio and ends at the clock tower in the park."

He must've been watching her, and picked up on Mattie's fascination with the statues. He turned his gaze toward the open book in his hands.

"What do you mean, a ghost walk?" she asked.

"The statues," the young man said, his gaze still fixated on his book. "Each is a replica of a murder victim from surrounding counties. You should come. I'll be there," he said. Then he turned, squaring his backpack across his shoulders, and exited the library. She saw him descending the steps and then he was gone.

Mattie fell asleep early that evening, but awoke around 11:45. She was breaking free of a dream in which the clock tower bells were summoning her. A chill swept across her flesh and she got out of bed. She pulled on a lightweight hoodie and shorts, and carried her rollerblades down the outdoor steps of her apartment. Gray clouds surrounded the moon. She sat on a bench, tying the laces of her blades. The strap under her neck felt too tight, and she adjusted it. She moved down the deserted street, and in the streetlights saw a small crowd had formed in front of the dancer at the entrance to the studio. She recognized the man from the library, still holding his book. He waved at her.

The bell tower struck midnight.

"Thank you all for being here tonight," the tour guide said. His long silver hair shimmered under the street light. But his face looked handsome and young. Chiseled. "Here you see the replica of Sage Founder, sister of the artist. She was seventeen years old when she was murdered walking home from this very dance studio. Pitch Founder became obsessed. He used his skill to create this statue. Using a lock of her hair, her favorite pair of ballet slippers, and the wax from dozens of prayer candles, he hoped to communicate with her from beyond the grave."

Mattie looked around at the crowd. She saw a man in some kind of uniform, *a cop maybe?* An old woman near an old man. The guy was holding some kind of kit or box from a handle in his hand. There was even a dark-haired girl in a pink leotard and tights. *Great, a ghost walk fan.*

"His goal was to find out who murdered her, and to avenge her. When he discovered that he could communicate with her, he realized she had no recollection of those last painful moments on earth."

Mattie stood silent as the man from the library approached her. He adjusted his glasses.

"Glad to see you here," he whispered. He looked at the speaker in awe. "I still can't believe he actually did it."

"Did what?" Mattie whispered back.

He looked at her. "Found a way to talk to the dead." Mattie shook her head, indicating she didn't know what he was talking about. "He communicates with them in order to see the future. He's a necromancer," the man said, as though it were the most obvious thing on Earth.

The crowd was moving down the street now, and stopped in front of the library.

"Craig McBroom," the guide said. The bookworm looked up. The speaker went on. "A sophomore at the campus over in Partridge Meadows. Came across a drug deal gone wrong. Bled out from numerous stab wounds before anyone even knew he was missing."

The man next to Mattie clenched his stomach. She felt like doing the same thing. The thought of being stabbed to death was horrifying.

Next they came to the old woman carrying her groceries. She'd been mugged over in Carlsberg, and died from blunt force trauma to her skull. Then the crossing guard at the park entrance. He'd been run down on purpose by someone angry about property taxes, randomly taking out a county employee.

"Each time the artist heard of another victim, he created a bronze statue, using personal items and a part of the corpse, hair, nails, blood, tissue, to put in the kiln. But each time he realized they

The Ghost Walk

were no help in solving their own murder. They could, however," and the handsome man with the long silver hair paused, his eyes sweeping the small crowd, "sense a murder that was imminent. With no conscious recollection of their own demise, they nonetheless could sense danger approaching. Could smell murder brewing. Each statue was a victim. Each victim in turn becomes a watcher. A guardian. Their last moments on Earth, they smelled the predator. They know what to look for, and are drawn to a killer on the cusp of his crime as a moth to the flame."

As the speaker continued to tell the story, Mattie realized that only the dancer had been murdered right here in town. The rest all occurred in surrounding counties. Twin Oaks hadn't had a murder since Sage Founder died. But, according to their guide, there had been eleven missing persons, including a drifter who'd been seen lurking near the church choir director's cabin, a high school swim coach who spent too much time alone tutoring students, and a city councilman who'd taken out a large insurance policy on his wife. The tour stopped in front of the clock tower. The crowd parted, and the guide made his way toward Mattie.

His sudden approach startled her, and her wheels began to roll. He steadied her, then laid his hands gently on her shoulders.

"Mattie," he said. He looked upon her like a father might look at a child, still awestruck that in a way he'd had a hand in the creation of this amazing being. "Each of the dead saw something to warn me who the next murderer was. While he was fishing, Charlie saw the drifter near the choir director's cabin."

Mattie watched the old man, realized it was a tackle box he held in his hand.

"And Madge saw the councilman coming out of the insurance agent's office down on Main Street."

Mattie looked toward the old woman, who had a bag of groceries clutched under one arm.

The guide's gaze penetrated into Mattie. "I need to know what you've seen since you've woken up."

Woken up?

He gripped her shoulders more firmly. "You wouldn't have joined us on the ghost walk if you hadn't sensed something. You've been drawn to someone, someone evil, who is about to commit a most reprehensible crime. I'm sorry there was no way to save you. The police report said you'd been rollerblading at night. You'd left a half-empty coffee mug at home, probably didn't even intend to be gone long. Your attacker gagged you with a leather strap during the assault, then used it to strangle you before dumping your body in the frigid water of a drainage ditch. Don't let that happen to someone else. Please," he begged, "please tell me what you've seen."

Mattie sensed someone behind her, watching her. She spun out of the man's grasp and saw a woman sitting on a park bench. She was wearing a helmet, and was frozen in time, tying the laces of her rollerblades.

"No," she said. Then she screamed it, to the tour guide, to all of them. "*No!*"

She sped away, racing down the path. At the water fountain, the little girl dropped her skateboard, and tried to come after Mattie. Mattie could hear the whirring of the wheels on the path behind her. At the entrance, the crossing guard held his hand out, and brought the whistle all the way to his lips, blowing it, screaming and shrill in her ear. She moved into town, and saw the old woman. Hailing a cab.

What have you seen Mattie? *What have you seen?*

I know you. *Unbuttoning your shirt, smoking your weed.*

Footsteps slammed the pavement behind her in the dark. Mattie turned and saw him. Pitch Founder. The artist who had molded her. His eyes searched hers and his eyes alone asked the question.

What have you seen Mattie?

"The cab driver," she said, sounding defeated. The way he watched that girl. *The way I watched him.* "He's going to murder the teenager who runs through town."

Headlights rounded a corner up ahead. Madge moved a step closer to the curb, hailing the taxi. Mattie could hear the voice from

THE GHOST WALK

inside the dark den of the cab growling, "Where to?"

"Founder's Park," Madge said with a smile.

Mattie and Pitch made their way back to the park entrance. The whole crowd was there when the cab pulled up. Madge asked the driver if he could help her out.

He pulled himself out of the car and slumped around to the passenger door. He swung it open, and gave Madge a hand. She stepped from the car. Mattie watched as Madge's white hair turned to bronze in the moonlight.

"What the—?" the cabbie said. He turned to the others, as if to ask, *do you see this?* But then he saw *them.* All of them were turning to bronze. The ballerina stepped forward, raising one delicate arm toward him. The man's eyes grew huge.

"Sage? That's not possible. You're dead, I made sure..." He lunged as if to make for the safety of his cab, but several statues blocked his way. He ran. Into the park.

Mattie led the pack, speeding ahead of everyone on her roller blades. She instinctively chased him to the clock tower. There, she grabbed him by the wrists, locking herself in position until Pitch and the others arrived.

Craig, the bespectacled bookworm, opened the door at the base of the tower.

Pitch turned to Mattie in the moonlight. "It's okay. We'll take it from here."

She looked beyond the door, and saw a glowing, pulsing light. "What's in there?" she asked.

"My kiln." Pitch looked thoughtfully at the blubbering cab driver, relief at having found his sister's killer obvious on his face. "You know, sometimes a piece just doesn't make the grade, and ends up as a big bronze blob at the bottom of the lake."

She released the man into the waiting hands of the others. After the door closed, she heard a skateboard roll up to her. She answered the question on the girl's face by nodding. They took off together down the path, making the rounds of the park.

As the clock tower struck one, she froze in mid-stride. But

she could feel a perpetual warm breeze on her face, and the power of her momentum. When the first rays of the dawn glinted in her eyes, she smiled.

And she watched.

ABOUT THE AUTHOR:

Marianne Halbert is an author from Central Indiana. She has had numerous short stories published in various magazines and anthologies. "The Ghost Walk" is dedicated to Steve, for being such an awesome husband. http://halbertfiction.webs.com. Wake up and smell the creepy.

BLOOD BROTHERS
J. Matthew Saunders

"I can't believe I'm doing this," he says. "I swear, Mark, if this is a sick joke—"

I cut him off. It's about the fifth time he's threatened me in the last two weeks. "It's not a joke, Brad. Did you bring what I asked?"

He reaches into the plastic bag he's holding and pulls out a shirt—her shirt. I don't want to know how he got it. He hands it to me.

"Well?" he asks.

In his jeans and faded t-shirt, he looks like he just stepped out of a J. Crew catalog. Brad is comfortable in his own skin in a way I'll never be. Not too hard when you're the quarterback of the football team and girls throw themselves at you all day.

There's only one girl either of us cares about right now, though, and she's buried in the ground. The marker on her grave says:

Emily Anne Fletcher
July 20, 1992-April 18, 2010
Our Beloved Angel Gone Back Home to Heaven

She died in a car wreck a couple of weeks ago. It was raining. She took a curve too fast and skidded off of the road down an embankment and into a tree. Her mother has already started a campaign to have the state's driving age raised to eighteen. I think she just needs something to do. I understand that. I needed something to do, too.

I rip the shirt into little pieces while Brad watches. I arrange the tatters of Emily's shirt in a pile on top of her grave, and pull the rest of what I need out of my backpack: chalk, courtesy of the school gym's supply closet; salt, courtesy of that new yuppie grocery store that just went in downtown; a branch from a hawthorn tree, courtesy of the school's botanical garden; and a book. I put the hawthorn branch on top of the shirt. I open the book to a page I've marked, one with a diagram drawn on it. I mix the chalk and the salt together and spread it in a circle around the grave, like the diagram shows.

"This isn't going to be like some bad horror movie, is it?" Brad asks. "We're not going to get stalked and killed by some creepy freak because we're cheating death, right?"

"We're not cheating death."

The whole school came to Emily's funeral. Everyone loved her. Everyone wanted to say goodbye to the golden-haired girl whose life was tragically cut short. Brad even cried. The last time I saw him do that was when his pet turtle, Freddie, died. We were six. Our families all lived on the same street. Hell, we still live on the same street. We used to do everything together, the three of us. We climbed trees. We rode our bikes. In the winter, we built snowmen. In the summer, we caught fireflies. Every Wednesday, rain or shine, Brad and I went to the comic book shop. Sometimes, Emily even came with us, though she always went for the girl comics.

When I told Brad at the funeral what I was going to do, I though he was going to punch me out until I reminded him about something that happened when we were ten.

"Do you remember, the dead bird, Brad?" I asked. "Do you remember how we were both into role-playing games? Do you remember how we went online looking for cheats and shortcuts and found those sites about real magic? Do you remember the little ritual we performed and how the bird opened its eyes and fluttered around before falling over again? You were scared. I wasn't. It's been eight years. I can do a lot more now than revive a bird for a few seconds."

Blood Brothers

After that, he listened to what I had to say.

I complete the circle, and I start to draw the first of the five glyphs spaced around the outside, again just like the diagram.

"What's that?" Brad asks. "Zodiac signs or something?"

"Or something."

The truth is I don't really know. I don't know what the glyphs stand for, or what language they are, or if they're a language at all. All I know is what they're supposed to do.

Everything changed when we started middle school. I don't know why. Brad stopped going to the comic book shop with me after he tried out for and made the middle school football team. He had practice on Wednesdays. Me and sports; we don't get along. My hand-eye coordination sucks, and I'm a beanpole. Always have been.

Emily started hanging out with other people, too; some girls in our class. She didn't want to talk about comics, even the girl ones, or ride bikes, or climb trees. She also started dressing differently: skirts, boots, clingy sweaters. I can't say I didn't enjoy the view, but sometimes I missed the Emily who would jump out of the big oak tree in her backyard any time anyone dared her to. We still said, "Hi," when we passed each other in the hall, but sometimes I heard the other girls snicker behind my back. Eventually Emily stopped saying, "Hi," and soon after, she started snickering as well.

After I finish the glyphs, I turn to Brad. "I need you to step inside the circle."

"Why?"

"Because it's what the book says, that's why."

"That just looks like one of your stupid role-playing books."

I pick it up. "It's not. It's a copy of the Munich Handbook. The original is over six hundred years old, and it says to get in the circle."

Brad rolls his eyes and walks toward the grave.

"Wait." I can't forget the most important part. I fish my Swiss Army knife and a book of matches out of my pocket. I hand them to him.

"What's this for?" he asks.

"God, can't you be a little patient? You'll see."

He steps inside the circle. "Now what?"

I don't answer him. I begin to read the incantations written in the book.

"That sounds like some Harry Potter bullsh—"

I wave my hand to shut him up. I have to get this right. I'm only going to have one chance.

Funny thing is he's actually sort of right. It's Latin, but it's some weird offshoot, not the Latin we're supposed to be learning in Mr. Dade's class and certainly not any the boy wizard would be using.

As I say the words, I hear another voice, low and gravelly, saying them with me. I can't tell where it's coming from, only that it's somewhere close by, though Brad doesn't seem to hear it. I chant faster. The voice begins to anticipate what I'm saying, and soon I'm not even paying attention to the book. I'm just repeating what the voice says. I chant faster. I close my eyes. I see the glyphs in my mind glowing white-hot, searing away everything until all that's left is the voice whispering in my ear. I chant faster.

A few minutes pass, or an hour. I'm not really sure. I finish the incantations and open my eyes. Brad claps slowly. "Bravo. You trying out for the drama club?"

"I'm just doing what I'm supposed to," I say.

The real break with Brad came toward the end of the sixth grade. He was hanging out with some of his football buddies after school one day. We hadn't talked in a few months. Deep down, I knew something was wrong, but in my cluelessness I had convinced myself it was because of football. The season was over, though, and I wanted to ask him to go to the comic book shop with me that Wednesday.

"Hi, Brad," I said.

One of the others punched him in the arm. "Hey, Brad, Goth boy's talking to you."

Brad sighed. "Guys, it's just Mark." He turned to me. "What

Blood Brothers

do you want?"

I shrugged. "Nothing. Just saying, 'Hi.' We haven't hung out in a while."

"There's a reason for that, emo," another one of them said. "Don't you have to go cut yourself or something?"

They all laughed, even Brad. Goth. Emo. Just because I happened to be wearing a black t-shirt. I walked away without another word. Brad called me that night. He told me he didn't want to be friends anymore. I didn't talk to him again until Emily's funeral.

"So what do we do now?" he asks.

"Take the knife and cut yourself. The palm doesn't hurt as bad as you might think. I need you to bleed on the tree branch and the shirt."

"What? I'm not going to do that."

"It's what the book says. Do you want Emily back or not?"

"Why don't you do it?"

"I can't. I read the incantation. You supply the blood. That's the only way it works."

He glares at me as he opens the knife. He swipes it across the palm of his hand. On his first attempt, he barely breaks the skin. He tries again and winces as the blade creates a red gash. A trickle of blood oozes out of the cut. He holds his hand over the tree branch. The blood falls drop by drop.

"That's enough," I say after about a minute. I may have let him bleed a little longer than he needed to. "Now take a match and light the branch and the shirt on fire."

He does it. His blood gives the tiny fire an acrid, rusty smell. It only burns for a few minutes. Soon the shirt and the branch are just ashes.

He looks up at me. "What happens now?"

"We wait."

Our freshman year in high school, Brad and Emily started dating. A little part of me died every time I saw them together in the cafeteria, in the hall, on the bus. Every day they paraded it in front of me, that I wasn't part of their world anymore. I made other friends, losers and freaks like me. There's definitely strength in numbers. Still, Brad and Emily were my first friends, and as far as I was concerned, they didn't have the right to exclude me.

Five minutes pass. Ten minutes. Twenty. Nothing happens. Brad starts giving me dirty looks. After thirty minutes, I can tell he's about to leave. I need him to stay, though. Emily needs him to stay. So I talk to him.

"What went wrong, Brad?" I ask.

"What do you mean?"

"We used to be friends. Me, you, Emily. Why did we stop?"

Brad shrugs. "We don't have anything in common anymore, Mark. We grew up. At least me and Emily did. You still like all the same things we did when we were ten. Come on, don't you think it's ridiculous sometimes?"

I don't answer.

Brad swears. "This is stupid. I'm done. I can't believe I fell for this. Don't you breathe a word, Mark. I'll make you regret it."

He moves to step out of the circle, but the earth itself rears up and knocks him backward.

"What the f—" he yells.

Another roll of the ground swallows his voice. The earth shakes so much I have trouble standing. Brad doesn't have a chance. He tries to get up, but he keeps getting thrown back on his ass. When the ground finally stops moving, Brad lays with his face inches from a small hand with long, delicate fingers sticking up out of the ground. The flesh has decayed off of the tips to reveal the bones. The rest of the hand is a whitish-blue color. Brad yelps and jumps up. He nearly falls backwards over the gravestone. The fingers move weakly.

"Dude, what the hell is that?" he screams.

"It's Emily," I say.

"What? You didn't tell me she was going to come back like that. Are you sick?"

"She's not going to stay that way. She'll be just like she was before she died, I promise. We might have to help her, though. You know, pull her out."

Blood Brothers

"You want me to touch that?"

He's about to retch. I can tell.

"You want her to suffocate?" I ask. "How badly do you want her back, Brad?"

"More than anything."

"Then you've got to do it."

He takes a deep breath. "I guess I should thank you for bringing her back to me."

He grabs the hand. The rot immediately begins spreading up his arm. He screams and tries to let go, but he can't.

"I didn't do it for you, you son of a bitch. I did it for *her*."

He's not really focusing on what I'm saying. His body is convulsing. He's bleeding out of his mouth, his nose, his eyes, his ears. His skin grows blotchy. As his lungs putrefy and fill with fluid, his screams turn into watery groans.

"You see, Brad, Emily and I were just getting to know one another again," I say. "She called me the day after the division football championship. She told me what you did. I told her she needed to go to the police, but she wouldn't do it. She said you didn't know what you were doing because you were wasted. She said you didn't mean it. She said she knew you loved her. After that, we talked once every week or so, usually about something you did. I told her to break up with you. I told her she was too good for you, but she always had an excuse for the way you treated her. She called me again the night of the wreck after you tried to do it to her again. She couldn't see the road, Brad, because her left eye was swollen shut, and the other was filled with tears. I told her she had to press charges. At the very least, she had to get away from you. And you know what she said? She said she felt bad for making you upset. I got so mad I hung up on her. I didn't say goodbye."

He can't hear me. His eardrums have probably disintegrated. His skin has split open and is peeling away from his face. He isn't groaning anymore. Now he's just letting out weak croaks, but that's mostly from the involuntary twitching.

The earth heaves again. This time, it's enough to throw me

to the ground and knock the wind out of me. It takes me a couple of seconds to get up again. I look back at the grave and see Emily crouching next to her own gravestone. She has on a blue dress, the one she was going to wear to prom. It's tattered and dirty. She's missing a shoe. Her hair is a mess. The makeup the funeral home put on her is smeared across her face.

She's beautiful.

Next to her, Brad's decayed hand juts up out of the dirt; the hand that threw the football for the winning touchdown at the division championships; the hand that pushed me into a mud puddle on picture day in the seventh grade; the hand that shook mine when we were eight after we pricked our fingers, smeared our palms with the blood, and swore we'd be blood brothers forever.

I wasn't lying when I said we weren't cheating death. We made a bargain, a life for a life, a contract signed in blood. Brad's going to have a much harder time breaking *this* promise.

Emily sees me and runs to me. She buries her face in my chest sobbing. I put my arms around her. Her body feels warm. I don't know if she's thinking about the car accident, or wherever she's been for the last two weeks, or what just happened. Right now, though, I don't really care.

About the Author:

J. Matthew Saunders grew up in Greenville, South Carolina. He attended Vanderbilt University and Chapman University School of Law. He is currently a writer trying to be an attorney in Charlotte, North Carolina.

BEQUEST
Greg Mellor

The trucks rolled in along the empty streets, kicking up a cloud of dust like smoke from a funeral pyre. There were three of them—long, articulated, 56 wheelers—covered in road grime and graffiti. They were called road trains in another time and now the sound of them rumbling into the city stirred our bellies.

"Mommy, the trucks are here."

I stood behind Claire at the apartment window. "I know, dear, I can see them too."

From this height, they looked like segmented caterpillars, their pitted chrome and steel turned gray beneath a leaden sky. They hauled into old Elizabeth Street, crumpling empty boxes that littered the road from their last visit, and weaved their way slowly into Hyde Park. They came to rest under the stunted trees, brakes hissing and echoing around the buildings that lined each side of the park.

Claire was jumping up and down. "Can we go now? Can we?"

"Not yet, sweetheart," I said gently. "They need time to unpack."

She raced to her bedroom and brought out her recycled teddy and a doll with a missing arm and a glitzy smile that seemed like a travesty.

"Can I bring Baggins and Jemima?"

"Of course."

"What about my crayons?" She turned back to her room with a small frown of indecision. I could see a hint of her tattoo beneath the cuff of her sleeve. The skin was still a little raw.

"Leave them here, it will be dark soon. Take your jacket though; it's going to be cold tonight."

I watched the unpacking from the window until the sun cast a red pall across the Sydney skyline. The underbelly of the clouds looked like an artist's palette, swirling with the hues of sunset. Faint memories began to swell at the back of my mind, but the colors in the sky quickly bleached away and I cursed the creeping tendrils of night, for they always made me forget.

I could not contain Claire any longer so I lit the candles and we left the building by the emergency exit, the sound of our shoes slapping on the steps became a cacophony as we joined the other tenants pounding down the narrow stairwell.

We emerged like lines of fire flies from all around the inner city—maybe ten thousand. It was hard to tell whether our numbers had dwindled. I looked over at the other parents and teenagers. We were all caught up in our private apprehension. A few women were pregnant, which perhaps was a good sign that some of us still knew how to dream, or maybe it was just a reflection of our blind tenacity.

Claire raced ahead to the bands of orange light that were bursting out between the gnarled silhouettes of the trees.

"Slow down," I said in a futile attempt to curb her excitement.

"They're lighting the fires," she squealed, and raced on ahead with the other children.

We all paused at the clearing in the center of the park—a ring of pale faces—mesmerized by the flames that licked but never quite usurped the night. The three grills were grease spattered and blackened steel, about two metres high, sitting over the bonfire and accessed by a long ramp. The smell from the grills was incredible, nauseous, liberating.

The drivers had finished unpacking our ration of boxes—so few, but enough still. They loaded the boxes onto trolleys and wheeled them up the ramp.

Bequest

The heat from the fire began to build, it seemed like so long ago since I last felt it, and that stirred something deeper in me, a longing that dampened the constant ache of hunger. Is this the night? Is it really time?

But where was he? Each truck had three occupants—a driver, co-driver and a cook. Only the lead truck had a fourth ... there ... a flash of red on the other side of the grills, but the crowd cheered and surged, and I was caught up in their excitement as the cooks strode up the ramps on and began opening the boxes. I craned my neck, but there were so many people around me.

Then I remembered Claire.

I shouted her name, but my voice was drowned out as the crowd began to sing, discordant at first, but the rhythm was soon remembered, and then their stamping feet added a resonating undertone. I looked around, frantic. Something nagged at the edge of my senses. Where was she? And what was that annoying bumping? "Stop it—"

Claire was tapping me on the arm, pulling my sleeve.

I reached down and picked her up. "I'm sorry, honey," I said, but I could hardly hear my own voice.

She leant in close to my ear. "Why are you crying?" She wiped my cheek. Baggins and Jemima dangled from a string around her waist.

"It's okay, I thought I lost you." I stroked her hair.

The chant eased and faces turned expectantly. "Oh, look," I said, pointing, "they're cooking."

We watched as the cooks placed the first batches of meat on the grills.

"Smells delicious," Claire said, captivated by the way the cooks skilfully turned the pieces with large tongs that looked like mandibles strapped to their forearms.

"Go on," I said, letting her down. "Why don't you get some. I'll be over in a minute, but make sure they scan you first."

"Okay, I will."

The meat lying there in the boxes looked black from this

distance, but I knew it was just a trick of the constantly changing light. It was certainly black once it came off the grills, spitting and dripping juices.

The first group of children were scanned by the co-drivers at the base of the ramps. The cooks checked the printouts from the scanning devices then sorted the plates in order and handed them out, laden. The children moved away and sat under the dead trees and ate. I checked to make sure Claire was settled then, with my heart pounding, I drifted through the crowd to the far side of the grills near the trucks.

The chanting eased as the adults surged forward to be fed. I was giddy with hunger and the noise and smells and the rush of the crowd. My stomach felt like a knife was twisting inside, but I resisted the urge and pushed against the bleak tide. I needed to know, tonight, so I pushed harder against the crowd until I found a clearing. I emerged, breathless and sweating. I bent over at the waist and rested my hands on my knees.

Then he appeared, standing in front of me, and the sound of the crowd seemed to dim, but I knew it was just my mind trying to get perspective, focus. His face was half-lit by the fire: one side cast orange, the other a silhouette. It mirrored my inner turmoil. I so wanted to be here, yet there was something deep inside of me, screaming.

He reached out and cupped the back of my head in his huge hands. The sleeves of his red overalls stretched to reveal the quilt of tattoos on his arms—contorted, naked bodies, intertwined and blending, floating on a sea of skulls. He turned my head left then right, his eyes scrutinising my face, my jaw line. I started to shake, but his hand held me firm.

He pulled off my jumper and the screaming rose like a banshee inside, but I dared not move. I reached down and unzipped my trousers and let them fall to my ankles. He checked my wrist and then roamed his hands up my arms and down my ribs. I had tried to keep toned, but it was almost impossible. My ribs stuck out, my belly was bloated and my breasts had almost

Bequest

vanished.

He knelt down and his hands roamed all the while, over my buttocks and thighs and down to my knees and calves. He sniffed once as he stood up, and then, as if it were some afterthought, he leant forward and checked through my hair, then his eyes latched on to mine. They looked like deep pits in the shadows with only a glimmer of white crescents.

I felt his body heat and the bulge in his overalls pressed firm against my stomach. The tension in his arms and shoulders was incredible.

He suddenly took a step back. "Not this time."

"You can't be serious?"

His eyes widened in surprise. "Don't question me."

He began to walk away as the sounds of the crowd started to bleed back in.

"Wait," I said, and caught him by the sleeve.

He turned as if to hit me, but something in my eyes held him. I pulled him close, pressed his hand down between my thighs.

"Choose me," I said. "There's life in me yet."

"That's the problem," he said, though he didn't pull his hand away.

"Then fuck it out of me," I sneered, and slapped him hard.

He laughed and pushed me down onto the ground. "All right then," he said, wiping blood from his lips. "If that's what you want."

He shrugged the top of his overalls down. His chest was covered with the same unearthly tattoo. In his anger he fumbled with his buttons, his hands shaking, but I reached out and covered his hands with mine, undoing one button at a time, until he was free. His anger seemed to melt away but his breathing quickened and I pulled him down until he was sitting, then I shuffled forward onto his lap.

He entered me then and the sounds of the crowd carried a new urgency as they began to dance and sing and fuck in the firelight under the dead trees beneath a dead sky. He did not last long, but I kept up my tempo well after he had spilled into me, until I too wearied and finally flopped over him.

"Will you honor our deal?" I whispered as shadows of the celebration flickered on our skin.

His eyes were blue. He looked up at me with a mixture of guilt and sadness. The tension in his upper body had eased, but the skulls still looked at me, grinning. "Of course," he said, "but I still don't think you are ready."

"Is anyone ever truly ready?"

He thought about it then said, "I suppose not."

"When will it happen?"

"Soon," he said, his eyes calculating something. "The next visit or the one after, but we are loath to leave children alone."

"Claire will be fine. She has her aunt to stay with. And in any case, I'm doing this for her."

I buried my face in the necromantic quilt of his chest to stave away the cold, but it seemed that nothing now would ever thaw the chip of ice lodged in my heart. Soon the fire began to dwindle as all our meat had now been cooked. The grills cooled and ticked on into the night and I awoke, alone, to a lustreless dawn.

I dressed and found Claire huddled close to the other children under the trees. Her face was smeared with grease and charcoal. She must have heard me tip toeing between the sleeping children and she greeted me with a smile and bleary eyes.

"Hi, mom."

"Hi, sweetie, how are you feeling?"

"Sore," she said. "I think I ate too much."

"That's okay, it will pass."

"What's this?" I said, tapping the plastic horse in her hands.

Her eyes brightened. "The driver gave it to me. There were boxes and boxes of them, lots more than the meat boxes, but he

Bequest

said that there was only one toy each." She lifted up Jemima. "But look, he found a new arm for Jemima."

"That's great," I said, not looking at the grinning face of the doll. The new arm was a little longer than the original.

The other children began to stir.

"We should clean up," I said.

I began to search through the discarded plates and remnants of the meal. There was an ulna on the plate next to Claire, picked clean. A pile of blackened skin lay on the ground. She hated the skin. I picked it up carefully and turned it over in my hand. I recognized the half seared bar code on what had once been a wrist. I breathed a sigh of relief and quickly turned away from Claire and hugged the skin close to my chest.

That skin had once felt sensations, that arm had once embraced me, had belonged to the only man I had ever loved.

"I will be with you, soon," I whispered.

The tears came freely then.

"What's the matter, mummy? Are you still hungry?"

"No, I'm fine."

But we'll make sure you are fed, Claire—that was our pact, our bequest to you—in this pathetic, ravaged world where food doesn't grow any more, but meat still does. We'll keep you as long as we possibly can.

The trucks began rolling out at mid-morning. I saw the butcher once, still in his red overalls, sitting high up in one of the cabs. He nodded to me and I knew that I would see him again.

What more could he do?

I had risen, I was his now.

About the Author:

Greg Mellor is a business consultant living in Canberra, Australia. This is his first story accepted for Pill Hill Press anthologies. He has published stories in Cosmos Magazine, Cosmos Online, Aurealis, Simulacrum, Deep Space Terror

GREG MELLOR

anthology and Novus Creatura anthology. Greg was a finalist in the 2009 Aurealis Awards Best Short SF category and has reached the quarter finals of the Writers of the Future contest on four occasions, plus one Honorable Mention. He is an associate member of the SFWA.

9 MYSTERY ROSE
Eden Royce

Gabe scrawled an address on a faded coffee shop receipt and passed it to the man across the table. He gave a luxurious cough.

Mike LaVarr slipped the paper into his suit jacket pocket. "Are you sure about this?"

"If there's any help for you, it's there. But I don't know, Mike." He shook his wooly head like a broken puppet left to dangle without a master. "I...don't know." The empty coffee cup sat between the men, ignored.

"So, you think this woman can do it?" He frowned at the diner's laminated menu and tossed it aside.

"Maybe." Gabe chewed at his cuticles. A strip of dirt lay under his nails. When the waitress refilled his mug, he grasped it with both hands and held it against his lips. "So warm."

"Look. If I'm gonna get involved in this kind of thing, it needs to work."

"I hear you."

"How did she move all those accounts without me noticing? I wonder if she found out about..."

Gabe grimaced. "You didn't exactly try to hide it. Why'd you do it? You had it so good with her."

"You don't understand." He paused when the bell on the door tinkled and three squealing teenagers in shorts and flip-flops tumbled into the all-night grease bucket. Mike continued in a hard whisper. "Can this witch—"

"Mambo."

Eden Royce

"What?"

"She is a mambo, not a witch. A priestess, a vessel for—"

"Whatever she is. Can she raise Karen?"

"I think so. You just have to pay." Gabe pulled the dusty, wrinkled coat closer around his thin frame and shivered.

Mike stood and threw a twenty on the Formica tabletop. "Go get yourself some rest, bro. And a shower. You reek."

***

Mike programmed the address into his car's GPS. Gabe's scribbling made the words look as though they read: 9 Mystery Rose.

"It's 'Road'. Damn drunk." Mike relaxed into the plush interior of the midnight blue coupe as it slid through the half-lit streets. Litter danced macabre steps with the wind in the shadows of the abandoned buildings.

A silhouette darted in front of the car.

"Holy shit," Mike stood on the brakes. A symphony of screeching tires and florid curses severed the silence. The hunched figure skittered away and faded from view.

"Unable to locate address." The guidance system blinked, as if confused.

"Piece of crap. You had the address a minute ago." Mike pressed every button, but the machine refused to respond. He looked around. No one in sight to ask.

A cloud shifted, leaving the moon exposed and brighter than the flickering streetlights. "There it is."

Number nine crouched at the end of Mystery. A lonely lamp fought to illuminate the shop's front window. He peered inside, and a fluttering movement made him jump back. The door opened and the sweet heat of oranges and chili powder wafted onto the balmy air. "Michael. Come in."

He walked into the shop, ducked under the bundles of dried herbs hung upside down from the ceiling. One wall displayed amber bottles in various sizes, all without labels. On a stand in the corner,

9 Mystery Rose

swung a large crow, whose gaze followed him as he moved. A candle glowed next to the bird and he could see his reflection in its unblinking eye. He took a step back.

The nut-brown woman motioned him deeper into the murky room. Her skin, while no longer taut, remained unlined. Two salt and pepper plaits escaped from the patterned headscarf.

"What can I do for you, *mon fils*?" She didn't smile as she settled her stooped frame onto a stool next to an antique secretary's desk.

"Um, yes. I was told to come here for—" Words failed him when he saw her slice the pad of her thumb and add a few drops of blood into a ceramic bowl. "Actually, I'm just looking."

Her rheumy eyes turned sharp and pinned him like an insect. "Everyone come here for something. You don't find Zéphyrine less you need her."

"My wife died and I was told you could…could…" He swallowed with difficulty.

"Bring her back to life."

"Yes. I need to talk to her one more time."

Zéphyrine didn't reply, but continued to grind the blood into the contents of the bowl. No other sound except the rustling of bird's wings. "Gabriel tell you this?"

Mike nodded, but spoke when the woman frowned. "Yes, ma'am."

"What else?"

"He said I had to pay you."

"Umm hmm. Always payment."

He rocked back and forth on his heels while the woman continued to add pungent items from the drawers in the desk to the bowl, heedless of his impatience. Unused to waiting, he looked around the store. A bowl of pomegranates rested on a window ledge, their coarse skins dried and tight. Drawn to the supple finish on a ring box covered in pale, soft leather on a side table, he reached for it.

"Don't touch that."

He yelped and spun around. The mambo, fists on her generous hips, stood toe to toe with him. The top of her head came up to his shoulder.

"How did your wife die?"

"She got sick an—"

"You killed her."

Mike's jaw dropped and he looked around him, as if he could locate a camera hidden among rows of incense cones and twirling dreamcatchers. "No, I didn't kill her. Of course not. I loved her."

She flicked her tongue at him. Thick and black, it left the scent of wet ashes on the air. "I can taste your lie." She advanced on him and he banged against the table.

A screech came from the box as it fell to the stone floor and cracked open. Thin, dark liquid seeped from the damaged corner. "I'm sorry."

"*La verité*, Michael." Her accent deepened; its richness covered him, lulled him. "I hear only the truth."

Mike's vision swam and he swallowed hard. "I never could keep a job. But I love expensive things. Clothes, cars, trips. I was drowning in debt when Karen came along, with her convertible and her trust fund. She spent a fortune on me." His eyes locked with the crow's unblinking gaze. "When we got married, it changed. She put me on an allowance. Said I was burning through her family's money. Said I needed to be a man and get a job and stop bleeding her dry. That set me off. I started planning after that."

When he returned his eyes to Zéphyrine, she was nodding. "How long ago?'

"About eight months."

"And you want to know how she hide the money from you? Where it is now? So you don't have to hit a lick at a snake for the rest of your days? I never understand a man don't want to work."

"But I—"

She held up a hand. "Don't matter. Don't care." She went back to the desk and poured the contents of the mortar into a pouch and secured it around her neck. "Payment is due when I do the

9 Mystery Rose

work."

"You don't care that I killed her? Don't you want to know how?"

"Can you pay?"

"Of course." They'd had close to fifteen million the last time he saw a bank statement.

She pointed to a dim corner. "*Bon.* Let us go."

He took the shovel she indicated. There was no sign of the box, save for a smudged trail of dark liquid where it had fallen.

***

Mike followed the old woman as the full moon guided her through the cemetery. She navigated weary tombstones, making sure her steps never fell on a grave. The moon stopped and hovered over an unmarked section of the well-kept graveyard where the grass had just begun to grow in.

Zéphyrine snorted in disgust. "You didn't even buy a stone for her?"

"I—I didn't have time. I was waiting until I had the money to do it right."

"Michael."

He wouldn't meet her eyes.

"Umm hmm. Dig."

Mike took off his suit jacket and rolled up his sleeves. Piles of earth grew higher behind him. His back throbbed, but thoughts of a nubile masseuse in less than a bikini drove the shovel deeper. Sweat poured from him. Fine-grained dirt abraded his face and arms. A metallic thud. He forced the blade of the shovel into the corner of the casket and wedged it open.

Karen lay in the unlined casket, hands folded on top of her white dress, her dusky skin ashen. Lank black hair rolled in waves past her shoulders.

Decomposition had yet to eat away her serene face, but her hands were shrunken into claws. Zéphyrine leaned in and sprinkled the contents of the pouch onto the body as she murmured in a melodic French patois. *"Réveille."*

Karen's eyelids flipped open.

Mike pressed against the back of the coffin-shaped hole to reassure himself of an escape route. "K-Karen? Honey?"

Her jaw opened with an audible pop. She struggled to sit up. Her right hand caressed her left. "Where is…my ring?"

Terror sliced his flesh and crawled in. "I had to pawn it to pay for your funeral. You were gone so fast."

"What…do you…want?"

He thought of what he would do if Karen lunged at him. He could use the shovel. Or if he couldn't get to it in time, he knew his hands fit around her neck.

"Michael, the dead do not breathe, " Zéphyrine said.

Shit. He turned his attention back to his late wife. "Karen, I miss you…dear. I can't be with you, but I need to ask you a question."

The corpse waited.

"Where did you move our money, baby? I went to settle up some bills and it was gone. Our accounts had barely enough for your funeral." Sweat ran down his face, but he wouldn't wipe it away, in case Karen thought it was tears.

"I moved it…from father's bank. I thought…you were… cheating on me. Stupid…"

"No, it wasn't stupid. I should have paid more attention to you. I'm sorry."

Karen's face contorted in an attempt to smile. "The…money is at…Central Credit…Union. In my…maiden name. Ask for…the manager." She creaked her head to look at Zéphyrine. When she faced her husband again, the smile turned frightful and knowing. "Don't worry, love. We'll be together soon."

Mike slammed the coffin shut. As he clambered out of the dank hole, he could hear Karen's cackling laughter. "Jesus. Crazy bitch." He brushed dirt from his slacks and tried to catch his breath. "I'm getting as far away from this freak show as possible."

"There is still the matter of my payment."

9 Mystery Rose

"Right. When I get the money tomorrow, you'll get paid."

"Payment is due when I do the work."

"Look, I don't have it right now. But I'll get it to you, I swear."

"You have it."

She reached out to him and he knocked her hand away. "Unless you want fifty bucks, I don't have it. What do want from me, anyway?"

"Your eternal servitude." Zéphyrine bared her teeth in a grin.

Mike ran.

Arctic wind flew in from behind the witch and tore the scarf from her head. Long, thin braids cracked whip-like in the now frozen air. Icy mist rose from the ground. Her eyes rolled back in her skull, white against the walnut skin as she stretched her bare, fleshy arms to the torn sky. The wind shrieked. A high, keening cry rose up as the earth lunged and snapped like a rabid dog on a leash. She released its chain. "I call you forth, my legion. The hunt is now."

Mike's dress shoes slipped on the moist dirt. He panted and his body dripped cold sweat. He stepped in a hole, hidden by the cemetery's long grasses, and went down. He clawed at the ground as it retched and split open beneath him. Rot and decay rolled into his mouth as he tried to scream. He spat, rubbed his tongue on his filth-crusted sleeve.

A skeletal hand closed around his ankle, the flesh on the bone slick with the ooze of decay. Mike stared, as it pulled itself forward and opened a mouth teeming with bloated maggots. "So warm."

He howled and kicked off the thing's grip, scrambled to his feet and fled toward the open gate. He dodged the grasping hands where they emerged from the dirt. He looked behind him. They were lumbering toward him, hundreds of them, stinking and leaking putrid gore. He ran harder, trying to outdistance the rotting corpses as they swayed to Zéphyrine's eerie song.

Mike turned to see a milk-white form rise in his path. He could not avoid it. He went through the spirit and gasped at the achy weakness it left. His hope of escape withered. More hazy forms emanated from the frosty slush, each taking a turn ripping away hunks of his soul. He wobbled, unable to keep his footing. *Can't. No strength.* His steps faltered as they circled back for another pass, their banshee wails gluttonous and gleeful.

His legs, leaden now, sank deeper into the tortured soil with each step. It was getting closer, the rattle of bone, the tattered mutterings…Above it all, the scent of wet ashes. He began to sob.

***

Anthony strolled into the diner and looked for Mike. He found him at a corner table hunched over a cup of steaming coffee. His navy suit jacket was grayed over with dust and his hair stood at odd angles. Mike pushed a thin strip of paper with an address scrawled on it across the table. Anthony looked around before he pocketed it. "Man. You look like you been through hell."

About the Author:

Eden Royce (www.edenroyce.com) is the pseudonym for a stockbroker living in North Carolina. In addition to writing, her passions include roller-skating, thunderstorms, and exceptional sushi. She fully expects her mutant powers to manifest any day now.

In the Dark Kingdom
Brandon Berntson

The dead had life.
Impossible for rotting eyes to see?
Rotting eyes, especially now, *could* see. They opened—despite their degenerate decay—to a world of light. Limbs, long dead, learned to move again. Sounds like brittle paper shuffled between the trees. Slippery maggots writhed in thick, noisome patches. Beetles lumbered over cheekbones and jaws.

Signs of death were everywhere. But so where the signs of life. They'd learned to breathe, found the answer to their plights. This light, they realized, was no ordinary beacon. In the blackness of the tombs, they'd been given a glimpse of Heaven.

The night air was crisp, the perfect evening for finding themselves on the road to salvation. Families, friends, lovers, even lost acquaintances, gathered for the exchange. Didn't this warrant redemption? Weren't they angels now? Heaven spoke to each of them lovingly, and its words brimmed with comfort and light.

One by one, they clambered from their shallow graves. The centuries had been long. They had suffered, but they emerged into the night now, placing one skeletal foot in front of the other.

This is how it felt to live again! This was how it felt to... *breathe!*

They lurched forward, caked in mud. Some had forgotten how to walk. How could they not, all this time in the grave? Living—especially now—was like riding a bicycle.

Seeing? Love? This suffocating slumber, breathing sour,

spoiled meat! Listening to the maggots swarm! Who allowed this reign, this passing salvation into Heaven's light?

It was a miracle, nothing more. How could it be anything else?

Mouths grinned. Lips split. Some were fresh, some old. All of them gathered for the dance of life. Blood had hardened over the years, some still glistened fresh and scarlet. Skin had shriveled, cracked, and withered over time, while some, though dead, still lay warm.

These forgotten bones had turned to magic. Thoughts of an old life granted them access. Death hadn't established a miracle: they remembered the lives they'd lived. They'd been forced, unfairly, to suffer under the hands of their Maker.

Remembering? How was that possible? Hadn't worms and other vermin devoured their brains?

To move, to think, to feel, newborns for another age…What a grand and cryptic world it could be!

The dead banded together like a close-knit team, a colony of leprous chaos. They owned a single-minded purpose. Being dead had taught them patience.

Thousands already congested the roads and highways, the powerful, assaulting aroma of rot spreading through the night air.

As the shuffled along, others emerged, cracked fingernails, green fingers, pushing dirt aside. The night caressed them, adding strength. Breathing in the summer wind, they were able to move, able to stand, to…*see.*

Death had proposed a bad beginning, but destiny drove them now.

These carrion forms did not feed off the brains of the living. Bigger, grander designs motivated them, and they were restless, anxious to begin the night's endeavors…

The dead smiled at one another across the roads, through the forests and trees. Disintegration didn't matter, weak sinews snapping, falling—appendages forgotten—to the pavement, across the woodlands. Even the legless—still determined—dragged

In the Dark Kingdom

themselves along by skeletal hands.

Brighter territories loomed ahead, new sights to discover. Life in death began in a starless world.

They sensed one another, a shuffling mass, elbow to elbow, by the thousands. They had a job to do.

From a black wonderland, they placed their decaying feet—one in front of the other—on the road to salvation.

They had some unfinished business, these dead things, lain for centuries across the miles. Everyone—they realized with a smile, at some point in their lives—gets their day in the sun.

***

Charlie Silverthorn had everything he'd ever dreamed. He lived for passion's kiss. The Dark Kingdom had granted him *access*. Angels and demons had made every dream come true. He was part of the known universe.

Take your pick, he thought, smiling.

He was walking down the sidewalk of just one of the world's many cities.

Did it matter? he wondered. *Aren't they all the same?*

The masses hemmed him in from all sides. People were everywhere.

Charlie was the ruler of the Third Gate in The Dark Kingdom, a region of time and space divided from the 'real' world. Pain and lies shadowed this haunted land. Its walls were built with madness, lust, and murder.

His reigning position was one to be proud of, and Charlie Silverthorn loved his job.

Access fitted his hands, the mercy binding him to The Kingdom. He proved his worth for magic, his name now synonymous with murder. Power kept him shadowed by his hands—his passion, his drive—for slaughter. It granted him power in the Third Gate. Each death made his realm more powerful, darker than before, and Charlie Silverthorn was the reigning Heavy Weight Champion.

He was obscene in his obesity at 360 pounds. His hairless crown was a halo of pink under the noonday sun. His attire was always white shirts, sweat pants, and comfortable shoes, sometimes plain bib overalls, depending on his mood. He knew he owned the weight of intimidation. He had a mean, yet alluring quality to his features. Dark brows permanently furrowed, eyes penetrating, large, soulless black (because of The Kingdom), he surveyed the populace, not missing a beat. He smiled among the masses.

He owned a quaint, comfortable house on the outskirts of Bakersfield. He drove a midnight blue van. The home and the van, the comfortable shoes, were also—as strange as it seemed—tokens from The Kingdom.

No one had a clue as to what he was. He blended in except for the weight of intimidation. The thought made him laugh. He performed dark duties for The Kingdom: drive the populace mad, add them to the dark, making The Kingdom...*blacker.*

The Dark Kingdom prized him. Charlie Silverthorn was one of their favorites.

He laughed aloud, idling alongside the passersby, down the city streets in the middle of day (any place of his choosing in the known world, another of the Kingdom's miracles). He was not shy. He wanted the attention. He announced himself almost gaily to the world. Some bumped into him accidentally, cursing this careless, overweight giant. He recorded their faces, looked for them later. *Remember me?* he'd say when he caught up with them years down the road.

He could slip from one world to the next without anyone knowing, the fortune of owning the Third Gate. The Kingdom and Charlie Silverthorn solved riddles together.

Over the years, he'd mastered the use of countless instruments. His hands being the first. Charlie loved blades— hatchets most of all—though, he was not averse to razors, crowbars, piano wire, saws, hammers, chisels, lawnmowers, weed-eaters, and swords. Each death lasted a lifetime. The longer they suffered, the more powerful the Kingdom became. Instruments didn't matter. His

In the Dark Kingdom

hands were the catalyst for the Kingdom's power.

Life and death were not a riddle to Charlie Silverthorn, however. The Kingdom had not only made his dreams come true, it had answered the most elusive questions.

Still, bewildering thoughts prodded his brain, the outskirts of his perception, as though The Dark Kingdom were deliberately keeping secrets from him. Whenever he got close to solving the riddle, The Kingdom slipped the wool over his eyes.

Charlie shook his head. Best to leave it be. The miracles would reveal themselves in time. It couldn't afford to lose its most devout follower.

He'd grown up shaped by dark deeds. Even as a boy, he'd mutilated and tortured small animals. He'd been made for this since time began. The Dark Kingdom had been waiting for him. After time, of course, those animals turned into people. He'd made the Kingdom proud.

He chalked them up, the masses, made them numbers in the world (soon to become the Dark Kingdom itself). Charlie was a giant walking the earth. The Dark Kingdom had instructed him, told him how to perform, and he was obedient to every whim. Enough slaughter and blood would bring the division back together again, making Earth and The Dark Kingdom one again

He couldn't remember the shift, the change that had brought him here exactly. Miracle? Death? He didn't know. It was a blur, like the riddle, the answer to the mystery. It didn't matter, he supposed.

Maybe he'd been born in The Kingdom. Why else did he have power, the position he did?

What a day it will be when I'm crowned, Charlie thought. *What a day it will be!*

He had a job to do on a grand scale. He put passion into his tasks, even a loving touch. His position was unruly—his name, powerful. He had never—that he could remember—owned such promise before.

Before? he thought. *Before what?*

Still the question...the riddle. He tried to ignore it.

Death had its comforts, and Charlie provided. He granted mercy and love, impossible as that seemed. He was entitled to show, to display compassion, but sometimes this confused him, too. Hadn't he been thinking about cruelty just seconds ago?

The dead had needs. He eased them gently into the dark after burying the hatchet in their brains. Black tears spilled from his eyes. He was provider and killer. Ah, he understood now! He was merciless *before* the kill. *Afterwards,* he showed compassion. No wonder he was so unique!

Power moved through his hands. When they looked at him—the chosen—their eyes grew wide in shock. Only then did they recognize who and what he was. He said a silent prayer to The Kingdom, closing his eyes, then eased them into their graves.

Slipping from the black world to the other took only a small amount of concentration, a single thought. The next thing he knew, he was walking among the populace, anxious for the night, as he was doing now, meandering along the streets of the world's cities, bumping into them as they passed. They had no idea. He was a magician, a God among them.

Charlie waited patiently. The Dark Kingdom had granted him immortality as well. What gifts, what power he had!

He believed in service. He was dedicated. The dead would understand, they'd be thankful *he'd* been the one to dispose of them. They were helping build The Kingdom, bringing it to life.

Someone bumped into him again, a man in his mid thirties, wearing glasses.

"Asshole," the man said, looking at Charlie with a scowl.

"A fabulous day to *you,* sir," Charlie said, putting on the biggest, most enormous smile he could muster.

***

Endless possibilities! Answers didn't concern them as they shuffled along. Some left their legs behind them, yet still they pulled themselves along. Concern was feeble. The thought made them

In the Dark Kingdom

smile.

They shared the same purpose, expressing their desires not with words, but single thoughts. They made friends along the way.

Life! Again? Was it possible? Was this unnatural drive for real? Volition here to stay?

They could remember the lives they'd lived. Part of the blessing, perhaps. They'd had friends and families, lovers, at one time. They could remember it all: the holidays, walks in the park, prom night, and shopping. Now, they owned a renewed sense of hope and ambition. Woebegone funerals, decay, the sweet and gentle partings—all things of the past. Their loved ones would be proud knowing life had been granted them again...

His smell is strong, they thought with one mind, and followed...

What a perfect joy to walk in the arms of mercy! It was here now. Impossible? The dead laughed in Heaven's light.

They weren't without complete joy, a shred of wanting. They were selfish in their purpose. Heaven told them it was okay to want. *Wanting* was the reason they were here, able to live again...

They could *feel* as well, another aspect of fortune's promise. Nerves wove themselves together again, the summer night air, like a balm against their smiling faces, and the love they shared, the emotions assaulting them, the fear and loneliness.

Justice in the dark, they thought, and smiled.

Across the thoroughfares—hit by cars, chaos, shouting, guns sounding in a ricochet of fire—the dead ambled on, undeterred. The populace tried to stop them to no avail. Their numbers were simply too great, an unstoppable virus of dead things. They would avenge their fallen comrades. They mocked the disbelieving, impossible world as they watched them walk by. They'd prove these skeptics wrong!

The redolence of decay spread with liquid fingers. Fistfuls of maggots lie in bloody clumps along the road. The Kingdom was channeling the dead toward their Maker.

They marched in succession, driven by one, too-familiar

smell...

They weren't concerned with *how* this had come to be. Miracle lay in the chance for redemption after all.

One by one, they awakened to a sensation of writhing, swarming in various cavities of their flesh. Parasites nested in open wounds, laid eggs, breeding on bacteria and disease. They swarmed with maddening, itching propulsion. Microscopic claws picked heedlessly at their remains with hands similar to precision doctors, tearing them apart piece by piece. They whittled at perversions, vices, their senses of mortality, taking them back to blood-soaked memories and shameful guilt. The dead tortured themselves with humiliation as if posed atop the Eiffel Tower, the Statue of Liberty, mortifying themselves with their own reflections. Nothing made them gasp in more lunacy and trauma.

Once entombed, they'd had no idea death was so voraciously busy!

They mocked the night's cameras as they moved along. The dead—at least to the rest of the world—were harmless, despite their appearance. They only wanted to do what they came here for. These mortal spectators were of no concern. The dead even laughed, voices of dirt, at each shocked and disbelieving expression.

Die again.

They voiced these words to the bewildered citizens, countryfolks, the passersby who stood gawking by lampposts, rooftops, parked cars. Within hours of their waking, the dead packed the roads by the thousands.

Eternity walks...

Tanks positioned, blowing them to bits. Fighters dropped bombs. The coverage was on every channel, visible to a mortified, stricken America, yet the dead had gathered in such numbers, defense was useless.

It'll be over soon anyway, the dead thought. *None of this matters. We're just passing through.*

The stars were bright in a clear, luxurious night over Bakersfield. The moon was full, rising to the east. A cool breeze of

In the Dark Kingdom

ocean salt and wet sand purified the air, if only briefly.

If they could run, they would have. What a sight it would be, a marathon, cross-country race of the dead! Patience made them savor each lurching step, however. Some rolled decapitated heads alongside them with sticks, as if they couldn't forge ahead without them; others dragged themselves by two crusted, bony arms, pulling along what remained of their carcasses. Others opened simply opened their dead jaws wide and moaned in ecstasy and joy.

Sour odors flourished through the night breeze, a choking sense of unholy rot. The scent was a reminder as well. It hugged them closer to their promise, convinced them of their purpose, a question eternally unanswered.

They drifted into a more defined point of travel, zeroing in on their Maker. Some locked themselves together arm, cracking smiles of teeth, bugs, and dirt. They nodded, recognizing their purpose with anticipation.

Each, in turn…

Sharing confirmation all around, they nodded.

It felt good to laugh again.

A jaw descended to the pavement and shattered to brittle dust. Lungs exploded, splattering black and scarlet slugs across the road.

Their imprisonment had gone on long enough. It was time for progress, to keep the wheel moving. The Dark Kingdom could be good to those it housed, to those to whom it was faithful. Only *they* deserved the throne, the right to The Kingdom, it told them.

The dead had…*access*.

The patrons—those lost and idly confused, watching this nightmare unfold—felt a chill in the air, blood hemming them in from all sides. The cold emerged in the distance from every direction. Murder and corruption stained the air.

Burning carcasses, acts of atrocity came to life. Some citizens—boys and girls, loiterers, and trespassers—gasped and fell to the ground, buckling with the shock and horror, a world of impossibility proved real.

The dead knew where to go and how to get there. Night's thick, oppressive shadow pinched the lights, encasing society in a helpless wonder of panic and fear.

Passion returned with love and determination, not to the denizens, of course, but to those already departed.

Something about eternity...

Something about slumber...

In the wake of the dark, the doors of Heaven revealed its bright corridors, opportunity and redemption of every kind. The dead moved into the darkest shadows, clearing a path for each in turn.

And below, a single candle flickered in the window of a lone house in Bakersfield, on the verge of winking out, anticipating a permanent extinction.

How appropriate, the dead thought

Smiling at one another, the dead moved on...

***

It was funny, Charlie thought, *how they waltzed in without suspecting, the senseless way they went about their lives.* They never understood how such a bloody nightmare could unfold until they met him.

The bar, The Country Gopher, was loud and smoky. The smoke irritated Charlie's eyes. How he detested the smell of cigarettes! The music twanged loud and obnoxious, which was just as bad. He was not a country western fan, but he didn't like to single anyone out, which was the reason he chose the bar in the first place. End this Country Gopher madness and the rednecks it bred.

Country boys stood drinking along the bar, their accents thick. Many wore tight blue jeans, cowboy hats, large silver belt buckles on display. Several men played pool under a bright Budweiser sign.

The patrons ushered in and staggered out, some helpless, some brawling, some lost to their libidos on the dance floor.

Charlie didn't understand it. He never had, for some bizarre reason. It had never made sense to him. Was it a ritual for

In the Dark Kingdom

entertainment's sake? Is this what they did best? They had to learn at some point in their lives, though, didn't they?

Death, after all, *should* be unexpected.

The hunt was his favorite part, walking in undetected from one reality to the other. They never knew whether he materialized out of thin air or simply emerged from around the corner. Charlie loved it.

Picking out his first sheep for the evening, he shifted his massive bulk on the barstool, making it creak.

He wore black sweats today, brand new comfortable Nikes, and a tight white T-shirt. He sipped a cold, draft beer. He'd shaved earlier and silkily polished his head. It was a bright, gleaming crown under the lights of the bar. He laughed at himself, looking in the mirror behind the bar. Charlie Silverthorn had a halo on his head.

Already, the men veered away when they saw him, giving him a wide berth. *Let the big man at the bar have all the room he wants,* they seemed to say. The bar shifted to one side when they did this, it seemed, leaving Charlie to occupy the other. Already, the Country Gopher was wary of him.

Yes, he thought, *they know who's in charge.*

Charlie wiped foam from under his nose with an index finger. He smiled at the patrons, the drunken, red-faced cowboys.

Someone at the Country Gopher will lose their way, he thought.

All sizes, shapes, and dramas. It didn't matter. He enjoyed men and their lack of control, their willingness, helplessly begging for mercy, for God's sake…*please!*

He enjoyed their obviousness, their ridiculous naïveté.

A heavy-set blonde woman waddled up to him, asking him if he wanted to dance.

Ah! *This* kind! They were *fun* to shock!

Portly and almost an insult if he hadn't been so charming, but just enough on the oblivious side. It was all he could do *not* to pass it up!

She wore lots of colorful make-up, tight jeans, and cowboy

boots. A frilly white blouse hugged her enormous bosom. Charlie liked her right away. They had something in common.

He shook his head in disappointment, though, wanting to give her a makeover.

"Sweets, sweets, sweets," Charlie said, smiling.

The woman raised her eyebrows.

Charlie shook his massive head. "So primitively *unfashionable,* darling," he said, with all the charm he could muster. It was amazing how high his voice could go when he tried. "Now, now, now. *Whatever* must we do? Charming thing like you? We have to teach you etiquette, my dear, on perfect originality. Now, let's try again, shall we?"

The woman gawked like a parrot. Notwithstanding the make-up, the tight jeans, the heavily, muscled upper-body—she, this model of woman—*was* alluring in her own right. For Charlie, she was a 'shoe-in.'

She smelled of ambrosia, making him swoon. Charlie smiled again.

"What's your *name,* darling?"

Mouth gagged and tied, she was helpless, poor thing. Charlie's heart went out to her.

He put a hand on her shoulder. She was warm.

"Miss, are you all right?" he asked, with genuine concern. "Can I get you a glass of water?"

The woman came back to herself. She blinked, focused on her surroundings, looked at him, then managed to smile. She had dark blue eyes. Charlie was enchanted.

"Cynthia," she said, her voice sweet and girlish. She held out her hand. Charlie liked her even more. Two things in common. Weight and letters of their first name. Charlie took her hand, soft and warm. "Sorry, there," she went on. "I…uh…gee. I think I took a little vacation. You want to go on a boat ride or something?" Cynthia cackled at her own humor, a trifle drunk.

Charlie squeezed her hand with both of his and beamed. Letting out a guffaw—that sent the entire bar into terrified silence—

In the Dark Kingdom

Charlie reeled back on the barstool, kicking out his feet. He covered the top of her hand with his and laughed as if nothing pleased him more.

"See, now *that's* the proposal I'm talking about," he said. "You didn't even know you could do it, did you? You are *deviltry*, Cynthia! You cast a *spell!* You weave a sparkle of witchcraft about you, young lady, order me to do an about-face, begging for more!"

"*Stop* it!" Cynthia said, blushing, and waving his charm away.

Charlie suddenly roared: *"Can I get a beer over here?"*

The entire bar shook and trembled. The bartended procured a beer in seconds flat.

"*And* for the young lady?" Charlie asked, turning his malevolent gaze on Cynthia.

"I'll have the same," she said.

Cynthia was a fish on a hook, attached to his eyes everywhere they went. Charlie dragged, pulled, and reeled her in every direction.

"What's *your* name?" Cynthia asked.

"Charlie."

"Good and old fashioned," she said, smiling and nodding.

"Yes," he said. "And you are *quite* the becoming young lady."

"Nice to meet you," she said.

"Your pleasure can in no measure equal mine."

Cynthia shook her head and raised her eyebrows, unsure how to respond.

Come on out to my van, darling. Let us do what can become of you. Now, I will begin your makeover here, just below the jawline.

"I come here all the time," he said, smiling

"You do not!" Cynthia said.

"Why not?" Charlie said, enjoying himself.

"Because *I* come here all the time!" she said.

Charlie raised his eyebrows. "Is that a fact?"

Cynthia realized what she'd said, what it implied, and

blushed. "Well. Not *all* the time. I like the music mostly."

Charlie nodded, playing along, but didn't believe her.

"Really!" she said, and laughed.

"Don't try and fool me, honey," Charlie said, gazing into her soul. "I know the *whole* lot. *I* have eyes and ears."

"Wow," Cynthia said, feigning surprise. "Everyone else on this planet has eyes and ears, *too!* What a coincidence. Well, mostly. I guess not all if you think—"

"Cynthia, dear," Charlie said, star-struck. "You are a bowl of sunshine. You make the *best* witticisms without even knowing. *However* do you do it?"

"Just in the genes, I guess."

Charlie downed the rest of his beer and slammed it on the counter. Cynthia seemed to forget one was still waiting for her.

"Damn," Charlie said, looking at his wrist. He wasn't wearing a watch. "I told the Confession's Factor I'd be at the church by seven. It's already a quarter to eight. They must think *awful* of me!"

"The Confession's Factor?"

"A little group of sporting agents I like to call home," Charlie said, knowing he wasn't making sense.

"Well, gee," Cynthia said, suddenly crestfallen. "I hope you don't have to run off. I was...huh, well, yeah. I mean...I guess I'll see you later."

"Well, you could always come *with* me," Charlie said. "But, hey..." he laughed, holding his round belly. "Sorry, awful dense of me, not realizing you—"

"If you wait here," Cynthia said, holing up a finger. "I'll tell my girlfriends. Let me just get my coat."

Charlie watched her hobble away. He turned his eyes to the smoky atmosphere.

Technique, fashionable skill.

Cynthia hurried back, holding a black jacket over her arm.

"You never finished your beer," Charlie said.

"Huh? Oh. Uh—?"

In the Dark Kingdom

"Just teasing. Let's get out of here." He put his hand on her back, steering Cynthia toward the door.

Patrons looked his way. Everyone let out a long, anticipated breath once he exited the bar.

It was chilly and wet outside. Sheets of rain were visible in the light of the streetlamps. Charlie, the perfect gentleman, put his jacket over Cynthia's head.

"Watch your step, darling," he said.

Laughing in the rain, he opened the door to his van, helping her up and inside. He shut the door after her. Charlie nodded and smiled at Cynthia through the window. He hurried to the other side, pretending to be outwitted by the rain. He opened the door, climbed in, and shut it behind him, silencing the rain.

"I thought it was a clear night!" he said.

Cynthia shrugged and giggled, raising her eyebrows

"You never know *what* to expect in this town," he said, slipping the key in the ignition.

Charlie turned to Cynthia, beaming with majesty. He started the van. "You ready?"

"Let's go, Charlie!"

"Spoken like a true player," he said, and put the van in drive. "Buckle up, darling! This party has only *just* begun!"

The van lurched into the street with a loud squeal. From one world to the other, Charlie Silverthorn drove into the night.

***

A consuming stench took control of the atmosphere. It swelled inside the van. It leaked in from the murky fields beyond the road. Cynthia wasn't sure what it was exactly, but she knew it wasn't a good thing. In fact, once she thought about it, the smell could only be coming from something dead, something that had been dead and rotting for a long, *long* time.

The headlights depicted every detail of the dirt, rocks, and surrounding fields as Charlie drove. The tires moving over the unimproved road were the only sound. The radio was off. In the Dark Kingdom, the only fault was the lack of reception.

"This is the Confession's Factor?" Cynthia asked, narrowing her eyes. She looked through the window at nothing but blackness.

Charlie didn't reply.

To her right, the area was one she didn't recognize. Thick fog and overhanging trees obscured a swampy, poisonous landscape. This was like no place she'd seen around Nashville.

Eventually, she could hear the sound of crickets, their chirps adding to the sound of the tires moving over the road. Her heart was beating fast. Her palms were sweaty. She took a deep breath, trying to calm down. She realized suddenly that was not just worried, she was scared.

Something hit the passenger window, startling her. She put a hand to her throat. Whatever it was rolled up onto the roof, bouncing with successive drags. It tumbled and fell on the road behind the van. Cynthia looked in the side mirror, saw it vividly in the red break lights, and screamed.

An arm, severed where the shoulder began had just plopped onto the road. A bracelet encircled the wrist, fingers puffed, bloodied with chipped nails.

"What the hell was that?" Cynthia looked at Charlie, eyes wide and terrified. For some ridiculous, nightmare reason, he'd metamorphosed in size, an exaggerated, blacker version of himself. His skin was a dull, cast-iron black. His eyes were the same, not a single shred of white. His leer revealed successive points above and below his lips. His ears were pointed. Two aligned horns, the size of shot-glasses, topped his obsidian crown. His muscles were massive, hugely barbaric.

Cynthia wailed. She grabbed the handle on the door and pulled, but it was locked! She beat and pounded on the window, scraping her nails against the glass, making the shrillest, most piercing shrieks she could muster.

A picture of herself on milk cartons danced through her mind. She saw it in the junk mail no one recognizes.

In the Dark Kingdom

"There there," Charlie said, in his normal voice. "There's a lot of strange things happening on the other side. There's nothing to be scared of."

When she looked, it was the Charlie she'd met at the bar. The sight actually reassured her. He smiled and nodded. What a charmer! A midnight pundit on Halloween.

Or was he grimacing? Had she only imagined him as a black-skinned monster?

Cynthia looked out the window again. From what she could see, there were no stars at all, no road behind her. A small house sat surrounded by thick trees roughly thirty yards in front of the van now.

This isn't Nashville, Cynthia thought. *There isn't a place like this around Nashville at all.*

She had the impression they were traveling underground.

What was the first warning sign? Hadn't she learned enough?

Panicking again, but forcing herself to stay calm, Cynthia thought of her options…

"Ummm," she said.

Don't make him mad, don't make him angry…

Charlie eyed the road, not looking at her. An intent, contemplative look crossed his face.

"Do you mind if we turn around?" Cynthia said. "I just realized…I mean…I changed my mind. Is that okay? I just…don't think this is a good idea. I'll give you all my money."

She trembled. Her eyes were wide.

A sympathetic look crossed Charlie's face. It surprised her. He slowed the van to a stop, then shocked her by putting it in reverse just that fast.

"Well, yeah," he said, looking her way, the perfect gentleman. "I mean, I don't want you to feel uncomfortable. I'd want to go back, too, if *I* felt uncomfortable. Jeez, I'm sorry. Did I scare you?"

Charlie looked in both side mirrors and steered the van in the opposite direction, moving slightly off the road, and into the murky land of fog.

Oh, God, is this—can it be—

Cynthia felt a pang of guilt for not trusting him. She wanted to grab his hand and squeeze, lean closer—

She closed her eyes and put her hands together in prayer. In the next second, a steel beam collided into her brain. A bright, white light split her vision in half, sending her into darkness. Her head bounced off the window, and she slumped, unconscious, against the door.

Charlie shook his hand after hitting her. The blow had stung. He redirected the van and drove toward the house.

As he nosed the van into the yard, he sighed, shutting the engine off.

Taking a second to bask in his glory, he closed his eyes, and gathered his thoughts.

Charlie pulled the keys from the ignition, hopped out of the van, and moved to the passenger's side. He opened the door, and Cynthia sprawled into his arms.

It was time to get to work.

***

Newport, Havenworth, and Merryside. Shreveport was here now, too. The public continued to gawk in the beleaguered mist, the triumphant, mesmerizing spectacle. What was the world thinking, the broadcasts on CNN? No nationwide event had ever seen the likes of this before.

The initial shock had bypassed them, a mute acceptance into blacker things.

Thousands, millions now, flocked the roads and fields. The firepower and helicopters were useless. Spotlights flashed, but all it did was depict the dead in their multitudinous glory. The people would have to wait and see. Many prayed for deliverance. Many predicated the end of times.

Down the slopes and into Bakersfield, the dead continued their lurching journey toward their Maker. The more terrain they

IN THE DARK KINGDOM

traveled, the more they began to excavate themselves, adding countless lumbering bodies to the already shuffling convoy.

An eyeball split open with pus as it hit the road. It sluggishly rolled to a stop, and was squashed by a heedless, bony foot.

Birds picked at discarded appendages. Flies hummed in the air. Mongrels followed, looking for scraps, grabbed a piece, and bolted.

This time they'd crush his throat with *their* hands. Each in turn...like a child waiting for a ride at the amusement park.

Shuffling along, the dead smiled. His scent was virtually overpowering. They trusted their senses now. He would not get away. In The Dark Kingdom, everyone was welcome.

***

Charlie Silverthorn and The Dark Kingdom—this sable slab of earth—were made for each other. No other place spoke with such volume. No other place made him feel more at home.

It was too bad they were what they were: weak, timid, helpless creatures. He shuddered, sickened by the revulsion they made him feel. He was doing them a favor by sheltering them coldly in the ground. Didn't they understand that? Merciless now, compassionate later.

I'm showing you a peaceful way into the dark, he told them. *Take my hand; you'll see it's not so bad. It's your duty to The Kingdom. Death is good. See, how your blood paints these walls blacker?*

She is venom, Charlie thought, looking at Cynthia, bound and gagged, prostrate on the floor. *She is a reeking cavity. She has no more right than the rest of them.*

A wail echoed in from the distance, a bemoaning lamentation miles outside his home. He cocked his head and frowned, brows coming together as he sat in a lone wooden chair in the basement. Charlie ignored the sound. Sometimes, The Dark Kingdom could get a little creepy, even for him.

A single, 60-watt bulb dangled over Cynthia's still form.

She'd wake soon. He was patient. On his lap, he gently caressed a hatchet.

His victims were merely numbers, a notch in the over-all expanse of life and death. His mission never saw an end. He had plenty of work to do.

He'd donned an older pair of gray, soiled sweats, a dirty white T-shirt. He didn't want to ruin his nicer apparel. He was not wearing his comfortable Nikes now. He was barefoot

Cynthia's breath hitched for oxygen. He'd heard the sound before, and it had always bothered him. Her body jerked. He felt sorry and hated her at the same time.

"You're a prisoner," he said, looking at her. "I'm setting you free."

Cynthia shifted and made an unintelligible sound.

Smiling, Charlie stood up, and moved toward her. The hatchet dangled by his side.

***

Her left eye had swollen shut. Her hands were bound, chafing her wrists. Ropes dug painfully into her skin. There was a gag in her mouth. Another thick strip of cloth dug into the back of her head where he'd tied the knot. A bright light above made her head throb. The only thing that felt good was the cool, concrete floor against her cheek. A puddle of warm saliva pooled from her mouth. Or was that blood?

What...where...how...is...???

She knew what had happened once the shadows came to life. It was everything she hoped it wasn't: barren, cold, lifeless...

She tried, mentally, to put herself somewhere else. The pain, the vomit, the squirming defenselessness of her position—the shocking reality of what he was about to do—limited her options.

Bite back on the pain, sweetheart. Steel your mind against it. This will never be a memory. It's going to be hellish, evil, and

In the Dark Kingdom

maddening, but if you try hard, you can get through it, and we will not allow you to live with the memory. Tell my mom and dad I love them so.

OH, GOD, NOOOO!!!

She squirmed while on the ground, fighting the ropes that bound her. She tried to focus on her surroundings: concrete gray and bright light.

She wished Charlie had already killed her.

She saw him now, though. He was sitting in a chair just behind her. Something was on his lap. Her eyes widened when she recognized the lost, soulless look on his face: pure evil. Her mind reeled with panic and terror. She could do nothing but make helpless, mouse-like noises. Cynthia squirmed on the ground, trying to crawl away.

Laying here about to die wasn't horror alone, not mere fear, terror, or simply being afraid.

This was worse.

Charlie stood, walking toward her, carrying a hatchet.

Oh God oh God oh God oh God, no, please!

Cynthia whimpered and began to cry.

Part of her tried to deny it, *refused* to believe it!

He's not gonna chop me in pieces! He's not gonna cut me apart! He's not gonna kill me, please! Yes? Right? He's not gonna chop me in pieces! He's not gonna chop me in pieces! He's not he's not he's not he's not he's not! I don't believe it! Don't believe it! Please, God, he's not!

Why had she turned into this promiscuous, easily delved-into girl? Why had she defiled herself this way? Why had she given this ruinous, jumbled maniac the satisfaction?

Because you're a fat girl, easily pleased, always wanting. No one chances it. It's all a game. You got unlucky honey, but you'll go straight to the top when it's over!

Part of her believed this.

With full force, the entire night came back—what she'd seen in the brake lights, where they'd been: the swamplands, his house coming into view, the darkness that followed when he'd clocked her...

His feet were just inches from his face now. Blood caked his toenails. Cynthia trembled and looked up with stricken eyes.

"Shhh," Charlie said, looking down. Yes, his eyes were solid, shiny black. "This is all a blur. You're not in this now. Sometimes it's an awful way to go, but it has to be done. This is it, the spring of things. You'll be amply rewarded. I promise."

Sirens wailed in Cynthia's head. She clenched her eyes shut. Her massive bulk trembled in panic. She braced herself for the bloody violation, the rape, the unwelcome pain about to come. She sent her thoughts out into the universe and grasped at everything but the moment: amusement park rides, cotton candy, the time daddy pushed her on the swing when she was ten...

Please God, make it quick! Brace against the pain! Have him kill me quick, not juicy, not slow, but I know it will be! It will be worse, worse than I can imagine, worse than any pain, but please! God! If You're there, please! Have him kill me quick!

Distancing herself from it was all she had. The farther she put herself, the more tolerable it would be. She needed all the help she could get.

Charlie knelt on the ground. He put his flabby, beefy arm around her. She couldn't tell what smelled worse: him, the room, or her own quivering flesh.

Her lips trembled, drool pooling on the floor. Her breath quickened. Cynthia kept her eyes closed.

Keep them closed, just keep them closed. Don't let him have any part of you. You are already gone!

No answer, only her silent prayer in space...

Go away! she thought. *Go away! Go forever into the black of cold wonder, and remember you lived a good life. People will miss you, but you won't feel anything here...*

"Don't you see," Charlie said. "There's no reason to be afraid? You're scared. That's to be expected. This is gentle sway. It's revolving slowly through time. The Kingdom is proud of you,

In the Dark Kingdom

Cynthia."

Charlie put his hand on her head, petting her wet, matted hair. He cooed softly, a lullaby, brushing her blonde locks behind her ear.

Cynthia wept and imagined candy, popcorn, and ice cream. She imagined merry-go-rounds, rabbits, frogs, and sunshine. She thought of gorgeous sunsets, laughter, and colorful balloons sailing into a bright, wonderful sky…

She was at the circus. Carnival music surrounded her. She had successfully reached a plateau away from the nightmare. Now, all she had to do was keep herself here.

Charlie rolled her onto her back, bringing Cynthia back (if only for a moment) from the circus. She opened her eyes in time to see him raise the hatchet. The next second shocked her, the sheer brutality of the moment. Not wasting a second, he swung the blade into the cavity of her chest, making her squeal. She wailed in wide-eyed pain and horror, the hatchet digging deep. Blood gushed from her bosom like a geyser.

Charlie fought and tugged at the hatchet, trying to pull it free. Jagged lightning bolts of pain shot through Cynthia's chest.

Charlie clenched his tongue between his teeth, and swung the hatchet into her a second time.

Balloons gone, the carnival. Only horror, the shock of his brutal behavior. The stars disappeared. She did not close her eyes. Charlie did that for her, trying to show her compassion even in death.

***

Seconds savored, Charlie thought. *Lasting moments.*

This is what he lived for.

This is real, this madness. This is the darkness where real madness is. This is how the Kingdom is built. This makes everything a little better, a little brighter all the way around.

The night was still young.

Cynthia was resting in the peaceful arms of Heaven, Charlie

thought. Or The Dark Kingdom, depending on how you looked at it.

He set the hatchet on the ground, his face and arms coated in blood. He put his fingers to Cynthia's eyelids, closing them with a gentle touch.

The Kingdom smiled at Charlie. A sense of aloneness filled the room. A silent, dark wonder invigorated his being. With each kill, he moved deeper, turning blacker, reigning more supreme in The Dark Kingdom, and that electric current of magic was coursing through him now.

The blood helped, of course. He never minded the fresh, wet aroma of a recent kill, the shimmering scarlet drenching his arms, shirt, and face.

Charlie closed his eyes and breathed it in, smiling.

"This is your gentle sway, your simple breathing," he said. "My meditation. You had no reason to be afraid."

Charlie shifted and moved awkwardly to his knees.

Under him, Cynthia's eyes sprang open. She reached for the hatchet.

Glass shattered upstairs. Charlie snapped his head toward the basement door and frowned.

Something about a riddle...

Footsteps sounded, a stampede across the ceiling. To his right, the basement window shattered.

He looked around him, frowning, puzzled.

What the hell was *this?*

Cynthia reared up, chest still spilling blood. Charlie barely saw her out of the corner of his eye. Like a blur, in violent fury, she drove the hatchet into his chest.

He wailed in agony as the blade tore through him, shocked, dumbfounded. He opened his eyes, staring in betrayed, motionless shock. Cynthia was smiling.

Was The Dark Kingdom turning against him?

She pulled the hatched out and drove it into his chest again. Cold steel sunk into his heart. Charlie reached up, trying to grab the handle, to pull it free, but he wasn't strong enough

In the Dark Kingdom

Cynthia was mad with delight. She laughed like a lunatic. Blood bubbled over her lips. She spat in Charlie's face.

He was stunned. He couldn't believe it! Surely, he couldn't die! He was too powerful a figure in The Dark Kingdom! He was... *immortal!*

Yet, he met this dazed, bewildered reality: *Have I failed? Why would they do this to me?*

They shuffled down the stairs, mad with glee. Their timing was perfect. They thrashed at the doors, breaking windows, a leprous scent growing more powerful as they moved in, encircling him in his very own home.

They'd waited lifetimes—deaths—for this very moment...

Every one he'd plucked from the world—every one he'd laid to rest—was here. Their dead, skeletal faces encircled him, and they asked a single question:

Did you think we would forget?

The pain in his chest ebbed to a dull, ceaseless flow. His reason, why he could never remember his life, his birth, or death was because it was happening still. The smell of dried, moldy bones, stale, papery crust moved through the basement of his house.

The dead, Charlie realized, had been brought back to life. Somehow, someway. It could only happen, he realized, in The Dark Kingdom.

He'd been usurped, betrayed by his masters. His reign was officially over. What a cruel, unmerciful trick.

Charlie fell over, trying to pull the hatchet from his chest. The concrete floor was slick with blood. Bugs and insects dropped onto his face as the dead moved in.

But the practice, the time and patience...

Had someone made a deal to dispose of him? So much for building deeper and darker shadows...

Charlie felt his life slip away, outdone by the very things he'd lived to destroy.

But he didn't die, not quite, and that was the horror. That was justice, he supposed, the answer to the riddle. He *was* still here. Why did he get the feeling he should've predicted this?

Various implements and tools appeared before his eyes. He could not *close* his eyes, another rule, apparently, from The Dark Kingdom. Cynthia had already obtained her redemption. She smiled at him as the dead lurched closer, one after the other, taking their turns. Each held a particular device for the occasion. One clung feebly to a butcher knife, he saw, another, a fork. One held a simple spoon; another clutched the handle of a saw.

The line of dead things traveled from the basement and up the stairs, and surrounded the swampy lands outside his home. He saw each of them in turn, and in turn, a separate implement to his destruction: picks, shovels, ropes, plastic bags clutched in decaying, skeletal hands, piano wire, a hatchet, the one he'd used on Cynthia, the one she'd used on...*him.*

Cynthia's voice emerged:

"Say goodnight, you ruthless fuck. Say goodnight a thousand times, you rotten, black bastard. I hope you have the stomach for it."

Laughter—not his own—surrounded him.

He'd never owned a thing. He wasn't meant to manipulate the shadowed world he'd helped create.

Once again, the hatchet dug into him, burning repeatedly into his chest. Every ounce of scarring pain roared through each nerve ending and muscle. Blood continued to flow. His life did not run out, however, not completely...He could still smell himself.

Unlike him, these creatures *did* possess light, a strange, incandescent hue.

Was this what his nightmares had been about, the elusive thing puzzling him since time began?

Tears sprang to Charlie's eyes. He knew the dead, their suffering holocaust, their yielding flesh. Every nerve screamed with electric currents more unbelievable and traumatic than the last...

His bones shattered, tearing, clawing through him. One of the dead things crushed in his skull with a large rock. Another put a plastic bag over his head, making it impossible to breathe. A wire dug into his throat, digging into the folds of his neck.

In the Dark Kingdom

Charlie screamed and struggled, but to no avail. He knew now...He was meant to die a thousand, million deaths...

Strangely, he traveled into the darkness after an interminable suffering. He moved slowly, unendingly over each second of his demise.

There are many, he thought. *My demise is not a single event...*

They killed him one by one, time and time again, and he awoke to a newer, more revolting horror than the last. He underwent the same treatment, only in a slightly different, more modified way.

Daggers of fire ripped through his groin, splitting his torso in two. His brain whined under a crushing blow again.

But the lights never went out. Not completely. Death was never *quite* complete, never final. Death, apparently, in The Dark Kingdom, was never...*absolute.*

Another diseased and maimed corpse stared down at him, anxious for its turn. When it was finished, another replaced it...then another...the unending line, like an amusement park ride, never ending.

Would this candle *ever* go out?

Another dead thing loomed above, widening its stagnant maw. A clump of writhing maggots spilled onto Charlie's face. He choked and gagged, tried to scream...

Bony hands gripped his windpipe and squeezed...

From all sides, darkness gathered, clogging his senses.

He would spend the rest of eternity opening his eyes to a new death, praying and hoping for something new. They were anxious, happy to deliver this pain, make him suffer and bleed, put him through the same torment he'd put *them* through...

One of them pulled his pants down, and the rest of them giggled...

Oh, God! he thought. *No. Please! Anything but this!*

The rugged, rusty teeth of a saw dug into his enormous belly...

This is not *how it's going to end! Please! This is not an end at all! This is* not *death! You* tricked *me!*

He did own the ability to scream, and maybe that was mercy. Maybe that was their compassion for him. He screamed whenever he could, but it didn't alleviate the horror, the realization he'd been cruelly, viciously deceived. It didn't help at all.

This was mutiny.

What had once been his refuge was now kicking him off the throne of the Third Gate in The Dark Kingdom.

Some waited patiently, hands across their chests, nodding and ushering to the ones standing nearby:

After you. I insist.

Thank you. That's very kind of you.

Centuries waited, lifetimes, places and dimensions Charlie never knew existed. What he experienced was perfectly cruel, the most painful of fates. Even his darkest desires failed to expose this nightmare.

He had to find a way to get comfortable...It was his only hope...

Accusations, insults, mocking laughter rattled him...

Charlie Silverthorn blubbered like a school boy. A stranger's hands fitted warmly cold and, somehow, warmly dead around his throat.

We can humiliate, too, they said. *Look, he has a tiny wee-wee.*

They roared with laughter.

Something about another world, a chance of escape...?

He tried to close his eyes, but it was no use. Death had many guises. The lies and tricks were endless.

His position had never meant a thing. It had been a ruse since the beginning, since he'd come into existence. His existence, in fact, had been a joke the entire time.

Would it make a difference if he tried to get to know them now?

Something about compassion, that sway, like a lullaby...?

In order to receive an answer, he realized, he'd have to be given...*access*. Since he'd owned it once before, he thought he

In the Dark Kingdom

knew the answer already. He tried to accept his forgotten position, but that, too, was no easy task.

If only he could see the humor…If only a lot of things…

Charlie tried, but he didn't have the stomach to laugh.

The Dark Kingdom had no patience for mercy. It believed in salvation, except where Charlie Silverthorn was concerned.

The Dark Kingdom and Heaven worked side by side. In the dark. In Heaven's light. For them both, it was one and the same.

Thus, the answer to the riddle…

About the author:

Brandon Berntson has been writing speculative fiction for almost 20 years. Published in several anthologies and magazines, and with a recent novella, he is a member of the Horror Writer's Association. More about him and his work can be found at www.bloodredtales.com.

Jenna's Awakening
TW Brown

For the third night in a row, Jenna heard the faintest of scratches coming from her closet. At twelve years old, she didn't believe in Santa, the Tooth Fairy, the Easter Bunny, or the Closet Monster. This was what Doctor Lenn diagnosed as her mind dealing with "loss of a close sibling".

Five days ago, she'd stood over a too-precisely-cut rectangle in the ground and let a handful of dry earth crumble between her fingers. The sound of it cascading over the shiny, black capsule sounded an awful lot like…the scratching coming from her closet.

Squeezing her eyes shut only made things worse. Her mind immediately painted a picture, using her closed eyelids like a high-resolution movie screen. The hole seemed a mile deep, yet the coffin was close enough to touch. She knew what was inside: Julia, her twin sister.

She'd found Julia. She knew why the service was a close-casket affair. The local news always issued a warning if they were going to talk about Julia. The first night, Sylvia Stinson, the pretty brunette anchor, cried. Everything just seemed so mashed together after that.

Mistress.

Jenna's eyes popped open. As with the previous nights, the voice came. Not a proper voice. Rather, like the one in her head when she thought…only…different. This voice was flat, higher, and without emotion. It came from everywhere and nowhere.

This is stupid, Jenna thought. She sat up, looking around the

Jenna's Awakening

room. It was the same. Nothing magical or sinister had happened in the brief moment that she had closed her eyes. Now her eyes flicked to the closet door, and the scritching sound...stopped.

Throwing back the covers, Jenna swung herself around, her feet dangling over the side of the bed. *Nothing.* No clawed, fanged, or furred nightmare-come-to-life grabbed hold of either bared, slender ankle. Slowly, she slid to the cold, hardwood floor. There had been a carpet, only...Julia...

Mistress.

Creeping to the closet, she glanced back once at her bed in spite of herself. Nothing looked out at her. There were no glowing, red eyes blazing up from the darkness. Just the black shadows that exist under every bed. Returning her attention to the closet door, she reached out with one hand and clutched the doorknob.

Realizing that she'd been holding her breath, she let it go and turned the knob. The door opened with only a slight creak. Nothing too scary. Inside the closet Jenna discovered...

Nothing.

Just as she suspected. The recent events had become too much. She was, after all, only twelve. Days ago, she'd discovered the remains of her twin sister on the floor of their bedroom, splayed open with her insides in a dark stinking pile beside her. And whoever had done this, had done...*other* things as well. Before or after gutting Julia was not exactly known. Still, did it matter?

Mistress.

The voice hadn't changed in pitch or tone. Yet, there was something in the urgency. As if it sensed her and now needed her attention. Jenna peaked around inside the closet. There was still no sign of...

"Down here," a voice beckoned.

Looking down, Jenna saw what looked to be some kind of lizard. Only it was standing on its hind legs, and its head seemed just a bit too large for its body. Jenna knelt down. Should she be afraid? She didn't think so. This tiny thing didn't seem like it could hurt much more than a fly.

"Are you talking?" Jenna whispered.

"Yes! Yes!" the thing said, clapping its tiny claw-like hands.

Now that the voice was not just simply in her head, it was different. It carried a strange clicking that popped in and out between words. Also, there was a peculiar whistling sound.

"Why are you in my closet?"

"Sent with a gift!" the creature replied.

"Gift?" Jenna sat down, yet, still she towered over the creature.

"I feel your pain…your anger," the creature said, venturing closer, stepping from the darkness and into the soft light that came in through the window. "I can help. You have…the *qualities* that will let you call The Magic."

"Magic?" Jenna scoffed. There was no such thing as magic. Not *real* magic. Then again, there was no such thing as six-inch tall, talking lizardy things either. "What sort of magic?"

"The kind that will bring you peace."

"I don't understand."

"Time," the creature seemed to whine. "Time is our enemy. I have but three hundred seconds. Tomorrow, when I call, hurry."

"Wait!" Jenna cried.

There was a sound, like when her dad would put his thumb in his mouth and flick it out like a champagne cork. Then, the faintest hint of something that reminded her of burnt eggs. The creature was gone.

Jenna looked at the glowing red numbers of her digital clock: 12:05. Standing up, she closed the closet door and padded back to bed. As she drifted off to another fitful night's sleep she kept hearing the words, *The kind that will bring you peace.* How would that thing know what would bring her peace?

In the morning, Jenna woke to the sound of rain…and her mother crying in the background. Something nagged at the back of her mind. A dream that she could not recall. The harder she tried, the more elusive the dream remained.

It was Monday. She didn't have to go to school for another

Jenna's Awakening

week if she didn't want to. Doctor Lenn had said so. Only she didn't want to stay home and listen to her mother cry. Or worse, be smothered by her all day. Pulling her hair back into a ponytail and finding her black jeans that she'd bought with her birthday money along with the black hoody, she snuck downstairs. She left the house using the back door, grabbing her red beanie, tugging it over her ears and stuffing her ponytail inside before stepping out into the rain.

School seemed different. Everybody looked—stared was more like it—but Jenna ignored it the best she could, simply trying to make it through the day. Every single teacher gave her a double-take during roll call, and none of them called on her in class. Not even Mister Koehne, who *always* called on people who didn't raise their hands during history class.

When the final bell rang, she walked home in the rain. Alone. Something in the back of her mind continued tugging at her all day. She knew she was forgetting something. If only she could remember what.

When she got home, her mother was sitting on the couch in the living room. The curtains were drawn and the lights were out, making it very dark. There was something about that darkness that called to her. It made that itching in the back of her mind start to form and take shape. Maybe if she went in there and sat, she would remember.

"Mom?" Jenna stood in the arch of the entry way.

"Doctor Lenn called," Jenna's mom slurred. She'd been drinking again. "He says your next appointment is tomorrow instead of Friday." Jenna sighed and went upstairs. It was no use trying to talk to her mom in this condition. Plus, whatever she was struggling to remember simply wasn't coming to mind. And now she wasn't even sure that there *was* something to remember.

She went into her room and closed the door. Suddenly, she was very tired. Sitting her book bag next to her desk, Jenna laid down. She must have drifted off, because at some point, she heard her dad come home. There was an argument and door slamming, but that was it. Nobody came up and asked if she wanted dinner, and she never smelled the slightest hint of something cooking. For the rest of the evening, Jenna drifted in and out of sleep; at some point she exerted enough energy to kick her shoes off and climb all the way onto the bed.

Mistress.

The voice woke her from a restless sleep where the horrifying images of her sister refused to go away. Jenna sat up noticing that absolute silence had descended on the house. She glanced at her clock: 12:00. It was exactly midnight.

Outside, the rain had ceased, but it was still dark and gloomy, no sign of moonlight. The only light was from the hallway. The small crease of light coming from under her door seemed blinding when looking directly at it.

Mistress.

Jenna scrambled out of bed and hurried to the closet. She opened the door to discover the little creature from last night standing on an overturned shoebox.

"Time is against us, mistress," the creature said begging her to come closer.

"Why did you go away last night?" Jenna asked, only briefly aware that she now remembered everything from the previous night's encounter and that *this* was what had been eluding her all day.

"I must be bound to one that is unsullied," the creature explained in its peculiar voice. "Only one that had known great pain and sadness can call so that I may answer. I have waited over six hundred and seventy years for the call from someone with the gift that was pure."

"Pure?"

"Virgin," the creature said, and made a sound like rocks being rubbed together. Jenna thought it might be laughter, but wasn't sure. Still, that word made her blush.

"How do you know I'm a virgin?"

"I can smell it on you just as you can smell the sweetness of a flower, but we can speak of this later...time is short." The creature

Jenna's Awakening

hopped off the box and moved closer. "I must be bound to you to stay."

"How?"

"Blood."

"Then what happens?" Jenna asked suspiciously.

"Then I may remain to serve."

"But—"

"No time, mistress," the creature's voice rose in pitch, almost a squeak.

"And what do I do?"

"Give your finger to me."

"Cut off my finger?" Jenna scooted back quickly.

"No." The creature made that rock grating sound again that Jenna was now certain to be laughter. "A poke, no more than a pin-prick."

Jenna glanced at her clock: 12:03. She thrust her hand forward to the creature, but it scrambled away from her.

"You must do it yourself."

"Jenna jumped up and ran to her dresser. She was suddenly thankful that her mother insisted that she keep things so orderly. The small sharpener to her eyeliner pencil was right where it should be. She grabbed it and ran back to the closet.

"Hurry, mistress," the creature urged. "We have seconds."

Jenna smashed the tiny, plastic sharpener and picked up the shiny razor blade that it contained. With a quick flick of it across her thumb it was done.

"To me, mistress," the creature beckoned. "Give me your hand."

Jenna thrust it at the creature who grabbed it with its scaly clawed hand. Its mouth closed over her thumb, and for an instant she felt an intense heat fill her as if her blood had turned to molten metal. Jenna wanted to scream, but before she could muster a breath, the pain was gone.

"So now what?" Jenna asked skeptically.

"Do you wish to see your sister again?" The creature climbed

199

up onto Jenna's leg.

"What do you mean?"

"You have the power," the creature's voice became quieter, barely above a whisper. "You carry the gift."

"What gift?"

"You can call the dead."

"But—"

"Would you not like to find the person responsible for your sister's death and make them pay?" the creature asked, tilting his head up to Jenna.

"I don't understand."

"Your blood calls the dead. If you call your sister, she can find her killer, and all your pain will go away."

Jenna considered the words. It all seemed ridiculous. *Any more ridiculous than sitting in front of your closet at midnight, talking to a lizard?* Jenna thought.

"How?"

"I will show you. I will give you the words."

"And my sister will come back?" Jenna felt her throat tighten at the thought.

"She will not be able to refuse the sound of your voice and the draw of the power in your blood," the creature said.

She considered it for a moment. Then nodded. "Show me what to do."

"Excellent, Mistress," the creature hissed.

"Hey," Jenna paused, bringing her face down so she could look into its red, beady eyes. "Do you have a name?"

"I have many," the creature chuckled as if at some wonderful joke. "You may call me Mmirg."

"Murg?" Jenna asked.

"Through the nose more…Mmirg."

"Mnmurrg," Jenna repeated trying to mimic the sound.

"Better." Mmirg climbed up to her shoulder. "Now, there are a few things we must gather before fetching your sister.

Jenna's Awakening

***

Two hours later, Jenna climbed off her bicycle and leaned in against the steps. Pulling her pink backpack off her shoulders, she unzipped it.

"Mmirg?"

A tiny head popped up and two hands gripped the edge. "Perhaps I should have ridden inside your jacket." Mmirg said, pulling himself out and scrambling up Jenna's arm to perch on her shoulder like a featherless parrot.

"We're at the cemetery," Jenna said with a touch of uncertainty. "What's next?"

"We go to Julia so that you may call her," Mmirg urged.

Jenna looked around, ensuring that nobody was coming, and then scrambled over the fence. Mmirg remained on her shoulder, so light that she stopped noticing him shortly after he'd taken perch. *He*, Jenna pondered, at some point deciding that the creature was a 'he'.

As she wove through the headstones and monuments, she tried to understand what was happening. Somehow, someway, she was supposedly going to call her sister from the grave. The tiny voice in her head protested the impossibility of it. But the past couple of days had stretched what was believable. More than anything, Jenna was curious.

Without realizing it, and paying very little attention, Jenna had arrived at Julia's headstone.

Julie Rose Jamison
Born May 20, 1998 Died June 8, 2010
Beloved daughter and sister

Jenna considered the tiny monolith. *This is what it all comes down to,* she thought. Nowhere did it say that she loved chocolate chip cookies fresh from the oven, or that she had a gift when it came to finding music that nobody her age listened to, and introducing it to her sister with absolute confidence that she would love it. Nothing here told passers-by that Julia was the twin who laughed while Jenna was quiet. Outgoing while Jenna was shy.

"What do I do?" Jenna asked, not bothering to wipe away the tears that were trickling down her cheeks.

Mmirg gave instructions, each one painstakingly exact. The funny thing was, it all made sense to Jenna as each new component was used or arranged. Even the symbols that she was required to scratch in the ground seemed obvious once she began etching each one. However, there was one thing that Jenna couldn't be sure if she liked or not. The best way she could describe it to herself was the sensation to be able to actually *feel* the blood coursing through her veins. She could feel each precious drop. And there was something more. She felt power…power in her blood that felt like touching her tongue to a battery.

"Very good, Mistress," Mmirg whispered in her ear.

Jenna blinked her eyes and looked around. The pale glow of the moon, along with a light post made to look like an old-fashioned gas light, cast a bluish hue over everything. She'd created a complex pattern of glyphs at each of the points of the pentagram, accented by candles at the junction where each line crossed another. For some reason, she could not recall doing much of any of it.

"How—" Jenna began.

"No time for questions tonight, Mistress," Mmirg was almost purring. "Must be done before sunlight. Not even our bond allows me to stay in the sun."

Mistress. Jenna felt the voice in her mind again. Yet, there was something more. A connection like a plug in a socket. Something in that moment connected her to Mmirg in a way that they hadn't been just a second ago. She could physically feel him wading through her memories. It was a sensation that Jenna decided that she didn't care for.

The feeling ceased just as suddenly as it began. Mmirg's feet scrambled a bit, seeking to regain purchase on Jenna's shoulder. Jenna felt a tug of her hair as the tiny, lizard-like figure righted itself.

Jenna's Awakening

"What was that?" Jenna insisted.

"Mistress?" Mmirg whined. The pitch of his voice rising so that it was almost painful to hear. "No time. We must join for this. I cannot speak the words aloud. They must only come from you, carried by the night air to the ears of the dead."

"It felt like you were…spying on my memories," Jenna accused. She felt silly saying it, but she could not think of another way to describe the feeling.

"Pardons, Mistress," Mmirg pleaded stroking Jenna's cheek. "I only sought to know you better, and thus know Julia better in order to help you focus your energy."

"Well, it felt…" Jenna considered her next words for a moment, then decided on the one that best fit, "…dirty."

"Mistress, I once more beg your pardon," Mmirg rose to that unpleasant whine again, "but I must insist we hurry. The rise of the sun will make this all for naught."

"Fine." Jenna nodded. "But no poking around where you don't belong."

Yes, Mistress. Now repeat the words I give. At each break, during silence, you must allow a drop of blood from your finger to fall into the flame of the candle. Start at the one atop the grave marker, and move left after reciting each phrase.

The first words felt strange and awkward in Jenna's mouth, but soon began to remind her of music. Just like the often strange music Julia would find and play for her.

She didn't like the fact that she had to poke her fingers every couple of phrases to renew the flow of blood. Also, she was certain she could feel a distinct loss with each drop. She imagined that this would be what it felt like to be a battery…if batteries had feelings.

She hadn't realized that there were so many candles. Yet, eventually, she reached the last one. As the words rolled off her tongue, and the final drop of blood landed on the flickering orange flame of the candle with a hiss, there was a sensation like being in an elevator that was dropping way too fast.

She sensed the shift, a change like when you first open your eyes in the morning when the sun woke you. Just like that. At first she was disoriented, unsure as to what she actually saw or felt. Then, a wave of coldness hit her from all sides.

Force it back, Mistress, Mmirg's mind-voice echoed. *Think just as you did a moment ago when you broke our connection.*

Jenna did as she was told, focusing on the coldness. At first it felt like trying to keep sand out of a hole dug at the beach. Very slowly, she began to push it back. She could still sense the coldness, but now it was different. It was hundreds of individual pieces, varying in size, and even in degree of cold.

Superb, Mistress, Mmirg ran a scaly claw along the outer curve of Jenna's ear. *Now focus on Julia, and bring her to you.*

Even though the instructions seemed simplistic and vague, Jenna understood. He 'waking vision' was clearing of sleep. She *knew* this power. She had always known this power.

And just like that, she found Julia. She felt *her* coldness, *her*...emptiness. Jenna knew what Julia needed without being told. She poured her own warmth down the invisible line that ran between her and her sister.

Yes, Mistress. Now call her to you.

She didn't remember kneeling, but now she was in the center of the large design, directly above where her sister's coffin rested underneath six feet of earth. Inside a dark box, scared and alone. Jenna began to cry as she thought about how Julia would feel waking in such a place. As she did, her focus began to waver.

Now she could feel the *others*. So many of them, cold and alone, some felt sad, others angry, but all of them felt...cold. She reached out to one, then another, only wanting to comfort, to share a little warmth.

***

Mmirg slowly skittered down the girl's arm so as not to disturb any of the lines drawn in the ground, left the area of the giant *Glyph of Summons*. His work here was finished.

Jenna's Awakening

Moving to a granite statue of a weeping angel, he watched and waited. Once again, he had chosen correctly. The girl was a natural. The powers of Necromancy sang in her blood louder than anything he had ever encountered. If she grew to be of age, and learned to control her powers…even the demons of The Pit would have reason to fear.

It would be a few hours before any of those summoned would break through the soil. From what he was feeling…there would be many answering The Call. That was why he chose her.

Had it been a boy, it would have likely gone differently. A boy would have most likely brought back only one. A boy wouldn't have stretched out and thought of all the others lying in the cold earth.

That had been the problem the last time. Mmirg had done this once before. The year—according to human standards—had been 1333. He'd discovered a peasant boy in some remote place in a part known as Central Asia. Sadly, the boy was killed while their bond remained. That had confined Mmirg to a lengthy sentence in The Pit.

When he'd finally been released, and returned to the plane of mortals, he'd been amazed at how the ignorant creatures had progressed. And multiplied. There were so many now. This might actually make his task easier. Scouring the world, he had searched for his Source. The one who could make the dead rise. It had taken almost thirty years. During that time, he'd learned some interesting facts about humans. The biggest was that they loved to be able to explain everything. Especially those things that had no explanation. They'd called his last attempt The Black Plague. Blaming it on a flea!

This time there would be no excuses. Blinded by their own eyes, hiding behind the protection of their so-called technology, they would not be able to explain this until it was too late.

Mmirg sat back, pleased. He could feel them clawing through the earth, seeking the warmth of human flesh and blood. He hadn't *lied* to the girl. Whoever had brutally raped and murdered her sister would die at the hands of what was coming. Just as they all would… all these humans.

    Eventually.

About the Author:

    TW Brown is the author of Zomblog and Dead: The Ugly Beginning. An editor, he is the president and editor of May December Publications. When not writing or editing he tries to divide his time between family and playing guitar. He can be found at www.maydecemberpublications.com.

Queen of Bones
Aubrie Dionne

The hoof beats startled Alaria from her daydreams of her new found love. She glanced up from the tomato patch, curious and a little annoyed as a rider crested the ridge. He rode toward her with reckless abandon, trampling the crops and stirring up wheat dust in his wake. The man slumped in the saddle, the reins falling from his hands. Her irritation turned to concern.

"It's Elric." She dropped her basket and the tomatoes tumbled in the muddied field. The other harvesters followed her as she raced up the hill. Farmer Jet overtook her pace, reaching the teetering rider as he fell off his wheezing horse.

Alaria approached, winded as Jet laid him on the ground.

"What's wrong with him?"

She needn't have asked. Peering through the circle of gathering villagers she saw an arrow protruding from his chest like a stake through the heart. She covered her mouth and stifled a cry.

"We need help," Jet held Elric and gestured to the village below the rise. Two women nodded, taking off in a sprint toward town. Elric shifted in his arms and attempted to sit up.

"Don't move," Jet instructed, holding him down with steady arms. The old farmer tore a piece of fabric from his shirt and wound the white cotton around the young man's chest.

"He's trying to speak," Alaria pushed through the others and knelt beside him. She'd known him her entire life. He was practically a brother. If he was to say anything, he'd say it to her.

She took his hand, "Go on, Elric, I'm listening."

"Must...warn..."

The onlookers huddled around them and bent down, harkening his last words. The world stopped, going mute but for the howl of a wicked wind.

Alaria squeezed his pale fingers, "Elric, listen to me, who did this to you?"

His gaze wandered as he flickered in and out of consciousness. A woman from the crowd spoke, "Leave the wounded boy alone."

While Alaria shot her a reproachful stare, Jet examined the arrow shaft, running his fingers through the violet plumes of the fletching. "The feathers are from the Windrunners in the North and the wood is a crudely cut by a blunt hand."

"Death trails his heels..."

Alaria's heart tightened. The description could only mean the enemy of legend loomed at their doorsteps. But she had to be certain. She cupped his face in both hands, forcing his faltering gaze to look into her dark eyes.

"Tell us what you saw."

Elric coughed, blood streaming from his lips. "The barbarian horde. They overtook the sentinels."

Gasps sucked the air around her head. Someone cursed under their breath and another whispered a prayer to the gods. The woman beside her spoke in denial, "But the King's army defeated them. I saw them ride triumphantly into port."

"Trickery it was," Jet swiped back Elric's sweaty hair. He spoke in a strong and certain tone but Alaria spied fear in his eyes, "A diversion." Her concern for Elric spread to envelope the entire town and the one person that meant everything to her. The poor young man was but a pawn in a larger, more tragic scheme.

Elric's eyes closed and Alaria shook him. He needed to stay awake. The question deciding all of their fates hung unanswered.

She whispered, her voice cracking, "How long before they reach us?"

Elric's eyelids fluttered, "They'll be here when darkness falls."

Queen of Bones

***

The streets streamed with chaos as able-bodied men donned armor to defend the village, and elderly men, women, and children packed their belongings to escape in the forests of the Southern border. Alaria sprinted through the madness, scanning faces both distraught and resigned. In desperation, she pulled one man aside, grasping his arm, "Calen. I'm looking for Calen."

The man looked down as if tattling. Alaria wondered if he knew of their courtship. "He's over at the Smithy's, sharpening his long sword."

"Damn." Alaria released her grip and threw herself into the swarming crowd, leaving the man without saying farewell. She tripped over a goat, stumbling onto a market stall and fell amongst baskets of apples and thyme. Wiping her bruised knees, she expected a harsh retort, but the owner of the stall was long gone, his wares left untended. Alaria leapt up and regained her bearings. As she bolted around the corner, a hanging canary cage slammed into her head, feathers flying. Its owner hunched over a pile of parcels and pack bags. Alaria wondered if she carried everything she owned on her back.

"Ma'am, are you okay?"

She rubbed her temple as the woman grabbed her arm, "Watch where you're going, missy!"

"I'm sorry." Alaria steadied the cage, wondering if the old woman would make it far enough with all her baggage before the onslaught began. She pulled away, "Your bird is unharmed. Good luck to you."

The smithy lay a block away and Alaria saw men waiting in line on the cobblestone. As she took off, the old woman called after her, "You're going the wrong way!"

But Alaria knew very well where she was going. Cutting through the line, she entered the main forge. The tang of metal and sweat clogged the air. Iron clanged and sparks flew as each farmer was outfitted into a makeshift soldier. Men of all shapes and sizes stared back at her. She darted through the clamoring, ignoring the strange looks.

A large hand clamped on her shoulder. Alaria turned to see the blacksmith holding a hammer glowing red from the coals. "You should be running to the cover of the woods, young lady."

She yanked away, "I need to see Calen Rue."

He smeared a streak of soot across his brow as he wiped his sweaty face. His beady eyes bore into her, condemning her plight. "This is no place for a lady."

"I need to see him one last time." She said it with a fiery gaze and a tone hard as the anvil he struck.

The smithy shrugged as if she were a crazy horse he couldn't tame and gestured to a bunch of men standing around the hearth. "The lad's over there."

Alaria's eyes fell once more on her love. He stood amongst the other young men, putting his arms through a gleaming breastplate of armor. His long sword rested at his feet. He looked older, his tanned face shining in the bronze light of the hearth and more handsome than the first day she saw him fishing at the banks of Innis brook.

"Calen," she ran into his arms.

He embraced her for a moment before pulling her back to look into her face, "Alaria, what are you doing here?"

She sniffed back tears, "I've come to stop you. You mustn't go."

Calen's face was stoic, his eyes, unwavering, "I cannot forsake my duty."

He nestled her arm in his and coaxed her forward. With bewildered dismay, she realized that he led her out. She tugged back, but her resolution faltered, "It's a fool's quest. You'll all be killed."

Calen nodded, "So be it. I will not leave my brethren to die alone."

Alaria's heart raged. Her hope of their future lives together seeped away as he guided her back to the threshold. She tried once

Queen of Bones

last time, "We can both forget this place. Please, Calen, run away with me."

"And live with no honor? I can't." He placed her outside the darkness of the forge into the afternoon's bright light. She watched with pleading eyes as he brushed back a strand of her auburn hair. He looked like he was saying goodbye. "You must run as far away from here as you can. We can stall them, but only for so long."

"Calen, no."

Her love ran a tender finger along her cheek, "Dear Alaria, you will see me again. If not in this life, then the next."

After a quick brush of his lips to hers, he turned and disappeared into the blackness of the forge. For the first time in her life, she felt helpless and alone. Alaria stumbled away and dropped to her knees. She'd rather stay and have her heart slashed open than live a life without her love.

Curling up in an alley, she sobbed while the crowd passed and the streets grew silent as a ghost town. She couldn't bring herself to stand and walk away, she couldn't leave Calen to face his death. The sun hung low, casting the scene in crimson light.

Alaria watched Calen's silver helmet gleam as the troops march in tragic steps toward the hills on the horizon. She followed their tracks one block behind, until they reached the open field where she could trail them no more.

Alaria stood on the outskirts of town, kept company by the howl of wind and something more: a strange rattling of bones. Below her, in the valley to the West lay the Land of the Dead. In the daylight, it seemed only a mist covered shadow, but in the darkest hours of the night, when all was still, she could hear minions crossing into the town's cemetery, searching for more unfortunate souls to join their ranks. Today they stirred in the fading rays of sunset, eager to collect the remains on the battleground.

Alaria perked up, wiping her tear stained face. Below her hid an army, a massive front of undying soldiers. One woman stood between her and the unlikely saviors of the town. She stifled a shudder and rose up on both feet. She would pay a visit to the Queen of Bones.

***

The grass turned white as the hair on an old man's head as Alaria descended into the valley of the forgotten. The earth felt cold and still as if time had ended long ago and the place hung in suspension, a nether land between worlds. Misty tendrils reached out from the twilight fog and crept around her legs. She kicked them away and pulled her sweater close around her neck. In the distance, she could see the obsidian towers of the palace where the Queen of Bones performed her rites.

Twigs snapped behind her, followed by a long, low moan. Alaria took off into a sprint and ran toward the spiraled towers. Gnarled branches tugged at her hair and yellow eyes blinked from the shadows. The land turned from barren earth into cat tailed marsh, thick with a veil of white weeping willows. She stumbled forward on a precarious mound of raised earth, weaving through the moors.

As she ran closer, she heard a distant cackling laugh like the crumpling of shriveled leaves. Was it a lost soul gone mad? Or had the Queen heard her footsteps?

The sludge from the swamp rose, slickening her path. She slowed to a jog, her feet sticking in the muck. The mist pressed in and she heard the melancholy call of a lost whippoorwill. Chancing a glimpse into the murky waters, she saw the back of a viper rise up from the depths. She pulled away from the edge and forced herself to focus on the path forward.

As she rounded the bend the palace loomed over head, protected by gates like sharp pins jammed into the earth. Alaria wrapped her porcelain palms around the rust-caked iron and heaved. The hinges creaked and the entrance swung open with a sharp shriek of grinding metal.

Suddenly, the sounds of the bog were quiet as if every slimy animal watched and waited for her next step. Alaria found herself in a garden where skunk cabbage festered and the roses bled black.

Queen of Bones

Thorny shrubs lined a walkway of ash leading up to crumbling palace steps. Statues stood on either side of the path like lost souls trapped in eternal torment. Their stony eyes stared blindly as their frozen hands reached out, grasping mist. Alaris stayed clear of their reaches as she walked up to the palace steps.

The door to the palace was locked. Alaria took a deep breath and knocked. The sound echoed in the stillness like rude clatter and she winced. Moments later, the entrance creaked open to reveal more shadows.

"Hello?"

No one was on the other side. Alaria stepped into a large antechamber of cold marble and stone. A pulsating greenish light emanated from the staircase above. She followed it, ascending the steps until she reached a balcony. A doorway led to a throne room with cathedral ceiling high as the church steeple tops framed by rows of triangular windows, draped in black velvet.

"What do you seek?"

Alaria gasped and shrunk back. The Queen of Bones emerged from the shadows behind her throne, cradling a crystal ball. She wore a black, leather gown with a collar so tall that it framed her high cheekbones and pointed nose. Spikes like the ridges on a dragon's back adorned her arms, trailing down from her shoulders to her hands. Her hair was dark as a raven's wings and slicked back with oil to a tightly knit bun. Eyes, bright as emeralds, peered through the darkness with a feral spark of inner light.

Alaria summoned her courage. She didn't travel all the way to death's doors to leave empty handed. "Your Highness, a mass of barbarians rides from the North. Tonight they attack our town."

"And what of it?" She tapped tapered fingernails on the stone rest of her throne.

"I've come to ask your help."

"Ha!" The Queen walked toward her and strings of crystals clinked around her neck, "You are an interesting young woman to journey all the way down here for a mere mortal's squabble."

"If they attack, every man in town will die."

"Hmp...." Her eyes sparkled, "more for my army, then."

Alaria was losing. She'd assumed too much and thought too little. Why would a Queen of the Dead want more people alive? Her mind searched frantically for any kind of excuse. She couldn't stand the thought of Calen as a zombie, roaming this wasteland at the Bone Master's command.

Her voice was haughty, "If the barbarians win, they'll come here next."

"Very clever, your ploy." the Queen raised her eyebrows, "but I have an army to defend my Kingdom. Although, I appreciate your concern."

Alaria felt like she grasped at spider webs trying to climb a mountain. She fell to her knees, "Please, I'll give you anything. Anything at all."

The Queen turned and her leather gown rustled like whispers at night. "What would a young woman like you have that I want?"

Alaria's tears burned hot in her eyes. She had failed. She'd come all this way for a lunatic's gambit. And she'd called Calen the fool. Wiping her face, she turned back toward the doorway. Maybe there was still enough time to throw herself in the battle. They couldn't stop her from picking up a fallen soldier's sword, even though she'd had no training. At least she'd die at his side.

"Wait."

Alaria whipped around. The Queen held a pointed a claw-like finger to her chin. "I like you. You're a clever, driven girl. I have a bargain: my army for you."

She swallowed, "You mean, my body when it's dead?"

"No. I need an apprentice, one to carry on my legacy."

Alaria's mind scrambled, trying to make sense of the deal. "You want me to sell my soul to necromancy?"

She nodded, "One ritual and a blood pact."

Alaria's answer hung in the air. This moment would decide the rest of eternity. She would never see the light of day or sleep in her family's cottage by the lake. She wouldn't marry in the town church or have her children frolic at the harvest festival. The thought

Queen of Bones

of Calen and his body, lifeless and bloody on the battlefield was all she needed to decide.

"I accept."

***

Alaria rode a horse with green-glowing eyes and hair dark as ash up the hillside to the swords that clanged in the crux of night. Behind her swooped the spirits of the fallen, followed by the clattering bones of the dead. They approached the battle in a shroud, carrying darkness over their shoulders and casting shadows in the moonlight.

Dark power surged through her veins as she commanded her army wordlessly to the front lines. As her minions approached, the soldiers fell back, some frightened and others in awe. The barbarians gawked, their axes held in mid air. Some retreated, but Alaria was unforgiving. She chanted a war cry and the minions surged around them, enveloping them with the stench of death.

They swiped at the spirits in vain as the wispy tendrils dove down, blowing shadows in their eyes. Their axes sent the skeletons flying in pieces. With a flick of her wrist, the bones reassembled and rose back up in an endless tide. The bodies with flesh still clinging were the strongest, spearing the barbarians with their own swords.

Her horse charged to the middle of the horde and she challenged the leader, a man big as an ox with a horned helmet and a beard thick as bracken. His brown charger was no match for a horse of the dead.

He swung up his axe and her steed leapt, kicking the weapon from his hands. She circled round and came up behind him, grabbing his throat with her bare hands. The skin where she touched turned purplish-black, spreading venom outward in wiry veins. He choked and grabbed at her with hairy hands, but her gown was slick with snake oil and his hands slipped, pricked by small pins in the fabric. He roared in frustration as the venom spread and fell off his horse with a thud.

Each barbarian that died in the battle rose up seconds later to fight against their own blood. The army grew greater each minute that passed, and the living dwindled one by one.

The battle was won. Alaria scanned the crowd, pursing her now blackened lips. All of the soldiers stood unharmed, staring at her and her army of minions like small boys at festival time. A few of them cowered and closed their eyes. Alaria's eyes darted uneasily until she found her love. A wave of relief washing over her like rays of the sun see would never see again. Calen stood out from the army like a Grecian God in a throng of beggars. He locked eyes with her and his own gaze flared in recognition and denial.

"Yes," she mouthed with her black lips, "It is I."

Just as sudden as the army came, the moon waned and the night gave way to morning dawn. A fateful wind blew around her, warning her to return to the Land of the Dead. Alaria gave Calen one last, longing look before she spirited away. The dark army disappeared in a cloud of smoke.

***

Elric walked along the street, one arm tied in a sling and the other holding a bottle of festival wine. The streets were alight with late night revelers as the village celebrated another bounteous harvest season. Bulging pumpkins lined the cobblestone and warted gourds decorated windowsills. Everything had taken a turn for the better, and he'd even had the extra coin to buy a new suit to match his blue eyes. Maybe Rudy would notice his efforts. Perhaps, if luck was on his side, she'll sip his wine.

A shadow caught the corner of his vision and he whirled around to see a familiar silhouette dash toward a back alley behind the baker. He raised his arm with the bottle and shouted, "Calen, come join me, friend."

Calen froze, pondered a moment, and turned around. He was holding a bag of sweet bread and a bouquet of jasmine and periwinkle. He pulled down his hood, his face falling into the golden torch light. He smiled, but his eyes were tinged with sadness.

"I can't."

"What do you mean? The festivities are just getting started." Elric took a few steps toward him. He still walked with a limp, but his right side was getting stronger each day.

"My night's just getting started as well."

"Then join us. Rudy's baked a dozen of her delicious wild berry pies. I'm going over there now to try one out!"

"Eat a big piece for me," Calen reached out and put a hand on his shoulder. "Glad to see you feeling better."

"Glad to be better. Listen, I hardly see you anymore. Ever since that battle…" His words trailed off and he didn't have the courage to finish.

"I know," Calen interrupted, "and I'm sorry." He looked over his shoulder, distracted. "Look, I've got to go."

"By all means, go." Elric's tone was emphatic. "I don't want to keep you."

"Thanks, my friend." Calen raised his brows and for a second, the old friend Elric missed so dearly resurfaced.

"Fishing isn't the same without you."

Calen laughed but there was no humor in it. "See you around."

"All right, then." Elric felt wounded and this time it wasn't from the tip of an arrow. Calen had been his best friend before that strange battle, and now he was secretive and shy. Dark circles plagued his eyes as if he never slept at night.

Looking back at the bonfire that raged in the center of town, Elric decided that partying could wait and followed his friend. Calen walked swiftly through the back alleyways and Elric huffed and panted, trying to keep up. His leg grew sore and the hole where the arrow was removed ached.

Turning the corner, he saw Calen jump the fence to the cemetery. A shiver brought up goose bumps on his skin. Ever since the dead rose from the grave he'd stayed far away from anyone buried. But he didn't want to party while his friend brooded alone, and in the cemetery no less.

Calen had disappeared over the far ridge, where the outskirts of the village mingled with those of the shadow land. Taking a circuitous route around the main part of the cemetery, Elric peered over, into the valley of mist.

Calen ran to a dark hooded figure perched atop a demon horse. Elric took in a breath, ready to scream to save his friend, but just then, the hooded rider turned in his direction and cast a green glowing eye and he was stilled. Calen jumped on the back of the horse and, like magic, they vanished into the shadows.

About the Author:

Aubrie Dionne is an author and flutist in New England. Her writings have appeared in Mindflights, Niteblade, Silver Blade, Emerald Tales, Hazard Cat, Moon Drenched Fables, A Fly in Amber, and Aurora Wolf. Her ebooks are published by Lyrical Press, SynergEbooks, and Gypsy Shadow Publishing. Her epic fantasy, The Voices of Ire, is published in print by Wyvern Publications. Aubrie teaches flute at Plymouth State University and the Manchester Community Music School. Please visit her website: www.authoraubrie.com and her blog http://authoraubrie.blogspot.com.

Small Matters of Immortality
Michael R. Colangelo

When Peter was an infant, everyone who encountered the baby suggested that he would grow up and move on to do great things. He was a handsome and healthy child, very robust in comparison to the other village newborns, and he was bright. He was walking on two legs when he was only eight months old.

The village elders—with their prophecies and divination magic—also made this observation about the child, and so it was that this young boy born of unremarkable parents became something of a totem to the people of the village. It gave them something to cling to, at least for a little while.

But near the end of his first year, just a few days before his first birthday, Peter's life met an unfortunate and early ending.

But what an end he did meet, at least.

He was eaten by a vampire.

There were some things in Peter's world that were not of the ordinary way of things. In fact, there were many things that were quite extraordinary about the ways of life in his dimension. The people, the normal ones who were not touched by such things, developed a sort of resistance to the unnatural by creating myth and storytelling around its various components and facets. These were legends about spirits and magic and Gods that walked the planet.

One could live one's whole life without ever encountering such things face-to-face, but just like Peter's unfortunate turn for the worst, that was about to change on a grand scale.

The local lord who controlled the lands that surrounded the land where Peter's village sat were no greedier than the other local lords from the areas that touched its borders. It was common for the rich, who had access to things such as literacy and education, to pursue the unspeakable in hopes of turning lead into gold and developing siege trebuchets that launched dragon fire into the skies. They sought other magic too—elixirs that made one irresistible to the opposite sex or ones that made you live forever, once imbibed. It was, ultimately, less evil and simply shallower than it sounds, except for the really evil nobles who sought out bad magic explicitly to meet their own despicable means.

The local lord was not an evil man, but he was interested in the power and control brought by bigger treasuries and more land. And while he did dabble in magic, as most noblemen did, he hardly took it seriously. He was more interested in swordplay and mead drinking and servant chasing. He was hardly a disciplined man.

When he decided to arrange a marriage between himself and the daughter of one of the merchant lords of the southern islands, (thus controlling many of the trade routes—which thus resulted in more power and control), he did, unfortunately, run into some very powerful and very real magic—of the very evil kind.

Her name was Sadinkalya, and she looked to be only sixteen. In actuality, she was approaching her thirtieth birthday.

Her parents and her tutors had dabbled in bad magic in pursuit of immortalizing their future merchant-queen. Sadinkalya had indeed, been bestowed the gift of immortal youth at the age she presently appeared to be, but it came at a terrible price.

From that age, onward, she was consumed with a terrible urge to eat newborn flesh. Infants were the fuel that bound the dark magic to her soul. Worse, she had grown to enjoy her own perverse nature. So much so that once she was married, she demanded from her new husband a monthly tribute of newborn babies from the village below his hold.

He was weak-willed and greedy enough to go along with her

Small Matters of Immortality

plans.

So the baby Peter never really grew to his full potential. He was one of the first children snatched by the lord's men. He became part of the original baby tax. He was stolen from his home in the dead of night by garrison soldiers disguised as hill bandits, and he was whisked away to Sadinkalya's inner chambers where she consumed him on her canopy bed of yellow satin. The sheets were changed and everybody went about their normal business. Nobody dared utter a whisper about the lord's unspeakable new bride, especially his lordship himself.

Everybody except for the handmaiden, that is.

Initially, when she caught wind of the lord's marriage, she thought with excitement that she would finally have something to do inside the castle. She was also a little relived that she would not become a surrogate of any type. Lords who did not marry often turned their female servants into concubines.

She was as horrified as anyone else when the true nature of the lord's new bride was revealed. She was even more horrified when she realized that Sadinkalya had taken the special boy in the village for her first meal.

And while she kept her mouth shut and her head down like all of the others, she did formulate a plan. While it wasn't perfect, it was the only plan that she had. It was a desperate move that used magic against magic. She hoped for the best, and carried it out.

The night after Sadinkalya had devoured the infant Peter, the handmaiden crept into her bedchamber at night. The room was thick with incense that obscured the senses. While the lord's monstrous bride slept in her bed, the handmaiden found the remains of baby Peter in the chamber pot. He was just a pile of red and raw bones. There was nothing left of him.

She snatched the pot from beneath the bed and hurried from the room, fearful that Sadinkalya would awaken. Then she smuggled it out of the keep and headed down to the bend in the riverside where the forest grew thickest.

Here lived a madman in a crude clapboard shanty. Everyone

in town knew that he was a wizard.

She passed the red bones of Peter to him in her wicker laundry basket. They did not discuss payment for the boy's resurrection. Payment would come later, and it would be whatever the hermit pleased. This was silently understood. He took the bones from the basket and went inside his crooked abode while she camped outside for three days and three nights in waiting.

The swamp pests were bad and she was bitten by insects and drenched by the periodic and cold downpours that plagued the region. But three days later, the swamp hermit exited his home carrying the baby Peter in his arms. She placed him back inside the basket and followed the wizard back inside. She trembled, knowing that his price would be a steep one, but still she walked forward. She knew that she was performing a deed that was greater than she was as a single person.

Later, she stumbled through the swamps away from the cabin. She had barely enough strength left to lift the baby and basket away from the place. The hermit's magic, like most magic, had cost her dearly. Raising the dead was not a lighthearted matter. The price of returning baby Peter's flesh to his frame had cost exactly that—somebody else's flesh in return—and three days to extract it from the handmaiden. It was exactly the amount of time it took to bring Peter back to life.

But what would she do with the baby now?

She knew that she had done the right thing. The lord's new bride was a monstrous aberration, and she would only bring strife and death to the people of the land. That said, she couldn't bring Peter back to his parents in the village. Word would spread quickly of what had occurred. Sadinkalya would hear of it, and her fury would only fall upon the people. The baby would be eaten for a second time, along with everyone else, no doubt.

The handmaiden also knew that she could not keep the child. The hermit had injured her beyond repair while extracting his payment. Even if she survived, she would never be the same, and she certainly would not be in a healthy enough condition to raise a

Small Matters of Immortality

baby into a man.

There was a monastery that took in the poor and the sick and the orphaned—and it was separate from the state—protected directly by the King himself. Not even the lord and his corrupted new bride would dare encroach upon the monks that lived there. The monks, in turn, had taken vows that would not allow them to reveal the true nature of the boy—should they even discover it.

She travelled a day through the swamps and reached the muddy hill upon which the monastery sat. It was a weather-worn and dome-shaped building that was badly in need of a stone mason's touch of repair. She dragged herself and the basket up the hill in the dead of night. Upon arriving at its steps, she discovered its titan-sized stone doors barred from the inside. She did not have the strength to knock loudly and so she waited on the steps.

In the morning, the brothers of the monastery found the baby in basket. Peter was healthy and awake. He giggled at them when they lifted its wicker cover off. Beside him, the handmaiden's icy corpse lay sprawled on the stone steps. The blood from her injuries, also frozen, had stained the steps with a splay of red ice.

They brought the baby inside and then peeled her body from the granite. Whatever had happened, it was not their concern. They buried her in the barren garden at the center of their temple. The baby would be taken care of here until he was old enough to venture forth into the world, or become a brother himself and stay to tend the temple grounds.

***

As the seasons passed, and while the boy was educated by the monks of the shrine, Lady Sadinkalya came to realize that her hunger for children might also become her undoing.

For while she imposed iron law over her husband and servants, so that they would never speak ill of her, she was consuming children faster than the people of the northern backwater could produce them.

Michael R. Colangelo

She longed and pined for her father's great city in the desert, where the burden of her curse could go well-sated and below suspicion. But it was not possible to return. Whatever the sheik's Byzantium scheme, he needed her to remain married as long as the lord lasted.

It was thus that Sadinkalya plotted to develop a cult, and then proceed to use the tool of religion to control the people and farm human infants to sate her own hunger.

She would need to develop a core of soldiers and persuaders first, and later, fanatics to her cause. She could get these men and women from the dungeons beneath her father's palace. Prisoners had a funny way of exchanging their sentences for exile and servitude, and their lives for their belief systems.

Sadinkalya also realized that she would need a false idol for the people to worship—and for that she would need to bind a spirit. Since her transformation, she had avoiding magic of any kind, but she realized that if her hunger was to ever reside, she would need to delve back into the black knowledge of her homeland once again.

She sent a courier to the land of her birth, requesting her father and his circle of magicians send both men willing to work for her cause, and a deity for them to worship. Then with her own hands, she fashioned a crude idol from the clay that could behind in the rancid moat of the keep. It was a squat female deity with exaggerated breasts and hips to symbolize fertility. In the place of its head, however, was a open and gaping maw. This signified its eternal and ravenous hunger.

She named it Hazzakka—a goddess of birth and hunger, and then she waited for its newly minted followers to arrive.

In less than six months time, her father sent a boat carrying trade goods and followers for Sadinkalya's new religion. The foreigners were strange and alien to the servants of the lord's castle with their sweet-smelling perfumes and brightly colored desert robes and dull iron jewelry.

Also arriving with the others was a bronze lamp that had been blackened in a fire. A slender gold chain hung from its handle

Small Matters of Immortality

to which was attached a single and small azure gem.

Inside the lamp was a spirit trapped by her father's magicians. A minor devil they'd discovered by accident while attempting to communicate with other, more malevolent powers. It was cunning and dangerous, but it was hardly strong enough to break free from its imprisonment. Sadinkalya could easily control it—she was versed fairly well in the dark arts. They were not worried it might overtake her mind and then control her with its meager willpower.

In a short, three-day ceremony, Sadinkalya managed to transport the spirit from the lamp into her handmade idol with little difficulty. When she was finished, she hid the idol in her chambers and sent the depleted lamp back with her father's returning vessel. They would want the lamp back as a sign that no harm had come to her during the transfer process.

The final step was to establish a place of worship for her new cult. It needed to be a place that was recognizable to the locals, but secretive enough that she could establish breeding and birthing chambers undetected within its walls. It was over dinner when she brought the need for a temple space up to her husband.

"We don't have enough masons on hand for such a venture," he told her. "I can't afford to import any more from the front lines, either. The King's at war, you know."

It was then that she suggested using an existing structure within his land. After all of the years they had spent together, he was even more weak-willed and feeble-minded than when they had first married. He hesitated, thinking of something disposable.

"You could use the monastery, perhaps. I can't forcibly evict them because they're under protection of the Union—but they don't pay tithes to me. That means that I'm hardly under pressure to offer them any sort of military protection. Do you understand?"

His eyes wandered to a group of cultists who were standing nearby. They were torturing a dog in a darkened corner of the keep. The bunch her father had sent away from his prisons were the worst of the worst. She was certain that they could handle a bunch of garden-tending monks. They would probably relish the opportunity.

Michael R. Colangelo

It also occurred to her that she would need a base of breeding slaves to get her operations underway. The monks were all males and they would do.

The men sent from the south had organized themselves into loose hierarchies. Gangs of the thugs had congregated individually under the more powerful personalities among them. These men, in turn, had agreed to cooperate with one another rather than fight—as fighting would have them executed or simply returned to their homeland to rot in the prisons there.

She sent for the men, four in total, and organized an attack on the monastery. The monks were unprepared and untrained in the arts of war. It would be a straightforward assault under the cover of darkness, and it would happen in three days.

***

The Cult of Hazzakka struck the monastery before dawn. Peter was in the cramped lower chambers below the great oven where they baked their bread. He was on his hands and knees, sifting through the ashes that fell through the fire grates. He was searching for a key that he'd lost to the temple bullies days before.

It was a simple box key crafted from silver, and nobody knew what it opened. Nobody could remember where it came from. He'd had it since he was a boy—taken from a shelf in the back of the temple. He hoped that one day he'd find the container to which it belonged.

Today was not that day.

He heard the muffled shouts of warning coming through the stone before the cultists reached the lower chambers, intent on finding any stragglers or early risers in the depths of the shrine. The temple was usually silent, and so the sounds of alarm instantly made Peter think the worst was happening.

He quickly forgot his search for the lost key and scrambled from the ashes to run the narrow basement corridors. He was looking to make it upstairs, hopefully, and out of the temple if they were being attacked by bandits.

The monks were not faring well on the upper floor. Surprised as they were, among their numbers were very few with even rudimentary combat skills. The cultists, many of whom were ex-military or ex-mercenary at worst, quickly overcame them armed with cudgels, steel nets, and long pole axes topped with blunted iron hooks.

Peter reached the top of the stairs and stepped surprised into the chaos. He was quickly spotted by three men, beaten to the floor, and netted. They were dragged outside to the courtyard where wagons fixed with iron cages awaited them. Those that could not be dragged were carried. By sunrise, the cages were packed full of wailing monks and the monastery largely overtaken. Those that managed to escape were not chased if only for the lack of imprisonment space.

Finally, the seniors of the monastery were picked out from their cages and slaughtered there in the garden in front of the rest of the monks. They used axes. The grievousness of the killing blows, which broke bones as well as cut through flesh, was to strike fear into the hearts of their prisoners to make them more compliant. The plan worked. The monks abided.

Sadinkalya arrived a day later.

She examined the monks as if they were meat, the building as if it were made of diamond. The monks were less virile than she had hoped for, the building was less spacious than she imagined. It was of no consequence, though, this was only the beginning of her expansive plans.

She went through the monks one at a time, having those that were too old or otherwise undesirable executed in the garden in the same manner that they executed the senior members of the monastery. She paused when she came to Peter. There was something about his eyes...something familiar.

"Have we met before?" She asked him. "Perhaps in the southern desert?"

He was too scared and despondent to respond to her question, but her familiarity rang true with Peter as well. He didn't dare speak, however. To speak might bring an axe blow.

She decided to keep him. Not for breeding, however. He would be a consort of types. She did not recognize his face, but there was a familiarity to his eyes. It was one that she couldn't shake.

So it was that the cult was established and Peter became a member of Sadinkalya's innermost court.

***

The swamp hermit had found immortality as well, but of a different type. For him, while he aged at an incredibly slowed rate—so much so that by the time Peter was a handsome youth, he was still the same old man he appeared to be when the handmaiden first delivered Peter to him.

This time distortion could make seasons feel like days, or days feel like seasons had passed. So it was only fitting, that, so many years after he had struck his bargain with the handmaiden, that he should get the idea in his head that he was owed more than what he had taken.

He was not an evil man, but he was a greedy and powerful one. Why should he settle for mere reagents, he eventually decided, when he could have a whole woman, or many whole women, for himself? One he could keep alive over time indefinitely—from which he could take what he liked. He had noticed that the handmaiden was from the keep. She still wore its colors on her outfit—forbidden unless one was employed by nobility, or was actual nobility.

So it took him many long years to make up his mind, although in his own thoughts this process may have taken all the total of a week. Once he decided to return to take more, he carefully dressed in his best robe knitted of swamp leaves and rodent skulls, put on his leather skullcap, and picked up his walking staff. Then he strode from his hovel and made his way across the inhospitable landscape towards the keep in the mountains.

When he reached the gates of the keep, there was an uproar of sudden activity. The gatemen recognized his coming,

Small Matters of Immortality

and superstition had long held that the swamp hermit's appearance indicated a disaster of some sort was soon to follow in his wake. They immediately sounded the alarm, and, with great hesitation and regret, demanded that he wait outside the keep.

"I've come for what is rightfully mine." The hermit told them.

The lord himself came out to meet him. There was no one in the castle brave enough for such a task, and he was hardly brave enough, either. But he could not lose face in front of his own servants, especially with his wife's servants—the rough and mercenary southerners—lurking about.

"I've come for what is rightfully mine," the hermit told him. The lord, quite unfortunately, had no idea to what the hermit referred. He wasn't supposed to be here, demanding things. It was common knowledge that the hermit merely wanted to be left alone. It was the safety of the realm that the hermit did not wish for land or power or blood. It was unheard of for him to deposit himself like some beggar at the foot of the castle gates—completely unheard of.

"Whatever you'd like, but I do ask that you return to your swamp peacefully. Your mere presence here worries my men—it worries me too."

The hermit smiled at him. His teeth were still as strong and white as they had been when he was a young man. He had taken good care of himself across the span of centuries.

"To rid yourself of me, this is what you must do." The hermit told him. Then he leaned in and whispered his dark instructions into the lord's ear.

***

Sadinkalya returned to the keep a fortnight after the hermit had appeared at the gates. She brought Peter back with her, and only a small entourage of bodyguards. Most of the men stayed behind to convert the monastery into a more appropriate prison for the cult's new slaves.

Michael R. Colangelo

"This youth will be our son," she told her husband. "I've a strange affinity for him that I cannot explain."

The lord was relieved to hear her news. As murky and muddled as his mind was, he had always secretly feared the noble acts of childbirth and child rearing with his wife. Despite all of his attempts to hide the truth from himself, he still knew what went on in her chambers on a regular basis. This boy, whatever her fascination with him, was not within an appropriate age category to be of danger to her hunger. And while Peter would not be of his own blood, the lord could fake it. He had faked many things for many years, after all.

Of course, all of this would be over soon, anyway.

***

At night, the hermit waited patiently for her to fall asleep. He had been hiding inside her boudoir for three long days and was rightfully more cantankerous than usual.

What better tribute to pay the swamp hermit than a woman who could not die by rightful means? What better way to lift the sorrow from his shoulders?

***

In the morning, at breakfast, the lord summoned Peter to the banquet hall.

The two of them ate bread in silence.

They sat at the opposite ends of an empty and cold hall.

About the author:

Michael R. Colangelo is a writer from Toronto. Visit him at www.michaelcolangelo.blogspot.com.

THE STONER BRIDE
Matthew Fryer

Jimmy slid the key into the door and shivered, silently cursing his nerves.

There was no sound from inside his box room. Maybe she was asleep? Or perhaps she was simply still *dead*, and this whole ritual thing was exactly the load of bullshit he suspected.

"Sarcana?" He gripped the handle, his palm damp against the metal, and pulled the door open a couple of inches. The cramped room was dark, soft moonlight drizzling around the boards nailed across the window. Something stirred in the shadows.

No way...

"Sarcana?" he whispered. A pungent aroma assaulted his senses, like a sweet, chemical wine.

He cried out as she burst from the darkness, charging the door wide, a naked blur of pale skin and black, twisted lips. Her hands curled into claws, reaching for his face. Jimmy staggered backwards into the hallway as her fingernails gouged his cheek. He batted her hands away and punched her hard in the mouth, feeling a couple of teeth crack beneath his fist. Sarcana tumbled backwards into the darkness of the room.

Jimmy slammed the door, quickly engaging the lock. She clattered into the other side, her fists battering the wood, and the door trembled in its frame.

What the fuck was wrong with her?

He backed away, tentatively touching the pink furrows her nails had raked across his face. Slowly, the shock relented to anger.

He'd almost lost an eye! What use was she to him in this state?

"La Croix," he breathed. The bone conjurer had some questions to answer. This wasn't what he'd paid for at all.

Pulling out his phone, Jimmy quickly selected La Croix's number. He couldn't shake the image of Sarcana's face; a rictus of mortal terror and hatred. The sheer *rage* that boiled behind those dead eyes had iced his blood. It was exactly how she'd looked as she'd died.

After a couple of rings, La Croix picked up.

"Jimmy Bates." The man's soft, sinister accent curled from the earpiece. "How is your new girl this fine witching hour?"

"She's gone batshit crazy, foaming at the mouth! She just tried to rip my face off!"

There was a contemplative pause. "That should not be."

"Well it *is!*" Jimmy checked his watch. It was two minutes past midnight. "I just opened the door, after twenty-four hours, like you said. She went for my eyes like a fucking harpy!"

"The ritual was routine. Are you sure that she passed away peacefully?"

Jimmy licked his lips, hesitating a moment too long. "Of course. Why?"

"The undead return exactly as they departed. If Sarcana died calmly from a drug overdose, as you say, her brain loaded with serotonin and endorphins, then that temperament should be preserved. I don't understand the fury."

Jimmy cursed silently, wishing La Croix had told him that before. The overdose story was a load of crap. He'd only spun the yarn so that the necromancer would agree to bring her back without any awkward questions.

Sarcana was one of his best customers, a chain-smoking pothead who lived in a communal squat just down the road from his flat. A petite brunette with Disney eyelashes and an ass to die for, she never gave Jimmy a second glance. She'd tolerate whatever banter was necessary to score dope, occasionally turning on the seductive charm if she was broke, but clearly had no interest in friendship,

The Stoner Bride

let alone anything more. Jimmy was a necessary evil, and only the potency of his home-grown White Widow kept her coming back to his squalid little den.

Yesterday afternoon, he'd returned from the pub to discover that somebody had broken in and rifled his stash. Moments later, he found Sarcana half way out of the toilet window. He'd dragged her back inside by her ankles, and made her turn out her pockets. She pulled out several ounces of pilfered skunk, followed by a large bowie knife. Before Jimmy could react, she went for his heart. He dodged the strike, but she kept coming, slashing his arms and almost slicing off his left ear. Fueled by several pints of strong continental lager, and more than a little hurt by the betrayal, Jimmy strangled her to death.

It was pretty much self-defence, and the mercenary bitch had certainly made her own bed, but he'd decided that La Croix didn't need to know the details. Admitting to murder hardly seemed like the best opening gambit.

Jimmy shook his head as the door rattled on its hinges beneath Sarcana's demented assault. The residents of this God-forsaken block were used to antisocial disorder well into the early hours, but she was creating quite an impressive din. At least she couldn't scream. Jimmy supposed you needed breath to do that.

"What if I give her some heroin?" Jimmy asked. "Or rohypnol? Something to chill her out?"

"Sarcana is dead," La Croix said gravely. "She has no ability to ingest and her heart doesn't beat. Drugs don't work unless injected directly into the brain, and even then, the effects are very weak and temporary."

"So what do you suggest?"

"Buy a leather bit and a strait jacket."

"That supposed to be funny?"

"No. It is grim reality."

"Shit!" Jimmy kicked the wall. Sarcana's rabid onslaught was already making his head throb, and he worried that somebody might eventually call the police. Not out of concern—the amoral indifference of his neighbors was spectacular—but just out of spiteful revenge for the disturbance.

La Croix lowered his voice, and Jimmy could almost *taste* the suspicion. "Reanimated corpses only go berserk when they died full of survival adrenaline."

"Well, I...I wasn't actually there when it happened," Jimmy said, floundering for an excuse.

"What?"

"I found her sprawled on the couch. She looked peaceful, like she'd just slipped away. I just guessed it was an OD."

"You *lied* to me?" La Croix boomed. "Reckless fool! The dark powers are not to be trifled with, and you dabble with them like a stupid schoolgirl with a Ouija board!"

"Watch your mouth, La Croix." Who did he think he was, all smug and superior, insulting Jimmy like he was some stupid street skank? Nobody got away with that, necromancer or otherwise. "Okay, I lied. But we need to decide what the hell we're gonna do about this."

"We?" La Croix laughed, his rumbling baritone vibrating the phone in Jimmy's hand. "This is *your* problem, Jimmy. And your fault. The girl clearly died kicking and screaming."

Jimmy remembered how she had writhed on his bathroom floor, locked in a grimace of dread and sheer loathing, thread veins rupturing in her eyes. Now she was stuck like that forever.

"You should have told me the truth," La Croix said.

"*You* should've explained!"

"I don't have to explain anything to anybody."

Jimmy sighed. That figured.

La Croix was a local underworld legend, and clearly basked in his aura of mystery. A tall, square-jawed man, he shaved his perfectly round head, and always wore a long black coat like some kind of fetish priest. Rumor had it he was some kind of renegade Haitian, and had brought several flat-lined junkies back from the other side. Some feared him and whispered his name with absurd reverence. Others thought he was a pompous prick. He'd never

The Stoner Bride

believed the stories, and until tonight, assumed La Croix was simply a disgraced but gifted doctor with a flair for resuscitating people from scag-induced comas. And clearly liked to inject a bit of theatre into his illegal practice with all the hokey ritual bullshit.

His old mate Skinny Dave was one of the necromancer's previous patients, and seemed to be a success.

Dave lived in a grubby bedsit with his girlfriend on the other side of town, and last month, had gorged himself—allegedly to death—on morphine. Ever since the La Croix treatment, he just sat on his couch like a hippy on the last day of Woodstock. According to his girlfriend, he never spoke, ate, slept or even took a piss. He was zoned-out but happy enough, and she swore he was cold to the touch and didn't have a pulse.

Jimmy had guessed the poor kid was just brain damaged from his overdose, and the pulseless chill was just a result of low blood pressure and a fried metabolism. But suddenly stuck with a dead body in his bathroom, Jimmy decided to give the necromancer a shot. His hopes weren't high, but he'd nothing to lose and didn't give a toss whether La Croix's gift was voodoo magic or medical science; he might be able to help Jimmy dodge a murder investigation. And as a bonus, he'd have his own little stoner bride.

Jimmy's dingy flat was a lonely place. A dumb zombie babe like Sarcana would be the perfect partner. He'd always dreamed of bagging a gorgeous girlfriend, somebody to get high with, and maybe even get the occasional blow job. Was that too much to ask? But you needed money, looks or talent for that, and Jimmy was dismally lacking in all three. He smoked most of his profits, and had no abilities other than avoiding the law and his rival dealers. The biggest problem was his looks. Nicknamed *Jimmy the Hutt* at school, he was dog-ugly, with a mouth too big for his head, third world teeth and a limpid gaze. People were forever mocking him because he couldn't get a girlfriend, and the only girls he'd ever slept with had done it for cash or drugs.

So rather than trying to dump Sarcana's body, he'd given La Croix a call, faintly hoping the cocky weirdo could resurrect her as a similar creature to Skinny Dave. He could then move her in, and her cute ass would certainly silence his sniggering mates, and provide a bit of company around the house. She might never speak, but he wasn't one for relationship small talk anyway.

La Croix had declared a fee of two grand, oozing smug self-importance like sweat, and Jimmy almost told him to piss off on the spot. Now he wished he had. Instead, he'd managed to round up the cash and reluctantly handed it over. La Croix's instructions were simple. Leave the flat and return in twenty-four hours.

Last night, he'd crashed over at Skinny Dave's, and curiosity had led Jimmy to check his friend's pulse while he sat smiling blankly at MTV. He couldn't find one; Dave's wrist was cold and lifeless as a slab of fish.

Jimmy winced as Sarcana stopped pounding her fists on the box room door and began scratching deliriously at the wood. The raw squeak of her nails set his teeth on edge.

"So there's nothing I can do?"

"She might respond to familiarity. Personal desires and fears sometimes linger in the undead. Considerably reduced, of course, but there nonetheless."

"She used to smoke weed. Big time."

"I see. Well she obviously can't inhale, and any actual physiological effects will be minimal due to the stagnant inertia of her lungs and bloodstream. But lingering memories of the aroma may calm her. Did she have a favorite type of music?"

"Not sure. I remember her once saying she was on her way to a techno gig. You think that'd help?"

"It often does."

"Oh, great. I fucking *hate* dance music, and now I'm gonna have to play it 24/7 for the rest of my life just to keep the murderous lunatic away from my throat?"

"No. Just for the next couple of years."

"What happens then?"

"The effects of the ritual will wear off, and Sarcana will succumb to death a second time."

The Stoner Bride

"Two years?" Jimmy mumbled, then jumped at the sound of cracking wood. Sarcana had ragged a small hole in the door, and was tearing at the edges like a rabid mandrill. She pressed her face to the gap, wild eyes burning in the darkness, and started to gnaw at the jagged wood, tearing her gums on the splinters. He certainly wouldn't be putting his dick anywhere near *that* mouth from hell. "Is it possible to kill her?"

"Possible, but very difficult. Until the spell abates, she will never *truly* die. Life's essence remains in every single cell."

"Could I just tie her up and bury her in a field somewhere?"

"Of course, but should she escape or be discovered, the trail might lead back to you."

Jimmy frowned. He didn't like the sound of that, and entombment did seem rather cruel. She might've tried to thieve his stash and kill him, but he was no torturer, and Sarcana was clearly having a pretty bad time already.

"What if I burn her? Or just pound her to dust with a sledgehammer?"

"That would certainly be more practical."

One of Sarcana's slender arms shot through the gap in the door, snatching blindly at the air with pale, bloody fingers. "Can you come and give me a hand? I don't fancy taking her on without some back up."

"I am a very busy man."

"Fuck you, La Croix. *You* resurrected her, you creepy voodoo bastard! You're up to your neck in this too. And who else can I ask to come and help me take down a psycho zombie?"

"Very well. But it will cost you, Jimmy."

He'd never feed the necromancer's ego by telling him this, but Jimmy would pay whatever it cost for his cool expertise right now. "Whatever. Just get down here before she breaks out, or you'll be watching her rampage on the evening news."

"Five minutes," La Croix promised, and hung up.

Jimmy slipped his phone away as Sarcana savaged the hole in the door, ripping off fat splinters, her broken nails leaving crimson smears on the wood. She managed to force her head through the gap, clumps of hair tearing out on the spiky edges, baring her teeth through mincemeat lips.

Jimmy remembered what La Croix had said about residual fears and desires. He knew Sarcana was afraid of fire: the ghost of some childhood trauma she'd never revealed. Now she couldn't even blaze up a bong without using one of those flameless electric lighters.

Jimmy took out his zippo and flipped the lid; this should stall her until La Croix arrived. Igniting the flame, he carefully stepped forward.

Before he could lift the flame to the gap, the lock popped free from its moorings and the door burst open.

Jimmy leapt back as Sarcana scrabbled towards him, her ashen breasts jiggling in the gloom. He thrust the zippo in panic, and there was a deep *whump* as she was immediately engulfed in fire.

Jimmy kicked her in the stomach, sending her careering back into the box room. He watched as she spun in a macabre dance, windmilling her arms, the eerie orange flames licking hungrily up her body. It was lucky there was nothing that could catch fire; he'd emptied the room completely, as instructed, for La Croix's ritual. The air thickened with black smoke, and Jimmy's stomach squeezed at sickly-sweet stench of burning flesh. Sarcana's skin sloughed off in crispy strips as she bounced off the walls, fat spitting onto the floor like kebab grease: a ghastly but hypnotic display.

Soon Jimmy could see nothing but smoke, and he snapped from his trance and dashed into the kitchen, desperately looking for something he could fill with water. He grabbed the washing-up bowl, tipped a week's worth of dirty plates onto the floor, and shoved it beneath the tap. It seemed to take ages to fill, but by the time he hurried back to the room, the raging fire had burned itself out, leaving a strangely tranquil hiss and pop of cooked meat.

He put down the bowl of water and peered into the billowing murk.

"Sarcana?"

The Stoner Bride

The smoke parted and she lurched from the pit, little more than a flame-grilled skeleton.

Charred innards sloshed behind her ribcage, bones held together by lugs of gristle and blackened sinew. Jimmy's bladder flushed hot. The oily, leering skull of her face was the most grisly thing he'd ever seen in his life. And he'd seem some *seriously* messed-up stuff.

Sarcana lunged for Jimmy with pincer fingers, tumbling them both to the floor. She caught his bottom lip in her teeth and bit down hard. Jimmy shrieked at the white-hot pain and jerked his head away, tasting blood, and managed to grab the greasy bones of her upper arms, pushing her back. She was light as a feather, but somehow terrifyingly strong. How the hell could she fight without any muscles?

Life's essence remains in every single cell.

Jimmy hefted the thrashing skeleton up in the air, her spindly limbs kicking and stabbing at his body. The stew of cooked guts slithered from her ribcage, piling in Jimmy's lap.

"Aw, gimme a break!"

Through the corner of his eye, Jimmy saw the front door of his flat swing open. La Croix stood on the threshold, blinking with incredulity, his long black coat undulating around him like a robe. *That was quick.*

"Don't just fucking stand there!"

The necromancer strode down the hall, dragged Sarcana off Jimmy's struggling form and hurled her back into the box room. He slammed the door, thumping his boot up against it. He turned to Jimmy, dark eyes blazing. "What happened?"

Jimmy swayed to his feet, dabbing at his torn lip. "Christ, that hurts!"

"What *happened?*"

"I set her on fire."

"Inside? Are you quite deranged?"

"It was an *accident.*"

"The chemicals used in the ritual are highly flammable."

"No shit! *Now* what do we do?"

Sarcana flailed at the door, skull knocking against the wood, teeth clacking like clockwork. She started to stab her fleshless fingers through the wood, and one of them snapped off. It stuck there, protruding like an ivory coat-hook.

"We have to subdue her," La Croix said calmly, and Jimmy wondered if this wasn't the first time he'd had to battle one of his more ill-advised creations. "Do you have something we can use as a club? A hammer or a baseball bat would be ideal."

Jimmy nodded and hurried into the kitchen, fished his old tool box from beneath the sink, and pulled out a couple of weighty claw hammers. He returned to La Croix and handed one over.

"Perfect," La Croix said, raising the weapon. "Are you ready?"

Jimmy braced himself. "As I'll ever be."

La Croix nodded sagely, then heaved the door wide.

Sarcana blundered out, more sluggish than before. One of her femurs had cracked, and she lolled on the ruined limb like a drunk. Jimmy giggled at the horrific sight, and wondered if he was close to breaking.

The two men battered Sarcana's skeleton to the ground, pounding at the torso and limbs, shattering the ribs to kindling. One of her hands grasped Jimmy's hammer, and when he tugged it free, it tore off at the wrist with a jellied crunch. Taking a deep breath, Jimmy swung the hammer into the side of Sarcana's skull with everything he'd got. It connected with a solid squelch and knocked it clean off her shoulders. The skull bounced across the floor and came to rest facing the wall, as though unable to watch the destruction of its body. But still the decapitated skeleton fought and squirmed, the seared remnants of muscle twitching in spasm.

Jimmy screamed, no longer caring about the neighbors as he swung the hammer. He didn't rest until there was nothing left but scorched fragments of bone and shreds of cooked tissue strewn through the hall.

La Croix stepped over to where the skull lay in the corner.

The Stoner Bride

He nudged it with his boot, and it rolled over to face him, broken teeth still snapping like some ghoulish novelty toy. La Croix raised his boot.

"No!"

The necromancer hesitated and frowned.

Jimmy dropped his hammer to the floor. "I'm going to keep it."

La Croix pondered this for a moment, then shrugged. "Very well. But be extremely careful. She is still dangerous."

"I know. But I might as well get *something* out of this mess."

"A living skull?"

"Why not?" Jimmy walked over and picked it up, carefully keeping his fingers away from the manic jaws. "And it doesn't seem fair to kill her a second time." He cursed inwardly, realizing what he'd said the moment the words had passed his lips.

La Croix narrowed his eyes.

Oops. You and your big mouth. "Just joking."

La Croix shook his head, towering above Jimmy. "I couldn't understand how the victim of an overdose could be full of such... *wrath*. Now it all makes sense."

"Look, it was self-defense, okay. She tried to kill me first."

La Croix reached into his jacket and produced a dagger. It had an ornate handle engraved with arcane symbols, and the foot-long blade was viciously serrated. He levelled it at Jimmy's face. "I do not care about the whys and wherefores. You lied to me, disrespected my powers, and caused a world of trouble. She could have slaughtered us both, and exposed our craft to the world."

"*Our?*"

"I am not the only one of my kind. Our ancient order has lain dormant for many centuries, but now the time has come for the black dawn." La Croix drew himself up. "The practitioners of the necromantic arts will rise again!"

"Sure you will," Jimmy scoffed. "With your army of lazy smackheads, who'll be able to stop you?"

La Croix scowled. "The addicts were just practice. As *you*

will be."

"Me?"

"I'm going to kill you, Jimmy. Then I shall reanimate your filthy corpse, and kill you again."

Jimmy held the skull tight. He ducked low and whispered into the seeping cavity that was once Sarcana's ear. "You ready babe?"

"What did you say?" La Croix demanded.

Jimmy hurled the skull at his face. Sarcana's jagged teeth clamped onto the necromancer's nose with a wet crunch, biting deep, and blood jetted up into the air. La Croix squealed, dropped his dagger and crashed to the floor, both hands gripping the sides of the skull's head as though he was trying to French kiss the abominable thing. He gurgled and begged as Jimmy picked up the dagger, knelt beside the struggle, and plunged the blade down into his heart.

If anything, he was doing the world a favour. This reanimation game was bloody dangerous, and they were all better off without his craft. Rise of the fucking necromancers? Not if *he* had anything to do with it.

Once a final breath had bubbled from La Croix's crimson lips, Jimmy lifted Sarcana's skull from his face. She hung on, and La Croix's skin stretched then snapped free like a strand of cheap mozzarella cheese. Her jaw pointlessly chewed what was left of his nose.

"Good girl," Jimmy smiled. "You deserve a reward."

He carried her reverently across to the coffee table, and took the lid off his home-made bong. Jimmy could be quite innovative when it came to indulging his appetite, and had built this one using an old goldfish tank. "I'm not putting any techno on, but I'm sure you'll like this."

Sarcana's skull slotted neatly inside the chamber, her restless jaw rattling against the glass. Jimmy replaced the lid and wiped his sticky hands on his trousers.

"Shhh. Daddy's got ya." He took out a baggie, stuffed a fragrant bud of White Widow into the bowl, and blazed up. The

The Stoner Bride

chamber filled with creamy smoke, curling around Sarcana's teeth and into the black hollows of her eyes.

She calmed immediately. Perhaps it was Jimmy's imagination, but it looked as though her charred, demonic grin had relaxed into a contented smile.

He laughed with delight.

Never mind the cute stoner bride. This was going to be *much* more fun.

About the author:

Matthew Fryer was born in Sheffield, England, where he lives with his wife, Allison. As well as writing, he spends too much of his time losing at poker, listening to loud music, and hoping it will rain so that he doesn't have to mow the lawn. Visit his website, *The Hellforge*, at www.matthewfryer.com.

SEDENBERRY'S PEST
Jon C. Forisha

There was a pest growing in the town of Sedenberry. It was not a plague or an infestation of rodents; it was something much larger, much more intelligent, and much more apt to breathe fire.

Wadlen had been the mayor of Sedenberry for three years at the time of the pest's appearance. The town itself was small, nestled between two large hills, and Wadlen had been pleased to find that his job generally required minimal effort from him.

Curled knuckles rapped upon his large oak door one gloomy morning.

"Who is it?" Wadlen shouted over his shoulder.

"It's Doon, sir," came the reply.

"What is it, Doon? I'm quite busy."

"Well, sir. Could I come in, sir?"

Wadlen finished the sentence he was on and laid his quill pen on the ink reservoir so as not to spoil the letter he'd been writing. As usual, Doon took Wadlen's silence as acquiescence and let himself in. The mayor turned in his chair to see his second-in-command standing motionless in the doorway, his face quite pale.

"Well, then? What's the matter, Doon?" Wadlen said as he stood and straightened his robes.

"You remember, sir, when a few of the farmers complained last week of something in the hills?" Doon spoke from the doorway, his exaggerated sense of privacy laid bare.

"Yes, what of it?"

"They're complaining again, sir. And, well, sir, I saw it."

Sedenberry's Pest

"Saw what?"

"Sir, I believe it's a dragon."

***

The meeting that afternoon was the most raucous assembly that Wadlen had presided over in his duration as mayor. He had asked Doon to bring the victimized farmers so they could explain the damage to their crops. As he looked down from his large wooden desk on the shouting men, however, he began to feel that was his first mistake.

"Gentlemen!" he shouted, but no one paid him any attention. He turned to Doon, who was speaking with a man some five feet away, and tugged on his arm. "Take care of this nonsense, will you?"

Doon nodded, moved away from his conversation, and pulled his flintlock pistol from his belt. He pulled back the hammer and aimed the gun at the ceiling, pulling the trigger. The many conversations in the room abruptly ceased at the sound of the deafening gunshot and all eyes (wide as they were with hitherto absent fear) went straight to Doon.

He pulled his handkerchief from his back pocket and began to wipe down the gun. Though he had fired the gun devoid of any gunpowder, cleaning and oiling his gun after each use was a habit that he'd found was hard to break.

"Glad to have your attention, everyone," Wadlen said with a smile as he glanced around the chamber. "As Mr. Danell was saying," he swept his arm toward Mr. Danell, the elder of the three farmers in the chamber, "the *pest* has been eating his crops in the dead of night. It's not limited to one crop and burns appear all around his farmland. Though he's stayed awake three nights of the past week to try and spot the pest, he has not yet been successful. Am I correct in my understanding, sir?"

Mr. Danell nodded, his long gray beard moving with his head. "Quite, sir."

"And you believe this pest to be a dragon, do you not?"

"I do, sir."

"And you are aware, I presume, that dragons have been out of these lands for quite some centuries, yes?"

"Yes, sir, I knows that. It's just that I been looking at all of the signs around me farms, and all's I can see is a whole bunch of burns. In *Raxon's Journal*, Sir Raxon hisself outlines how the dragons behave. It seems to fit, sir."

"This proves nothing!" shouted Tarea, a nobleman who owned a good portion of southern Sedenberry. "We all know that *Raxon's Journal* has largely been proven to be fictional."

"Quite true," Wadlen said, keeping his voice bold so that he might stay above the growing volume of the assembly. "However, who amongst us has seen a dragon? In the flesh—or scales—I mean?"

One hand was raised into the air. Everyone turned and glanced at Glamacian, one of the newly promoted guardsmen. Voices rose all around and a general sense of jealousy began to seep into the air.

"Glamacian, is that so?" Wadlen asked, searching his memory of the man and finding that he knew frighteningly little of a guard so high up in the city's hierarchy.

"It is, sir. I was in Yarkyt three summers past. One attacked a nearby city."

"Did you have anything to do with its slaying?" Wadlen asked.

"Nay, sir. It was, regrettably, not slain." Glamacian stood proud, but the simple fact that a living dragon crossed his path and continued to live very obviously put a damper on his pride. He was a fighter to the end, as evidenced by the many scars that crossed his muscular torso, a few of which managed to creep out from beneath his modest green tunic.

The meeting was adjourned and Wadlen requested a smaller assembly with just a few men in his office. He particularly hated loud situations, and when he knew that half of the conversations in the assembly had nothing to do with burning crops or a dragon of

Sedenberry's Pest

any kind, he found that he became almost incapacitated with anxiety.

Wadlen sat in a large red chair by the fire of his office, Doon next to him on a blue chair and Mr. Danell on a sofa across from them. There was a knock upon the door and Wadlen's servant opened it, motioning for Glamacian to step inside.

"Sirs," Glamacian said to his superiors with a nod as he took a seat next to Mr. Danell upon the sofa.

"Glamacian, I don't know about Yarkyt. What happened when the dragon attacked?" Wadlen asked, having long ago established a reputation for skipping pleasantries.

"Well, sir, the guards were mobilized. They created lures for the beast, but it didn't take to them. They shot arrows, but even those that cut the beast did little but draw a few drops of blood. It seemed quite invulnerable."

"Sirs, if I may," said Mr. Danell. "*Raxon's Journal* tells how they can be beated."

"That's true," Doon said. "Magic, is it not?"

"Not just magic," Glamacian said regrettably.

"No, not just magic," said Mr. Danell. "Raxon wrote, in his book, that a real dragon needs to be killed by necromancy. Only can a necromancer kill one o' them."

"Again, though," said Doon with a smile, "Raxon's been proven as not the most factual of sources."

"Sadly, it seems to be all that we have to go on at the moment," said Wadlen as he turned to face the fire.

The four men sat for a moment in silence, the only audible sounds in the room being the screams of the dying log and the sounds of its innards being torn apart by the merciless fire in the fireplace.

"I would rather not use a necromancer, gentlemen," Wadlen said into the fire. They all nodded at that, having heard things from sources more reliable than *Raxon's Journal* that led them to draw an unsavory picture of the average necromancer.

"Shall I assemble the guards, sir?" Glamacian asked. "I could have them to Mr. Danell's farm by nightfall."

"No," said Wadlen, "I fear that this, if it is a dragon, will be a bit tougher than swords and arrows."

"Shall I send for Lady Calafar then, sir?" Doon asked.

***

Lady Calafar lived in a small tower near the eastern edge of Sedenberry. She was one of the wealthiest citizens of the town and voluntarily abstained from joining in the politics of the area, choosing to spend her time doing more worthwhile things, as she called them.

As Wadlen, Glamacian, and Doon mounted the winding walkway to the front door of her tower, it became clear that excessive gardening was one of those worthwhile things that she preferred over politics. Ivy clung to every stone surface surrounding her tower and flowers of all shapes and colors decorated her yard like it were some kind of perverse flag to be viewed from on high.

Lady Calafar, it was quite certain, was the only magician in Sedenberry. Since the town was rather small and remote, magicians were seldom of much use, but if one were to travel to the larger surrounding cities—such as the sprawling Dranbe or the long and skinny Uryt—then one would encounter more magicians than one would know how to employ.

"Greetings," said a voice from behind them. They all turned at once to look but saw no one there. A giggling was audible from far off, and once they all began to glance around for Lady Calafar, she appeared quite suddenly behind them, at her front door, though no one had heard the door open.

"Hello, Lady Calafar," Wadlen said with a bow. The others followed his lead. "We have a proposition for you."

"By all means," she said, sweeping her hand at the doorway, inviting them in.

The door was not open but still she was able to walk through the doorway, the door appearing to be naught but a trick on the eyes. The three men followed her into her tower, each in turn mesmerized by the authenticity of her illusion.

Sedenberry's Pest

She sat in a large chair and motioned for each of them to do the same. Ivy had crawled inside her tower in the same manner that it had conquered the exterior, and it showed no signs of stopping—though Lady Calafar also showed no signs of wanting it to.

"Have you ever dealt with a dragon before, Lady Calafar?" Wadlen said.

"Is that what Danell has up there?" she asked inquisitively.

"We think so," Glamacian put in.

"You've seen it?" Doon asked.

"Only heard things. Sounds that don't belong to any wolves. So let me see, gentlemen. You came to my lovely tower to pluck me from my peaceful existence so that I may vanquish your dragon before it takes your town?"

"Our town, Lady Calafar," Wadlen reminded.

"Right you are, since I suppose I still reside in the boundaries of Sedenberry." She stroked her graying hair with her skinny fingers.

"You wouldn't go alone," Glamacian said. "I and a group of my best guardsmen would accompany you."

"Where is its den?" Lady Calafar asked.

"We're not sure," said Wadlen. "Though Mr. Danell's farm seems to be its preferred hunting grounds, so it must be nearby."

Lady Calafar looked around her sparsely decorated drawing room and began to nod her head slowly.

"What will you do for me, if I vanquish your monster?" she asked.

"Mr. Danell has already posted a substantial bounty on the beast's head," said Doon.

"Not to mention the fame that would come with killing the first dragon to be seen in this area in quite some time," Glamacian said.

"Though it may not be a dragon," said Wadlen quickly. "You could have anything you desire, Lady Calafar."

"There's the problem, friends; I have all that I desire right here."

The three men collectively let out a sigh.

"However," she said, "I will help you with this. Of all the things I have done during my years, sparring with a dragon has, regrettably, not been one of them."

"You have our most gracious thanks, Lady Calafar," Wadlen said.

***

By the time the sun left the sky, Lady Calafar sat in a wooden chair in the middle of the burnt fields at Mr. Danell's farm. Glamacian and five of his most valued guardsmen sat with Mr. Danell and his wife around their dining room table. All eyes were upon Lady Calafar.

In one hand she held a clay pipe and in the other was one of the vines that used to hold some of Mr. Danell's fledgling pumpkins. She had initially been inspecting it for signs of burns, but after a while, the feel of it in her hand gave her a kind of relief that she hadn't known she needed.

She'd been there for an hour already, and though the sun had only just left the sky, something ominous in the hills seemed to almost be daring her to venture into them. She had decided to instead remain in her chair.

"She'll get rid of it?" asked Mrs. Danell.

"Don't worry about her," said Glamacian. "She'll bring it down before her pipe runs low."

Lady Calafar began to search for familiar star patterns in the heavens above her when, all of a sudden, an earth-shattering roar fell over the farm. She perked up and glanced all around the hills, which were only barely visible in the moonlight.

"You announce yourself, my friend," she said to the night. "You say hello as if I were an old rival, and yet we've never met."

A great gust of air from behind sent her hair flying all around her face, and by the time Lady Calafar had stood from her chair, nothing was visible. She began to pace across the charred crops, her eyes going from cloud to cloud and then finally to the hilltops themselves, though nothing was visible to her.

Sedenberry's Pest

Another rush of wind startled her and she dropped her pipe to the ground. She muttered a spell and tossed the vine into the sky. At the top of its arc it burst into radiant light twice the strength of midday sunshine and it continued to glow fiercely as it fell back to the earth.

It was about twenty feet overhead when Lady Calafar caught a glance of the beast. It was blacker than the night, as large as three or four of her towers combined, and was deviously eyeing Mr. Danell's farmhouse.

She quickly muttered another spell and projected her voice into the farmhouse. "Get out, quickly," she said to those inside, and then watched as they all scrambled from the house.

The roof caved in, two huge legs taking its place, and a wide swath of fire was sent pouring all over the small house. The guardsmen and farmers dove out just in time and continued to run towards Lady Calafar, too dazed and scared to trek the two miles it was to the next closest building.

She muttered another spell and brought a massive ball of fire from a different plane of existence, holding it in between her two hands as she stalked closer to the monster. The dragon had flattened the house and continued to stand in its flaming remains, staring, unmoving, at Lady Calafar even as she let fly her fireball.

The dragon seemed to snicker (it's what the guards would tell the other townspeople later), and with a flash of its long tail that was almost too fast for the eye to see, the great fireball abruptly changed its direction and came flying right back at its creator.

***

Wadlen held his head with both hands.

"We barely got out," Glamacian said with a shake of his head. "It was faster than I thought, sir. I think it was just toying with us. It could have easily taken the rest of us if it had wanted to."

"This is awful," Wadlen said. "Lady Calafar dead and our crops turning to dust."

Doon sat beside him with a pile of papers in his lap. He was shuffling through them loudly when Wadlen asked him what he was doing.

"The last thing I can, sir. We need a necromancer."

Wadlen let out a lengthy sigh and brought his mug to his lips. As he let its contents slosh down his throat, easing the distress that the latest news had brought him, he knew that Doon was right.

***

Fralack was in the chamber before anyone had even told Wadlen that he was in town. He was there so fast, in fact, that the guardsman working the door to the chamber asked him who he was.

"Your saving grace, sire," replied the necromancer as he brushed past him.

The hall was louder than before, fright evident in most of the loudest voices, and as Fralack brushed past them, each person would stop speaking for a moment and wonder what that awful smell was.

"Good afternoon, sirs," he shouted from the direct center of the chamber. "My name is Fralack, and I will slay your dragon."

"You're the necromancer, then?" Wadlen asked from behind his large desk.

"Indeed I am, sir. You must be Mayor Wadlen. You look mightily distressed, if you don't mind my saying. Put your mind at ease."

"Have you ever slain a dragon, sir?" Wadlen asked the curiously dressed man.

"I have slain them and I have even brought them back to life."

The chorus of voices erupted once more.

"However," shouted Fralack, but no one would let him speak. He glanced at Wadlen, who shrugged, knowing full well how it felt to be drowned in voices. Before Doon could pull back the hammer of his flintlock pistol, Fralack had uttered a spell and effectively taken the voice from each and every person's throat.

Sedenberry's Pest

"However," he said, ignoring the panicked expressions from the men closest to him. "I will need to know every detail of our situation."

Wadlen started to respond, only to find that his voice had also left him. Fralack shrugged, spoke a few words, and then offered his apologies.

"Not a problem," Wadlen said, his voice returned. "It's a trick I wouldn't mind learning myself." He looked out over the noblemen and women of Sedenberry, all grasping their throats as if they were choking, though Wadlen knew as well as they that their lungs were perfectly functional.

"Our mage, Lady Calafar, was sent to dispose of the beast last night. Sadly, she failed," Wadlen said with a pang of regret.

"She is dead?" Fralack asked hungrily.

"Indeed she is."

"You still have the body?"

"Sir, I'm unsure of what you mean by that, but I assure you that Lady Calafar had a unique and respected station in our town and we fully intend to respect her in death as well." Wadlen glanced at the outraged expressions on the faces of the other people in the chamber and wondered what they were thinking.

A few people began to grab Fralack and shake him in an effort to gain their voices back, to which he smiled and gently removed them, finger by finger, from his dark and layered robes.

"You can respect her spirit all you'd like, mayor. What I'm proposing would be a surefire way to dispose of your crop killer. If this—Lady Calafar, was it? —was really as powerful in the magic arts as you and your townspeople seem to think, then my bringing her corpse back to life should be more than sufficient a solution."

Wadlen's eyes went wide and suddenly Doon was at his shoulder, silently yelling in what he could only guess was the same kind of remonstrance that the others in the chamber were shouting.

"I'm afraid that's quite out of the question," Wadlen said slowly.

The necromancer nodded solemnly and glanced in annoyance

at the nobles around him. He uttered another spell and a small sphere grew around him, keeping those more physical persons in the chamber from setting him off on a bout of claustrophobia.

"You've heard that necromancers kill dragons, and you've thus called in myself, a necromancer. My good sirs of the chamber, what then were you expecting?"

Wadlen watched as the silenced critics of his chamber bumped up against the nearly translucent bubble surrounding the necromancer and fell back, unscathed and surprised. He couldn't help but wonder if he'd made a mistake.

"While we're on the subject, my good sir, how large is the graveyard of your lovely town?" Fralack asked as a devious grin crept across his face.

***

"The man stinks of death, sir!" Doon said, pacing back and forth in Wadlen's office.

"Yes, I've noticed," Wadlen said. "But we have no other options."

"He will defile all of our dead just so that he can kill the beast. And then what? Why, he'll take our whole treasury! He'll make off with the riches of the whole town!"

"We have few riches to begin with, and all those that matter are being burned nightly by that damned dragon. We need to kill it soon or we may as well lay down next to our dead and surrender our bodies along with our food." Wadlen drew in a long breath and glanced at a hair of his which had fallen on to his lap. It was quite gray, a reminder that he was not built for the kinds of scenarios that involved dragons or necromancers.

"How many bodies does he wish to raise?" Glamacian asked, standing next to Wadlen's chair with a pensive look across his scarred face.

"He said the more, the better," Doon said, spitting the words as if they were lies so volatile that keeping them in his mouth for too

Sedenberry's Pest

long would scald his tongue.

"And so what do you propose, sir?" Glamacian asked.

Wadlen glanced again at his fallen gray hair and shook his head. In the year leading up to the dragon's appearance, the largest problem in Sedenberry had been a minor pickpocket that had become too ambitious. That problem had been squelched by a single sword.

Now, for all Wadlen knew, that very same pickpocket would be rejoining them to march in Fralack's army against the dragon.

***

For the rest of the day, Wadlen avoided the townspeople as much as he could. An overwhelming sense of regret and fear had been steadily rising in his stomach, and as he felt it slither up his throat like some evil bile, he knew that adding any more stress to his life could be fatal. He went with Fralack to the cemetery, at which the necromancer couldn't stop smiling.

"What, might I ask, is so funny, sir?" Wadlen had finally asked him.

"Nothing is funny, mayor," he replied. "Nothing. I'm thinking to myself what a joy it will be to march against the devil on your hills."

"I see," Wadlen said, not entirely convinced.

"So this grave is the one that belongs to your deceased mage?" Fralack asked as he came to a stop in front of a freshly dug hole.

"Indeed. I can get some men to dig her up," Wadlen said softly, as if he were afraid Lady Calafar would hear him and think less of him.

"No need of that, sir, no need at all. When I bring them up again, they'll have quite enough strength to get out of the earth on their own," Fralack said with an unnerving wink. He walked in another direction, reading headstones aloud to himself, and the overwhelming musk of death leapt off his thick robes again, forcing Wadlen to breathe through his mouth.

"So you will use them all?" Wadlen motioned to the cemetery, which was comprised of roughly two hundred graves.

"Oh yes. I will need all of the undead fighting power your town can scrape together. In fact, I wish you had more bodies for me to dance back to life."

The man threw back his dark hood and reached down the front of his robe, pulling a necklace from inside of it. The necklace had a star inside a circle, a symbol that Wadlen knew little of, save that it was a mark used by necromancers and contained great power in their arts.

"Shall we begin?" Fralack asked, his pale skin and dark eyes looking unnatural in the evening sunlight.

***

The ground had begun to shake at that point and Wadlen had not hesitated to leave the area. He watched from a block away, feeling as if he were quite on the verge of tears. Fralack motioned and danced all over the cemetery, his arms moved in arcs while his feet hopped and skipped over the headstones and graves as if they were his dancing partners.

The ground shook and rocks fell aside. A few headstones fell over. And then the dearly departed began to rise. At first, the most recently deceased were the only ones whose graves showed any signs of renewed life. After a moment, though, all of the two hundred and thirty-four graves had hands and arms breaking through their dirt ceilings, shoulders appearing in varying degrees of decomposition and yet still managing to keep the sometimes skinless heads atop those all-too-visible spines.

Fralack's voice became louder and louder as the ceremony continued, his dance becoming more intense, as if it took quite a bit of persuasion for the long-deceased to come back and fight a dragon.

Wadlen was sitting at his vantage point, though he couldn't quite remember when he had decided to sit down. His eyes were wider than they'd ever been as he watched the most famous and mythologized of necromancy's ceremonies happening in the graveyard of his own town.

A roar rode the wind down from the hilltops and sent his head glancing up in the direction of Mr. Danell's farm. He told himself once again that it was necessary and stood up on shaky legs, glancing again at Fralack as his dance began to slow, several concentric circles of standing corpses already surrounding him.

He turned away from the grisly scene and noticed for the first time that many others were watching it with similar mixtures of fascination and disgust. Doon was nearby, as he always seemed to be.

"A perfectly vile man, isn't he, sir?" Doon said without removing his eyes from the cemetery.

"Indeed, he is. I think I'll refrain from asking you, for the moment, where you found him."

"I didn't, sir. Glamacian found this one."

"If he can bring down the dragon and we can eat our crops again, I don't care who brought him in." Wadlen began to walk away, back towards his office, not choosing to watch the battle on the hill for fear that he would recognize too many of Fralack's army recruits.

***

A peculiar mist had a way of forming along the hills that flanked Sedenberry, and the night that Fralack marched against the dragon was no exception. Mr. and Mrs. Danell had abandoned the ruins of their farm, and sadly, no one remained on the farmland to watch the undead army rise through the mist.

Regardless, many of the townspeople, including a large percentage of the youth (choosing to ignore their parents' strong admonitions against going anywhere near Fralack) had decided to cautiously follow the army up the hillside. They kept their distance and chatted with one another in low voices. All eyes remained on the gruesome army ahead of them.

Jon C. Forisha

Fralack walked at the front of his group, the corpse of Lady Calafar walking next to him, her incredibly charred skin and hair being the only things that gave away her undead nature. Behind them marched rows upon rows of the town's dead. None of them bore weapons, but the supernatural glow in each of their mostly empty eye-sockets seemed, to the townspeople, proof enough that they were capable of more than their frail appearances seemed to suggest.

Another roar issued from the sky, though the sun had left it at that point and the beast was reportedly pitch black. Fralack seemed entirely at ease as he brought the army to stand right on the spot that Lady Calafar had died the previous night, her wooden chair and clay pipe still present upon that charred farmland.

Fralack looked at the sky for a few moments and then sat in the wooden chair. He looked to his army and then at the townspeople, who all backed up a few steps upon drawing his glance. He smiled and surveyed the sky again.

"Calafar, if you would?" he said.

Lady Calafar's corpse lifted her charred arms to the sky and spoke foreign words in an otherworldly voice, and suddenly the sky was illuminated.

"That's better," said Fralack. "I've got to ask, just why didn't you do that last night?" he asked the corpse next to him.

He smiled maliciously and looked up again in response to the townspeople's collective gasp of surprise. The beast was in full view, flying in the illuminated sky, its large eyes focused on Fralack sitting in his wooden chair.

"Finally!" he shouted at the dragon, which lazily touched down on the ground some hundred feet from the necromancer's army.

Fralack stood and began to walk toward the monster, which continued to stare only at him. The townspeople slowly began to advance as well, their curiosity gaining the best of them.

Suddenly, with the gap between them diminishing, the dragon ran on all of its legs straight at the army. Fralack laughed loudly and motioned in an elaborate arm movement at the monster. The first two waves of corpses ran full speed at the beast and Lady Calafar's corpse quickly spoke some words in her odd voice. The sky's illumination turned hazy as a rain cloud appeared directly overhead. It rapidly morphed into a lightning cloud and sent pulses of crackling lightning at the dragon.

The dragon pounced on several corpses and blew fire at them, but then a lightning bolt crashed into its left wing and caused it to roar in pain. Fralack laughed again, sending the next two waves of corpses at the dragon. He spoke some words that made those already knocked over by the dragon reassemble themselves and again join in the fight. Another bolt of lightning fell into the dragon and it let forth a mighty burst of fire that lit most of the corpses aflame, though they didn't seem to mind much.

The corpses crawled all over the dragon, and as much as it thrashed, it couldn't quite knock them off. They began to tear at its scales with their unnatural strength, their bony fingers proving quite adept at removing the beast's armor and penetrating its fragile skin underneath.

It continued to roar and flail. It tried to fly again, but with its left wing injured, it was only airborne for a moment before it clumsily crashed into Mr. Danell's ruined farmhouse. The corpses chased it and another bolt of lightning soared into its eyeball, stealing its sight and zapping a good portion of the beast's motor functions from its rather intelligent brain.

The townspeople began to cheer, the dragon obviously conquered. Fralack heard their cheers and began to walk towards them, his last two rows of corpses following he and Lady Calafar as he made his way to them. They again began to back up, but Fralack was laughing so hard at that point that a few of them refused to move, so curious were they as to what was funny about the situation.

A lightning bolt fell from the ominous clouds overhead and sent five of the townspeople sprawling on the ground. Upon Fralack's orders, two waves of undead charged at their own kin, some of them running to attack their own children and grandchildren, and all the while the necromancer giggled like a child.

***

Glamacian sat in Wadlen's office, neither man speaking and both desperately hoping the thunder and roars would soon cease.

"I think we did the right thing, sir," Glamacian said for the third time that night. "I'm not sure how else we could have gotten rid of the dragon. We may have ended up like Yarkyt if we hadn't taken the risk we took."

"I trust you, Glamacian. If Fralack hadn't come to us with your blessing, I would by no means have gone forward with this." Wadlen again sat in his large chair by the fireplace. His nerves were effectively frayed, a condition that he tried to remedy with the glass of scotch that he held in one hand.

Glamacian shifted uncomfortably in his chair. "I'm not sure what you mean, sir."

The only light in the room was the fireplace, which crackled occasionally but was less intrusive than in nights previous.

"I never brought this necromancer," the guardsman said slowly. "I didn't even know one was coming."

"Then who contacted that man?" Wadlen asked, his mouth suddenly almost too dry to speak.

His question was answered by a flash of lightning that struck down in the center of the room, Lady Calafar's blackened body letting itself through the door just behind the remains of Wadlen's own sister, long dead. She hadn't been a fighter in life, but in the afterlife, she appeared to have quite a bloodlust.

Wadlen's fear at last rose to his mouth. He found that it tasted not unlike how Fralack smelled.

ABOUT THE AUTHOR:
Jon C. Forisha is currently a senior Creative Writing major at the University of North Texas. thecolorsplorge.wordpress.com.

A History of the Wraith King
Chris Poling

It is with the utmost horror and guilt that I scribble these words so that the truth may be known of our immortal Lord: horror at what he has become of recent, and guilt because I know my part in facilitating his succession. I know speaking of this, what will surely be blasted as heresy, will lead to my death, but I scarce think I have long to live as it is. I, First Councilor of the Crown, write these words so that in some distant future, the truth may be known of the ascension of the Wraith King.

My life before being introduced to the King's alchemist is of little importance. Suffice it to say that I performed various roles in the court, none of which garnered promotion or deference from his majesty. I was to watch over the alchemist and learn his secrets. The elders had noticed my ability to learn, which had raised me from farm peasant to royal errand boy. I did not know it at the time, but there was distrust of the alchemist on the King's part—a fear that he was a rebel and dallied on useless prospects; this is what I had been told.

His name was Donovan, and nothing more. He was a young fellow for such an esteemed alchemist. I later discovered that he had had no formal training in the art. He had been found in some distant land during the Gilrothian Crystal Wars by the grand-elder. The grand-elder recognized the boy's talent immediately and had him sent to the King's court. There, the masters of alchemy attempted to teach young Donovan their secrets, but were left in stupor when the young whelp bested their magics. It should have been a sign of curses to come, for no mere child should ever be blessed with such gifts.

Upon my first visit to the alchemical tower, which had been fitted similar to a dungeon since Donovan's reign as the King's alchemist, the young man said only this to me, "You are here to attempt at my designs. You will fail. If you wish to be of use to me then sit quietly."

The quarters were compacted to such a degree that the modest desk at which Donovan studied seemed vast by comparison. The only furnishings in the room were a simple bed, the desk and shelves lining the stone walls filled with ingredients. Most of these I could recognize while others bore foreign names that time had forgotten.

Days would pass between Donovan and me with no words. My entry would always be greeted by his cold stare and my exit by his vulgar demands to see the King. Of what their feud was I learned later and gained a heavy heart in the doing. It was several weeks into my assignment that I gained courage enough to ask Donovan what his current task was. He told me it was an elixir for 'his *mortal* majesty'. When I asked him why he described the King as such, he only shrugged his shoulders without taking his gaze off his distillery.

"Some things are not meant to be tampered with."

I scoffed at him, ridiculing him for doing the work despite his disagreement. It led to what would be the first time Donovan threatened to kill me. He was not larger than myself and had no weapon, but I feared what toxin he may slip into my body. Toxins, how I wish I could suffer such a sweet death.

It was a cold winter day when I rose to the alchemist's tower to find Donovan shouting at the door guards. They were laughing and prodding Donovan back into his cell with their halberds. Donovan refused to give up so easy and threw a small glass ball at one of them that shattered and spewed a vicious liquid that melted the man's

A History of the Wraith King

face. The other guard swung the butt of his weapon and knocked Donovan hard off his feet. He locked the door promptly and dragged his comrade down the steps past me. He died later that night. Only the skull remained.

Donovan was unresponsive the next day. Over time, we had developed a modest acceptance of each other. I had become fascinated with the man, the only one I knew who held ill toward the noble king. I think I in turn had become the nearest thing he had to a friend. He had even ventured so far as to tell me some rudimentary potions and their applications. When I repeated this to the elders, they greedily scribbled the recipes down on parchment.

The day after his assault however, he was silent. He did not toil at his desk, make demands of me to pass on to the king, or entertain himself in chiding my limited knowledge of alchemy. He remained deathly silent gripping his head in his hands. The sun was setting beyond the tower window: Donovan's only view outside the tower. I began to take my leave. Just then Donovan gripped my arm with bare white knuckles and muttered what became the collapse of my loyalty to my king.

"My wife lies in the King's dungeons."

I sat back down and listened. Donovan told me of my king's coercion at the suggestion of the elders. They had found the most beautiful girl in the land and given her to Donovan. Their love was true, and they enjoyed some small part of life together. However, it was a ruse, and they trapped her so that Donovan would use his gifts in the name of the king. I did not sleep well that night, for I had worked in those very dungeons Donovan could only speculate on. The ground was always slick with blood and screams were rampant.

It was spring when Donovan had completed his elixir and moved on to experimentation.

"It is meant to prolong life," he said.

I had in the weeks since that dreary winter day come to bond with the young alchemist, for his life at court was opposite to mine in every way. I felt he had removed a cloth from my eyes that had me blind. The elders refused the elixir at first on the grounds it could be a poison and demanded intensive testing first. Rats and all other kinds of vermin were brought to Donovan's tower to take the amber liquid. Donovan hated performing his duties for the King, but even still, he could not hide his excitement at his own work. We both watched excitedly as the first rat took bites of bread laced with the elixir, which proved to be a terrible poison. The rat ate the cube of bread happily, but no more than a second later did its eyes sizzle in their sockets and bleed puss. The stomach of the thing bloated to thrice its size and ruptured, oozing its molten entrails across the desk and onto the floor. Donovan was in a rage and smashed his mortars, distillers, and wares with bare and bleeding hands. I knew his mind too well by that time: he feared he would never see his wife.

Donovan reworked his calculations, read the ancient tomes again and again; yet, the same event occurred with the rest of the vermin test subjects, all of them dying in the same violent fashion. I stayed with him longer those days, sometimes till sunrise. I had taken it upon myself to assist him in every way: checking his work, studying other tomes, securing special ingredients from the markets that the elders did not know Donovan used. I had in effect become his apprentice without ever taking the oath. I never told the elders of this because I had unknowingly shifted allegiance. I wanted to see Donovan reunited with his wife. In the course of my studies and lectures from the master alchemist, I learned potions and elixirs unknown to the rest of the alchemical school. Donovan taught me the acid he had used against the guard. It could be made into a gas as well, he said, and could kill an entire court.

It was the first day of summer when Donovan and I resumed our tests. We were equally excited, for this time we surely had the components correct. Oh, how horrible it was to see Donovan's face when the first specimen died. The death was not as dramatic this time. The eyes shot out followed by liquid brain matter. I silently left the chamber to Donovan and his terrible visage. For surely if I had stayed the rage that inhabited the deep recesses of his soul would have found me.

When I returned the following day, I was witness to a

A History of the Wraith King

gruesome sight. Donovan, in his mindless bloodlust the night before, had slaughtered all of the vermin. Some were flattened on the floor and others strung open on the walls. As I entered, he finished dissecting another rat, neatly folding the flesh back so that all of the entrails could be seen. He had a vial of the amber liquid on the desk as he mockingly explained to me that we might as well see the action as clearly as possible. I remained by the door solemnly and watched my dear friend carefully administer a drop of the elixir on the rodent's tongue. He sneered as he did so, as confident as I that the result would be all too familiar. But nothing happened. The brutalized rat remained as it was, succumbing to no further punishment. We waited till the guards changed shift and still no development was seen. Had Donovan changed the recipe? He assured me he did not and was as baffled as me at the lack of a sight. Just then as we stared at the deceased vermin the eyes of Donovan went cold and his voice callous.

"Bring me another test," he demanded.

I told him all of the rodents had been used up; we had no animals save the King's hunting dogs. Donovan went into a rage.

"Then bring me the dogs!" he shouted and threw me out of his tower.

I returned later with two of the King's prized creatures. The elders were angry with this intrusion, but I did my best to defend Donovan and claimed no knowledge of improvement of the elixir. Donovan had a mallet, for smashing nuts and herbs, gripped when I entered. He instantly struck one of the dogs on the head with a powerful blow. I stood shocked. He dragged the other from my hands and forced the elixir down its throat. Why did it not fight back? I can only say that the beasts of this world have perception beyond our knowing, and I speculate it saw in my friend what I dared not. The dog died, as Donovan predicted. Its death was just as grisly as the other specimens. He poured the liquid down its throat, even after its demise, resulting in no change. He threw the head down against the stone and turned his attention to the dog he had struck moments before.

Donovan had tested tirelessly on the living subjects granted to him. They had all died gruesome deaths. There was no reason, save the dissected rat, that should have alerted him to try the elixir on the dead. Why he thought of it, or why it was practical I do not know. I speculate he considered it a step towards purifying the elixir and, thus, obtaining his beloved. Donovan lifted the dog's head into his lap and gently trickled a few drops into its throat. I could only stare at my friend and wonder at the madness that had possessed him. The shock I had when that dog began to open its eyes is beyond description. The color of the eyes had turned to amber. The beast lifted its head to my friend and stared into the deep recesses of his soul.

"Bring me more," he said.

I backed my way to the door, quivering all the way down the tower steps and finally collapsing when I found the bottom.

***

Within a single week, Donovan had killed and revived half of the King's prized hunting dogs, nearly fifty in all. My soul recoiled at the sight of them. The things stood guard all throughout the tower, in Donovan's chamber and occasionally wandered the castle grounds. The things were monstrosities. The beasts seemed to be more aggressive. I cannot recall a single moment when upon encountering one not being viciously growled at. Only Donovan held sway over the creatures, only he controlled them. What troubled me most about the beasts was that they did not breathe. Their chests never flexed with the exhalation of air. It was like they were still dead but clung to life by some unnatural means. I never dared try to touch one. I still do not to this day, but I swear if I were to put my hand at the throat I would feel no beating of life in their veins. There was surely something arcane at work.

I had brought Donovan what creatures I could since he revived that first beast, but I never stepped foot in his chamber. I knew he had great success with the beasts I brought him, my god

A History of the Wraith King

they littered his tower, but it was near a month before I went into his chamber to see him. The room itself had changed little. Jars still lined the wooden shelves and a single cot and desk made the rest of my friend's cell. The beasts, some laying on the cold stone floor and others standing as if ready to attack, all eyed me hungrily as I stood in the threshold. Saliva dripped from their mouths.

Donovan turned his head from his labors and smiled at me. Bloodshot eyes and heavy bags hanging from them told me of his exhaustion. He must not have slept the entire time. I had come to tell him about the summons of the elders. They wanted him to give a report on the elixir and his progress. Normally such demands would be kept silent out of the respect for the alchemist's intensive work, but it was impossible to hide Donovan's success when his creations wandered the castle grounds freely. The guards that had stood post outside his door for so long moved to the base of the tower and shuddered every time one of the beasts wandered past them. They had no qualms about keeping Donovan in his tower, but they refused to even try to keep the monstrosities within the same confines. They feared Donovan may make them into his puppets; they were not very far off.

Donovan refused to give any report or lecture to the elders. He said his task was done. He had found the way to cheat life and live forever. He wanted his wife.

I cautiously resumed my apprentice duties with Donovan. I tried as best I could to help him refine and reproduce more of the elixir, but I was kept at bay most of the time by his dogs. The elixir worked simple enough. If taken by a living thing, it died rather grotesquely. The amber liquid only revived the dead, but the dead had to be relatively intact. Donovan explained it once to me.

"If the flesh is too far corrupted, the elixir holds no gain."

It was why the dissected rat underwent no change. It was dead so the elixir could not kill it, but too far mutilated that it could revive it. The first of Donovan's dogs suffered a blow to the skull, fracturing it and killing the beast. The lethal wound was not great enough, though, to keep the elixir from working. Donovan assured me that had we cut open the beast's head to see the bludgeoning wound ourselves, the elixir would have yielded nothing.

It was late into the summer, and the grand-elder came with me to the alchemist's tower. The grand-elder made his case to Donovan citing that his work was not complete. The elixir worked on mongrel animals but that it was no assurance to work on human flesh. There was also worry, though he did not say it, that Donovan could make the King his dog. The grand-elder stated that for Donovan to see his wife he would have to prove the elixir worked on humans as well.

I cringed at the idea of the elders taking someone's life for Donovan's experiments. Though he was my friend, I had begun to build a reservoir of fear toward him. I had no doubt he would do whatever grisly task necessary to achieve his goal. What his goal was, I told myself, was to see his wife again, but in the back of my mind I suspected the quest for the elixir had begun to take a greater hold.

Donovan did not change his expression but stared with callous eyes at the grand-elder. He asked who he would be given. The grand-elder tried to hide a grin and said it would be one of the damned in the King's dungeon.

The next day, the grand-elder arrived with an entire troop of guards at his beckoning. The undead beasts in the alchemist's tower eyed them suspiciously and kept close watch with malice. The guards were obviously disturbed by the dogs but tried their best to stay disciplined. Donovan had cleared his cot, ready to receive the human specimen. I had helped him prepare most of the night, even to my great horror of what we were doing. Donovan had altered the elixir to better suit a human. The grand-elder stood at the threshold and smiled like a jackal. He reached into his cloak and withdrew a small leather bag which he tossed at Donovan.

"Here is your subject," he said laughing.

Donovan opened the bag and a finger fell out and smacked the ground. A simple silver ring encompassed it. Donovan collapsed and gripped his head and began shrieking.

"At least what is left of her," the grand-elder finished.

A History of the Wraith King

 I am unsure of what happened next. I had been horrified at the sight of the finger and what it meant the King had allowed. I felt the greatest sorrow for my friend and did not give attention to the grand-elder or the amber eyed beasts until they had begun their attack. The savage animals had sensed their master's grief and anger. The creatures in Donovan's chamber had leaped at the grand-elder and ripped his flesh to pieces. One had grabbed him by the throat with its fangs and released a torrent of blood. The guards were shocked and took too long to react. The dogs from Donovan's chamber pursued them into the tower cloister and attacked the armored guards at their necks, groins, and hands. The dogs that waited on the tower steps leaped at the men and ravaged their heels, causing many of them to fall down the hard steps to their death. But there were more guards than dogs, and by a narrow margin they overpowered them. The tower had become a place of death and decay within a few minutes, and the blood flowed down the steps.

 After the conflict was over, the remaining guards beat Donovan. He was knocked unconscious and bruised severely. They took what the grand-elder had come for: the elixir prepared for the human host.

 I spent days treating the wounds of my friend. The guards had broken several of his ribs. He never once spoke to me. How could he after such traumatic an event? He only stared into the empty air, his thoughts unreadable. His emotions were clear enough, however. The dirt on his face was streaked where tears ran freely at night. During those dark hours, his screams could be heard throughout the wings.

 I was pleased on the fifth day after the bloody event when Donovan spoke. He asked if I knew the ultimate fate of his wife. I told him that she had been beheaded, her finger removed afterword, and buried in an unmarked grave. Donovan hid his face in his hands. As terrible the tale I told was, it was a lie. I had to invent a fate horrible enough that Donovan would accept it and not press further, for he surely would have detected the falsity. I never knew what had happened to his beloved, but the rumors in the servant quarters were too ghastly. It was said that the ring finger of his beloved was pulled out of its socket and torn from the flesh, and the guards relished in her death. As reprimand for taking half of his hunting dogs, the King ordered the remains of the woman given to those dogs which remained. I never told this to my friend for I feared it would break him. I left my friend then to his sorrow.

When I returned the next morning, I was shocked to see Donovan hunched over his desk at work. I was perplexed and angry. Why should he be working for the monster who had killed his wife? He silenced me with a hand and gently told me his deductions. The King's alchemical court would study the elixir, not use it. They would in time become able to reproduce it and enhance it. Donovan believed his days were running few. It was only a matter of time before the King would have his elixir of long life, without Donovan's assistance. I then asked why he struggled to hasten his death. He told me he only had vengeance left now, and he needed to stay an asset to his merciless majesty.

"I need to have an audience with the King," he said. "I need to see him be tormented as I have."

I was at a crossroads: Donovan spoke of blatant treachery and murder, but he was my friend and I had grown close to him and shared in his torment. My time with him had shown me the true nature of the kingdom I had once loved. I reluctantly agreed to assist him in whatever way I could. After swearing to this, he sent me away so he could be left alone to his studies.

The next day, Donovan displayed two vials. I recognized both instantly. A powerful poison filled one vial and the infamous amber liquid filled the other. Before he said a word, I knew his plan. Why did I do it? The reasons are too many and are insignificant anymore. I did it in the service of a friend, to retaliate against a tyrant, it does not matter. Donovan confirmed what I feared. He lay on his cot and whispered to me his instructions once more; his last living words. He held the poison firmly in his hand and slipped the liquid down his throat. He closed his eyes and shivered only a little. He grimaced with pain that soon passed and then he was dead.

A History of the Wraith King

This was the moment I doomed the land and the living. I had the choice to obey my friend or my conscience. I knew what I did was horrible, an abomination. It would be better to endure one tyrant than to trade one for another! But my emotions overcame me, convinced me it was for my friend that I did this. And so, with tears in my eyes, I cradled the head of Donovan and carefully slipped the amber liquid into his mouth. I backed away from his cot and watched from the center of the tower chamber.

The skin turned ghastly white and shrunk to the muscles underneath. The body on the cot began to shake and then bolted up with a deafening cry. The hair on the scalp turned white in a blink and then fell to the ground. The thing before me resembled a ghoul. It then stood on weak legs and walked to me. It had Donovan's face and that was the only thing that kept me from running. The face was Donovan's, but the eyes were alien. The white of the eyes had been replaced by pure blackness, and the color of the iris was a brilliant deep blue. Amber streaks crisscrossed his eyes.

"Come friend," he said, "we have work to do."

Rumors spread through the castle that something had happened to Donovan, something terrible. None of the rumors involved my aid. I was never recorded as the mechanism of Donovan's transformation, but I make it plain here as my final atonement. Donovan worked furiously for days. I found myself unable to keep up with him in the end for he worked too fast, without even consulting the ancient tomes he possessed. He told me that his brief period of death had changed him; he knew things that no living mortal ever had. His intellectual revelations, that he would come to display often, were the least of what frightened me. It was the simpler things. He never drew a breath of air, never ate or drank. He explained to me that he no longer needed these pleasures.

A month to the day of his wife's demise, Donovan made an official proclamation that his work was done and ready to present to the King. The elders refused to allow Donovan presence with the King, but after he threatened to destroy his notes and let the other alchemists spend a generation to complete his work, they subsided.

Chris Poling

I bear witness to the horrors of that day. I walked just behind Donovan as he made his way through the court to present himself before the King in the grand hall. The King, middle-aged and watchful, peered down from his throne. He glanced once at the new grand-elder who nodded. Donovan had been searched before being allowed to enter. The grand-elder waved Donovan forward.

He walked silently, seemingly gliding across the carpets. I did not know his complete plan, but I knew the objective plainly. As he passed I could hear whispers in the crowds about his appearance, especially the eyes. Donovan stood ten paces from the King and from his robe revealed a vial containing the elixir he promised to deliver. The King stared greedily at it, but not as much as the elders who waited at the side. To all others in the chamber it must have been a magnificent sight. To myself, however, it was terror. The liquid in the vial was not amber, it was completely different from what I had helped him prepare. Part of me wanted to rush forward and throw the vial to the floor, oh how I wish I had, but loyalty to my friend kept me in check.

The grand-elder broke the gaze of the crowds. He demanded that Donovan provide proof of the elixir's work lest it be poison. Donovan grinned and uncapped the vial. He took a single drop on his tongue and turned to the crowd raising his hands.

"I am your proof," he said to them.

The elders whispered to themselves. I heard some of their misassumptions, *"He drank from it.", "It cannot be poison.", "He has not proved it works, only that it does not kill.", "What harm will come then to try it?"*. The grand-elder then pointed at me, and for a second time I chose the path to damnation.

He asked me for my testimony that the vial Donovan held truly was the elixir of longevity. Donovan peered over his shoulder at me, his eyes intensely focused. I steeled myself and said it was the elixir we had toiled over. The grand-elder smiled hungrily. This was, after all, why they had appointed me to be the alchemist's assistant. They had thought of me as a pawn too loyal to disobey the King. They had wanted me to be the final assurance of Donovan's

A History of the Wraith King

obedience. I instead became the instrument of their doom.

Donovan handed the vial to the grand-elder who then passed it to the King. The King, without thought, emptied the liquid. The vast audience was quiet, and the elders waited with clasped hands. The King rested back in his throne content. He prepared to say something but hesitated.

His eyes darted to Donovan, the elders and to me. He clutched his throat and gagged. He stuck his tongue out; it was black and bloated. The elders backed away and the audience looked on in horror. I remained sentient, knowing this was just as much my doing as Donovan's. The King's eyes swelled in their sockets and became violently bloodshot. His hair fell to the ground in clumps. Soon the King was unable to gag for his tongue rotted in his mouth. His skin became putrid. It slumped and became more like a liquid. Then it oozed off of him and became a steaming puddle on the throne. The stench was overwhelming for most. In a matter of seconds, the skin and muscle of his majesty rotted off and revealed his skeleton. The grotesque spectacle was not the worst of it. All of the audience gathered there could see in the moving swollen eyes that the King was still aware. He was still alive. The eyes frantically moved from person to person before settling on Donovan.

Donovan, gliding up the steps to his throne, leaned in close to the King and whispered words where there were once ears. He then gripped the skeletal king by the neck and threw him across the chamber. The skeleton shattered into a thousand pieces. The skull, with eyes still moving, came to a rest at my feet. The remains of my former lord then disintegrated into smoke.

The elders regained themselves and summoned the guards. Donovan pulled from a hidden pocket a small glass globe. It contained a gas that I had come to know all too well. The guards came streaming through the crowd. Donovan threw the globe high and it cracked against the ceiling, releasing its deathly cloud. The guards were focused on Donovan and the audience was too transfixed to move. I was the only one who ran out of the chamber and shut the large doors behind me. I waited for several minutes until I heard no more screams.

I opened the large doors. The toxic gas was still present, but only in a harmless low fog. The acidic cloud hid most of the ghastly remains of the once living, women and men alike, innocent and guilty alike.

Donovan picked the crown out of a puddle of flesh and sat on the golden throne. I walked to where I had bared witness to the King's demise and now stood to witness to the rise of the Wraith King. He did not see me but stared past the hall unto the land that would become his nightmarish empire. What was left of my friend Donovan had died that day and had been replaced by the creature I saw rise upon that throne.

As I write these final words, I can hear the undead guards shouting for me at the base of the tower. I wrote this testament in the former alchemy chamber, where I can still sometimes think of him as the man Donovan, my friend. The guards will surely kill me and revive me to serve unquestioningly for their master. The amber elixir idles by my hand and I shall finally take it, after so long refusing, to receive what waits in the next world.

ABOUT THE AUTHOR:
Chris Poling has written many stories over his life, but this is his first publication. He graduated from Washington State University with a degree in Civil Engineering and is living with his fiancée in Colorado.

And Greatest of these is Love
David McDonald

When he awoke, he awoke to darkness. It was not merely the absence of light, though there was none, but an absence of any awareness of self, of who or what he was. In this strange state time had no meaning, as there was nothing to measure it against, until change came.

Gradually, he became aware of a lessening of the pressure bearing down on him, a shifting and moving of weight he had not been aware of until it left him. As whatever it was above him was slowly lifted away, light began to filter down and shapes began to come into focus. With dawning horror he realized that he was buried beneath a mound of corpses. Claustrophobia rose within him, and an overwhelming desire to escape, but to his shock he found himself unable to move, his body refusing to obey his commands.

Move.

The command resonated through his body, and he felt muscles contracting and nerves firing in response to its irresistible power. With no conscious command from his own will, his body struggled to its feet, unthinkable fluids squelching beneath his hands as he climbed down a wall of death, coming to rest on ground ripped and torn as if with battle. Notched weapons and shattered helms littered the blood soaked grass around him, where it had not been churned into mud by hundreds of feet. His body marched him further on, towards a group of motionless figures, neatly arrayed in lines.

David McDonald

As he came closer, he became aware that their lack of motion went beyond any military discipline. Each figure bore a mortal wound, crushed skulls stood next to cloven chests. Flies buzzed around them, landing on unblinking eyes. He fought his body every step of the way, desperate to stay away from the grotesque statues, but powerless to halt until he found himself in line towards the back of the neat square. The sun beat down as he stood there, the only thing to break the monotony the odd fly that crawled across his vision. He could sense other figures falling in behind him but he could not even turn his head to check.

Motion towards the front caught his eye, and he saw a figure working its way up and down each row, pausing to inspect each statue. Occasionally it would halt and reach out and touch the corpse before it, which would fall noiselessly to the ground. As it approached, he realized that the chosen cadavers were those with the most battle damage, some with missing limbs, while one was missing half its skull.

Soon the grisly reaper was close enough to distinguish his features. He was an older man with cruel thin features, a hooked nose over thin lips, a mangy white beard descending in wisps from his chin. He was dressed all in black wool with a leather vest, the only ornamentation a gold chain with a gold disc attached. In the centre of the disc was a green gem which pulsed with a febrile, diseased light. There was something about the old man that nagged at his mind. He knew he should know him, and his lack of memory added to his unease.

By now, the old man was right in front of him, and their eyes met. There was a sensation of intense heat burning into his chest, then blackness as all around him faded away and he fell into memory.

The sound of festivities filtered through the walls as the guests continued to feast and drink, but his thoughts were only with the beautiful woman before him. The women of his tribe were known for their golden hair and sky blue eyes, but she was different, raven tresses cascaded over her shoulders while deep brown eyes gazed

And the Greatest of these is Love

up from under long lashes. Her looks had occasioned resentful murmuring from some of the younger women who had perhaps hoped to snare the hand of the chieftain's son, but it was other differences that had set the village elders to dark mutterings. The folk who lived deep in the woods had long been considered fey, and many tales were told of their affinity for dark magics.

But he cared nothing for such stories, and from the first moment he had seen her, shyly peeking through the curtains of the caravan her father brought into the village full of trade items, he had been determined she would be his. And now he had her, and his world was complete.

She drew something from the folds of her robe, a chain that glimmered a ruddy gold in the torch light. From its end dangled a crescent moon. She reached up and fastened it about his neck, the metal warm against the skin of his chest.

"Promise me you will never take this off, my love." She murmured. "Wear it for me, Osric, and I will always be with you. While my soul lingers on this side of the veil so shall yours and we will pass together when the time comes, but not before and not apart."

Her words made little sense to him, but she was beautiful and his thoughts were on the sweet anticipation of what lay next and it was an easy promise to make. So, he smiled and nodded and promised and kissed her, and soon the festivities were drowned out by her cries of pleasure.

He was dragged out of pleasant memories, and the horror of his present situation crashed down upon him. If he had been able he would have sobbed, but instead he could merely stare unblinking into the eyes of the old man before him. There was a look of slight puzzlement on that face, as if the old man could sense something strange, but with a slight shake he seemed to shake it off and he moved on to the next corpse, leaving only one thing behind. A triumphant thought rose. I am Osric!

The sun moved lower in the sky and around mid afternoon the columns began to move, marching towards some distant, shared goal. Osric was a passenger in his own body, unable to control his course or alter his pace. The corpses moved in unison, the ground rumbling as a thousand feet hit the ground in time. Occasionally one would drop out of formation, collapsing as some previously unseen wound or fracture gave way, but there seemed to be no hesitation in whatever will guided this macabre army.

But, it was as if self awareness had unlocked some door, and as the day progressed Osric found that memories began to return, and that he had some slight control over his own body. While he could not stop his march or change direction, he could look around and perceive familiar faces, men he had fought and feasted with. The soldier closest to him was a short, dark man that he knew as Hevan.

Osric tried to speak, but found his throat blocked. With great difficulty he coughed up a plug of blood and mucous, and tried again.

"Hevan?" His voice sounded like think croak in his ears. "Hevan? Can you hear me?"

The corpse gave no response, or even any indication that it had heard him.

He tried again. "Hevan, are you in there? Please, man, blink or something if you can hear me!"

There was still no response, the corpse looking straight ahead. Osric begged and pleaded with the unresponsive figure but it was futile. None of the others around him were any different, and soon Osric subsided into a morose silence. It seemed that he was alone, that only he had kept hold of anything of himself.

They marched through the night, stopping for no obstacle. It was flat ground for miles around, and the deathly host had simply trampled down any hedges in their way, and forded one or two shallow streams. Other than the thump of their footfalls, they had preceded in a silence that was eerie to a seasoned campaigner like Osric. No whispered conversations, or muffled laughter at private jokes, no curses as a man stumbled. No animals could be heard in the darkness around them either, whatever else that might be prowling the night was obviously giving them a wide berth.

And the Greatest of these is love

Dawn found them on the edge of a open field. A few hundred meters away stood another group, this one of obviously living men. Bright banners fluttered in the crisp morning air, and snatches of low conversation rode the dissipating fog. To Osric's experienced eyes there appeared to be even numbers on both sides, but there was a sense of vitality in the group across the field compared to Osric's companions. As he watched them draw up into formation he felt memories come bubbling up to the surface of his mind.

Osric watched as his father strode up and down in front of the massed ranks of soldiers, his armor flickering in the light of the bonfires that surrounded them. Men from every village for leagues were represented, some from well organized militias clutching swords or axes, others simply carrying scythes or wooden clubs. All bore the same grim look, of men pushed to desperation and living in fear of what was to come.

Despite their disparate loyalties, there had been been no real arguments when Oswald had been appointed commander of this ragtag army, aside from a few grumblings from one or two who had wanted the glory for themselves. Even those had been subdued because Oswald was acknowledged as the greatest fighter in the land, and in thirty years of conflict he had never led men to defeat. But, Osric knew his father well and could see a new uncertainty in the way the great warrior spoke and moved, because the foe they would face tomorrow was like no other they had ever faced before.

The old man would never let the men see his doubts though, and he began to speak, exhorting them to face their fear with courage.

"My friends!" Oswald bellowed, deep voice cutting through the cold air. "We face a terrible enemy. Ever since he raised his black banner the Necromancer has swept all before him. Not only has he left death and destruction in his wake, but with his black magic he has raised the bodies of the fallen to fight in his army against those they once called brothers."

Muttering rose from the ranks, punctuated by the odd gasp of horror at this news.

David McDonald

Before anyone could speak, Oswald continued. "But, what is magic against the bravery of the free folk of the plains? He may have his magic but we have our strong arms and the courage of our hearts!" He raised his axe above his head, shaking it at the heavens. "Tomorrow we stand between darkness and our families. This is the greatest host ever assembled here, the first time we have put aside our petty rivalries and stood together.

Oswald grinned. "I know your worth because I have fought with you, or against you all over the years." He pointed his axe at a hulking man with a tattered patch over one eye. "Ulric One Eye, I have seen you crush one of my soldier's skulls with your bare hands!" Moving it he pointed it at another short, lean man with a baldric full of daggers. "Dirk Nightghost, I have seen you slit the throats of five men before the first hit the ground!"

Both men grinned, delighted to be singled out.

"If we fall then our families will know horror. But, we will not fall. With men such as these, with men such as you, who can defeat us? Some moldering old book worm who reeks of sulphur and bat dung? Never!"

Oswald took a deep breath and raised the axe back over his head. "Who will stand with me? Who will stand for freedom?"

With one voice the men roared their challenge into the darkness, shaking weapons over their head. Osric heard his own voice join them, and he knew that tomorrow would bring victory and an end to this Necromancer.

Osric was awoken from his reverie by another command echoing through his mind.

Attack.

He heard the sounds of movement all around him as the undead host began to advance towards their enemy, slow steps speeding up until they were sprinting. Osric heard heard howls of rage rise from dead throats around him, tentative as if from disuse at first, but growing louder, filled with hunger and hatred. With a start of horror, Osric realized his own voice was raised with them, a terrible sound that filled him with revulsion. The grim ululation

And the Greatest of these is Love

echoed across the battlefield and he could see the front ranks of the foe shifting uneasily. Profane curses competed with the shrieks of the dead as grizzled sergeants sought to maintain order, and maintain it they did. The ranks held firm as the wave of corpses crashed against them, like waves falling upon the beach.

It seemed a mismatch at first, the dead bore no weapons while the living seemed well equipped. Blows from swords and axes rained down up on the undead, while they could only retaliate with nails and teeth. But it soon became apparent that the advantage lay with Osric's unwilling confederates. Wounds that would have slain a normal man instantly seemed to have little effect on the undead. Osric himself felt a sword cleave deep into his side, but there was no pain. The sword was lodged deep inside him, and the soldier who had struck him grunted as he tried to pull it free. Osric felt himself reach out and place a hand on either side of the soldiers helm. Pulling him close, Osric sank his teeth into the unfortunate warrior's throat, silently sobbing as he felt warm, salty blood gush into his mouth. Against his will, Osric gulped it down until the stream died to a trickle and the soldier went limp in his arms. Dropping the limp form to the ground, he moved on to his next opponent.

All around him Osric saw the scene repeated, as living soldiers fell beneath rending claws as they sought to trade blows in an exchange they were doomed to lose. He watched as a golden haired youth wielded twin swords in a glorious dance that took him through the ranks of the dead, shining blades flickering out to deal what would have been mortal wounds had his foes been other men. The part of Osric that was still his own admired the skill of his cuts and thrusts, but the dead shrugged off his blows, open gashes leaking no blood. The last Osric saw of him, the youth was screaming in terror and pain, trapped in the arms of one corpse while another ripped off his face and devoured his eyes.

And so the battle went, the living beaten down by inexorable foes, until finally the only ones that stood were the dark army. No crows dared approach, and the only sounds were the moans and sobbing of the conquered.

David McDonald

Feed.

As one the undead moved towards the fallen, and obeyed the silent command. Osric beat at the confines of his mind, trying to resist but he could not and soon he was crouched over a body, jaws burrowing into soft flesh, unspeakable meat sliding down his throat. While his body was intent on its grisly feast, Osric looked around at the other feeding creatures and noticed that as they fed their wounds began to heal, gashes closing, crushed skulls filling back out. He sobbed as he continued to feed upon the once brave warrior, until mercifully unconsciousness claimed him and everything went black.

When he awoke, they were back in formation, standing before the battlefield. There were new additions to their ranks, warriors Osric remembered facing as enemies. Despair filled Osric as he realized that with each battle the Necromancer would grow stronger, and that no one could stand for long in his path.

And so it continued. Each day brought a new battle against a new force, each smaller and more ragged and more desperate than last. All fell before the undead host, their bodies either feeding the dead and healing their wounds, or rising to swell their ranks. Day blurred into day as Osric sank into a black depression which no atrocity or foul sight could shake him from, until one day he stood before his own village, with all that faced them a cluster of old men, boys and women clutching farm tools. Osric had thought he had fought the dark commands before, but now he strained every ounce of will power, trying to spare his home the horror he knew was to come.

But it was futile, and soon they were sweeping through the village, massacring the men and boys. But the voice commanded them to spare the young women, and they were captured easily by the cadavers, arms pinned by cold hands as they struggled uselessly to escape.

"Osric?" A familiar voice rang out. "Osric? Is that you?"

His eyes found the source of that cry, and a gasp of horror managed to wring its way from his throat. It was his Edith!

"Help me, Osric, please. I know you are still in there."

And the Greatest of these is Love

He took one wavering step towards her, before the compulsion that bound him fast brought him to halt.

His movement, small as it was, had attracted unwanted attention. The Necromancer strode over to where Edith was held. Placing his hand under her chin, he forced her face up, her gaze meeting his.

"A rare prize indeed. One of the witch women. How did you end up here, I wonder?" he murmured.

Osric felt mental claws scrabbling at his memories, searching for the information the dark mage desired.

"Ah, how delightful. Young love reunited," the voice gloated. Edith sobbed as he continued. "Well, a bride like this is wasted on some bumpkin, I can think of better uses for such a prize." He leered down at Edith. "I will have her, then I will have her power."

Bring her.

Osric stepped forward, and took her from the corpse that held her. He had thought he had known despair before, but that was nothing compared to the torment he now felt as Edith's sobs rang in his ears. All through the night she sought to reach him as they marched towards the Necromancer's castle, but he was unable to do anything more than listen to her pleading. Osric screamed inside, but his mouth would not answer.

The Necromancer's throne room was as black as his heart, torches sputtering in sconces dotted about the room doing little to illuminate. But, from the strange rustlings and movements in the shadows, Osric was not sure that was a bad thing. There were some sights no man was meant to see, and he could already feel his sanity stretching perilously close to snapping. On a raised dais at one end of the room stood the Necromancer's throne, made from bones that came from no creature that Osric had ever seen. Before him stood a golden stand, holding a huge green gem that pulsed in time with the stone hanging around the wizard's chest.

Bring her to me.

Despite his attempts to fight the command, Osric found himself dragging Edith by the arm, leading her towards the throne and its withered occupant.

Edith began to whisper. "Osric, I know you can hear me. You can fight him, I know you are strong enough." She licked her lips nervously. "The stone, it is the source of his power. He has fed too much of his life force into it, I can sense it feeding on his evil and feeding him in return. Break it and he is doomed."

They moved closer. "I love you, Osric, I always will. We of the woods know that love is stronger than any magic he can command. It is my love that has kept you here, the other creatures are merely vessels for his will. It is our love that means that our souls will never be parted." Her hand caressed the cold flesh of his face. "Free us both, Osric."

Finally, they reached the steps of the dais, and stood before the Necromancer. His eyes glowed with a necrotic emerald light, and Osric felt his hands let go of Edith.

"No!" he screamed silently. "Don't leave me!"

But Edith moved forward jerkily, like a clumsy puppet until she stood right in front of the Necromancer. He stood and took her head in his hands.

"Now, I will have you and you will sit beside me until I tire of you. "

Rage blossomed in Osric, anger that he had never felt before. That was his woman and no one would take her from him! He managed to take a step towards the gem, then another, the Necromancer too distracted to see what he was doing. Dead flesh sizzled as he reached out and lifted it from its frame, raising it above his head.

"No!" The Necromancer's scream rang out, echoing from the rafters. "Don't! You can't!"

"Do it, Osric!" Edith yelled. "Do it for me!"

PUT IT DOWN!

The command hit him with unimaginable strength, rocking him on his feet. He could not resist, and with one last look at Edith he obeyed the Necromancer's final command.

Shards of green crystal flew in all directions as he put

And the Greatest of these is Love

the crystal down, hurling it with all his strength into the granite flagstones. A despairing wail erupted from the old wizard as he burst into viridian flame. The walls began to shake, rocks raining down upon them, and he barely had time to murmur "Edith" before whatever force that had animated him dissipated and he collapsed as a lifeless bundle of flesh.

He floated in darkness, lost and despairing and alone. He had defeated the Necromancer, but victory tasted like ashes in his mouth as he realised that there was no way Edith could have survived and that he had lost her. What use was anything without her?

Suddenly, a small hand took his and a voice filled his mind.

"I told you we would never be parted."

Together, they flew out from the darkness and into light.

About the author:

David Goodwin is a professional geek from Melbourne, Australia who works for an international welfare organisation. When not on a computer or reading, he divides his time between helping run a local cricket club and dreaming of publishing his bestselling novel. http://camaris.easingthebadger.com.

Pill Hill Press
For the BEST in speculative fiction!
www.pillhillpress.com

How the West Went to Hell
by Eric S Brown
ISBN-13: 978-1617060120

Eric S Brown, horror author extraordinaire, takes readers on an Old West adventure of epic proportions in his novella, How the West Went to Hell.

A bookish editor travels to Reaper's Valley, a small town set in the Wild West, to finish the macabre manuscript of a recently-deceased novelist. He arrives by stagecoach, where he is introduced to a classic bevy of characters who will join in the fight against the yellow-eyed demon bodysnatchers overtaking Reaper's Valley.

A gun-toting, six-gun blazing tip of the hat to both the horror and Western genres.

Kinberra Down
by Eric S Brown & Jessy Marie Roberts
ISBN-13: 978-6167060168

A sci-fi horrorfest set on a glacier-covered alien planet. The crew of *Kinberra* emergency lands on a life-sustaining planet in the unchartered wilds of outer space. The icy world is teeming with terrifying creatures desperate for human flesh.

Will the unlucky crew of *Kinberra* survive the arctic planet? Or will the snow-burrowing monsters satisfy their hunger by feasting on the survivors of the starship?

Find out in *Kinberra Down*!

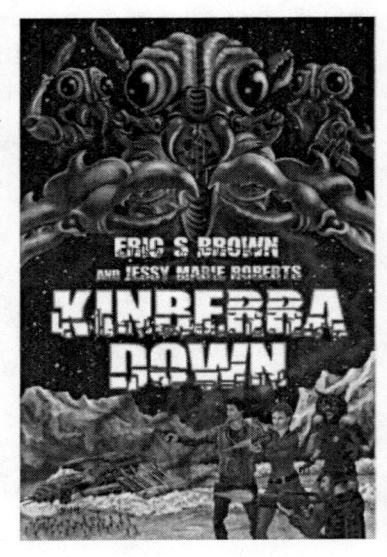

Pill Hill Press

For the BEST in speculative fiction!
www.pillhillpress.com

Twisted Legends: Urbanized & Unauthorized
Edited by Jessy Marie Roberts
Release Date: October 2009
ISBN-13: 978-0984261017

"Do you know what happened to a friend of mine?" You know the stories, you know the outcomes...or do you? Now you can enjoy twisted versions of classic urban legends in Twisted Legends: Urbanized & Unauthorized. From crocodiles in the sewer to stolen kidneys, from Bloody Mary to ravenous housecats, this anthology will leave you breathless and asking yourself, "Aren't you glad you didn't turn on the lights?" Authors in this anthology include: Christopher Jacobsmeyer, Jameson T. Caine, Laura Eno, J. Troy Seate, Michael A. Kechula, Bradd Parton, Jennifer Greylyn, Jessy Marie Roberts, Kevin Brown, Jessica Brown, Jodi MacArthur, Ennis Drake, Anthony Giangregorio, Jennifer R. Povey, Chris Bartholomew, Liz Clift, Jacob Henry Orloff, Jessica A. Weiss, Natalie L. Sin, Jason Everett Morris, Sam Cox, Brian M. Sammons, John Pupo, John Pennington, Jerry Enni, Sam Battrick, Charles West, Alva J. Roberts, Bill Mattox, Sean Logan, Bill Ward, Michael Penncavage & Ruth Imeson.

Silver Moon, Bloody Bullets: An Anthology of Werewolf Tails
Edited by Jessica A. Weiss
ISBN-13: 978-0984261093

Silver Moon, Bloody Bullets is a collection of twenty-five claw-biting short stories that explore the myth of the werewolf and the lure of the full moon.

From gladiator fights and cursed blood lines to secret societies and anonymous meetings, the following talented authors have turned the mysteries of the werewolf inside out: Matthew S. Dent, Jay Raven, Kelly Metz, Christopher Jacobsmeyer, Mark Souza, Dale Carothers, David Bernstein, Scott M. Sandridge, Marianne Halbert, Donald Jacob Uitvlugt, J. Leigh Bailey, Dylan J. Morgan, Edward McKeown, F.J.R. Titchenell, Patricia Puckett, Jessy Marie Roberts, Ben Langhinrichs, Kiki Howell, D. Nathan Hilliard, Frank Summers, Christopher Heath, Rob Rosen, Carl Hose, Stephanie L. Morrell, and Lawrence R. Dagstine.

Pill Hill Press
For the BEST in speculative fiction!
www.pillhillpress.com

Love Kills: My Bloody Valentine
Edited by Jessy Marie Roberts
ISBN-13: 978-0984261055 (Softcover)
ISBN-13: 978-0984261062 (Hardcover)

Featuring 20 pulse-pounding short stories, including Mark Souza's "Cupid's Maze," Love Kills: My Bloody Valentine celebrates the sinister side of romance. Forget flowers and candy-scare your lover into your arms this Valentine's Day.

Including the talented works of Mark Souza, Lily Harlem, Phyllis Humphrey, Michael R. Colangelo, Marianne Halbert, Jack Horne, D.B. Reddick, Jessica A. Weiss, Jeffrey C. Pettengill, Neil Coghlan, Adrian Ludens, Harper Hull, David E. Greske, J. Troy Seate, Rebecca J. Vickery, John Pennington, C. Douglas Birkhead, Matthew Dent, Ruth Barrett and Rich Sampson.

This macabre collection of Valentine's Day horror is a devil of a good time.

The Bitter End: Tales of Nautical Terror
Edited by Jessy Marie Roberts
ISBN-13: 978-0984261024

Have you ever been afraid something is lurking beneath the murky surface of the water? In this horrifying anthology, something is!

Behold twenty six short stories of nautical terror and prepare yourself to come face-to-face with The Bitter End. From ghosts to sea creatures, talking fish to shark attacks, cannibalism to man-eating bacteria, this horror anthology has something for anyone who has ever been nervous to get their feet wet. Authors in this anthology include: Patrick Rutigliano, Jameson T. Caine, Lucas Pederson, Laura Eno, Sam Battrick, Stephen D. Rogers, John McCuaig, Jessica A. Weiss, Jacob Henry Orloff, Christopher Jacobsmeyer, Kelly M. Hudson, Michelle Bredeson, Miles Boothe, Allen Wise, Alva J. Roberts, Anthony Giangregorio, Anne Maclachlan, C.A. Verstraete, Joel Arnold, Mike Chinn, Kassi Shimek, D. Nathan Hilliard, Scott Harper, Bill Ward, Rachelle Reese & Flora Winters.

Pill Hill Press
For the BEST in speculative fiction!
www.pillhillpress.com

Zero Gravity: Adventures in Deep Space
Edited by Alva J. Roberts
ISBN-13: 978-1617060007

This thrilling collection features thirteen fantastic adventures set in the cold vacuum of space. Read about rogues, scoundrels, aliens, robots, heroes, junkers and priests as you explore the rich and creative diversity of the following stories:

Junker's Fancy By Rosemary Jones, Leech Run By Scott W. Baker, A Space Romance By Paul A. Freeman, Hawking's Caution By Mark Rivett, Parhelion By David Schembri, To Stand Among Kings By Kenneth Mark Hoover, The Unicorn Tree By Alethea Kontis, The Beacon of Hope By Gregory L Norris, Tangwen's Last Heist By C.B. Calsing, The Stand-Ins By Gef Fox, Glacier Castle By Will Morton, Rescue By Margaret Karmazin, At One Stride Comes the Dark By Murray Leeder

---

Patented DNA: A Catastrophic Clone Collection
Edited by Jessy Marie Roberts
ISBN-13: 978-1-61706-023-6

Thirty fictional short stories about the speculative consequences of human cloning. Includes stories by John Walters, Eric Dimbleby, Mark Souza, Diana Catt, Tony Schaab, Frank Roger, Miguel Lopez de Leon, Stephanie L. Morrell, Jonny Kelly, Glenn Lewis Gillette, Ross Baxter, Mark Taylor, Matt Nord, Jason Barney, Martin T. Ingham, Michael W. Garza, Kevin Bloomfield, William Wood, Marianne Halbert, Shane McKenzie, David C. Renfrow, Alethea Kontis, Rachel Bailey, Larry Lefkowitz, A.D. Spencer, Ellie Garratt, Shawn Cook, Scott Taylor, Ben Langdon & Matt Carter.

Pill Hill Press
For the BEST in speculative fiction!
www.pillhillpress.com

Ruthless: An Extreme Shock Horror Collection
Edited by Shane McKenzie
ISBN-13: 978-1617060175

"With Ruthless, Shane McKenzie has proved yet again that politesse is overrated, that it's not necessary to be smooth and restrained, that sometimes horror needs to be rough and messy...this is the real deal. Hardcore, kick-ass, take-no-prisoners horror. It's gross, it's disgusting, it's rough, it's raw."—Bram Stoker award-winner Bentley Little

This shocking short story collection includes sick and twisted tales by the following disturbed authors: John McNee, Daniel Fabiani, Lucas Pederson, Danny Hill, Jessy Marie Roberts, Shane McKenzie, Jared Donald Blair, Lesley Conner, David Bernstein, AJ Brown, Tom Olbert, Nate Burleigh, John "Jam" Arthur Miller, Thornton Austen, Aaron J. French, Eric Stoveken, Alec Cizak, D. Krauss and Airika Sneve.

With introduction by Bentley Little.

Pandora's Nightmare: Horror Unleashed
Edited by Jessica A. Weiss
ISBN-13: 978-0984261079

The mystery surrounding Pandora has spanned the ages. The first woman. A seductress. Releaser of all evils. But was she motivated by curiosity or malice? Find out in this terrifying collection of twenty-eight horror stories inspired by the myth of Pandora's Box. From a malevolent ghost town to a doomed archaeological dig, from a haunted fortress to an alien planet, discover the depths of insatiable human depravity in these fresh twists on a favorite story—where the only thing left behind is hope.

Authors in this anthology include: D. Nathan Hilliard, Peter Charron, JW Schnarr, George W. Morrow, Neil Coghlan, A. Lee Manton, Matt Becht, J.R. Rodriguez, Scott Taylor, Jacob Bayne, Nye Joell Hardy, Chris Bartholomew, Ruth Imeson, Alva J. Roberts, Emma Kathryn, John "JAM" Arthur Miller, Bruce Memblatt, Eric W Jepson, Rebecca J. Vickery, Jessy Marie Roberts, M Sullivan, Blake Casselman, Jay Raven, Thomas M. Earnhart, Jessica A. Weiss, Laura Eno and Belen Lopez.

Pill Hill Press
For the BEST in speculative fiction!
www.pillhillpress.com

Impossibilities
by Craig Booker
ISBN-13: 978-1617060359

Welcome to the peculiar world of the Winters family!

Meet Cassandra Winter, a resourceful PI with a penchant for stumbling across murder mysteries which defy rational explanation. Along with her grandfather, Penderel Winter, a brilliant hypochondriac, and wisecracking Rufus Knight, a wheelchair-bound whizzkid with an IQ of 150, the three sleuths unravel impossible crimes, locked-room murders and bizarre mysteries.

Included in this collection: Sweet Miriam, The Regency Room, The Deveraux Staircase, Murder in Waiting, Grand Guignol and Spindleshanks.

Immerse yourself in the delightfully oddball universe of Impossibilities, where there is a solution to every perfect crime!

A Whodunit Halloween
Edited by Jessy Marie Roberts
ISBN-13: 978-0984261086

A spook-tastic collection of eleven mysteries that celebrate Halloween and the "whodunit" genre. Includes: Brain Food by Paul A. Freeman, Murder in the Corn Maze by Joan Bruce, The Canton House by Jessy Marie Roberts, Slightly Mummified by Diana Catt, A Bolt from the Blue by Craig Booker, Dad's Favorite Holiday by Rebecca J. Vickery, Resurrection Man by Tim Champlin, The Trick-or-Treat Killer by Mark Souza, The Murder of Charlie Dekker by Donna Dawson, Trapped Under Glass by Jessica A. Weiss & Cornfield Crucifixion by Gwen Mayo.

Pill Hill Press
For the BEST in speculative fiction!
www.pillhillpress.com

The Weaving
by Gerald Costlow
ISBN-13: 978-1617060076

All the witch wanted was romance. All the demon wanted was the world. Their battle would challenge the Gods...

Rose, the Witch of the Woods, twists destiny when she embarks on a campaign to find true love. During her quest for happily-ever-after with her familiar-turned-husband, Tom, Rose accidentally releases Lilith, a powerful demon, from her ancient prison.

Rose and her allies battle Lilith in an epic struggle of destinies woven together by fate. With help from the Three Ladies, telepathically linked oracles, Rose struggles to vanquish Lilith from the realm and restore peace to the kingdom. Throughout her journey, Rose discovers the true meaning of magic, devotion, and most importantly, love.

A Plethory of Powers
by Gerald Costlow
ISBN-13: 978-1-61706-031-1

A Plethory of Powers features two standalone adventures set in Gerald Costlow's fantastical world of *The Weaving*.

In "The Case of the Missing Succubus," Rose, The Witch of the Woods, uses her wits and magic to solve a murder mystery with the help of her old friend, Keyotie. The second adventure, "A Conference of Powers," is an old-fashioned pileup of mislaid plans and harebrained schemes gone awry. Witches, wizards, and other powers of the land are invited to the Royal Palace to partake in a conference, proving that anything that can go wrong will go wrong—with comedic results.

Reunite with old friends and meet new ones in this exciting prequel to *The Weaving*.

THE PLACE TO GO FOR ZOMBIE AND APOCALYPTIC FICTION

LIVING DEAD PRESS
WHERE THE DEAD WALK
www.livingdeadpress.com